The Best British Mysteries III

The Best British Mysteries III
edited by
MAXIM JAKUBOWSKI

This edition first published in Great Britain in 2006 by
Allison & Busby Limited
13 Charlotte Mews
London W1T 4EJ
www.allisonandbusby.com

A catalogue record for this book is available from
the British Library.

10 9 8 7 6 5 4 3 2 1

ISBN 0 7490 8253 4
974-0-7490-8253-6

Printed and bound in Great Britain by
Bookmarque Ltd, Croydon, Surrey

Contents

Introduction

Welcome to the third instalment in our annual collection regrouping the best mystery short stories penned by British authors during the course of the preceding calendar year. Yet again, it has proven a sterling twelve months with an embarrassment of riches to be found in magazines, books, radio and other sometimes unlikely places. Evidence renewed that in Britain crime still does pay, in subtle if metaphorical and fictional ways!

It has also been a year when historical crime fiction has proven increasingly popular with a score of excellent anthologies published in Britain and the USA set in the past, together with a bunch of most ingenious new Sherlock Holmes tales commissioned by BBC Radio and later made available on their website (bbc.co.uk), of which three have made the cut and are offered for the first time in book form here; all three have amusingly been authored by writers whose roots lie more in the horror or science fiction field but who have all mastered the mystery genre and its often attendant ironies with particular bravura.

We have tales of dastardly deeds, ingenious puzzles and bloodthirsty murder and intrigue by authors famous for their bounty of past awards as well as newer talents now making a name for themselves in our field. I'm particularly pleased to be featuring the first ever short story by Jake Arnott, author of the powerful novel *The Long Firm*, which became one of last year's most prominent and well-reviewed television series. Other newcomers to the series include Irish author Ken Bruen, who is making quite some waves in the USA, John Connolly, creator of the dark and atmospheric Charlie Parker series and a favourite on both shores of the Atlantic, first-time novelist Adrian Magson, Margaret Murphy, a rare short story by Barbara Cleverly, Peter Tremayne, Ian Morson, and many others. And, should any of you question the inclusion of the witty Michael Z. Lewin in our collection, I would respectfully point out that though born in the USA, he has now lived in the UK for decades and actually has dual nationality, so there...

Staple favorites like Mark Billingham, John Mortimer, H.R.F. Keating, John Harvey, Peter Robinson, Val McDermid, Anne Perry, Amy Myers, Diamond Dagger winner Robert Barnard, Keith Miles (also known as Edward Marston), Judith Cutler, Peter Turnbull and Martin Edwards also make welcome returns to the series.

So, all in all, I think a potent cocktail and a sometimes deadly brew, with tales to enchant, puzzle, and scare, and hours of rewarding reading for anyone who enjoys a good tale of crime and mystery featuring unpredictable twists, memorable characters and, as ever, excellent writing and atmosphere to spare.

Welcome aboard; your annual mystery cruise begins here, and from the safety of your armchair enjoy these journeys in murky, troubled waters.

Maxim Jakubowski

Sydney Carton sat alone at a table near the door of the Café Procope, staring at the dregs of the red wine in his glass. He did his best to ignore the voices shouting, laughing, swearing around him in the suffocating heat. It was the seventh of July, 1793, and Paris was a city oppressed by hunger and fear. In January the Convention had sent the strangely dignified figure of Louis XVI to the guillotine. Predictably, by February France was not only at war with Austria and Belgium, but with England as well.

In the Place de la Révolution the scarlet-stained blade rose and fell every day, and tumbrels full of all manner of people, men and women, old and young, rich and poor, rattled over the cobbles on their last journey. The streets smelled of refuse piled high and rotting in the heat. Fear was in the air, sharp like sweat, and people along the Rue St Honoré complained because the streets stank of blood. You could not drive cattle down them any more because the stench terrified them and they stamped out of control, mowing down passersby and crashing into house and shop windows.

All that Carton cared about was Dr Manette's daughter Lucie, whose husband was locked up in the prison of La Force, with no hope of escape. Carton would have done anything he could to ease her distress, but he was utterly helpless.

The café door was wide open to let in a little air, and he did not notice anyone coming or going until a small man with tousled hair and a cheeky, lopsided face sank into the chair opposite him, having ordered wine from Citizen Procope as he passed.

'At least there's still wine, even if there's no bread,' he said with a grunt. 'Do you know what they're charging for a loaf now?' he demanded Carton's attention. 'Three sous! Twelve sous for four pounds! That's more than a carpenter earns in a day, and twice a week's rent. And the laundresses down at the river are creating hell because there's no soap! Never mind a Committee of Public Safety! What's the point of being safe if the sides of your belly are sticking together?'

'I'd keep a still tongue in your head, if I were you, Jean-Jacques,'

Carton replied dryly. 'If you criticise the good citizens of the Committee, your belly'll think your throat has been cut, and likely it'll be right!'

Jean-Jacques's wine came; he thanked Citizen Procope and handed him five sous. He sniffed the bottle and pulled a face. 'Not bad,' he observed. 'Want some?'

Carton never refused wine. 'Thank you.' He held out his glass.

Jean-Jacques filled it generously. 'You know my sister?'

'Amélie?'

'No, no! Amélie's a good woman, she never does anything except what she's told. Marie-Claire.' He drank half of his glass. 'I wish I had some decent cheese to go with this.'

Carton liked Jean-Jacques. There was a good humour about him, an optimism, misplaced as it was, that lifted the spirits. He was pleasant company.

'What about Marie-Claire?' he asked, to be civil. He did not care in the slightest. To tell the truth there was very little he did care about. He had no belief in himself, nor any in justice or the goodness of life. Experience in London as a lawyer had proved his skill, but it had not always led to victory, acquittal of the innocent, or punishment of the guilty.

Jean-Jacques leaned forward over the table, his round eyes bright, his face alive with suppressed excitement. 'She has a plan,' he said softly. 'To get a whole crateful of cheeses, and not just any cheeses, but perfectly exquisite, ripe Camembert! And a side of bacon!'

In spite of himself Carton's imagination was caught. Even the bare words conjured up the fragrance of rich, delicate flavour, food that satisfied, that filled the nose and lay on the tongue, instead of the rough bread and stew with barely any meat in it that had become the common fare. Even though these days one was glad enough to have more than a spoonful or two of that. 'What sort of a plan?' he said dubiously. Marie-Claire was an erratic creature. Younger than Jean-Jacques, probably not more than twenty-two or three, small like him, with wide brown eyes and wild hair that curled just as hectically as his, only on her it was pretty. She had been one of the women who had marched on the palace at

Versailles demanding food and justice in the early days of the Revolution when the king was still alive – fruitlessly, of course. The king had listened to everybody, and then done whatever he was told by the last person to speak to him, which was always some minister who did not listen at all.

Jean-Jacques was still smiling. His teeth were crooked, but they were very white. 'There is a particularly large and greedy fellow called Philippe Duclos on the local committee,' he replied. 'The man with the cheese, whose name I don't know, has hidden them so well no one knows where they are, except that they are somewhere in his house, of course. Marie-Claire is going to use Philippe to put his men there, so that the good citizen can no longer get to his cheese in secret.' He smiled even more widely. 'Only he is, of course, going to warn Citizen "Cheese" beforehand, so he will have the chance to move them. Then…' He clapped his hands together sharply and made a fist of the right one. 'We have them!' he said with triumph. 'Half for Philippe, half for Marie-Claire. She will eat some, and sell some, which I will buy.' He opened his hands wide in a generous, expansive gesture, and his irregular face was alight with pleasure. 'In two days' time we shall dine on fresh bread. I have some decent wine, not this rubbish, and ripe Camembert! How is that, my friend?'

'Unlikely,' Carton replied ruefully, but he did smile back.

'You are a misery!' Jean-Jacques chided, shaking his head. 'Are all Englishmen like you? It must be your climate: it rains every day and you come to expect it.'

'It doesn't rain in London any more than it rains in Paris,' Carton answered him. 'It's me.' It was a confession of truth. His general cynicism stretched beyond his own lack of worth to include everyone else.

'Cheese,' Jean-Jacques said simply. 'And more wine. That must make you feel better!' He reached for the bottle and poured more for both of them. Carton accepted with a moment of real gratitude, not so much for the wine as for the friendship. He thought the plan was doomed to failure, but it would be pointless to say so.

* * *

Carton deliberately put the cheese out of his mind. Even in Paris torn apart by the violence of revolution and sweating with fear, it was necessary to earn a living. He could seldom practise his usual profession of law, but he had a superb gift of words, even in French, which was not his own language, and Paris was awash with newspapers, pamphlets, and other publications. There was the highly popular, scurrilous *Père Duchesne* edited by the foul-mouthed ex-priest Hébert, which slandered just about everyone, but most particularly the Citizeness Capet, as Queen Marie Antoinette was now known. The latest suggestion was that she had an unnatural relationship with her own son, who in the normal course of events would now have become Louis XVII.

And of course there was *L'Ami du Peuple,* edited by that extraordinary man, Jean-Paul Marat, who liked to be known as 'The Rage of the People'. Someone had had the audacity, and the lunacy, to haul him up before the Revolutionary Tribunal in April. He had stormed in, filthy and in rags as usual, carrying the stench of his disease with him. The whole body of them had quailed before him, terrified, and he had been carried out shoulder-high in triumph. There was now no stopping him. The Paris Commune was his creature, to a man.

Carton always took good care to avoid him. Even though Marat lived here in the Cordeliers District, as did most of the revolutionary leaders, it was possible to stay out of his way. Instead Carton wrote for small, relatively innocuous publications, and earned sufficient to get by.

So it was that two days later on July 9 he sat in the Café Procope again, near the door in the clinging, airless heat. He was eating a bowl of stew with rough bread – more than some could afford – when Marie-Claire came in. Even before she turned toward him he could see the fury in her. Her thin little body was rigid under its cotton blouse and long, ragged blue skirt, and her arms were as stiff as sticks. She looked left and right, searching, then turned far enough to see Carton and immediately came over to him. Her face was white and her eyes blazing.

'Have you seen Jean-Jacques?' she demanded without any of the usual greeting.

'Not today,' he replied, clearing a little space on the table so she would have room for a plate. 'But it's early. Have some stew while there still is some. It's not bad.'

Her lip curled. 'What is it? Onions and water?' She sat down hard, putting her elbows on the table and both hands over her face. 'I've lost my cheeses! That son of a whore took them all! It was my idea, my plan!' She looked up at him, her face burning with indignation. 'He didn't even know about them, Fleuriot, until I told him!'

Carton was disappointed. He realised he had been looking forward to the richness and the flavour of cheese. It seemed like a long time since he had eaten anything that was a pleasure, not merely a necessity, although he was aware how many had not even that. The crowds pouring out of the areas of factories, abattoirs, and tanneries, such as the Faubourg St Antoine, with their acid-burned, copper-coloured faces, hollow-eyed, dressed in rags and alight with hatred, were witness enough of that. They were the people who worshipped Marat and gave him his unstoppable power.

Citizen Procope came by, and Carton requested a bowl of soup and bread for Marie-Claire. She thanked him for it, and for a moment the rage melted out of her eyes.

'Forget the cheese,' he advised regretfully. 'There's nothing you can do anyway. It's gone now.'

Her face hardened again. 'The pig! Slit his throat, and he'd make a carcass of bacon to feed us for a year! He won't have got rid of all that food, he'll have it stored somewhere. The Committee could find it, because they'd take his house apart, if they had to.'

Carton's stomach tightened. 'Don't do it!' he said urgently. 'Don't say anything at all! It'll only come back on you. You've lost them – accept it.' He leaned forward across the table, stretching out his hand to grasp her thin wrist. 'Don't draw attention to yourself!'

She glared back at him. 'You'd let that pig get away with it? Never!' Her teeth were clenched, the muscles tight on her slender jaw. 'I'll make him sweat as if the blade were already coming down on his neck. You'll see!'

Citizen Procope brought her soup and Carton paid for it.

She took her bowl in both hands, as if it might escape her. 'You'll see!' she repeated, then picked up the spoon and began to eat.

The next morning Carton was again sitting at his usual table at the café with a cup of coffee that tasted like burnt toast, and possibly bore a close relationship. At the next table three men were laughing uproariously at the latest joke in *Père Duchesne,* and adding more and more vulgar endings of the tale, when Jean-Jacques came storming in through the open door, his hair tangled, his shirt sticking to his body with sweat. His face was white and he swivelled immediately toward Carton's table and staggered over, knocking into chairs.

Carton was alarmed. 'What is it?' he asked, half rising to his feet.

Jean-Jacques was gasping for breath, choking as he struggled to get the words out. 'They've arrested her! Marie-Claire! They've taken her to the prison! You've got to help me! They'll...' He could not bring himself to say it, but it hung in the air between them.

Carton found his own voice husky. 'What have they charged her with?' It was all unreal, like a fluid fear turned suddenly solid. He knew when Marie-Claire had spoken of it that it was a bad idea to seek revenge, but this was different, it was no longer thought but fact, shivering, sick and real.

'Hoarding food!' Jean-Jacques said, his voice rising toward hysteria, as if he might burst into mad laughter any moment. 'She doesn't even have the damn cheeses – or the bacon! Philippe has!'

'I don't suppose that makes any difference.' Carton sank back into his chair and gestured for Jean-Jacques to sit down also. It was always better to be inconspicuous. They did not want anyone looking at them, or remembering.

'That's enough to send her to the guillotine!' Jean-Jacques obeyed, the tears running down his face. 'We've got to get her out of there! You're a lawyer – come and tell them that she wasn't even there. If someone stands up for her, we can make them realise it's him. They'll catch him with the cheeses, and that'll be proof.'

Carton shook his head. 'It won't be so easy.' In spite of the heat there was a coldness settling inside him. 'Philippe will have thought of that…'

Jean-Jacques half rose to his feet, leaning forward over the table. 'We've got to do something! We've got to help! She didn't take them. There has to be a way to prove it!'

Carton rubbed his hand wearily across his brow, pushing his hair back. 'It isn't about them,' he tried to explain. 'It's about reporting Philippe. The cheeses are gone. He can't afford to be blamed, so he's blaming her. If they can't find them, who's to say which one is guilty?'

Jean-Jacques straightened up with a jolt. 'Exactly! No one at all! Come on! We've got to hurry. For that matter, who's to say there ever were any? Citizen Fleuriot can't admit to having lost them without admitting to having had them in the first place! It's perfect. Hurry!'

Carton stood up and went after the rapid and highly agitated figure of Jean-Jacques. There was a kind of logic to it. The only trouble was that logic counted for very little in Paris these days.

Outside the street was hot and the sour smells of rubbish and effluent assaulted the nose. The air itself tasted of fear. A wagon rumbled by, half empty, a few casks in the back. An old newspaper stirred a little in the gutter and settled again. There was a group of Revolutionary Guards at the corner, laughing at something, muskets slung idly over their shoulders, red, white, and blue cockades in their hats.

Jean-Jacques was almost at a run, and Carton had to increase his pace to keep up with him. They had not far to go; there were district headquarters and prisons all over the place. Carton's mind was racing, trying to think what to say that would help Marie-Claire now, and not simply make it worse. He would have to offer some explanation as to why Philippe was blaming her. And it would have to be a story that left no guilt with him! If only Jean-Jacques would slow down and allow more time to think!

They passed a woman on the corner selling coffee, and a group of laundresses arguing. There were people in queues for bread. Of course they were far too late! Or perhaps it was for the candle shop next door, or soap, or any of a dozen other things one could not buy since spring.

Then they were at the prison. A huge man with a red bandanna around his head stood outside the doorway, barring their entrance. Jean-Jacques did not even hesitate. 'I have business with Citizen Duclos,' he said confidently. 'Evidence in a case.' He waved his arm in Carton's direction. 'Citizen Carton is a lawyer...'

'We have no need of lawyers!' the man with the bandanna spat. 'Justice gets no argument here.'

'Never say that, Citizen,' Jean-Jacques warned, glancing over his shoulder as if he feared being overheard. 'Citizen Robespierre is a lawyer!'

The man with the bandanna rubbed the sweat off his face and looked nervously at Carton.

Carton cursed Jean-Jacques under his breath. 'We have our uses,' he said aloud.

'Go in, Citizen.' The man ushered them past.

Jean-Jacques obeyed with alacrity, Carton with great reluctance. The place seemed to close in on him as if the walls were human misery frozen solid. Their footsteps had no echo, and yet there were sounds all around them, snatches of voices, cries, someone weeping, the clang of a door slamming shut. He had been here only minutes, and he was already longing to leave, his body trembling, his stomach knotted tight. He thought of Charles Darnay locked in the prison of La Force nearly a year now, not knowing if he would ever leave, and Lucie outside, every day trying to see him, imagining his suffering, helpless to affect it at all.

Jean-Jacques had reached the official in charge and was speaking to him. He was a lean, ferret-faced man with a scar on his shaven head, and most of his teeth missing. What hunger and injustice there had been in his life one could not even guess. He gestured to Carton to come forward.

Carton obliged, his hands slick with sweat, his shirt sticking to him. How had he ever allowed himself to get caught up in this? It was insanity! He stood in front of the man with the scar and forced himself to speak.

'Citizen, I have certain information you may not have been

given regarding a matter of hoarding food. Cheeses to be exact.'

'We know all about the cheeses, and the bacon.' the man replied. 'We have the hoarder in custody. She will be dealt with. Go about your business, Citizen, and leave us to do ours.'

Jean-Jacques was fidgeting, wringing his hands, moving his weight from one foot to the other. It was hopeless, but Carton was terrified he would say something and so involve both of them. It did not need much to make people suspicious.

'Ah!' Carton burst out. 'Then you have recovered the cheeses! I was afraid you would not!' He saw the man's expression flicker. 'Which would mean you had not caught the principals in the act.'

Jean-Jacques froze.

The man scowled at Carton. 'What do you know about it?' he demanded.

Carton's brain raced like a two-wheeled carriage cornering badly. 'I think you are a just man and will need evidence,' he lied. 'And if goods are in the wrong hands, then the matter is not closed until that is put right.'

The man leaned toward him. He smelled of stale wine and sweat. 'Where are these cheeses, Citizen? And how is it you know?' His eyes were narrowed, his lip a little pulled back from his gapped teeth.

Carton felt his body go cold in the stifling heat. Panic washed over him, and he wanted to turn on his heel and run out of this dreadful place. Memories of past prison massacres swarmed in his mind like rats, the priests hacked to death in the Carmes in September of ninety-two, and the women and children in the Salpetrière. God knew what since then.

'We know where they were taken from, Citizen, and when!' Jean-Jacques broke in. 'If we put our heads together, find out who knew of them, and where they were, we can deduce!'

The man scowled at him, but his eyes lost their anger, and interest replaced it. 'Wait here,' he ordered. 'I'll go and find out.' And before Carton could protest, he turned and strode away, leaving them under the watchful eyes of two other guards.

The minutes dragged by. There was a scream somewhere in the distance, then dense, pulsing silence. Footsteps on stone. A door banged. Someone laughed. Silence again. Jean-Jacques started to fidget. Carton's fists were so tightly clenched, his nails cut the flesh of his hands.

Then there were more screams, high and shrill, a man shouting, and two shots rang out, clattering feet, and then again silence.

Jean-Jacques stared at Carton, his eyes wide with terror.

Carton's chest was so tight he was dizzy. The stone walls swam in his vision. Sweat broke out on his body and went cold when his wet shirt touched him.

There were footsteps returning, rapid and heavy. The man with the scar reappeared, his face bleak. He looked at Carton, not Jean-Jacques. 'You are wrong, Citizen lawyer,' he said abruptly. 'The woman must have been guilty. Maybe she gave the cheeses to a lover or something.'

'No!' Jean-Jacques took a step forward, his voice high. 'That's a lie!'

Carton grabbed his arm as the man with the scar put his hand on the knife at his belt. Jean-Jacques pulled away so hard he lost his balance and fell against Carton's side. Stumbling.

The man with the scar relaxed his hand. 'It's true,' he said, staring at Jean-Jacques. 'She attacked Citizen Duclos, then tried to escape. The innocent have nothing to fear.'

Jean-Jacques gave a shrill, desperate cry. It was impossible to tell if it was laughter or pain, or both.

Carton's lips and throat were dry. 'Did you get them back?' He had known this would be hopeless, whatever the truth of it. He should never have come. 'Maybe she was just...' He stopped. There was no air to breathe.

The man with the scar shrugged. 'It doesn't matter now, Citizen. She was shot running away. Your job is finished.'

He smiled, showing his gapped teeth again. 'I guess you won't get paid!'

Jean-Jacques let out a howl of grief and fury like an animal, the sound so raw even the man with the scar froze, and both the other guards turned toward him, mouths gaping.

'Murderers!' Jean-Jacques screamed. 'Duclos stole the cheeses, and you let him murder her to hide it!' He snatched his arm away from Carton's grip and lunged toward the man with the scar, reaching for his knife, both their hands closing on the hilt at the same time. 'Her blood is on your soul!' He had forgotten that in Revolutionary France there was no God, so presumably men had no souls, either.

The other guards came to life and moved in.

Suddenly Carton found his nerve. He put his arms around Jean-Jacques and lifted him physically off the ground, kicking and shouting. His heels struck Carton's shins and the pain nearly made him let go. He staggered backward, taking Jean-Jacques with him, and fell against the farther wall. 'I'm sorry!' he gasped to the man with the scar, now holding the knife with the blade toward them. 'She was his sister. It was his responsibility to look after her.' That was a stretching of the truth. 'You understand? He doesn't mean it.' He held Jean-Jacques hard enough to squash the air out of his lungs. He could feel him gasping and choking as he tried to breathe. 'We're leaving,' he added. 'Maybe we didn't really know what happened.'

Jean-Jacques's heels landed so hard on his shins that this time he let go of him and he fell to the ground.

The guards were still uncertain.

Philippe Duclos could appear at any moment, and Carton and Jean-Jacques could both finish up imprisoned here. Ignoring his throbbing leg, Carton bent and picked up Jean-Jacques by the scruff of his neck, yanked him to his feet, and gave him a cuff on the ear hard enough to make his head sing – please heaven – and rob him of speech for long enough to get him outside!

'Thank you, Citizen,' he called to the man with the scar, and half dragged Jean-Jacques, half carried him, to the entrance and the blessed freedom of the street.

He crossed over, turned right, then left down the first narrow alley he came to before he finally let go of Jean-Jacques. 'I'm sorry,' he said at last. 'But you can't help.'

Jean-Jacques shook himself. 'Let me go back and get her.' His voice was thick with sobs. 'Let me bury her!'

Carton seized his shoulder again. 'No! They'll take you too!'

'I haven't done anything!' Jean-Jacques protested furiously. 'For

what? For coming for my sister's corpse? What are you, stone?
Ice? You English clod!'

'I am alive,' Carton responded. 'And I mean to stay alive. And
yes, coming for her corpse would be quite enough for them to
blame you, and if you used a quarter of the brain you've got, you'd
know that.'

Jean-Jacques seemed to shrink within himself.

Carton was twisted inside with pity. He refused to think of
Marie-Claire's bright face, her vitality, the dreams and the anger
that had made her so vivid.

'Come on, friend,' he said gently. 'There's nothing we can do,
except survive. She'd want you to do that. Come and have some
wine, and we'll find a little bread, and perhaps someone will have
onions, or even a piece of sausage.'

Jean-Jacques lifted up his head a little. 'I suppose so.' He sighed.
'Yes – survive. You are right, she would want that.'

'Of course she would,' Carton said more heartily. 'Come on.'

They started to walk again, crossing the river and turning south
for no particular reason, except that neither of them was yet ready
to sit still. Finally they came to a wine shop with the door open.
The smell of the spilled wine inside was inviting, and there was
room to sit down.

The proprietress was a handsome woman with a fine head of
black hair, long and thick like a mane. She stared at them, waiting
for them to speak.

'Wine?' Carton asked. 'Start with two bottles. We have sorrows
to drown, Citizeness. And bread, if you have it?'

'You would feed your sorrows as well?' she asked without a smile.

'Citizeness…' Carton began.

'Defarge,' she replied, as if he had asked her name. 'I'll bring you
bread. Where's your money?'

Carton put a handful of coins on he table.

She returned with a plate of bread, half an onion, and two
bottles. Half an hour later she brought another bottle, and half an
hour after that, a fourth. Carton kept on drinking – his body was
used to it – but Jean-Jacques slumped against the wall and seemed
to be asleep.

Citizeness Defarge remained, and in the early evening brought more bread, but by then Carton was not hungry.

Jean-Jacques opened his eyes and sat up.

'Bread?' Carton offered.

'No.' Jean-Jacques waved it away. 'I have worked out a plan.'

Carton's head was fuzzy. 'To do what?'

'Be revenged on Philippe Duclos, of course! What else?' Jean-Jacques looked at him as if he were a fool.

Carton was too eased with wine to be alarmed. 'Don't,' he said simply. 'Whatever it is, it won't work. You'll only get into more trouble.'

Jean-Jacques looked at him with big, grief-filled eyes. 'Yes, it will,' he said with a catch in his voice. 'I'll make it work...for Marie-Claire.' He stood up with an effort, swayed for a moment, struggling for his balance. 'Thank you, Carton,' he added formally, starting to bow, and then changing his mind. 'You are a good friend.' And without adding any more he walked unsteadily to the door and disappeared outside.

Carton sat alone, miserable and guilty. If he had really been a good friend, he would have prevented Marie-Claire from setting out on such a mad plan in the first place. He had spent his whole life believing in nothing, achieving pointless victories in small cases in London, and now here writing pieces that did not change the Revolution a jot. It carried on from one insane venture to another regardless. The Paris Commune, largely ruled by Marat, whatever anyone said, made hunger and violence worse with every passing week. France was at war on every side: Spain, Austria, Belgium, and England. Since the hideous massacres last September when the gutters quite literally ran with human blood, Paris was a city of madmen. Charles Darnay was a prisoner in La Force, and Lucie grieved for him ceaselessly, every day going to wait outside the walls, carrying their child, in the hope that he might glimpse them and be comforted.

And here was Carton sitting drunk in Defarge's wine shop, sorry for himself, and ashamed that Jean-Jacques called him a friend, because he had no right to that name.

* * *

Two days later, on July 12, Carton was back in the Café Procope, taking his usual midday bowl of soup when two soldiers of the Revolutionary Guard came in, red, white and blue cockades on their hats, muskets over their shoulders. They spoke for a moment with the proprietor, then walked over to Carton.

'Citizen Carton,' the first one said. It was not a question but a statement. 'You must come with us. There is a matter of theft with which we have been informed that you can help us. On your feet.'

Carton was stunned. He opened his mouth to protest, and realised even as he did so that it was totally pointless. It was his turn. Sooner or later some monstrous injustice happened to everyone. He had been informed on and there was no use fighting against it. He obeyed, and walked out between the guards, wondering what idiotic mistake had occurred to involve him. It could be something as simple as the wrong name, a letter different, a misspelling. He had heard of that happening.

But when he got as far as the Section Committee prison where Marie-Claire had been shot, and walked along the same stone corridor, with the smell of sweat and fear in the air, he knew there was no such easy error.

'Ah – Citizen Lawyer,' the man with the scar said, smiling. 'We know who you are, you see?' He nodded to the soldiers. 'You can go. You have done well, but we have our own guards here.' He gestured toward three burly men with gaping shirts and red bandannas around their heads or necks. In the oppressive heat their faces and chests were slick with sweat. Two had pistols, one a knife.

The soldiers left.

'Now, Citizen Carton,' the man with the scar began, taking his seat behind a wooden table set up as if it were a judge's bench. Carton was left standing. 'This matter of the cheeses that were stolen. It seems you know more about that than you said before. Now would be a good time to tell the truth – all of it. A good time for you, that is.'

Carton tried to clear his brain. What he said now might determine his freedom, even his life. Men killed for less than a cheese these days.

'You don't have them?' He affected immense surprise.

The man's face darkened with anger and suspicion that he was being mocked.

Carton stared back at him with wide innocence. He really had no idea where the cheeses were, and he had even more urgent reasons for wishing that he did.

'No, we don't,' the man admitted in a growl.

'That is very serious, 'Carton said sympathetically. 'Citizen…!'

'Sabot,' the man grunted.

'Citizen Sabot.' Carton nodded courteously. 'We must do everything we can to find them. They are evidence. And apart from that, it is a crime to waste good food. There is certainly a deserving person somewhere to whom they should go.' The place seemed even more airless than before, as if everything which came here, human or not, remained. The smell of fear was in the nose and throat, suffocating the breath.

Along the corridor to the left, out of sight, someone shouted, there was laughter, a wail. Then the silence surged back like a returning wave.

Carton found his voice shaking when he spoke again. 'Citizen Sabot, you have been very fair to me. I will do everything I can to learn what happened to the cheeses and bring you the information.' He saw the distrust naked in Sabot's face, the sneer already forming on his lips. 'You are a man of great influence,' he went on truthfully, however much he might despise himself for it. 'Apart from justice, it would be wise of me to assist you all that I can.'

Sabot was mollified. 'Yes, it would,' he agreed. 'I'll give you two days. Today and tomorrow.'

'I'll report to you in two days,' Carton hedged. 'I might need longer to track them down. We are dealing with clever people here. If it were not so, your own men would have found them already, surely.'

Sabot considered for a moment. Half a dozen Revolutionary Guards marched by with heavy tread. Someone sang a snatch of 'The Marseillaise', that song the rabble had adopted when they burst out of the gaols of Marseilles and the other sea ports of the Mediterranean, and marched all the way to Paris, killing and looting everything in their path. Carton found himself shaking uncontrollably, memory nauseating him.

'Tomorrow night,' Sabot conceded. 'But if you find them and eat them yourself, I'll have your head.'

Carton gulped and steadied himself. 'Naturally,' he agreed. He almost added something else, then while he still retained some balance, he turned and left, trying not to run.

Back in the room he rented, Carton sank down into his bed, his mind racing to make sense of what had happened, and his own wild promise to Sabot to find the cheeses. He had been granted barely two days. Where could he even begin?

With Marie-Claire's original plan. She had intended to have Philippe tell Fleuriot that he was going to post guards, so he had moved the cheeses and the bacon to a more accessible place. Only he had done it earlier than the time agreed with Marie-Claire. Presumably his plan had worked. Fleuriot had moved the cheeses, and Philippe had caught him in the act, and confiscated them. Fleuriot had said nothing, because he should not have had the cheeses in the first place. So much was clear.

Marie-Claire had heard of it and attempted to accuse Philippe, but either she had not been listened to at all, or if she had, she had not been believed, and Philippe had silenced her before she could prove anything. According to Sabot, no one had found the cheeses, so Philippe must still have them.

Maybe Carton should begin with Fleuriot. He at least would know when the cheeses had been taken, which – if it led to Philippe's movements that day – might indicate where he could have hidden them. Carton got up and went out. This was all an infuriating waste of time. He should be working. His money was getting low. If it were not his own neck at risk, he would not do it. All the proof of innocence in the world would not save poor Marie-Claire now. And it would hardly help Jean-Jacques, either. No one cared because half the charges made were built on settling old scores anyway, or on profit of one sort or another. Those who had liked Marie-Claire would still like her just as much.

He walked along the street briskly, head down, avoiding

people's eyes. There was a warm wind rising, and it smelled as if rain were coming. Old newspapers blew along the pavement, flapping like wounded birds. Two laundresses were arguing. It looked like the same ones as before.

He went the long way around to the Rue St Honoré, in order to avoid passing the house where Marat lived and printed his papers. He had enough trouble without an encounter with the 'Rage of the People'. A couple of questions elicited the information as to exactly which house Fleuriot lived in, next to the carpenter Duplay. But Fleuriot was an angry and frightened man. The loss of a few cheeses was nothing compared with the threatened loss of his head. He stood in the doorway, his spectacles balanced on his forehead, and stared fixedly at Carton.

'I don't know what you're talking about, Citizen. There are always Revolutionary Guards about the place. How is one day different from another?'

'Not Revolutionary Guards,' Carton corrected patiently. 'These would be from the local Committee, not in uniform, apart from the red bandanna.'

'Red bandanna!' Fleuriot threw his hands up in the air. 'What does that mean? Nothing! Anyone can wear a red rag. They could be from the Faubourg St Antoine, for all I know. I mind my own business, Citizen, and you'd be best advised to mind yours! Good day.' And without giving Carton a chance to say anything more, he retreated inside his house and slammed the door, leaving Carton alone in the yard just as it began to rain.

He spent the rest of the afternoon and early evening getting thoroughly wet and learning very little of use. He asked all the neighbours whose apartments fronted onto the courtyard, and he even asked the apothecary in the house to the left, and the carpenter in the yard to the right. But Philippe was powerful and his temper vicious. If anyone knew anything about exactly when he came with his man, they were affecting ignorance. According to most of them, the place had been totally deserted on that particular late afternoon. One was queuing for candles, another for soap. One woman was visiting her sick sister, a girl was selling pamphlets, a youth was delivering a piece of furniture, another was too drunk to have known if his own mother had walked past him, and she had been dead for years. That at least was probably honest.

Carton went home wet to the skin and thoroughly discouraged. He had two slices of bread, half a piece of sausage, and a bottle of wine. He took off his wet clothes and sat in his nightshirt, thinking. Tomorrow was July 13. If he did not report the day after, Sabot would come for him. He would be angry because he had failed twice, and been taken for a fool. And what was worse, by then Philippe himself would almost certainly be aware of Carton's interest in the matter. He must succeed. The alternative would be disaster. He must find out more about Philippe himself, where he lived, what other places he might have access to, who were his friends. Even better would be to know who were his enemies!

He finally went to sleep determined to start very early in the morning. He needed to succeed, and quickly, for his own survival, but he would also like to be revenged for Marie-Claire. She had not deserved this, and in spite of his better judgement he had liked her. It would be good to do something to warrant the friendship Jean-Jacques believed of him.

In the morning he got up early and went out straight away. He bought a cup of coffee from a street vendor, drank it and handed back the mug to her, then walked on past the usual patient queues of women hoping for bread, or vegetables, or whatever it was. He passed the sellers of pamphlets and the tradesmen still trying to keep up some semblance of normality at what they did: millinery, barrel-making, engraving, hair-dressing, or whatever it was, and retraced his steps to the local committee headquarters. It was a considerable risk asking questions about Philippe Duclos, especially since he was already known and Philippe would be on his guard. He knew he had taken the cheeses and would see threat even where there was none. But Carton had to report to Sabot by midnight tonight, and so far he had accomplished nothing. It was not impossible that in his fear of Philippe, Fleuriot had already warned him that Carton was asking questions.

Affecting innocence and concern, Carton asked one of the guards where he might find Citizen Duclos, since he had a personal message for him.

The man grunted. 'Citizen Duclos is a busy man! Why should I keep watch on him? Who knows where he is?'

Carton bit back his instinctive answer and smiled politely. 'You are very observant,' he replied between his teeth. 'I am sure you know who comes and goes, as a matter of habit.'

The man grunted again, but the love of flattery was in his eyes, and Carton had asked for nothing but a little harmless information. 'He is not in yet,' he replied. 'Come back in an hour or two.'

'The message is urgent,' Carton elaborated. 'I would not wish to disturb him, but I could wait for him in the street near his lodgings, and as soon as he comes out, I could speak with him.'

The man shrugged. 'If you wake him you'll pay for it!' he warned.

'Naturally. I am sure his work for liberty keeps him up till strange hours, as I imagine yours does, too.'

'All hours!' the man agreed. 'Haven't seen my bed long enough for a year or more!'

'History will remember you,' Carton said ambiguously. 'Where should I wait for Citizen Duclos?'

'Rue Mazarine,' the man replied. 'South side, near the apothecary's shop.'

'Thank you.' Carton nodded to him and hurried away before he could become embroiled in any further conversation.

He found the apothecary's shop and stood outside it, apparently loitering like many others, occasioning no undue attention. People came and went, most of them grumbling about one thing or another. The pavements steamed from the night's rain and already it was hot.

Twenty minutes later a large man came out, bleary-eyed, unshaven, a red bandanna around his neck. There was a wine stain on the front of his shirt, and he belched as he passed Carton, barely noticing him.

Carton waited until he had gone around the corner out of sight, and for another ten minutes after that, then he went under the archway into the courtyard and knocked on the first door.

A woman opened it, her sleeves rolled up and a broom in her

hand. He asked her for Philippe Duclos and was directed to the door opposite. Here he was fortunate at last. It was opened by a child of about eleven. She was curious and friendly. She told him Philippe lodged with her family and he had one room. Carton asked if Philippe were to be given a gift of wine, did he have a place where he could keep it.

'He could put it in the cellar,' she replied. 'But if it is a good wine, then one of the other lodgers might drink it. It would not be safe.' Was there not somewhere better, more private? No, unfortunately there was no such place. Might he have a friend? She giggled. The thought amused her. She did not imagine his trusting a friend, he was not that kind of man. He didn't even trust her mother, who cooked and cleaned for him. He was always counting his shirts! As if anybody would want them.

Carton thanked her and left, puzzled. Again he was at a dead end. He went back to the neighbours of Fleuriot to see if he could find anyone, even a child or a servant, who might have seen Philippe's men moving the cheeses, or if not cheese, then at least the bacon. One cannot carry out a side of bacon in one's pocket!

He spoke to a dozen people, busy and idle, resident and passerby, but no one had seen people carrying goods that day, or since, with the exception of shopping going in. Even laundry had been done at the well in the centre of the yard, and the presence of the women would have been sufficient to deter anyone from carrying anything past with as distinctive a shape as a side of bacon, or odour as a ripe cheese.

He saw only one rat, fat and sleek, running from the well across the stones and disappearing into a hole in the wall. Then he remembered that there was a timber yard next door, belonging to the carpenter Duplay. Shouldn't there be plenty of rats around?

What if no one had seen Philippe move the cheeses because he hadn't? They were still here – the safest place for them! Fleuriot would guard them with his life, but if Sabot should find them, then Fleuriot would take the blame, and Philippe would affect total innocence. He would say he knew nothing of them at all, and Marie-Claire, the only person who knew he had, was dead and could say nothing. It made perfect sense. And above all it was safe!

Philippe simply took a cheese whenever he wanted, and Fleuriot was too frightened of him to do anything about it. Certainly he would not dare eat one or sell one himself.

Carton walked away quickly and went back to the Café Procope and ordered himself a slice of bread and sausage and a bottle of wine. He sat at his usual table. Every time the door swung open he looked up, half expecting to see Jean-Jacques, and felt an unreasonable surge of disappointment each time it was not. He had nothing in particular to say to him, apart from to forget his plan for revenge, whatever it was, but he missed his company, and he hurt for his grief. Perhaps he even would have liked to talk of Marie-Claire and share some of the pain within himself.

If the cheeses were still in Fleuriot's house, then it would take a number of men, with the authority of the Commune itself behind them to search. The local authority was no good, that was Philippe himself. How could Carton get past that? He stared into his glass and knew there was only one answer – the one he had been avoiding for the last half year – ask Marat! Marat was the Commune.

There must be another way. He poured out the last of the wine and drank it slowly. It was sour, but it still hit his stomach with a certain warmth. So far he had avoided even passing the house in the Rue des Médicines where Marat lived. He had rather that Marat had never even heard of him. Now he was about to ruin it all by actually walking into the house and asking a favour! Never mind drunk, he must be mad! He up-ended the glass and drained the last mouthful. Well, if he were going to commit suicide, better get on with it rather than sit here feeling worse and worse, living it over in his imagination until he was actually sick.

He went outside and walked quickly, as if he had purpose he was intent upon. Get it done. The fear of it was just as bad as the actuality. At least get this achieved.

He was there before he expected. He must have been walking too rapidly. There was an archway on the corner leading into a cobbled yard with a well in the centre, just like any of a thousand others. At one side a flight of steps led up to an entrance, and even from where he stood Carton could see bales of paper piled up just inside the doorway, boxes beyond, and printed newspapers ready to deliver. There was no excuse for hesitation. It was obviously Marat's house.

He took a deep breath, let it out slowly, then walked across and up the steps. No one accosted him until he was inside and peering around, looking for someone to ask. A plain, rather ordinary woman approached him, her face mild, as if she expected a friend.

'Citizeness,' he said huskily. 'I am sorry to interrupt your business. But I have a favour to ask which only Citizen Marat could grant me. Who may I approach in order to speak with him?'

'I am Simone Evrard,' she replied with a certain quiet confidence. 'I will ask Citizen Marat if he can see you. Who are you, and what is it you wish?'

Carton remembered with a jolt that Marat had some kind of common-law wife – Marat of all people! This was her, a soft-spoken woman with red hands and an apron tied around her waist. 'Sydney Carton, Citizeness,' he replied. 'It is to do with a man hoarding food instead of making it available to all citizens, as it should be. Unfortunately he has a position in the local committee, so I cannot go to them.'

'I see.' She nodded. 'I shall tell him. Please wait here.'

She was gone for several minutes. He stood shifting his weight from foot to foot, trying to control the fear rising inside him. It even occurred to him to change his mind and leave. There was still time.

And then there wasn't. She was back again, beckoning him toward her and pointing to the doorway of another room. Like one in a dream he obeyed, his heart pounding in his chest.

Inside, the room was unlike anything he could conceivably have expected. It was small, a sort of aqueous green, and the steam in it clung to his skin and choked his nose and his throat. The smell was ghastly, a mixture of vinegar and rotting human flesh. In the centre was a tin bath shaped like a boot, concealing the lower portion of the occupant's body. A board was placed across it on which rested a pen, inkwell, and paper. Even through the heavy steam Carton could see Marat quite clearly. His toadlike face with its bulging eyes and slack mouth was almost bloodless with the exhaustion of pain. There was a wet towel wrapped around his head. His naked shoulders, arms, and upper chest were smooth and hairless.

'What is it, Citizen Carton?' he asked. His voice was rough and had a slight accent. Carton remembered he was not French at all, but half Swiss and half Sardinian. The stench caught in his throat and he thought he was going to gag.

'Would you rather speak in English?' Marat asked – in English. He was a doctor by profession and had held a practice in Pimlico in London for some time.

'No, thank you, Citizen,' Carton declined, then instantly wondered if it was wise. 'Perhaps you would indulge me should my French falter?'

'What is it you want?' Marat repeated. His expression was hard to read because of the ravages of disease upon his face. He was in his fifties, a generation older than most of the other Revolutionary leaders, and a lifetime of hate had exhausted him.

'I believe a certain Citizen Duclos has discovered a quantity of exceptionally good food, cheeses and bacon to be exact, in the keeping of a Citizen Fleuriot, and has blackmailed him into concealing that food from the common good.' Carton was speaking too quickly and he knew it, but he could not control himself enough to slow down. 'Citizen Duclos is in a position of power in the local committee, so I cannot turn to them to search and find it.'

Marat blinked. 'So you want me to have men from the Commune search?'

'Yes, please.'

Marat grunted and eased his position a little, wincing as the ulcerated flesh touched the sides of the bath. 'I'll consider it,' he said with a gasp. 'Why do you care? Is it your cheese?'

'No, Citizen. But it is unjust. And it could be mine next time.'

Marat stared at him. Carton felt the steam settle on his skin and trickle down his face and body. His clothes were sticking to him. The pulse throbbed in his head and his throat. Marat did not believe him. He knew it.

'A friend of mine was blamed for it, and shot,' he added. Was he insane to tell Marat this? Too late now. 'I want revenge.'

Marat nodded slowly. 'Come back this evening. I'll have men for you,' he assured. 'I understand hate.'

'Thank you,' Carton said hoarsely, then instantly despised himself for it. He did not want to have anything in common with this man, this embodiment of insane rage who had sworn to drown Paris in seas of blood. He half bowed, and backed out of that dreadful room into the hallway again.

He returned to his rooms and fell asleep for a while. He woke with a headache like a tight band around his temples. He washed in cold water, changed his clothes, and went out to buy a cup of coffee. He would have to think about something more for publication soon, as he would run out of money.

It was half past seven in the evening. He had not long before he would have to report to Sabot.

He was almost back to Marat's house when he heard shouting in the street and a woman screaming. He hastened his step and was at the archway when a Revolutionary Guardsman pushed past him.

'What is it?' Carton asked, alarm growing inside him.

'Marat's been killed!' a young man cried out. 'Murdered! Stabbed to death in his bath. A mad woman from Calvados. Marat's dead!'

There were more footsteps running, shouts and screams, armed men clattering by, howls of grief, rage and terror.

Dead! Carton stood still, leaning a little against the wall in the street. In spite of all his will to stop it, in his mind he could see the ghastly figure of Marat in that aqueous room, the steam, the shrivelled skin, the stench, the pain in his face. He imagined the body lifeless, and blood pouring into the vinegar and water. And with a wave of pity he thought of a quiet woman who for some inconceivable reason had loved him.

He must get out of here! Maybe he would be lucky and the widow would not even remember his name, let alone why he had come. He straightened up and stumbled away, tripping on he cobbles as he heard the shouts behind him, more men coming. Someone let off a musket shot, and then another.

All his instincts impelled him to run, but he must not. It would look as if he were escaping. A couple of women accosted him, asking what was wrong. 'I don't know,' he lied. 'Some kind of trouble. But stay away from it.' And without waiting he left them.

When he finally got inside his own rooms and locked the door, he realised the full impact of what had happened. Marat, the head of the Commune, the most powerful man in Paris, had been murdered by some woman from the countryside. The revenge for it would be unimaginable. But of more immediate concern to Carton, he did not have Marat's men to search Fleuriot's house for the cheeses. And Sabot would expect an answer tonight or Carton himself would pay the price for it. He would have to do something about it himself, and immediately.

He dashed a little water over his face, dried it, put his jacket back on, and went outside again. The one idea in his mind was desperate, but then so would the result be if he did nothing.

Rats were the key. If he could not get Marat's men to search Fleuriot's house, then he would have to get someone else to do it. The carpenter Duplay, with his wood yard next door, was at least a chance. He could think of nothing better.

He walked quickly toward the Rue St Honoré, hoping not to give himself time to think of all the things that could go wrong. He had no choice. He kept telling himself that – no choice! It was a drumbeat in his head as he strode along the cobbles, crossed to avoid a cart unloading barrels, and came to the archway at the entrance to the carpenter's house. He knocked before he had time to hesitate.

It was opened within two minutes by a young woman. She was small and very neat, rather like a child, except that her face was quite mature, as if she were at least in her middle twenties. She inquired politely what she could do to help him.

'I believe the Citizen who lives here is a carpenter,' he said, after thanking her for her courtesy.

'Yes, Citizen. He is excellent. Did you wish to purchase something, or have something made, perhaps?' she asked.

'Thank you, but I am concerned for his stock of wood, possibly even his finished work,' he replied. 'I have reason to believe that food is being stored in the house next door – cheese, to be precise – and there are a large number of rats collecting…' He stopped, seeing the distaste in her face, as if he had spoken of something obscene. 'I'm sorry,' he apologised. 'Perhaps I should not have mentioned it to you, but I feel that the Citizen...'

There was a click of high heels on the wooden stairway and Carton looked beyond the young woman to see a man whose resemblance to her was marked enough for him to assume that they were related. He was about thirty, small and intensely neat, as she was, almost feline in his manner, with a greenish pallor to his complexion, and myopic green eyes which he blinked repeatedly as he stared at Carton. He was dressed perfectly in the manner of the Ançien Régime, as if he were to present himself at the court of Louis XVI, complete with green striped nankeen jacket, exquisitely cut, a waistcoat and cravat, breeches and stockings. It was his high heels Carton had heard. His hair was meticulously powdered and tied back. He fluttered his very small, nail-bitten hands when he spoke.

'It is all right, Charlotte, I shall deal with the matter.'

'Yes, Maximilien,' she said obediently, and excused herself.

'Did you say "rats", Citizen?' the man asked, his voice soft, accented with a curious sibilance.

With a shock like icy water on his bare flesh, Carton realised what he had done. Of all the carpenters in Paris he had knocked on the door of the one in whose house lodged Citizen Robespierre, and apparently his sister. He stood frozen to the spot, staring at the little man still on the bottom stair, as far away from him as he could be without being absurd. Carton remembered someone saying that Robespierre was so personally fastidious as to dislike anyone close to him, let alone touching him. He had constant indigestion for which he sucked oranges, and anything as gross as a bodily appetite or function offended him beyond belief.

'I am sorry to mention such a matter,' Carton apologised again. He found himself thinking of Jean-Jacques and his grief, and how alive Marie-Claire had been, how full of laughter, anger, and dreams. 'But I believe Citizen Fleuriot next door is hoarding cheese, and it is unfair that he rob the good citizens of food by doing so, but it is also a considerable danger to his immediate neighbours, because of the vermin it attracts.'

Robespierre was staring at him with his strange, short-sighted eyes.

Carton gulped. 'I have not the power to do anything about it myself,' he went on, 'but I can at least warn others. I imagine Citizen Duplay has a great deal of valuable wood which could be damaged.' He bowed very slightly. 'Thank you for your courtesy, Citizen. I hope I have not distressed the Citizeness.'

'You did your duty,' Robespierre replied with satisfaction. 'The "Purity of the People"' – he spoke as if it were some kind of divine entity – 'requires sacrifice. We must rid France of vermin of every kind. I shall myself go to see this Citizen Fleuriot. Come with me.'

Carton drew in his breath, and choked. Robespierre waited while he suffered a fit of coughing, then when Carton was able to compose himself, he repeated his command. 'Come with me.'

Carton followed the diminutive figure in the green jacket, heels clicking on the cobbles, white-powdered head gleaming in the last of the daylight, until they reached Fleuriot's door. Robespierre stepped aside for Carton to knock. The door opened and Fleuriot himself stood in the entrance, face tight with annoyance.

Carton moved aside and Fleuriot saw Robespierre. A curious thing happened. There could not be two such men in all France, let alone in this district of Paris. Fleuriot's recognition was instant. He turned a bilious shade of yellowish-green and swayed so wildly that had he not caught hold of the door lintel he would have fallen over.

'I have been told that you have some cheeses,' Robespierre said in his soft, insistent voice. 'A great many, in fact.' He blinked. 'Of course I do not know if that is true, but lying would make you an enemy to the people…'

Fleuriot made a strange, half-strangled sound in his throat.

Carton closed his eyes and opened them again. His mouth was dry as the dust on the stones. 'It's possible Citizen Fleuriot does not own the cheeses?' he said, his voice catching. He coughed as Robespierre swivelled around to stare at him, peering forward as if it were difficult to see. Carton cleared his throat again. 'Perhaps he is frightened of someone else, Citizen?'

'Yes!' Fleuriot said in a high-pitched squeak, as if he were being strangled. 'The good citizen is right!' It was painfully clear that he was terrified. His face was ghastly, the sweat stood out on his lip and brow, and he wrung his hands as if he would break them, easing his weight from foot to foot. But the fear that touched his soul was of Robespierre, not of Philippe Duclos. He gulped for air. 'The cheeses are not mine! They belong to Citizen Duclos, of the local committee. I am keeping them for him! He has threatened to have my head if I don't...' His voice wavered off and he looked as if he were going to faint.

Robespierre stepped back. Such physical signs of terror repelled him. The Purity of the People was a concept, an ideal to be aspired to, and the means to achieve it was obviously fear, but he did not want ever to think of the reality of it, much less be forced to witness it. 'Philippe Duclos?' he asked.

'Yes...C-Citizen...R-Robespierre,' Fleuriot stammered.

'Then Citizen Carton here will help you carry the cheeses out, and we will give them to the people, where they belong,' Robespierre ordered. 'And Citizen Duclos will answer with his head.' He did not even glance at Carton but stood waiting for an obedience he took for granted.

Carton felt oddly safe as he followed Fleuriot inside. Robespierre was a tiny man with no physical strength at all – Philippe could have broken him with one blow – but it was not even imaginable that he would. Robespierre's presence in the yard was more powerful than an army of soldiers would have been. Carton would not even have taken a cheese for Sabot without his permission.

When the food was all removed, the yard was completely dark, but Robespierre was easily discernible by the gleam of his powdered hair. Carton approached him with his heart hammering.

'Citizen Robespierre?'

Robespierre turned, peering at him in the shadows. 'Yes, what is it? You have done well.'

'Citizen Sabot of the local committee is a good man.'

His voice shook, and he despised himself for his words. 'I would like him to have an opportunity to be rewarded for his service to the people by receiving one of the cheeses.'

Robespierre stood motionless for several seconds. He drew in his breath with a slight hiss. 'Indeed.'

'He works long hours.' Carton felt the blood thundering in his head. 'I must report to him tonight, to show my honesty in this matter, or...' he faltered and fell silent.

'He does his duty,' Robespierre replied.

Carton's heart sank.

'But you may be rewarded,' Robespierre added. 'You may have one of the cheeses.'

Carton was giddy with relief. 'Thank you, Citizen.' He hated the gratitude in his voice, and he could do nothing about it. 'You are...' he said the one word he knew Robespierre longed to hear, '...incorruptible.'

He took the cheese and went to the local committee prison. Sabot was waiting for him. He saw the cheese even before Carton spoke.

Carton placed it on the table before him, hating to let go of it, and knowing it was the only way to save his life.

'I found them,' he said. 'Citizen Robespierre will arrest the hoarder. You would be well advised to take this home, tonight – now! And say nothing.'

Sabot nodded with profound understanding and a good deal of respect. He picked up the cheese, caressing it with his fingers. 'I will leave now,' he agreed. 'I will walk along the street with you, Citizen.'

Philippe protested of course, but it availed him nothing. Fleuriot would never have dared retract his testimony, and apart from that, there was a sweetness in having his revenge on Philippe for having stolen his hoard, and then terrified him into guarding it for him, adding insult to injury.

Reluctantly Sabot was allowed his one cheese in reward. It was all over very swiftly. Robespierre was not yet a member of the Committee of Public Safety, but it was only a matter of time. His star was ascending. Already someone whispered of him as 'The Sea-Green Incorruptible'. Philippe Duclos was found guilty and sentenced to the guillotine.

Robespierre never personally witnessed such a disgusting act as an execution. The only time he ever saw the machine of death at all was at the end of the High Terror still a year in the future, when he mounted the blood-spattered steps himself.

Carton had not intended to go, but the memory of Marie-Claire was suddenly very sharp in his mind. He could see her bright face under its tumbled hair, hear her voice with its laughter and enthusiasm, as if she had gone out of the door only minutes ago. Half against his will, despising himself for it, he nevertheless was waiting in the Place de la Révolution, watching with revulsion Citizeness Defarge and her friends who sat with their knitting needles clicking beside the guillotine when the tumbrels came rattling in with their cargo of the condemned.

As usual they were all manner of people, but not many of them wore the red bandanna of the Citizen's power, and Philippe was easy to see.

Carton felt a joggle at his elbow, and turning for an instant, he thought it was Marie-Claire. It was the same wide, brown eyes, the tangle of hair, but it was Jean-Jacques, his face still haggard with grief. He looked at Carton and his cheeks were wet.

Carton put out his hand to touch him gently. 'I'm glad you didn't try your plan,' he said with intense gratitude. He liked this odd little man profoundly. It was stupid to have such a hostage to fate, but he could not help it. Afterward they would go and drink together in quiet remembrance and companionship. 'It would never have worked,' he added.

Jean-Jacques smiled through his tears. 'Yeah, it did,' he answered.

You want to know why what happened last Wednesday night at the Roxette happened at all. You have to go back twenty years. To the miners' strike. They teach it to the bairns now as history, but I lived through it and it's as sharp in my memory as yesterday. After she beat the Argies in the Falklands, Thatcher fell in love with the taste of victory, and the miners were her number one target. She was determined to break us, and she didn't care what it took. Arthur Scargill, the miners' leader, was as bloody-minded as she was, and when he called his men out on strike, my Alan walked out along with every other miner in his pit.

We all thought it would be over in a matter of weeks at the most. But no bugger would give an inch. Weeks turned into months, the seasons slipped from spring through summer and autumn into winter. We had four bairns to feed and not a penny coming in. Our savings went; then our insurance policies; and finally, my jewellery. We'd go to bed hungry and wake up the same way, our bellies rumbling like the slow grumble of the armoured police vans that regularly rolled round the streets of our town to remind us who we were fighting. Sometimes they'd taunt us by sitting in their vans flaunting their takeaways, even throwing half-eaten fish suppers out on the pavements as they drove by. Anything to rub our noses in the overtime they were coining by keeping us in our places.

We were desperate. I heard tell that some of the wives even went on the game, taking a bus down to the big cities for the day. But nobody from round our way sank that low. Or not that I know of. But lives changed forever during that long hellish year, mine among them.

It's a measure of how low we all sank that when I heard Mattie Barnard had taken a heart attack and died, my first thought wasn't for his widow. It was for his job. I think I got down the Roxette faster than the Co-op Funeral Service got to Mattie's. Tyson Herbert, the manager, hadn't even heard the news. But I didn't let that stop me. 'I want Mattie's job,' I told him straight out, while he was still reeling from the shock.

'Now hang on a minute, Noreen,' he said warily. He was always cautious, was Tyson Herbert. You could lose the will to live waiting for him to turn right at a junction. 'You know as well as I do that bingo calling is a man's job. It's always been that way. A touch of authority. Dicky bow and dinner jacket. The BBC might have let their standards slip, but here at the Roxette, we do things the right way.' Ponderous as a bloody elephant.

'That's against the law nowadays, Tyson,' I said. 'You cannot have rules like that any more. Only if you're a lavatory cleaner or something. And as far as I'm aware, cleaning the Gents wasn't part of Mattie's job.'

Well, we did a bit of a to and fro, but in the end, Tyson Herbert gave in. He didn't have a lot of choice. The first session of the day was due to start in half an hour, and he needed somebody up there doing two fat ladies and Maggie's den. Even if the person in question was wearing a blue nylon overall instead of a tuxedo.

And that was the start of it all. Now, nobody's ever accused me of being greedy, and besides, I still had a house to run as well as doing my share on the picket line with the other miners' wives. So within a couple of weeks, I'd persuaded Tyson Herbert that he needed to move with the times and make mine a jobshare. By the end of the month, I was splitting my shifts with Kathy, Liz and Jackie. The four calling birds, my Alan christened us. Morning, afternoon and evening, one or other of us would be up on the stage, mike in one hand, plucking balls out of the air with the other and keeping the flow of patter going. More importantly, we kept our four families going. We kept our kids on the straight and narrow.

It made a bit of a splash locally. There had never been women bingo callers in the North-East before. It had been as much a man's job as cutting coal. The local paper wrote an article abut us, then the BBC turned up and did an interview with us for *Woman's Hour*. I suppose they were desperate for a story from up our way that wasn't all doom, gloom and picket line. You should have seen Tyson Herbert preening himself, like he'd single-handedly burned every bra in the North-East.

The fuss soon died down, though the novelty value did bring in a lot of business. Women would come in minibuses from all around the area just to see the four calling birds. And we carried on with two little ducks and the key to the door like it was second nature. The years trickled past. The bairns grew up and found jobs, which was hard on Alan's pride. He's never worked since they closed the pit the year after the strike. There's no words for what it does to a man when he's dependent on his wife and bairns for the roof over his head and the food on his table.

To tell you the God's honest truth, there were days when it was a relief to get down the Roxette and get to work. We always had a laugh, even in the hardest of times. And there were hard times. When the doctors told Kathy the lump in her breast was going to kill her, we all felt the blow. But when she got too ill to work, we offered her shifts to her Julie. Tyson Herbert made some crack about hereditary peerages, but I told him to keep his nose out and count the takings.

All in all, nobody had any reason for complaint. That is, until Tyson Herbert decided it was time to retire. The bosses at Head Office didn't consult us about his replacement. Come to that, they didn't consult Tyson either. If they had, we'd never have ended up with Keith Corbett. Keith Cobra, as Julie rechristened him two days into his reign at the Roxette after he tried to grope her at the end of the evening shift. The nickname suited him. He was a poisonous reptile.

He even looked like a snake, with his narrow wedge of a face and his little dark eyes glittering. When his tongue flicked out to lick his thin lips, you expected it to have a fork at the end. On the third morning, he summoned the four of us to his office like he was God and it was Judgement Day. 'You've had a good run, ladies,' he began, without so much as a cup of tea and a digestive biscuit. 'But things are going to be changing round here. The Roxette is going to be the premier bingo outlet in the area, and that will be reflected in our public image. I'm giving you formal notice of redundancy.'

We were gobsmacked. It was Liz who found her voice first. 'You cannot do that,' she said. 'We've given no grounds for complaint.'

'And how can we be redundant?' I chipped in. 'Somebody has to call the numbers.'

Cobra gave a sly little smile. 'You're being replaced by new technology. A fully automated system. Like on the National Lottery. The numbers will go up on a big screen and the computer will announce them.'

We couldn't believe our ears. Replacing us with a machine? 'The customers won't like it,' Julie said.

The Cobra shook his head. 'As long as they get their prizes, they wouldn't care if a talking monkey did the calling. Enjoy your last couple of weeks, ladies.' He turned away from us and started fiddling with his computer.

'You'll regret this,' Liz said defiantly.

'I don't think so,' he said, a sneer on his face. 'Oh, and another thing. This Children in Need night you're planning on Friday night? Forget it. The Roxette is a business, not a charity. Friday night will be just like every other night.'

Well, that did it. We were even more outraged than we were on our own behalf. We'd been doing the Children in Need benefit night for nine years. All the winners donated their prizes, and Tyson Herbert donated a third of the night's takings. It was a big sacrifice all round, but we knew what hardship was, and we all wanted to do our bit.

'You bastard,' Julie said.

The Cobra swung round and glared at her. 'Would you rather be fired for gross misconduct, Julie? Walk out the door with no money and no reference? Because that's exactly what'll happen if you don't keep a civil tongue in your head.'

We hustled Julie out before she could make things worse. We were all fit to be tied, but we couldn't see any way of stopping the Cobra. I broke the news to Alan that teatime. Our Dickson had dropped in too – he's an actor now, he's got a part in one of the soaps, and they'd been doing some location filming locally. I don't know who was more angry, Alan or Dickson. After their tea, the two of them went down to the club full of fighting talk. But I knew it was just talk. There was nothing we could do against the likes of the Cobra.

I was surprised as anybody when I heard about the armed robbery.

* * *

I don't know why I took this job. Everybody knows the Roxette's nothing but trouble. It's never turned the profit it should. And those bloody women. They made Tyson Herbert a laughing stock. But managers' jobs don't come up that often. Plus Head Office said they wanted the Roxette to become one of their flagship venues. And they wanted me to turn it around. Plus Margo's always on at me about Darren needing new this, new that, new the next thing. So how could I say no?

I knew as soon as I walked through the door it was going to be an uphill struggle. There was no sign of the new promo displays that Head Office was pushing throughout the chain. I eventually found them, still in their wrappers, in a cupboard in that pillock Herbert's office. I ask you, how can you drag a business into the twenty-first century if you're dealing with dinosaurs?

And the women. Everywhere, the women. Everywhere the women. You have to wonder what was going on in Herbert's head. It can't have been that he was dipping his wick, because they were all dogs. Apart from Julie. She was about the only one in the joint who didn't need surgical stockings. Not to mention plastic surgery. I might have considered keeping her on for a bit of light relief between houses. But she made it clear from the off that she had no fucking idea which side her bread was buttered. So she was for the chop like the rest of them.

I didn't hang about, I was right in there, making it clear who was in charge. Got the promo displays up on day one.

Then I organised the delivery of the new computerised calling system. And that meant I could give the four calling birds the bullet sooner rather than later. That and knock their stupid charity stunt on the head. I ask you, who throws their profits down the drain like that in this day and age?

By the end of the first week, I was confident that I was all set. I had the decorators booked to bring the Roxette in line with the rest of the chain. Margo was pleased with the extra money in my wage packet, and even Darren had stopped whingeing.

I should have known better. I should have known it was all going too sweet. But not even in my wildest fucking nightmares could I have imagined how bad it could get.

By week two, I had my routines worked out. While the last house was in full swing, I'd do a cash collection from the front of the house, the bar and the café. I'd bag it up in the office, ready for the bank in the morning, then put it in the safe overnight. And that's what I was doing on Wednesday night when the office door slammed open.

I looked up sharpish. I admit, I admit, I thought it was one of those bloody women come to do my head in. But it wasn't. At first all I could take in was the barrel of a sawn-off shotgun, pointing straight at me. I nearly pissed myself. Instinctively I reached for the phone but the big fucker behind the gun just growled, 'Fucking leave it.' Then he kicked the door shut.

I dragged my eyes away from the gun and tried to get a look at him. But there wasn't much to see. Big black puffa jacket, jeans, black work boots. Baseball cap pulled down over his eyes, and a ski mask over the rest of his face. 'Keep your fucking mouth shut,' he said. He threw a black sports holdall towards me. 'Fill it up with cash,' he said.

'I can't,' I said. 'It's in the safe. It's got a time lock.'

'Bollocks,' he said. He waved the gun at me, making me back up against the wall. What happened next was not what I expected. He grabbed the computer keyboard and pulled it across the desk. Then he turned the monitor round so it was facing him. With the hand that wasn't holding the gun, he did a few mouse clicks and then a bit of typing. I tried to edge out of his line of fire, but he wasn't having any. 'Fucking stand still,' he grunted.

Then he turned the screen back to face me and this time I nearly crapped myself. It was a live camera feed from my living room. Margo and Darren were huddled together on the sofa, eyes wide. Opposite them, his back to the camera, was another big fucker with a shotgun. The picture was a bit fuzzy and wobbly, but there was no mistake about it. Along the bottom of the picture, the seconds ticked away.

'My oppo's only a phone call away. Now are you going to fill the fucking holdall?' he demanded.

Well, I wasn't going to argue, was I? Not with my wife and kid facing a shooter. So I went to the safe. It hasn't got a time lock. Head Office wouldn't spend that kind of money. We're just told to say that to try and put off nutters like the big fucker who was facing me down in my office. I was sweating so much my fingers were slipping off the keyboard.

But I managed it at the second go, and I shovelled the bags of cash into his bag as fast as I could.

'Good boy,' he said when I'd finished.

I thought it was all over then. How wrong can you get?

'On your knees,' he ordered me. *I didn't know what was going on. Part of me thought he was going to blow me away anyway. I was so fucking scared I could feel the tears in my eyes. I knew I was on the edge of losing it. Of begging him for my life. Only one thing stopped me. I just couldn't believe he was going to kill me. I mean, I know it happens. I know people get topped during robberies. But surely only if they put up a fight? And surely only when the robber is out of control? But this guy was totally calm. He could afford to be – his oppo's gun was still pointing straight at Margo and Darren.*

So I fell to my knees.

Just thinking about what came next makes me retch. He dropped the gun to his side, at an angle so the barrel dug right into my gut. Then he unzipped his trousers and pulled out his cock. 'Suck my dick,' *he said.*

My head jerked back and I stared at him. I couldn't believe what I'd just heard. 'You what?'

'Suck my dick,' *he said again, thrusting his hips towards me. His half-hard cock dangled in front of my face. It was the sickest thing I'd ever heard. It wasn't enough for this fucking pervert to terrorise my wife and kid and rob my safe. He wanted me to give him a blow job.*

The gun jammed harder into me. 'Just fucking do it,' *he said.*

So I did.

He grabbed my hair and stopped me pulling back when I gagged. 'That's it. You know you want to.' *He said softly, like this was something normal. Which it wasn't, not in any bloody sense.*

It felt like it took a lifetime for him to come, but I supposed it was only a few minutes. When I felt his hot load hitting the back of my throat, I nearly bit his cock off in revulsion. But the gun in my chest and the thought of what might happen to Margo and Darren kept me inside the limits.

He stepped back, tucking himself away and zipping up. 'I enjoyed that,' *he said.*

I couldn't lift my head up. I felt sick to my stomach. And not just from what I'd swallowed either.

'Wait half an hour before you call the cops. We'll be watching, and if there's any funny business, your wife and kid get it. OK?' I nodded. I couldn't speak.

The last thing he did before he left was to help himself to the tape from the video surveillance system that is fed by the camera in my office. In a funny sort of way, I was almost relieved. I didn't want to think about that tape being played in the police station. Or in a courtroom, if it ever came to it.

So I did what I was told. I gave it thirty-five minutes, to be on the safe side. The police arrived like greased lightning. I thought things would get more normal then. Like The Bill or something. But it was my night for being well in the wrong. Because that's when things started to get seriously weird.

They'd sent a crew round to the house to check the robbers had kept their word and released Margo and Darren. They radioed back sounding pretty baffled. Turned out Margo was watching the telly and Darren was in his room playing computer games. According to them, that's what they'd been doing all evening. Apart from when Margo had been on the phone to her mate Cheryl. Which had been more or less exactly when I'd supposedly been watching them being held hostage.

That's when the cops started giving me some very fucking funny looks. The boss, a DI Golightly, definitely wasn't living up to his name. 'So how did chummy get in?' he demanded. 'There's no sign of forced entry at the back. And even though they were all eyes down inside the hall, I doubt they would have missed a six-foot gunman walking through from the foyer.'

'I don't know,' I said. 'It should all have been locked up. The last person out would have been Liz Kirby. She called the session before the last one.'

By that time, they had the CCTV tapes of the car park. You could see the robber emerge from the shadows on the edge of the car park and walk up to the door. You couldn't see the gun, just the holdall. He opened the door without a moment's hesitation. So that fucking doozy had left it unlocked.

'Looks like he walked straight in,' Golightly said. 'That was lucky for him, wasn't it?'

'I told you. It should have been locked. Look, I'm the victim here.'

He looked me up and down. 'So you say,' he said, sounding like he didn't believe a word of it. Then he wound the tape further back so we could see Liz leaving. And bugger me if she didn't turn round and lock the door behind her.

'How do you explain that?' he said.

All I could do was shrug helplessly.

He kept the digs and insinuations up for a while. He obviously thought there was a chance I was in it up to my eyeballs. But there was fuck all proof so he had to let me go in the end. It was gone four in the morning by the time I got home. Margo was well pissed off. Apparently half the crescent had been glued to their windows after the flashing blue lights had alerted them that there was something more interesting than Big Brother going on outside their own front doors. 'I was black affronted,' Margo kept repeating. 'My family's never had the police at their door.' Like mine were a bunch of hardened criminals.

I didn't sleep much. Every time I got near to dropping off, I got flashbacks of that sick bastard's cock. I've never so much as touched another man's dick, not even when I was a kid. I almost wished I'd let the sad sack of shite shoot me.

Everything I am, I owe to my mam. She taught me that I was as good as anybody else, that there was nothing I couldn't do if I wanted to. She also taught me the meaning of solidarity. Kick one, and we all limp. They should have that on the signs that tell drivers they're entering our town, right below the name of that Westphalian town we're twinned with.

So when she told me and my da what that prize prick Keith Corbett had planned for her and the other at the Roxette, I was livid. And I was determined to do whatever I could to stop it happening. My mam and da have endured too bloody much already; they deserve not to have the rug pulled out from under them one more time.

After we'd had our tea, Da and I went down the club. But I only stayed long enough to do some basic research. I had other fish to fry. I got on the mobile and arranged to meet up with Liz's daughters, Lauren and Shayla. Like me, they found a way out of the poverty trap that has our town between its teeth. They were always into computers, even at school. They both went to college and got qualifications in IT and now they run their own computer consultancy up in Newcastle. I had the germ of an idea, and I knew they'd help me make it a reality.

We met up in a nice little country pub over by Bishop Auckland. I told them what Corbett had in mind, and they were as angry as me. And when I set out the bare bones of my plan, they were on board before I was half a dozen sentences into it. Right from the off, they were on side, coming up with their own ideas for making it even stronger and more foolproof.

It was Shayla who came up with the idea of getting Corbett to suck me off. At first, I was revolted. I thought it was grotesque. Over the top. Too cruel. I'll be honest, I've swung both ways in my time. Working in theatre and telly, there's plenty of opportunities to explore the wilder shores of experience. But having a bit of fun with somebody you fancy is a far cry from letting some sleaze like Corbett anywhere near your tackle.

'I'd never be able to get it up,' I protested.

They both laughed. 'You're a bloke,' Lauren said dismissively. 'And you're an actor. Just imagine he's Jennifer Aniston.'

'Or Brad Pitt,' Shayla giggled.

'I think even Olivier might have had problems with that,' I sighed, knowing I was outgunned and outnumbered. It was clear to me that now I'd brought them aboard, the two women were going to figure out a battle plan in which I was to be the foot soldier, the cannon fodder and the SAS, all rolled into one.

The first – and the most difficult – thing we had to do was to plant a fibre optic camera in Corbett's lounge. We tossed around various ideas, all of which were both complicated and risky. Finally, Lauren hit on the answer. 'His lad's about twelve, thirteen, isn't he?' she asked.

I nodded. 'So I heard down the club.'

'That's sorted then,' she said. 'I can get hold of some games that are at the beta-testing stage. We can knock up a letter telling

Darren he's been chosen to test the games. Offer him a fee. Then pick my moment, roll up at the house before she gets home. She's bound to invite me in and make me a cup of tea. I'll find somewhere to plant the camera and we're rolling.'

And that's exactly how it played out. Lauren got into the house, and while Margo Corbett was off making her a brew, she stuck the camera in the middle of a dried flower arrangement. Perfect.

The next phase was the most frustrating. We had to wait till we had the right set of pictures to make the scam work. For three nights, we filmed Corbett's living room, biting our nails, wondering how long it would take for mother and son to sit down together and watch something with enough dramatic tension. We cracked it on the Monday night, when Channel Five was showing a horror movie. Darren and Margo sat next to each other, huddling closer as the climax piled up.

Then it was Shayla's turn. She spent the rest of Monday night and most of Tuesday putting together the short digital film that we would use to make sure Corbett did what he was told. Lauren had already filmed me against a blue background waving around the replica sawn-off shotgun we'd used as a prop last series. It hadn't been hard to liberate it from the props store. They're incredibly sloppy, those guys. Shayla cut the images in so it looked like I was standing in Corbett's living room threatening his nearest and dearest. I have to say, the end result was impressive and, more importantly, convincing.

Now we were ready. We chose Wednesday night to strike. Lauren had managed to get hold of her mam's keys and copied the one for the Roxette's back door. While the last session of the evening was in full swing, she'd slipped out and unlocked the door so I could walk straight in.

It all went better than I feared. You'd have thought Corbett was working from the same script, the way he caved in and did what he was told. And in spite of my fears, the girls had been right. My body didn't betray us.

I made my getaway without a problem and drove straight to Newcastle. Shayla got to work on the video, transferring it to digital, doing the edit and transferring it back to VHS tape again. I packed the money into a box and addressed it to Children in Need, ready to go in the post in the morning, then settled down to wait for Shayla.

The finished video was a masterpiece. We'd all been in Tyson Herbert's office for a drink at one time or another, so we knew where the video camera was. I'd been careful to keep my body between the camera and the gun for as much time as possible, which meant Shayla had been able to incorporate quite a lot of the original video. We had footage of Corbett packing the money into the holdall. Even better, we had the full blow job on tape without a single frame that showed the gun.

The final challenge was to deliver the video to Corbett without either the police or his wife knowing about it. In the end, we went for something we'd done on a stupid TV spy series I'd had a small part in a couple of years previously. We waited till he'd set off in the car, heading down the A1 towards our town. I followed him at a discreet distance then I called him on his mobile.

'Hello, Keith. This is your friend from last night.'

'You fucking cunt.'

'That's no way to speak to a man whose dick you've had in your mouth,' I said, going as menacing as I could manage. 'Listen to me. Three point four miles past the next exit, there's a lay-by. Pull over and take a look in the rubbish bin. You'll find something there that might interest you.' I cut the call and dialled Lauren. 'He's on his way,' I told her.

'OK, I'll make the drop.'

I came off the dual carriageway at the exit before the lay-by. I waited three minutes, then got back on the road. When I passed the lay-by, Corbett was standing by the bin, the padded envelope in his hand.

I sped past, then called him again a few minutes later. 'These are the edited highlights,' I told him. 'I'll call you in an hour when you've had a chance to check it out.'

He wasn't any happier when I made the call. 'You bastard,' he exploded. 'You total fucking bastard. You've made it look like we're in it together.'

'So we are, Keith,' I said calmly. 'You do something for me, and

I won't send copies of the tape to the cops and your wife.'

'You blackmailing piece of shit,' he shouted.

'I'll take that as a yes, shall I?'

You could have knocked me down with a feather. I didn't know what to expect when I turned up that Thursday for work, but it wasn't what happened. I knew about the robbery by then – the whole town was agog. I thought the Cobra would be pretty shaken up, but I didn't expect a complete personality change.

Before I'd even got my coat off he was in the staffroom, all smiles and gritted teeth. 'Noreen,' he said, 'a word please?'

'How are you feeling, Mr Corbett?' I asked. 'That must have been a terrible experience.'

He looked away, almost as if he was ashamed. 'I don't want to discuss it.' He cleared his throat. 'Noreen, I might have been a bit hasty the other day. I've come to realise how much of the atmosphere at the Roxette depends on you and the girls.'

I couldn't believe my ears. I couldn't think of a single word to say. I just stood there with my mouth open.

'So, if you'd be willing to stay on, I'd like to offer you your job back.'

'What about the other girls? Liz and Jackie and Julie?' I couldn't have accepted if they weren't in the deal.

He nodded, although it looked as if the movement gave him pain. 'All four of you. Full reinstatement.'

'That's very generous of you,' I managed to say. Though what I really wanted was to ask him if he'd taken a blow to the head during the robbery.

He grimaced, his tight little face closed as the pithead. 'And if you still want to do the Children in Need night, we could make it next Friday,' he added, each word sounding like it was choked out of him.

'Thank you,' I said. I took a quick look out of the window to see if there were any pigs flying past, but no. Whatever had happened inside the Cobra's head, he rest of the world seemed to be going on as normal.

And he was as good as his word. I don't know what changed his mind, but the four calling birds are back behind the balls at the Roxette. I still can't quite believe it, but as our Dickson reminded me, I've always said there's good in everybody. Sometimes, you just have to dig deep to find it.

Marilyn Todd
Thoroughly Modern Millinery

The Pink Parrot was buzzing louder than a barrelful of hornets when Fizzy Potter fluttered her fingers at Lennie the barman, tossed her feather boa over her shoulder and shimmied up the sweeping spiral staircase. Down on the dance floor, the exuberance of the Charleston had given way to pencil-thin couples fusing together for the Argentinian tango, a relatively recent import, but one which seemed destined to remain the chief talking point among the middle-aged and middle-classed for years to come. Sensitive to the dance's stillness and pauses, the conductor of the Pink Parrot Orchestra was milking its suggestiveness for all it was worth.

'I say, Fizzy!' A young man with a moustache that looked like an anchovy on his upper lip waved her over. 'Care to join me with a whisky and soda?'

'Sorry, darling,' she quipped back, 'but with you and me it'll only ever be gin and platonic!'

With laughter ringing in her ears, she made her way to the corner where her friends had set up their usual Friday night colony. All feathers and beads, cloche hats and silk stockings, Fizzy also happened to own the finest pair of knees this side of the Bosphorus. A point which rarely went unappreciated when she sat down, as now, and crossed her long legs.

'Jolly glad you made it, old girl,' Marriott muttered across his martini.

Impeccably turned out as usual, and with a crease in his trousers that could slice bacon, he twiddled the yellow rosebud in his buttonhole. Marriott Stokes was the only member of the group who didn't need to go out and earn his weekly envelope, his father having left him a packet several years previously.

'Rather hoping you can do something with old Catspaw,' he drawled.

'Yes, I'd noticed he's sporting a face like a vulture whose carrion has just made a miraculous recovery and is now dancing the fandango instead of providing him with a good supper,' she said.

'What's the matter?'

'Seems Bubbles gave him the raspberry,' Foxy Fairfax explained.

Like Fizzy, he was also an illustrator, only instead of working freelance for magazines, Foxy tended to restrict himself to children's books.

'Come off it, chaps, every girl gives Catspaw the bird,' she said, sliding her olive off its cocktail stick. 'Why should Bubbles be different?'

Anyway, Bubbles was married, and girls like that don't pass up on rich bankers in favour of a penniless cartoonist.

'Exactly what I told him,' Biff said. 'In fact, I seriously advised the old halibut to go and get stinko and forget all about popsies. Like the Mongol hordes descending from wherever it was they used to descend from, girls only bring grief on a chap.'

Adding, as Marriott ordered another round of drinks, 'I say, Fizzy. Given any further thought about swanning down the aisle with me?'

As a partner in the family firm of purveyors of quality pickles, Biff Kilgannon had no interest in art like the rest of the gang; in fact the nuances of Impressionism, gouache and the finer points of the Neue Sachlichkeit sailed completely over his head. He only tagged along because his sister, Lulu, was an artist and this way he got to mix with lots of Witty Young Things, something one tends not to do in the gherkin and piccalilli department. It wasn't that Biff wasn't a dish, Fuzzy mused, especially since playing prop forward had endowed him with muscles of steel. It was just unfortunate that he had a brain to match.

'Sorry, Biff.' Fizzy set to powdering the shiny spot on her nose. 'The answer's still no.'

The mirror in her cloisonné compact reflected a heart-shaped face with a much-kissed snub nose and big eyes enlarged further by finely plucked brows and heaps of soot-black mascara. It was only upon closer examination that one realised that one eye was brown, the other blue.

Fizzy's appointment diary rarely showed a blank spot. Snapping the compact shut, she slotted a cigarette into its holder. Simultaneously, a battery of clicks produced enough light to power up half of southern England and quite possibly a chunk of East Anglia, too. Thanking her gallant knights with an all-encompassing smile, Fizzy struck her own match and thought, funny how the entire male section of the Westlake Set was queuing to slip a diamond cluster on the third finger of her left hand – yet every time she pictured the hatload of kids she so desperately wanted, all the little beezers sported the same ski-slope noses, lopsided smiles and floppy fringes of the only man who'd never once jumped forward in a bid to light her gasper.

Damn you, Squiffy Hardcastle. Damn you to hell.

'— don't you think so, Fizzy?'

'Sorry, Kitty, didn't catch that.'

'I was just saying, sweetheart, that his work's far too Gauguinesque for my taste —'

Fizzy didn't bother asking whose work. 'Absolutely,' she replied, her mind elsewhere. On a certain painting, as it happened, in a gilt frame...

'— Matisse is living in the south of France, I hear —'

'— now does Lulu's stuff reflect Synthetic Cubism with a hint of Purist, d'you think, or pastoralism with a touch of Analytic Cubism?'

Snippets drifted past like ducks on the Thames, while Fizzy contemplated portraits in gilt frames...

'Sorry we're late, everyone.'

Her train was interrupted as Orville Templeton, Hon. Member for Knightsbridge & Chelsea, held out a chair for his wife.

'Traffic was an absolute stinker.'

'You haven't missed much,' Foxy told the newcomers. 'Chilton and his protégé haven't arrived yet.'

'Traffic, probably,' Orville said, shooting his cuffs.

Poor Orville. Noble, worthy, gallant, dignified – a hundred decent men packed into one – and duller than a miner's bathwater. Fizzy exchanged smiles with his wife and thought the same couldn't be said of Gloria Templeton. Fizzy's best friend was five years older than her and a study in understatement, from the simple wedding band to the pale cream silk she always draped herself in. Not half as modish as Fizzy's white cloche, Gloria's broad-rimmed hats were perfect for hot summer evenings like this, flattering her chestnut bob and emphasising her strong patrician features – though nothing could disguise the permanent sadness in her lovely green eyes.

That was the problem, Fizzy sighed, when one's still in love with one's first husband.

A husband, moreover, who was handsome and charming, gave one two gorgeous daughters, then betrayed all three of them by getting himself blown to pieces in the very last week of the war. Her blue-brown gaze rested on Orville, looking for all the world like a reject from a second-rate taxidermist's. Poor Orville. The Hon. Member for K&C worshipped his new family. Adored Gloria. Idolised his adopted girls. Would do anything for them, anything at all. Even to accepting that he would only ever come second best…

Second best, of course, was a concept far beyond the scope of Fizzy Potter and, along the banquette, Bubbles was slipping her Cartier-encrusted wrist through Teddy Hardcastle's arms.

'I say, were you *really* the youngest captain in the Great War, Squiffy?'

Any closer, dammit, and she'd be a tattoo.

'Too jolly right he was,' Marriott boomed. 'Gave him a gong for it, too.'

Hardcastle spiked his rebellious fringe out of his eyes, but made no effort to prise the limpet away.

'Take no notice of Marriott,' he told Bubbles, with a flash of lopsided grin. 'By the time I joined up they were running out of men. Another six months and they'd have made me a machine gun captain.'

'Don't be so damned modest, man,' Marriott snorted. 'It's the same with his bookbinding commissions, y'know, Bubbs. All that inlaying of coloured leather, gold fillets, whose wossnames in enamelled porcelain you mount on the covers —'

'Plaques.'

'Plaques, thank you, and that's without him encrusting the whole bloody thing with mother-of-pearl and those other wotnots.'

'Cabochons.'

'Cabochons, thank you, so don't let him tell you different, Bubbs. They're works of art he churns out.'

But Bubbles wasn't interested in Hardcastle's technical aptitude. Rich bankers are dandy when it comes to footing bills at the likes of Chanel or Van Cleef & Arpels, but the trouble is, they *will* spend so much time at the bank. Having given one beau the old heave-ho tonight, she was looking to plug the vacancy fast.

'Why "Squiffy", darling?'

With a glass of champagne permanently welded to one hand, even Biff could work out how she'd acquired *her* nickname.

'Not what you think, Bubbles,' Foxy laughed. 'It's from the way Teddy wore his cap at school, and damn if he don't still wear his hat at that angle.'

On anyone else, Fizzy thought, it would come over rakish. On Teddy Hardcastle, the pitched brim lent a certain equanimity and she quietly damned ski-slope noses to eternal hellfire and sent lopsided smiles down the piste after them.

'— so this exhibition tomorrow,' Orville said. 'Is everyone going?'

'Are frogs waterproof?' Foxy Fairfax retorted.

And as though a light had been switched on, the whole group became animated about Chilton Westlake's new prodigy.

'What's the verdict on this, then?' Kitty asked, unrolling one of the posters she'd designed to publicise the exhibition at their friend's gallery. 'Have I captured The Great Man, do you think?'

When Doc Frankenstein shot the first electrical bolt through his monster, it couldn't have made so much of a jolt.

'By Jove, Kitty.' Biff was the first of the group to recover. 'You've got the blighter off to a T.'

And how, Fizzy thought. Lank black hair, olive skin, stubbled chin, the slight sneer on his lips…dammit, this WAS Louis Boucard.

'Just as well one can't get scent off a poster,' Biff added, wrinkling his prop forward's nose.

'He's French, darling!' Bubbles protested. 'And an *artiste*, to boot. Parisians don't think the way we do.'

What she meant, Fizzy reflected, was that soap and Louis Boucard were strangers, whereas booze and cocaine were blood brothers. She considered all the other attributes of this artistic genius – his gambling, his womanising, his debauching of young girls – and wondered exactly how well Kitty Gardener had known Louis Boucard to be able to produce such an intimate representation.

Indeed, how well every other member of the Set had known him, to recognise what they were seeing…

'Can't stand the fellow, as y'know, but I do feel his work has an affinity with Chevaillier,' Catspaw Gordon remarked, emerging from his doldrums at last.

The Boucard effect, of course, Fizzy mused. The uncombed Parisian touched a nerve with everyone sooner or later, and her thoughts flashed back to that portrait in its gilt frame…

'— pronounced Symbolist influence, certainly,' Marriott was saying, 'with a touch of the new Classicism overlaid with subtle early Cubist House elements and, hmm, maybe the merest smidgen of the draughtsmanship one sees in Migliorini —'

'Tosh!' Foxy Fairfax interjected. 'Boucard's a bounder and a cad who corrupts everything he touches! He's a liar, a conman, a thief and a cheat, and by his admission, he trawls the gutters to paint —' he adopted an exaggerated French whine '— prozzitutes *et* felons.'

'Yes, darling, but there's something so utterly exciting about the demi-monde, don't you think?' Bubbles shuddered delightedly. 'I mean, all that naked flesh and loucheness? I find his work riveting. How about you, Squiffy?'

But before Teddy Hardcastle had a chance to venture his opinion on this blight on the moral and artistic landscape, Chilton Westlake, the gallery owner whose name the Set had adopted for their Friday night get-together, arrived wearing a mustard check suit, straw boater and a face like absolute thunder. He was also alone.

'Have you seen these?' His chubby fist pounded the newspapers in his hand. 'Have you?' He didn't wait for an answer. '*The Westlake Gallery is holding a exhibition of exciting new Parisian artist, Louis Boucard,*' he read.

'Sounds just about top-hole to me.' Orville explained. 'You wanted a plug for the old show.'

'Plug? PLUG?'

Chilton was in danger of testing medical science's latest advance in cardiac technology.

'*I* was supposed to be one doing the plugging here, matey. Instead, what happens? Boucard only gives me some cock-and-bull story about needing to borrow the key to the gallery to make a couple of last minute alterations, don't he?'

'Inviting the press for a sneak preview instead, I suppose?'

Trust Gloria to get there before anybody else.

'*Boucard's bold style pushed the boundaries of art déco to a new dimension, says the London Bulletin.*'

Chilton tossed the paper on the floor and ground it with his spatted heel.

'*A greater whiff of decadence than a hundred Tamara de Lempickas,* according to the Evening ruddy Witness, and I wouldn't have minded him stealing a march on my show,' he said, gulping down Marriott's martini. 'But get this.'

He hurled the paper at Foxy, who read aloud.

'*— Boucard has promised a work entitled "Revelation" in addition to the paintings listed in the catalogue. A portrait, the likes of which, he claims, has never before been on public display in this country – a portrait so daring, so scandalous that he's keeping it under velvet until the official opening. Even the gallery owner*…Oh, I say, Chilton, is that right?' Foxy goggled. 'That even *you* have no idea of this picture's content?'

Westlake glugged down Kitty's drink and even managed to prise Bubbles' bubbles out of her grasp.

'Couldn't be righter, old man. First I knew about this so-called "Revolution" was when I read about it in the bloody papers.'

His fat little hand lashed out to tip Catspaw's, Biff's and Teddy's drinks down the hatch, his expression brightening only slightly when he noticed a stupendous pair of knees crossed elegantly on the soft leather banquette.

'But the really galling thing,' he wailed, 'was that Boucard had the cheek to tap me for the fare back to the Gallery, and that's not the first time he's tapped me for a tenner, either!'

Fizzy's martini was the last remaining casualty and Chilton Westlake was in no mood for taking prisoners.

'I'll kill the little bashtard,' he said, his boater rolling under the table as he slid down the table. 'Sho help me, I'll shlit his dirty French throat and then I'll pull his bloody gizzards through the hole.'

At that stage, of course, no one actually believed him.

Three p.m. on a Saturday afternoon and the Westlake Gallery resembled more a tin of sardines than a preview of an exhibition by a hitherto unknown artist. No invitation had been refused, placing something of a strain on the nosebags and drink trays, since Chilton invariably considered himself lucky if one third of his invites turned up to these dos, most often only a quarter (and those usually only relatives and friends). Today the place was packed to the gunwales and, despite bloodshot eyes and an aversion to bright lights, he wasn't looking half as bad as Fizzy expected. That, she supposed, was because the gallery stood to make a mint from the sensational publicity and, to give Boucard his due, the Frenchman knew how to play the press.

'Not drinking, sweetheart? Splendid!' Kitty swapped her empty glass for Fizzy's full one. 'Stuff's in perilously short supply. Well, chin-chin.'

Straightening his purple bow tie, Chilton Westlake mounted the podium and launched into a speech about his exciting new protegé and Fizzy noted the care he took to plug the other artists he'd sponsored, clearly intent on shifting as much stock as possible today. Sadly, though, her little plump friend was better at evaluating works of art than talking about them and her attention wandered in the direction of a certain portrait in a gilt frame. Entitled *Woman in a Mask*, it was typical of Boucard's style in that—

'I'm not convinced Bubbles finds the demi-monde half as riveting as she'd supposed,' a wry baritone murmured in Fizzy's cloche-covered ear.

She followed Teddy's gaze to where the banker's wife was

sandwiched between a brace of hard-eyed villains and a group of women in red heels and even redder lips. In another surprise for Chilton, Boucard had mischievously invited several of his 'prozzitutes *et* felons', who were swigging champagne and helping themselves to cigars on an industrial scale. Bubbles' high colour showed she was finding it hard to reconcile the fact that, any minute, she'd be seeing these same people sprawled naked across the gallery walls.

Chilton cleared his throat.

'— I now call upon Louis to join us and declare this exhibition open!'

Nothing.

'I said,' he repeated, raising his voice, 'that I now call upon Louis Boucard to come out from the back room and open the exhibition held in his honour.'

Knowing glances rippled round the crowd, as well as one or two giggles. Drink, drugs, you name it, only a relentless optimist like Chilton could have seriously have expected the artist to be sober during the daytime. Louis Boucard was a creature of the night. In every respect.

'Haw, haw.' Chilton tried to cover the gaffe with humour, 'Not sure I'll understand you temperamental *artistes* —'

Bubbles seized the opportunity to detach herself from her underworld sandwich to fetch him, but she wasn't alone for very long. The shrill scream and the accompanying crash of crystal said it all.

Louis Boucard was dead.

'And you are, miss?'

'Phyllis Potter, 62 Northwell Mansions, Bayswater.' Fizzy's smile was directed straight at the constable, but her glance was slanted at the man standing beside her. 'Right between the museum and a gentleman's club, if you must know.'

'Thank you, sir?'

'Edward James Hardcastle, 17b Elton Square, Chelsea.' He kept his eyes straight. 'Too many stuffed shirts and old fossils for my taste.'

'Oh, dear. Elderly residents are they, sir?'

'Not exactly, constable. Is that all?'

'For the moment, yes, thank you. But we're asking people not to venture far from the scene, as there will doubtless be other questions we wish to ask. In fact, I understand there's a bar down the road —'

'Jo-Jo's,' Fizzy said. 'We know it well, constable. Regular watering hole,' she added, tossing her boa over her shoulder, but instead of following Kitty and Marriott out into the afternoon sunshine, she took advantage of the milling confusion to slip into the anteroom.

Ugh. Louis Boucard wasn't what one would call classically handsome in life. Grey and waxy in death, he was even more unprepossessing! She took care not to tread in the broken glass from Bubbles' champagne as she approached the desk where he was slumped. Someone, it appeared, had caved the prodigy's head in with a rather sleek black marble panther. The bloodied statuette lay on the desk among enough cocaine – she tasted the powder with a tentative finger – yes, with enough cocaine to supply a small continent for a decade, possibly two.

So then. Not content to take it himself. Louis had been pushing the stuff.

'You realise he was dead before he was beaned?'

Fizzy yelped, half of her livid that she hadn't noticed him leaning against the wall with his hands stuffed deep in his pockets. While the other half was too busy picturing her hatful of kids made in this man's wretched image...

'If you're telling me someone frightened him to death,' she said coolly, 'I'm not remotely surprised.'

A muscle twitched at the side of Teddy Hardcastle's mouth. 'Boucard, I fear, was more tormenter than tormented.'

He feared right. Louis could be facing an army of flesh-eating zombies and he'd con them back to the grave.

'Look.'

Teddy lifted a hank of dark hair to reveal a puncture wound in Boucard's dirty neck.

'The ice pick or whatever severed his spinal cord, paralysing all muscular activity. The lungs stopped functioning, so did the heart, but death, as always I'm afraid, comes slowly.'

Fizzy reeled and was immediately caught in a steel net that smelled of ski slopes and pine.

'Never fear, Phyllis Potter of 62 Northwell Mansions, Bayswater. Looks like he was unconscious when it happened.'

Fizzy disentangled herself from his arms, slightly surprised that bookbinders had so many muscles.

'Why aren't the police swarming all over this room?' she asked.

'Ah, well. It would appear our boys in blue haven't realised that there would be more blood, had Louis been alive when he was brained, and knowing the blunt instrument to be a favourite among the criminal underclass, they rather fancy one of those as the culprit.'

Solicitously, Teddy straightened her hat. Fizzy jerked away, hoping he couldn't see the furious blush that had suffused her cheeks.

'What guff,' she snapped. 'Those girls aren't on the game because they enjoy it. They're dishing out knee-tremblers because they've run out of options, and even if one of them *had* killed Louis Boucard, they'd never leave a fortune in cocaine lying around.'

Not when it would buy them their freedom – and no self-respecting thief would dream of walking away empty-handed, no matter *how* pushed they had been to commit murder!

'Precisely the argument I presented to His Majesty's law enforcers,' he began. But whatever else he was going to say was overtaken by the door bursting open and Chilton, Orville, Gloria and a uniformed inspector rushing into the room.

'This is an outrage,' Chilton was blustering. 'An absolute bloody outrage! Why should *I* want to kill him?'

'You have a persuasive line in arguments, Mr Hardcastle,' Fizzy muttered under her breath. 'You get them to abandon the criminal underclass, so they're pinching Chilton's collar instead.'

The inspector shot her a venomous glance and continued.

'You were overheard threatening the deceased in the Pink Parrot nightclub last night,' he told Chilton, leaving the assembled company in no doubt as to his opinion of such a den of tangoed iniquity. 'Lewis Buckard had given the press an authorised showing —'

'For heaven's sake, man, it's *Louis*,' Chilton protested, 'pronounced Boo-car.'

'— and he'd also been holding out on you with regard to a mysterious portrait. To wit, this.'

He indicated the easel in the corner draped in black velvet.

'Inspector,' Orville cut in, 'I have explained how Mr Westlake was in plain view of everyone at all times this afternoon. I don't see how you can possibly follow this ridiculous line of questioning.'

In true political style, the Hon. Member then rephrased his argument in fifteen different ways. Somewhere between the fourth and the fifth, Gloria came across and took both Fizzy's hands in hers.

'Are you all right, darling? You look terribly pale.'

'Yes, I'm fine, really, I am. Just a shock, that's all, seeing death at close quarters.'

She glanced at Teddy Hardcastle, who had seen more of it and at far closer quarters, then looked back into Gloria's permanently sad eyes.

They'd been laughing, that was the terrible part. Celebrating because Fizzy had landed her first job with *A la Mode* and Gloria had just received confirmation that baby number two, already well advanced, was healthy and ready to hatch out on schedule. Yes, they'd been laughing fit to burst when that telegram came...

Fizzy shivered. 'The police don't really suspect Chilton, do they?'

'Darling, if they had a man standing over the body waving a placard written in Louis's own blood which read "It was me", they'd still think the butler did it.'

Gloria glanced at her husband, boring the inspector into submission.

'Orville will set them right,' she assured her.

Shouldn't be hard, either, Fizzy supposed. To compensate for his physical shortcomings, Chilton upholstered himself in the loudest checks he could find. Top that with a purple bow tie and spats, and who could miss him?

'For goodness sake,' Chilton snorted. 'I'm hardly likely to kill the goose that lays my golden eggs, am I, you clod?'

The inspector, who wasn't entirely won over by being labelled a clod, didn't take to having his chest prodded either.

'You're wasting time,' Chilton snapped, 'and anyway, what about the theft of my picture, eh? Eh? Why aren't you investigating *that*?'

'What picture?' Fizzy asked Gloria.

Patrician eyes rolled. 'Wouldn't you just know that while this kerfuffle's been going on, someone would filch one of the exhibits? Of course, it'll be worth a fortune on the black market after today. Chilton's incandescent.'

'Nonsense,' Fizzy murmured. 'He probably snitched it himself, to drive up the price of the others.'

'So true, darling. No artist is ever worth so much as when he dies.'

Meanwhile, the combination of being branded incompetent, a dim-wit, having a finger poked in his breastbone and being blasted with the notion that theft ranked higher than murder was doing little to enhance the inspector's opinion of Chilton. Especially since the accusations were being made in front of the Hon. Member for Knightsbridge & Chelsea.

'What Mr Westlake is forgetting, sir,' he told Orville, 'is that apart from Lewis Buckard playing him for a sucker over the publicity, he'd borrowed money from him totalling nearly one hundred pounds, which he apparently had no intention of repaying, and we know he was holding out on him.'

He indicated the velvet-draped easel as he read from the press.

'*…the likes of which has never been on public display before in this country – a portrait so daring, so scandalous that he's keeping it under velvet until the official opening. "Revelation", Mr Buckard called it.*'

With a flourish that could only be described as smug, he whisked off the velvet.

Revelation indeed. Six pair of eyes gaped at the empty frame.

Teddy Hardcastle let out a soft laugh.

'B-but —' Chilton couldn't find words to express what he felt.

'Well, I say!' Orville could.

The inspector rubbed his jaw for what seemed like an hour,

pausing only to glower at Chilton in the way a lioness might watch her marked zebra leap the gorge into safety.

'Do you suppose,' he asked eventually, 'that it was within Mr Buckard's character to pull a fast one to drum up publicity? That there never *was* a scandalous portrait to unveil?'

Five voices responded as one, the verdict unanimous. Such a stunt was *well* within Boucard's capabilities, they replied.

Cue more jaw-rubbing by His Majesty's servant.

'Whoever killed Mr Buckard did so by holding the weapon in this —' he held up one of numerous soft cloths used in the gallery to dust the frames '— to avoid leaving fingerprints. Unfortunately, we have no witnesses to say they saw anyone go in or come out of this room.'

'Why would they?' Orville asked reasonably. 'We were all facing the podium, inspector, anxiously awaiting the moment when the doors to the exhibition would open and we could be one of the first to see, and hopefully grab a slice of, this new and prodigious young talent.'

'There were nearly eighty people crammed into my gallery,' Chilton snapped, 'and not all of them with gilt-edged invites, I might add. You mark my words, one of those low-lifes killed Louis.'

The inspector turned his scowl on Teddy Hardcastle, making it clear who was responsible for diverting precious resources on this ridiculous wild goose chase when the police had had it sussed all along. With a loud 'Harrumph' he stomped back into the gallery, trailed by Chilton and Orville, with Gloria adding poise to the rear and leaving Fizzy alone with Teddy once more. This time, though, the silence between them stretched to infinity.

'The question,' he said at last, 'isn't who killed Louis Boucard, is it?'

'No?' Frogs croak louder, she thought.

'No.' He let the wall take his weight at the shoulders. 'The question is, why should *two* people want to kill the same man.'

Turning out of the gallery into the glorious midsummer sunshine, a mischievous breeze whisked off Gloria's hat and carried it halfway down Mayfair. Biff, of course, would have tackled it before it had gone fifteen yards, but Biff was already ensconced in Jo-Jo's Cellar sinking his second martini and by the time the Hon. Member for K&C had picked up sufficient speed, a Ford with an unnecessarily heavy foot on its accelerator had flattened Gloria's masterpiece right between the tulle and the rosebuds. Another time and the group would have hooted with laughter. Today, though, a man's life had been taken and the crushing, in an instant, of something so vibrant and bright stood for all that had happened.

On the other hand, it's an ill wind. Fizzy couldn't help but notice the look of gratitude and affection that Gloria shot her husband as he handed the battered titfer back to his wife and her heart gladdened. He was a good egg, the Hon. Member, and whilst he wasn't – and would never be – the love of her friend's life, she'd always felt he deserved more than mere recognition.

'Well?' A long stride fell into step alongside her, its fedora angled low over one half of his forehead.

'Any more thoughts?'

In front of them, Orville had offered a chivalrous arm to his wife and although Fizzy had hoped for a similar offer from Teddy, none came. She adjusted her beads, smoothed her drop waistline, tucked her clutch bag under her arm and thought, who cares about floppy hair anyway?

'I mean,' he added evenly, 'you must know it's one of us.'

'Don't you mean two of us?'

Dammit, Pekinese dogs don't snap that hard, but if Teddy Hardcastle noticed, it didn't show.

'Foxy called him a cad and a bounder,' he said, 'and not without justification. Did you know Boucard conned him out of five hundred pounds?'

'How much?'

To an illustrator of children's books, that was a fortune, and Fizzy calculated that she'd have to work until she was a hundred and twenty-eight to cover that kind of spare cash. Oh, Foxy, Foxy, what have you done…?

'We've already heard the inspector's case against Chilton,' Teddy said, stuffing his hands in his pockets.

Pity, because they were nice hands, with just the right amount of crisp, dark hairs on the back, and she'd pictured them tooling, stamping, making intricate mosaics of metal and leather. Perhaps, in his painstaking artisan mind, magazine illustrators came in on a level with doodlers?

'Also, our Parisian friend helped himself to a whole pile of Bubbles' jewels in, quote, payment for services rendered, unquote. He derided Catspaw's cartoons in the press, got Marriot to underwrite an enterprise that didn't exist – this must go no further, please – he also got Kitty Gardener pregnant. That's the reason she zipped off to Zurich in the spring.'

'Not a poster designer's convention, then?'

'There's a clinic that deals with these things —'

She didn't dare ask how he knew.

'— and it's common knowledge that Lulu was engaged to friend Louis until she found him in bed with Bubbles, and you know how passionately Biff feels about his sister's honour. Damn,' he added lightly, 'if the list ain't just about endless.'

'Aren't you forgetting someone else with a grudge against Boucard?' Fizzy asked as they reached the steps of the Cellar.

'Someone, for instance, like you?'

Ahead of them, Orville was tipping the doorman and Chilton was checking in his boater, but Teddy remained behind on the steps.

'You don't say.'

'Oh, but I do say.' Suddenly the sunshine seemed terribly bright. 'I don't know where you gathered *your* gossip from —'

'Information,' he corrected mildly. 'We called it information in the Intelligence.' Adding, in response to her involuntary raising of eyebrows, 'There was a lot to sort out after the Armistice.'

The hundreds, no thousands, of atrocities committed after the surrender flashed through her mind as it occurred to her that maybe that's what inspired soldiers to become bookbinders. Intricate, absorbing, it makes one forget.

She coughed. 'Anyway, don't think I don't know that Louis got your kid brother hooked on a certain white powdery substance.'

And him only sixteen, poor sap.

'I see,' Teddy said slowly. 'So which do you have me pegged for?

The puncture wound, the blunt object or both?'

Fizzy took a step back up the stairs to meet him square in the eye.

'Louis Boucard,' she said stiffly, 'was a man with neither scruples nor conscience, but reasons to hate aren't motives for murder, and even if they were, then the killer would surely choose somewhere more private, wouldn't they, where they're more likely to get away with it?'

'Ah, but they are going to get away with it,' Teddy replied softly, holding her miscoloured gaze. *'Aren't they?'*

Down in the Jazz Cellar, it looked like a tornado had swept through the place, with the contents of handbags and pockets spilling over every table and chair as the police searched everyone who'd been in the gallery in an effort to find the missing portrait of a young woman wearing nothing but a painted Venetian mask. The sombre mood quickly gave way to hilarity as photographs fell out of wallets showing girls who were definitely not the title-holders' wives along with two cream buns discovered in the kitbag of a woman who constantly bored people rigid with tales of her regimented diet. But no paintings of women in masks!

Having been officially declared a Snitched-Portrait-Free Zone, Fizzy found a sudden need to sit down. As shaking hands slotted a cigarette in its holder, she found herself met with the usual click of a dozen offers for light and one noticeable absence.

'I say, Fizzy, are you free for the opera on Saturday?' Biff wanted to know. 'Well, how about the Saturday after?'

'Tough luck, old man,' Marriott cut in, 'because I've already got my offer in for a spin down to the seaside in the old jalopy. What d'you say, old girl? Are you up for it?'

'Excuse me.'

She had to pass Teddy to reach the powder room, but managed to do it without meeting his eye, though suddenly, there seemed to be something wrong with her breathing. Just not enough air in the club. Once inside the pink painted sanctuary, she sank against the door, the feathers on her white silk cloche hat fluttering with each tremble that she gave.

'Goodness, darling.'

Gloria, a vision in her customary cream silk, stopped abruptly from the business of applying lipstick to her perfect pout.

'You look like you've seen a ghost!'

A hundred ghosts, Fizzy thought, recalling laughter, first jobs, second babies. Telegrams.

Her legs felt like they'd been filleted. There was no blood in her veins. None at all.

'That gust of wind gave it away,' she said quietly.

The lipstick in Gloria's hand faltered, but only momentarily.

'In all the years I've known you,' Fizzy continued, 'you've always worn wide-brimmed hats, Gloria, but the one thing they need that a cloche doesn't is a hat pin.'

Not an ice pick.

Louis Boucard was killed with a hat pin.

'And when the wind took yours down the street, I knew.'

As did Teddy Hardcastle.

She drew a deep, shuddering breath. 'I presume it was because of your affair?'

Gloria swallowed. 'I went into that with my eyes wide open, darling, because whatever other faults Louis might have had, he...well, let's just say he didn't have them in the bedroom department.'

Fizzy felt it best to let that one pass.

'But he used you as a subject?'

That was his great 'Revelation' – and what greater dynamite for an advertising campaign than the wife of a respected politician on public display?

'Like the press said, he only ever paints nudes,' Gloria said ruefully. 'But the treachery is that he painted me while I slept. I hadn't an inkling until he started blackmailing me. He was always in arrears with the bookies.'

'He wanted more, I suppose?'

'No.'

Gloria fixed her perpetually sad eyes on her friend.

'Orville's positively swimming in lolly and quite frankly the amount I was paying Louis, Orville didn't even notice. Another frock, another hat – he didn't question it. No, the trouble started once people began to appreciate the genius of Louis's work. You see, the two things my lover wanted most in life were to be rich and famous, and that's when he decided to unveil his masterpiece. To propel himself into the limelight.'

She drew herself up to her full height.

'Me, I could have ridden the storm, I've ridden worse, and the girls are too young to understand. But Orville, darling – Orville's a good man, and to see him publicly humiliated as a cuckold…Well, he'd have stood by me, no question, but the scandal would have destroyed him. I couldn't let Louis do that.'

'So you did the only decent thing? Stabbed him with your hat pin?'

What little colour was left drained from Gloria's face at the sharpness of her friend's tone.

'It wasn't what I intended, believe me. The idea was to sneak in and steal the horrid thing, but when I slipped into the back room, he was collapsed over his precious cocaine and —' She made a brave attempt at a smile. 'Typical Louis. Never did know when to stop.'

'Why kill him, Gloria?'

'Why not, darling? If you'd only seen Kitty after she got back from Switzerland! The doctors say she'll never be able to have another baby, did you know that? And then there's Foxy. Five hundred pounds, can you imagine? He'd ruined poor Lulu, was blackmailing Bubbles, had said terrible things about Catspaw, so I thought, what the hell.'

Gloria pointed to a spot on the back of her elegant swan neck.

'I read that if you go right between the vertebrae it severs the spinal cord. He was out cold, Fizzy. I swear he never felt a thing, and if you ask me do I regret it, I can honestly put my hand on my heart and say it was no worse than putting a rabid dog down.'

Fizzy counted to three.

'Except you couldn't bring yourself to pull the pin out?'

Gloria shuddered. 'Could *you*?'

Fizzy doubted she could have driven it in in the first place.

But then she wasn't a widow still deeply in love with a dead husband doing the best for her two tiny daughters by marrying someone who worshipped the ground they all walked on. A rich man, moreover, who would do anything to protect them. Anything at all —

'Orville saw you, didn't he? Orville saw you come out of that room, no doubt ashen and shaking —'

'I didn't know.' Gloria collapsed onto the stool and buried her head in her hands. 'I swear, darling, I had no idea, not until they said he'd been hit over the head with that panther.'

It didn't take much working out, really. Orville saw his wife come out of the back room and wanted to know why Louis was upsetting his wife. What went through his head when he saw Louis dead and his wife's hatpin sticking out of his neck? Fizzy swallowed. Not such a dull stick, after all. Quite the hero, in fact, because it was Orville who pulled out the weapon, then disguised the method of murder by bringing the black marble panther down on his head.

'What did you do with the incriminating canvas?' Fizzy asked. 'Everyone's been searched.'

A hint of colour returned to Gloria's cheeks. 'What I planned from the outset.' She opened her bag to reveal a pair of nail scissors. 'I cut it into tiny pieces and flushed it back to the sewer where it belongs.'

Congratulations to Chilton Westlake, Fizzy thought. He'd been very insistent about having all mod cons installed at the gallery!

'What are you going to do now, darling?' Gloria asked.

This time Fizzy counted to ten. Then ten more.

'About what?' she replied steadily. 'I only came in here to adjust my suspenders. This left one's digging in like blazes.'

She swallowed two tablets for migraine.

'Is it my fault we ended up talking for ages about what hats we might be wearing for Ascot?'

It was gone midnight when the Set finally tumbled out of the Cellar, leaving Jo-Jo one very happy proprietor, having trousered twice the usual takings. The moon was full and waxy, inspiring stars to twinkle, cats to yowl and Foxy Fairfax to treat Londoners with a loud rendition of 'Danny Boy'.

'Fancy putting on the old nosebag with me, Fizzy?' Marriott asked, with a hopeful twiddle of the yellow rose in his buttonhole. 'Only there's this little French place I know round the corner that serves up some pretty nifty proteins and starch.'

'We could all go,' Biff said, elbowing Marriott out of the way.

'If you don't mind, I'll give the roasts and boileds a miss tonight, chaps. I rather fancy an early night is in order.'

And besides. There was a cold, twisted knot deep inside that wouldn't let her eat if she tried.

'Don't be a wet blanket, sweetheart,' Kitty said, pouring Bubbles into the back of her car. 'There's plenty of room with us girls.'

'I know!' Biff nodded towards his convertible parked with its usual insouciance half on, half off the kerb whilst managing to completely block a back alley. 'Let's all go to the Kitty Kat Klub!'

'Good idea,' Bubbles and Kitty chorused together.

'It won't be the first time you've sat on my knee, Fizzy,' Catspaw said.

'No, but it'd be the first time she's sat on mine, so don't be greedy, old man,' Chilton retorted.

'Actually,' a voice rumbled beneath a fedora set at a rakish (some might say dignified) angle, 'the lady's already accepted a lift.'

'Dammit, Squiffy, you always get the pretty ones,' Catspaw wailed, as Biff revved up the engine. 'See you up there, then, what?'

'Twenty minutes,' Teddy promised, as the convertible cranked off the kerb with a splutter. Across the way, Orville was opening the door of his Rolls for Gloria and Teddy watched impassively as the Hon. Member settled himself behind the wheel and purred off.

'Happy endings all round, then,' he murmered.

'Not for Louis Boucard,' Fizzy said.

Teddy pursed his lips, but only briefly. 'True, but let's face it, the world's one scoundrel lighter and none the worse for it, and what odds the police make six wrong arrests before they stuff the file in the "Unsolved" archive and forget it?'

'Is that your definition of happy ending?'

'Ask Chilton. He'll make four times as much dosh with his

prodigy dead and how fortunate there was no scandal to come out, that velvet-covered easel being nothing more than a practical joke and all that.'

'Oh, that sort of happy ending.'

Teddy leaned against the brickwork and stuffed his hands into his pockets. 'Actually,' he said quietly. 'I was rather thinking of Chilton's missing exhibit and the matter of true love running smooth.'

'There *was* no portrait, remember?'

'Not under the velvet, no. I meant the one you stole when everyone was crowding into the room when Bubbles found Boucard's body.'

Fizzy reached into her handbag for a cigarette and attached it to the holder with a surprisingly steady hand.

'I don't even like Louis's work,' she said. 'Why would I steal one of his beastly paintings? Cubist mixed with Symbolist —'

'— and just the merest smidgen of the draughtsmanship one sees in Migliorini. Yes, I know. Ghastly, aren't they? Especially the portraits of masked nudes with one brown eye and one blue.'

A lighter clicked in the darkness and suddenly Fizzy's hand was anything but steady.

'I saw it in his studio when I went round to persuade him to lay off my brother. Unfortunately, our French friend was out, so I never did get chance to exercise my knuckles. Shame, that.'

'Maybe that was another practical joke,' she said evenly. 'I mean, we've all been searched. Thoroughly, as I recall.'

A soft laugh echoed into the night. 'Ah, women! What cunning and devious creatures thou art, is it any wonder we men are in thy thrall? Gloria —'

'How did you know it was her?'

'Don't tell anyone, but His Majesty's Intelligence Service relies more on guesswork than they'd like people to think. But in this case, Miss Potter, I know Boucard, I know his type and more importantly —'

Before she'd even realised what had happened, she found herself in his arms.

'— I know how human minds tick. Not to mention,' he added

an eternity later, 'that there are widgets designed to stop ladies' hats from bowling down Mayfair that are called, strangely enough, hat pins.'

'And the panther?'

'Who else would cover up another person's murder? I suspect they'll both view each other differently from now on. A rather more balanced relationship, one would hope.'

'So that's what you meant by happy endings and true love running smooth.'

'Hadn't quite got to that last bit,' he said, kissing her again. 'Only it strikes me that Fizzy Potter is a nice enough name, whereas Fizzy Hardcastle tends to run off the tongue rather more smoothly, don't you think?'

She couldn't be hearing this right. 'Edward James Hardcastle, are you actually asking me to *marry you*?'

'Not tonight. Far too late to knock up a vicar. But yes. That seems to be the general consensus.'

But...Fizzy pulled away.

'What about the painting?'

'What about it?' he rasped, drawing her back, and when they finally came up for air, he said, 'I don't imagine you'll make a habit of stealing. I mean, the logistics of bringing the kids to visit you in the clink would be an absolute nightmare.'

'That's not what I meant,' she stuttered.

He gave her nose a little tweak.

'Like my kid brother, darling, we all have siblings.'

He tilted her chin up to face him.

'The eyes were the wrong way round, Fizzy. Yours,' he said kissing them in turn, 'are blue on the left, brown on the right and trust me, artists of Boucard's calibre don't get such details wrong.'

For the first time in her life, Fizzy knew what it was to be floating on air.

'I suppose I *might* consider marrying you —' she began, though her actual thoughts ran more along the lines of wild horses.

'Very kind.'

'— but what about money? Neither of us earns very much —'

'True,' he agreed, 'but don't you think this,' he whisked off her cloche hat and pulled out *Woman in a Mask*, 'should get us off to a good start?'

'Do you mind!'

Fizzy snatched at her sister's naked image and stuffed it back under the brim.

'It's worth a fortune on the black market,' he rumbled.

'Teddy Hardcastle, you aren't seriously asking me to weigh my sister's morals against cold hard cash?'

She rammed the cloche back over her bob.

'Because if you are, you ought to know right now that I won't use something as tawdry as this to pay my electricity bill!'

She adjusted the cloche and thought, silly cow. Shouldn't have posed for him in the first place.

'A honeymoon, on the other hand…'

Teddy's laughter echoed into the darkness. 'Which do you fancy, you wicked, wicked child? A fortnight in Antibes? Or would you prefer to see Venice?'

Fizzy snuggled back into his muscular arms. 'Don't care,' she murmured.

Because with that painting they could afford both.

Christopher Fowler
The Lady Downstairs

What annoys me most is that he doesn't notice.

There are so few females in his life, and the ones that he does meet are usually in distress or hiding something. They're titled, or troubled, or – well, one wouldn't use the word in polite company, but it also begins with a T, and may be preceded by the word 'Bakewell'. I see them all, because I see all of his clients. I open the door to them, I send them away or ask them to wait, or show them up the seventeen stairs to his room. You don't let a stranger into your house without noticing something about them, and there's usually something to notice. The ladies may have red-rimmed eyes and damp handkerchiefs, or may adopt a disdainful air to make me think they are the mistresses of their situations. The gentlemen are more obvious still, their rage barely concealed as they hop from one foot to the other, their eagerness to see my lodger brushing aside the most common courtesies. Sometimes our visitors are fearful, and search the street to make sure they have not been followed. These ones rush inside as if they have been scalded, and once my door is safely closed behind them, apologise for their behaviour, wringing their caps and glancing to the top of the stairs, half-expecting him to pop out of his rooms and solve their problems right in the hallway, as if I would allow such a thing.

I shouldn't complain, for a landlady's life is rarely interesting, and the comings and goings are a small price to pay for housing such a famous London figure. There are annoyances, of course; the infernal scratching of that violin, the muffled explosions from unstable compounds in the laboratory he has rigged up in my back room (without my permission), the immovable stains that appear on the carpets, the ghastly burning-cat smells that waft down from the landing, invariably at tea-time when I am about to tuck into a kipper, the unsocial hours kept by a man who finds sleep a stranger. Yet I am fond of him because his enthusiasm leaves him so unprotected. He knows the doctor is concerned for his well-being. But he never notices me.

Of course, he is the Great Detective, and I am only the landlady.

To hear him pronounce judgement you would think no one else was born with a pair of eyes. We don't all have to shout about it from the rooftops. But my job is to notice everything, though I get little thanks.

Allow me to present you with an example. Only last week, on a drizzling Tuesday night at half past ten, as I was readying myself for bed, there came a knock at the door. The girl had gone up to bed, and I was left to greet the caller, a frantic lady of some forty summers, in a dripping fur hat, clutching a wet fox-collar about her throat.

'Is this the house of Mr Sherlock Holmes?' she asked, without so much as a good evening.

'Why yes,' I replied, 'and I am his landlady, Mrs Hudson, but Mr Holmes has left strict instructions not to be disturbed.'

'I must see him,' said the lady. 'It is a matter of the utmost urgency.' I say lady, for I assumed her to be one though she was not wearing gloves, and the wetness of her clothes suggested that she had not alighted from her own carriage, or even a Hackney. She had a bearing, though, and a way of looking that I have seen too often when ladies look at landladies.

'If you'd care to wait in the front room I'll see what can be done,' I told her, and trotted off upstairs. I am nervous of no one in my own house, but sometimes Mr Holmes can be alarming. On this night he spoke to me rudely through the door, and finally opened it a crack to see what was amiss.

As I explained that a lady waited downstairs, I could see my lodger hastily rolling down the sleeve of his shirt, tidying something away and complaining that it really was too bad he should be disturbed in such a manner. Knowing him, I took this to be an agreement that he would see her.

'Is she in need of medical attention?' he asked briskly. 'Dr Watson is still away.'

'No,' I replied, 'but she is quite distraught, for she has run here in the rain without stopping to dress for visiting.' And I showed her up. As she passed me, I smelled essence of violets on her clothes, and something else I recognised but could not place, a nursery smell.

I stood on the landing, listening. She introduced herself as Lady Cecily Templeford, but then the door closed and I heard no more. Still, it was enough. I read the women's weeklies, so I knew that Lady Templeford's son recently married beneath him. It was quite the scandal among the leisured classes, which I am not part of, but I make it my business to read about their small sufferings, who is engaged to whom, and why they should not be.

I went to the parlour and searched through the periodicals in the fire bucket. I soon came to the story. The Honourable Archibald Templeford married Miss Rose Nichols after a brief engagement. His mother refused to attend the wedding nuptials on account of Miss Nichols' former profession, namely performing as a songstress in the twice-nightlies, where she was known as 'The Deptford Nightingale'. Miss Nichols subsequently gave birth to a baby boy named Godwin. I was still reading this item when the door to Mr Holmes' apartment slammed open.

'If you do not help me, I do not know what I shall do,' she said loudly enough to wake up the serving girl on the top floor. 'I have no one else to whom I can turn, and need not tell you what this would do to our family should the news be made public.' And with that she swept past me once more, almost knocking me flat, her grand exit only marred by her struggle with the front door latch.

'Allow me,' I offered, squeezing past to shove the lock, for the wood swells in wet weather, for which help I received a look that could freeze a pond in midsummer.

'The poor lady seemed very distressed,' I ventured, wary of my lodger's reluctance to discuss his clients. 'I do hope you can help her.'

'That remains to be seen,' said Mr Holmes, 'but it is nothing you should concern yourself with, dear lady,' and with that he shut his door in my face. This does not bother me, for I am used to his ways, and I am just the landlady. I open the doors and close them. People pass me by. I stick to my duty, and they to theirs.

The next morning Mr Holmes went out, and did not return until five. He appeared haggard, in low spirits, and I gathered from his mood that the investigation he had undertaken was not going well. I knew he had visited the home of the Honourable Archibald

Templeford because I heard him giving the cab driver the address, which was published in my weekly along with a fetching painting of the drive and grounds in Upper Richmond.

'How was your day, Mr Holmes?' I asked, taking his soaking great-coat to hang in the hall.

'Somewhat less productive than I had hoped, Mrs Hudson,' he replied, 'though I venture to surmise not entirely without purpose.' He often speaks like this, saying much but revealing nothing. Most times, I have little interest in my lodger's cases. He does not vouchsafe their details, and wishes to discuss them with no one but the doctor, but sometimes I glean a sense of their shape and purpose, although I see them through the wrong end of a telescope, as it were, the clients coming and going, the snatches of hurried conversation, the urgent departures late at night, the visits from policemen like Inspector Lestrade, full of cajoling and flattery, and when those tactics fail, threats and warnings. It is like being backstage at some great opera, where one only glimpses the actors and hears snatches of arias, and the setting is all around the wrong way, and one is left to piece together the plot. Like any stagehand I am invisible and unheard, but a necessary requirement in the smooth running of the performance.

My lodger spent the next morning locked in his rooms, banging about, the ceiling above my dining room creaking like a ship in a tempest. Resolving to see what caused his agitation, and knowing he had not eaten, I took him some beef broth, and was gratified when he accepted it, bidding me enter.

'I worry you are letting this business with Lady Templeford tire you,' I ventured, only to have him fix me with a wild stare.

'What on earth do you mean, Mrs Hudson?' he snapped, sipping at the broth before setting it aside with a grimace.

'I noticed that because she arrived here in such agitation, you were compelled to deal with her case, despite being busy with other work.'

To my surprise he raised his long head and gave a great bark of laughter. 'Well Mrs Hudson, you will surprise us all yet,' he said. 'First Watson, and now you. I shall start to wonder if my investigative technique is catching. So tell me, what do you discern about the lady in question?'

'It's not my business to voice an opinion,' I said, wary of incurring his displeasure.

'Let's say for a moment that it is your business. It would be intriguing to know the female point of view.'

'I know she is upset by the marriage of her youngest son to a girl she considers to be of low morals,' I replied, 'and is shocked by the early arrival of a child. More than that I cannot tell.'

'But you have said much, perhaps without even realising it.' He inclined his head, as if seeing me through new eyes. 'The night before last, Lady Templeford's new grandchild was snatched from his cradle, and no one has seen him since. What do you make of that?'

'Its poor mother must be quite mad with grief,' I said, remembering the picture of Rose Nichols in my paper. Then I considered the enmity that existed between the bride and her mother-in-law, and how the son must be caught between them.

Mr Holmes was clearly thinking the same thing. 'Then take pity on Archibald, trapped between them, Scylla and Charybdis. At six o'clock his wife Rose enters the nursery to wake and feed her son, and there where the child should be is only rumpled bedding. They search the house until half past six, when Archibald returns from the city, and are still searching when Lady Templeford arrives to dine with them.'

'There will be a dreadful scandal if you do not find it,' I said excitedly. 'Lady Templeford would naturally suspect her daughter-in-law, for a woman who sets a son against his mother will always be blamed, especially when there is a child involved.'

'Do you really think so?' Mr Holmes' eyes hooded as I continued.

'Mrs Drake, the lady who keeps house at number 115, informs me that Rose Nichols had a long-time suitor in the Haymarket, and there is talk that the child might be his.' I realised I had gone too far, offering more of an opinion than was wanted on the subject. 'Well, I must get on with my dusting,' I said, embarrassed. 'The parlour maid is off today and the coalman has trod dirt into the back passage.'

He showed me his back with a grunt of disapproval before I had even turned to close the door.

I know my place. Landladies always do. I cannot help but form an opinion when I see so much going on around me. And, dare I say it, Mr Holmes is so convinced of his abilities he sometimes takes the long route to solve a simple puzzle. The disguises, for instance. I have seen him enter this house as a tramp, a blind man, a war veteran, on sticks, with a funny walk, first hopping, then dragging, in hats, in beards, in rags and on one occasion with a wooden leg, and frankly I have seen better impersonations at the Alhambra. I wonder that his suspects are not put off by laughing too hard. What is wrong with simply keeping out of sight? It is what a woman would do, because they know the ways of men.

But Mr Holmes does not know the ways of women. Oh, he acts superior around them, opening the door in his smoking jacket, listening to their stories with his elbow on his knee and his hand at his chin, appearing the man of the world. Why, then, does he become flustered when Elsie offers to clean his rooms? Why does he watch her from the turn on the landing as she smooths beeswax into the banisters? I shall tell you; it is because he sees the female form from afar, and puts them on a pedestal, because they have never been close enough to disappoint him, and he will not let them nearer.

But I am speaking out of turn again, for which you must blame a Scottish temperament. Let me describe the conclusion in the case of Lady Templeford. The morning after I had spoken out of turn with Mr Holmes, Inspector Lestrade turned up on my doorstep. I took his coat and requested he wait in the parlour, for I do not want the police trampling mud upstairs. Mr Holmes came down presently. As my offer of tea was accepted, I stayed outside the door while I waited for the kettle to boil.

'Well, this is a fine business, Mr Holmes,' I heard the inspector complain. 'A baby kidnapped from its cot and no ransom note! It has been more than two days now, and I cannot hold off my men any longer for your shenanigans.'

'Your men will destroy any chance we have of uncovering the crime,' my lodger replied with ill-concealed temper. 'The answer lies in Rose Nichols' house, and I cannot have the scene damaged until I have ended my investigations.'

'But what have you uncovered? Precisely nothing, sir!'

'Not true, inspector. Rose Nichols' nursery is situated at the back of the ground floor. Its door was shut with keys belonging only to the master of the house, and the rear of the building is surrounded by flower beds. You will recall that rain has fallen constantly for the last few days, and the garden earth is soft. Yet not so much as a single shoe or bootprint has been left beneath any of the windows. Nor was any latch or lock on either the door or windows forced. I must conclude, therefore, that Lady Templeford has indeed been right in her suspicions, and that the crime occurred at home. It is now a matter of proving the wretched girl's guilt before she brings further disgrace to her new family.'

Well, when I heard this I nearly scalded myself. Entering with the tray, I set to providing some hospitality in that chilly room. 'Hot tea, inspector, and for you Mr Holmes.' As soon as I entered, my lodger ceased to speak. He was waiting for me to leave. 'Will there be anything else?' I asked.

'No, Mrs Hudson, we must not detain you. Go about your duties.' His long hands waved me aside impatiently. Unable to find a reason to stay in the room, I took my leave. Now, as if suspicious of my whereabouts, Mr Holmes rose and firmly shut the door behind me, so that I could hear no more.

But I had heard enough. The 'wretched girl' was obviously a reference to Rose Nichols. Lady Templeford was accusing her of maternal neglect at best and murder at worst, suggesting she was solely responsible for the abduction of the child. I may know nothing of the criminal mind, but I understand a mother's nature.

I thought of Rose, low-born and swept off her feet by a noble suitor. Soon she finds herself surrounded by new relatives who frown upon her profession and status in life, who doubtless try to prevent the marriage and stay away from the wedding, causing Rose great embarrassment. She is installed in a grand mansion, overseeing servants she has never before commanded. She is cut off from the theatre, forbidden to see friends from her old life. A child arrives with unseemly haste; the family cast aspersions on her honour – but what if the Honourable Archie Templeford has been forced to marry hastily to avoid a scandal? Even he would now be against her. No longer a star of the stage, admired by friends and suitors, Rose finds herself a prisoner in her strange new abode. Then calamity strikes. Perhaps she discovers poor Godwin smothered in its cot, and has hidden the body from shame – friendless and alone, she will be condemned by all those around her, including Mr Sherlock Holmes, who is himself in thrall to those of nobler demeanour, and believes all he has heard about women of Rose's class.

When I passed my lodger on the stairs a little later, I found myself speaking out again. 'I see the story of the missing baby has reached the noon papers, Mr Holmes. I heard the boy calling it out from the corner. I wonder if you have visited Lady Templeford in town,' I asked. 'Her husband is reported to be —'

'It is common knowledge that Viscount Templeford is in poor health, Mrs Hudson, and does not welcome the attentions of strangers at his Devon estate. Her ladyship is presently staying in Mount Row. Perhaps —' He turns and fixes me with an irritated look. 'Perhaps it is best for us both to stick to our respective professions. On my part, I promise not to attempt to polish the silverware, nor wax the banisters.'

He was right to scold me. I had allowed myself to assume a role I was unfit for. I returned to the tasks of the day, preparing the luncheon menu and arranging payment for the tradesmen.

Still, I could not rid my mind of the suspicion that there was more to the case than Mr Holmes assumed. As I fulfilled the morning's duties I thought the matter through most carefully. I myself am born of low parents, and have – to my shame – behaved poorly with women whom I regard as lower than myself. However, a mother's bond is strong enough to cut through any ties of class, and I could not believe that Rose Nichols took the life of her first-born child in order to spite her husband's family.

That afternoon, Elsie overturned a milk-can in the scullery, and we were forced to move the furniture to clear the mess before it curdled, so I missed hearing Mr Holmes' return from what I assumed to be a further trip to Richmond. That evening, at the more respectable hour of seven, Lady Templeford called again, and I was on hand to usher her in. She removed a brown corded top-coat and, and finding it too hot in the front parlour, un-buttoned a matching jacket, which I took from her and hung in the hall.

Her manner had changed. The almost theatrical panic in her eyes had given way to a steely composure. She was determined to see Mr Holmes, and would accept no refusal. Deciding to forego the rigmarole of ascending, awaiting a reply, then returning to the parlour, I sent Lady Templeford directly to the first floor.

But I stayed on the stairs, watching and listening.

This is what I heard. A creak of floorboards. Mr Holmes pacing back and forth. A stern, high voice. 'How you could allow the press to be informed...breach of confidence...this brazen woman paid her fancy man to take the child...public knowledge...drag my family name into the mud...cannot stay at Mount Street a minute longer.'

This is what I saw. The polished toecaps of my lodger's shoes, twisting past the gap in the door. The glint of his grey eyes. The switch of Lady Templeford's dress as she rose and turned, her buttoned boots matching the detective's pace. Her pale hand brushing at a mark on her blouse. Suddenly I had an inkling of the truth.

I hurried back downstairs as the door to Mr Holmes' apartment opened. There was barely time to find what I was looking for; Lady Templeford was already on the top stair, about to descend. I went to the cloak stand and removed her jacket, hastily searching the pockets. I knew she would see me with my hand upon her personal belongings and my reputation would be ruined, but was determined to prove my theory correct.

Thank heaven Mr Holmes called to her from the landing at that moment. 'Lady Templeford, I have decided to accede to your wishes and search the premises of this mountebank, if you truly believe him to be the mastermind of such a deception. I shall accompany you.' Clearly the finger of guilt now pointed to Rose's former suitor. But I had found what I sought, and knew the truth. It suggested one solution. I turned to speak, but Mr Holmes gathered the coats from the stand and helped his client into them before springing to the front door. Then the pair were gone in their haste to reach the Haymarket premises of Rose Nichols' supposed lover, leaving me alone in the hall.

With a sigh, I returned to my kitchen. The potatoes would not peel themselves, and Elsie could not manage alone.

I heard the rest from the newspaper boy outside Baker Street station. The evening papers were full of the story. The missing baby had been found unharmed on the premises of one Mr Arthur Pilkington of the Haymarket, formerly of Clerkenwell. Neighbours heard the baby boy crying on the step of his lodging house. The former suitor of the Deptford Nightingale had been taken into custody at Bow Street, though he denied any knowledge of the infant. He was to be charged with kidnap. It was alleged that Rose remained in love with her former paramour. The police were hoping to discover whether the mother colluded in the abduction of her child. Mr Sherlock Holmes was to be congratulated for the part he played in restoring the infant to its father, the Hon. Archibald Templeford.

I pursed my lips as Mr Holmes passed to his room that night, unable to congratulate him. He failed to notice the withheld compliment, but I managed to hold my peace. He had reminded me of my place often enough for one week.

The case was called to mind just once more, when Lady Templeford came again, this time at ten in the morning. Her mood was one of jubilation. 'I must speak with Mr Holmes at once!' she cried, as if announcing her intention to the street, and pushed past me on her way upstairs, as though I were a ghost and she had intended to pass right through me. She met him on the floor above. 'Happy news indeed! They have arraigned the blackguard and his mistress, and my son is preparing to commence divorce proceedings. None of this could have happened without your help.'

At the foot of the stairs, I trembled for what I was about to say. My sense of justice was strong, but so was the conviction that I would be going against generations of wealth and class. A woman of my position cannot afford to make mistakes.

'Mr Holmes,' I called out, 'I must speak to you plainly.'

'Mrs Hudson.' My lodger was taken aback. 'You must see that I am entertaining a most distinguished visitor.'

'What I have to say concerns her too,' I ventured, standing my ground, although there was a quaver in my voice. 'I fear you have been deceived.'

'What is this imposition?' Straight-backed and frowning, Lady Templeford drew herself up to her full imposing height and faced me upon the stair. I took an involuntary step back.

'On the night Lady Templeford arrived in distress, a smell clung to her fox-fur coat, something a mother would recognise. It was the smell of a baby. But there was something else, a chemical stronger than that secreted by an infant. When she returned, the second smell still emanated from her pocket. While this lady was in your rooms, I glimpsed something in the jacket she gave me.'

'Really, this is too much!' Lady Templeford protested. 'Mr Holmes, why do you allow your staff to behave in this unseemly fashion?'

'Laudanum, Madam,' I cried, forgetting the correct form of address. 'Every woman of the working class recognises its smell, a drink cheaper than gin and sadly in just as much use. An opium-based painkiller prescribed for everything from a headache to tuberculosis, fed to infants by their nursemaids in order to keep them quiet – often with fatal results. I hear the drug has found popularity among even the grandest ladies now. You cannot deny it – the bottle was in your pocket.' I had seen the octagonal brown glass and smelled its contents. 'It is my conjecture you paid one of your son's servants to remove the baby from its cradle and deliver it to your lodgings in Mount Row. But there are many apartments around you whose occupants might hear an infant cry, so you silenced the poor mite with laudanum. Shame upon you!'

'The woman is mad!' cried her ladyship. 'I shall not countenance such an accusation.'

'Then this will do it for you,' I told her, raising the bottle so that Mr Holmes could see it. 'Your name is written upon the label. Your doctor will verify the prescription, I am sure.' No man can survive without the influence of women. But we live in a world that belongs to men. Even our own dear queen has withdrawn completely from British life, her strength brought low by the memory of her husband. What hope can there be for other women without her?

The truth did indeed come to light, although I do not know whether justice will be done. It is not my business to know. Certainly, Mr Holmes was not best pleased. How could he be in his position? Still, I look up to him. And he must look down upon me.

To him, I will always be the lady downstairs.

Nobody knew his real name. Since he was in his seventies, kept all of his worldly possessions in a plastic bag, and had a paternal manner, he was known as Old Bag Dad. Everyone who visited the Memorial Park knew and liked him. He was an institution. Sitting on his favourite bench and wearing the same tattered clothes year in and year out, he was a familiar figure in the community landscape, a cherished eccentric who radiated a kind of gentle wisdom.

Children loved him, parents trusted him and Douglas Pym, the head park keeper, treated him with amused reverence. Old Bag Dad was not a troublemaker, or a wino, or a beggar, or a misfit, or a lunatic or even one of the many aimless drifters who wandered in from time to time. He was, by his own definition, a good, oldfashioned, unrepentant tramp.

The bag was incongruous. Emblazoned with the distinctive logo of Harrods, it was filled with the most amazing range of items. It was hard to believe that Old Bag Dad had actually shopped in London's most exclusive store, still less that he had bought there the penny whistle, the golliwog, the pack of Tarot cards, the straw boater, the magnifying glass, the tartan scarf, the alarm clock, the bicycle pump, the dog-eared copy of *War and Peace* or any of the other unlikely objects that he invariably carried around with him. He was a collector with random tastes.

Douglas Pym always teased the old man about the bag. When he saw his friend on his bench that morning, he could not resist a joke.

'What have you got in there today?' he asked, peering into the bag. 'Something from Harrods' Food Hall?'

'Loaf of stale bread, Doug. That's all.'

'Where did you get that?'

'I have my sources,' said the old man with a smile.

'They never seem to let you down. You always manage to get grub from somewhere. I saw you with a punnet of strawberries yesterday. Who gave you those?'

'That would be telling!'

Old Bag Dad was very fond of Douglas Pym. Though the park was locked every night, the old man was allowed to sleep there during warmer months, stretching out on his bench under a newspaper or two. On rainy days, Pym even left the door to his storeroom open so that his resident tramp could slumber under a roof for a change. What happened to Old Bag Dad in the winter was a mystery that Pym had never managed to solve. He repeated a question that he had asked a hundred times over the years.

'Where do you go, Bag Dad?'

'Here and there.'

'Come on,' said the park keeper, nudging him. 'You can tell me now. I retire next week. I'll take your secret with me. Scouts' honour! Where do you hide out in the winter?'

'I migrate south with the birds.'

'Can't you be more specific?'

'No,' said the old man. 'You'd only follow me.'

'What did you do before you became a tramp?'

'I lived a useless and unproductive existence.'

'And now?'

Old Bag Dad gave a throaty chuckle. 'I'm happy,' he said.

'I'm not sure that your happiness will continue,' warned Pym, sadly. 'My successor may not be as easy-going as me. Ex-army man. Does everything by the book.'

'I'll win him over, Doug.'

'You may find it difficult. Ken Latimer's a martinet. When I told him that I made a few allowances for you, he said that they'd have to stop right away. Watch out, Bag Dad. He's a bossy type. Likes to throw his weight about.'

Old Bag Dad grinned. 'I'll charm the pants off him.'

His voice was educated, his manners impeccable. It led many people to speculate about his earlier life. Some believed he was a university professor who had fallen on hard times, or a brilliant scientist who had had some kind of mental breakdown, or even a famous writer who could no longer get published. What set him apart from every other tramp was the pleasant aroma that always surrounded him. In a way of life not known for its attention to basic hygiene, Old Bag Dad was noted for his strong whiff of aftershave lotion, an odd choice for a man who had not shaved for years. It was almost as if he bathed in it.

'Good luck, anyway,' said Pym, offering his hand.

Old Bag Dad shook it. 'Thanks for everything, Doug.'

'I should be thanking you. Whenever you're around, the kids seem to behave much better. They wouldn't dare to use drugs or sniff glue while Old Bag Dad is watching them. You're a one-man police force.'

'I've been called worse.'

'Not by me.'

Douglas Pym gave him a salute before walking away. When he glanced over his shoulder, a young woman was asking the tramp to keep an eye on her baby while she went to the rest room. It was visible proof of the trust that he inspired. Singing a lullaby, Old Bag Dad rocked the child gently in its buggy. He was a picture of contentment.

Set in the heart of a large Midlands city, the Memorial Park was one of its finest assets. It contained three football pitches, two tennis courts, an open-air swimming bath, a well-tended bowling green and – a quaint survival from an earlier age – a magnificent wrought-iron bandstand that was an irresistible challenge to juvenile climbers. Older visitors preferred the botanical gardens but younger ones opted for the playground and its childsafe equipment. It was near the playground that Old Bag Dad liked to sit. Reclining on his bench, he was reading a book when he had his first encounter with the new head park keeper.

Ken Latimer did not believe in mincing his words. He was a tall, well-built man in his late forties with a military bearing. A tiny moustache bristled at the centre of a craggy face. Marching up to the tramp, he stood over him and looked down with disdain.

'So!' he sneered. 'You're Old Bag Dad, are you?'

'That's what they call me,' replied the other.

'Well, I don't care whether you're Old Bag Dad or Old Beirut. All I can see is a tramp who lowers the standards around here. My name is Mr Latimer and my aim is to lick this place into shape.' He leaned forward. 'You're not welcome here any more. Got it?'

'It's a public park. You can't throw me out.'

'I can, if you break the rules.'

'Is there a rule against reading *War and Peace*?' asked the tramp, holding up his book. 'I would have thought an army man like you would recommend such literature.'

'Don't try any backchat with me, old man,' cautioned the park keeper. 'I'm not a soft touch like Doug Pym. Try to be clever with me and I'll have you out of here in a shot. Got it?'

'Yes, Mr Latimer.'

'Law and order have come to the Memorial Park.'

'They never went away.'

'Oh, yes, they did. I'm no mug. I know what's been going on. Young kids playing truant so that they could hang around here and smoke. Couples groping each other in the long grass. Drunks puking all over the place. And a certain person,' he added, meaningfully, 'daring to spend the whole night in the park.'

'I had an arrangement with Doug Pym.'

'I've just cancelled it.'

'Why are you being so hostile, old chap?' asked the tramp, trying his warmest smile on the keeper. 'At bottom, I'm on your side.'

'Not from where I stand,' retorted Latimer. 'I work for a living, you don't. I contribute, you simply take. You're nothing but a parasite. A filthy, hairy, disgusting old parasite.'

'Bear with me and I'm sure that you'll learn to love me.'

'Never! I rule the roost now – got it?'

'I think so.'

'Well, remember what I said. When the bell goes this evening, you leave the park along with everyone else. Trespassers will be prosecuted. In your case,' he said, vengefully, 'you'll have a boot up your backside as well. Is that understood?'

'Tolstoy could not have put it more clearly.'

'Who's he? Another tramp?'

'Don't you ever read, Mr Latimer?'

'Only the Rule Book. It tells me all I want to know.'

* * *

Ken Latimer was a good as his word. A strict new regime was imposed upon the park but it made him few friends. The keepers were more vigilant and liable to chastise wrongdoers for the smallest misdemeanour. If anyone so much as let an ice cream wrapper fall inadvertently to the ground, they were pounced on and reprimanded. Suddenly, the Memorial Park was no longer a place for fun and relaxation. Even in the botanical gardens, the iron hand of Ken Latimer was in evidence. Every visitor, young, old or middle-aged, was aware of being under surveillance.

It was at night that Latimer claimed his greatest success. Fearing that the park was a meeting place for drug-users, he instituted nocturnal patrols and chased any youths away. Lovers were also put to flight, caught in flagrante and subjected to the ear-splitting sound of Latimer's whistle. Another victim was Molly Mandrake, a local woman of almost fifty summers, who regularly serviced her clients after dark, and who could somehow get in and out of the park at will. With his torch and whistle, Latimer soon put an end to Molly's lucrative nighttime ventures.

He congratulated himself on what he saw as a moral triumph. No drugs, no sex – free or paid for – and no tramps. On behalf of the local community, he had comprehensively cleaned up the park. It was true that he opened his office some mornings to be met by the faintest smell of aftershave lotion but he never for a moment connected it with a man he perceived as a filthy, hairy, disgusting old parasite. Besides, how could Old Bag Dad possibly gain access to an office that had three locks and a burglar alarm to guard it?

Ken Latimer was in control. The Memorial Park was run like clockwork and its dissident elements quickly driven away. The head park keeper could strut around as if he was still on the parade ground.

But then, the unthinkable occurred.

'Who first discovered the body, Mr Latimer?' asked the Chief Inspector.

'I did,' replied the park keeper. 'At 7.45 a.m. precisely.'

'How can you be so sure of the time?'

'Because I always arrive a quarter of an hour before the gates are unlocked. As soon as I entered the park, I knew that something was wrong. When I glanced towards the bandstand, I saw the body.'

'What did you do?'

'I ran across to see if there were any vital signs, of course,' explained Latimer. 'When I realised that she was dead, I took care not to damage the integrity of the crime scene.'

'Yes,' said Chief Inspector Fallowell, 'we're grateful to you for that. Did you, by any chance, recognise the lady?'

'She was no lady, Chief Inspector. That's Molly Mandrake.'

'Show her some respect, sir. It's a hideous way to die.'

'She had no right to be in the park.'

'That doesn't mean she deserves to be throttled,' said Fallowell with compassion. 'I know that you've been cracking the whip around here, Mr Latimer, but surely even you would not advocate that intruders should be murdered in cold blood.'

'I suspect that the blood may have been a little hotter on this occasion, Chief Inspector. Molly and her client did not come in here to discuss theology.'

'How do you know it was one of her clients?'

'Who else could it have been?'

'An angry park keeper, perhaps.'

Tom Fallowell, head of the Murder Investigation Team, did not like the man he was interviewing in the shadow of the ancient bandstand. Summoned by a call from Latimer, he had resented his hortatory manner. Fallowell had great affection for the park. He had played there as a child and was now captain of the bowls team. His own children had also enjoyed the amenities but they, like so many others, found the place far less welcoming than it had been. Latimer's reign had driven dozens of regular visitors away.

'I want this murder solved, Chief Inspector,' said the keeper.

'These things can't be rushed, sir.'

'I've gone to great lengths to sweep this park clean. The last thing I need is a dead body lying in the middle of it. It's bad publicity. Got it?'

'Molly Mandrake did not get herself killed deliberately,' argued the detective. 'I know that she had reason to hate you but even she would draw the line at being strangled so that she could ruin your nice, neat, well-behaved, spick and span park.'

'Don't be sarcastic with me, Chief Inspector.'

'Then don't try to tell me my job, sir. A murder investigation is a slow process. If we have to keep the park closed for a week, so be it. I'll not be chivvied along by you.' He closed his notebook. 'Have you spoken to Old Bag Dad yet?'

'No. Why should I?'

'Because he may be able to help us.'

'He's been banned from the park at night.'

'So was Molly Mandrake but that didn't stop her, did it?'

'Old Bag Dad was nowhere near the place last night.'

'Nevertheless, we'd like to have a word with him.'

'It would be a waste of time,' said Latimer, testily. 'After what I said to him, he wouldn't dare come here after dark. I put the fear of death into him.'

'I doubt that, sir,' said the other with a half-smile. 'You obviously don't know Old Bag Dad as well as we do. Did it never occur to you that Doug Pym let him stay here overnight for a reason?'

'Doug felt sorry for him, that's all.'

'No, Mr Latimer. Your predecessor had the sense to see how useful the old man could be. He was a sort of guard dog. There were no break-ins here when Old Bag Dad was on the prowl. And no drug-users either. Not because he'd try to arrest them – how could he? – but because he'd talk to them. He has a very persuasive tongue, you know. Old Bag Dad would do his damnedest to persuade them how stupid it was to rely on drugs for their kicks.'

Latimer was scornful. 'We don't need tramps here.'

'Fortunately, Doug Pym disagreed. That's why we caught the lads who tried to vandalise the bowling green. Old Bag Dad saw them at it. He also foiled thieves who attempted to raid the botanical gardens. And there were many other occasions when he was a key witness.'

Latimer was stunned. 'You'd listen to the word of a man like that?'

'With gratitude.'

'Well, he can't help you this time, Inspector.'

'You may be surprised on that score.'

Fallowell turned away to supervise his scene of crime team and the park keeper was left to ponder. He was seething with frustration. The murder had made nonsense of his claim to have cleaned up the park. It was almost as if someone were deliberately trying to get back at him. He could think of only one person who might do that – Old Bag Dad.

It was two days before the park was reopened. Visitors swarmed in, still buzzing with curiosity about the crime and anxious to see the exact place where it had occurred. Molly Mandrake's profession added a lurid glow to the whole affair. In their press statement, the police announced that the victim had suffered death by asphyxiation though they were reticent about any sexual abuse involved. Colourful theories abounded.

When the head park keeper did a circuit of his domain, he was taken aback to see Old Bag Dad on his favourite bench. The tramp was in the process of eating a banana. Ken Latimer bore down on him.

'Don't you dare throw that banana skin away,' he warned.

'You have enough of those already,' said the tramp with a glint in his eye. 'And it seems that you slipped on one of them. What happened to your nightly patrol, Mr Latimer? You boasted that you'd make the park safe after dark.'

'That's exactly what I did.'

'Try telling that to Molly Mandrake.'

'She had no business being in here.'

Old Bag Dad stiffened. 'I hope you're not going to tell me that she was asking for it,' he said, sounding a note of challenge. 'No woman should suffer that fate. Molly may not've been a saint but she's entitled to our sympathy. God bless her!'

'Have you spoken to the police yet?' demanded Latimer.

'Why on earth should I do that?'

'Chief Inspector Fallowell thought you might've seen something.'

'Yes,' said the tramp with a chuckle. 'I noticed that Tom Fallowell was in charge of the case. He's a friend of mine. Give him my regards when you see him again.'

'You're the one who should see him.'

'Am I?'

'Tell him what you know.'

'About what?'

'This crime,' said Latimer with irritation. 'You know this park, and the people who use it, better than anybody. You must have ideas.'

'Dozens of them,' admitted the other, getting up. 'Excuse me while I put this banana skin in the bin. You won't slip on it then.'

'Were you acquainted with Molly Mandrake?'

'Not in a professional sense.' He dropped the banana skin into the metal bin. 'But we often had a chat. Molly was good company. She used to be a bus conductor, you know. In the dear old days when we had such luxuries. Apparently, that's how it all started.'

'What did?'

'Her change of direction. When they switched over to driver-only buses, Molly was out of work. She'd been so popular with her male colleagues that she decided to start charging for her expertise. I recall her telling me that it was just like being a bus conductor,' he went on with a fond smile. 'They bought their ticket and she took them on a very pleasant journey.' He heaved a sigh. 'The other night, alas, she reached her terminus.'

Latimer eyed him shrewdly. 'You know something, don't you?'

'I know lots of things, my friend.'

'You have information about this murder.'

'How could I?'

'It's a crime to withhold evidence. Do you realise that?'

'What evidence could I have, Mr Latimer?' taunted the old man. 'I'm banned from the park after dark. You evicted me from my bench.'

'You might have sneaked back in here.'

'And eluded your eagle eyes? How could I possibly do that?'

'This is important. We're talking about a serious crime.'

'Nobody is as anxious as me to see the killer brought to book,' said the tramp, firmly. 'Molly was a friend of mine. She was so full of life.' He shook his head slowly. 'Molly was like me, Mr Latimer. A harmless soul who relies on the sympathy and understanding of others. She also relied on their weaknesses, I grant you, but that doesn't contradict my argument. Molly needed the kind of tolerance that Doug Pym used to give us. If he'd still been here, I have a feeling that she'd be alive to this day.'

Latimer blenched. 'Are you saying I am responsible for her death?'

'Not exactly.'

'My intention was to get rid of any crime.'

'That was tantamount to throwing down the gauntlet,' said the old man. 'Some people hate authority. When they're given orders, they have this tendency to disobey them. Molly had to go on coming here.'

'And what about you?'

'Oh, I'm much more law-abiding.'

'Don't lie to me.'

Old Bag Dad beamed. 'I always tell the truth to a man in a peaked cap,' he declared. 'And you look as if you were born with it on.'

Ken Latimer was stymied. He realised that bullying would get him nowhere this time. If he wanted cooperation from the old man, he had to trade. It was a bitter pill to swallow but the future of the park was at stake. He could not let an unsolved murder hang over it like a dark cloud.

'Right,' he said. 'Let's have it. What's the deal?'

'Deal?'

'You were a witness. We need you to come forward.'

'But I was forbidden to come here at night,' the tramp reminded him. 'If I give evidence, you'll prosecute me for trespassing on council property. My lawyer would never allow me to do anything like that.'

'There'll be no prosecution, Bag Dad.'

'What guarantee do I have of that?'

'My promise,' said Latimer, proudly. 'I'll stand by it.'

'I need something more. I want to go back to the old arrangement.'

'You, staying the night here? I won't have that.'

'Then there's no deal. Got it?'

'There has to be. My reputation is at stake here.'

The old man indicated the bench. 'So is my bed.'

'If I let you stay overnight, I'd be breaking the rules.'

'Join the club, Mr Latimer.'

The keeper's head sank to his chest. After a lifetime of enforcing rules and regulations, he was faced with an impossible dilemma. He could stay true to his principles and risk having an unsolved crime leaving a permanent stain on his park. Or he could compromise. It required a huge effort on his part.

'Very well,' he conceded, grudgingly. 'You win.'

'I'd prefer it if we could shake hands on that.'

It was almost too much to ask. Latimer was a fastidious man with a deep-seated hatred of tramps but he knew that Old Bag Dad was in a position to dictate terms. With severe misgivings, he extended his hand. The other man shook it then walked across to pick up his bag.

'I think I'll go and have a talk with Tom Fallowell,' he said.

When he arrived at the police station, Old Bag Dad was taken straight to the Chief Inspector. A mass of evidence had already been collected but no suspect had yet emerged. The police were baffled. The tramp was able to supply a crucial detail.

'I caught a glimpse of the registration number on the car.'

'What was it?' pressed Fallowell.

'This is only a guess, mind you,' said the old man. 'It was quite dark. Luckily, he left the door open when he got out of the car so the courtesy light was on. That meant I saw him clearly.'

'Did you recognise him?'

'Not exactly.'

'And the number of the car?'

'I think it was W848 MJK.'

'Any idea of the make?'

'A Mondeo. But don't ask me the colour, Tom.'

Fallowell wrote down the details on a slip of paper and handed it to a colleague. The latter immediately picked up a telephone to trace the owner of the vehicle. The Chief Inspector turned to Old Bag Dad.

'Why didn't you tell us this before?'

'I was held up by a legal technicality.'

'Would his name happen to be Ken Latimer?'

'No wonder you became a detective!'

'Thanks for coming forward, Bag Dad,' said Fallowell. 'This may be the breakthrough that we need. But next time you have evidence,' he stressed, 'make sure that you give it immediately. In a murder inquiry, we expect help from the public.'

The old man winked. 'Oh, I think you'll find that I've given that.'

Ten minutes later, Chief Inspector Fallowell was in a police car, leading a convoy to an address that they had been given. When they reached their destination, they found the house in a quiet cul-de-sac. Standing on the drive was a blue Ford Mondeo with the correct registration plate. The Inspector leapt out of the car and deployed his men around the property. He rang the bell but got no response. When he pounded on the door with his fist, he still elicited no reply. Standing back, he nodded to a waiting police officer who smashed down the door without ceremony. Armed detectives surged into the house to be met by a sight that made them stop in their tracks.

Chief Inspector Fallowell was as astonished as the rest of them. The man they wanted to interview could not have answered the door, even if he had wanted to do so. Sitting in an upright chair, he was bound and gagged. The look of desperation in his eyes was a confession of guilt in itself. He was untied, asked his name then formally arrested on a charge of murder. Fallowell ordered his men to take the prisoner out. Others were told to search the premises. One of the detectives sniffed the air. He wrinkled his nose. 'What's that?' he asked. 'Smells like aftershave lotion.'

'Funny,' said Fallowell with a knowing smile. 'Can't smell a thing.'

* * *

Douglas Pym soon got to hear how a brutal murder had been solved with the help of a tramp who was trespassing on council property. He was delighted to learn how Old Bag Dad had wrested a vital concession from the new head park keeper. The tramp had the freedom of the park once more. Pym caught his friend on his usual bench, finishing the last chapter of *War and Peace*. The old man let out a chuckle of satisfaction.

'I always wondered how the book ended,' he said.

'What's it to be with Ken Latimer from now on – war or peace?'

'Peace with honour, Doug.'

'Be careful. He bears grudges.'

'I fancy that he'll keep out of my way from now on.'

'Until the cold weather sets in,' noted Pym. 'Even you won't stay around the Memorial Park then. You'll be up and away.'

'Following the sun.'

'But where to? I do wish you'd tell me that.'

'Then I'll let you into the secret, Doug. I go to the Middle East.'

'The Middle East?'

'My spiritual home.'

'Are you pulling my leg?'

'Of course not. There's only one place I could go.'

'Is there?'

'Yes,' said the tramp with a grin. 'Old Baghdad.'

I

'We must be constantly on guard. Night and day. Vigilance is essential. I'm sure you would agree, wouldn't you, Luci?'

Soapy Sam Ballard, our always-nervous Head of Chambers, addressed the meeting as though the forces of evil were already beating on the doors of 4 Equity Court, and weapons of mass destruction had laid waste to the dining hall, condemning us to a long winter of cold meat and sandwiches. As usual, he longed for confirmation and turned to our recently appointed Head of Marketing and Administration, who was now responsible for the Chambers' image.

'Quite right, Chair.' Luci's north country voice sounded quietly amused, as though she didn't take the alarming state of the world quite as seriously as Ballard did.

'Thank you for your contribution, Luci.' Soapy Sam, it seemed, thought she might have gone a little further, such as recommending that Securicor mount a twenty-four hour guard on the Head of Chambers. Then he added, in a voice of doom, 'I have already asked our clerk to keep an extremely sharp eye on the sugar kept in the coffee cupboard.'

'Why did you do that?' I ventured to ask our leader. 'Has Claude been shovelling it in by the tablespoonful?'

Claude Erskine-Brown was one of the few barristers I have ever met who combined a passionate affection for Wagner's operas with a remarkably sweet tooth, continuously sucking wine gums in court and loading his coffee with heaped spoonfuls of sugar.

'It's not that, Rumpole.' Soapy Sam was getting petulant. 'It's anthrax.'

'What anthrax?'

'The sugar might be. There are undoubtedly people out there who are out to get us, Rumpole. Haven't you been listening at all to government warnings?'

'I seem to remember them telling us one day that if we went

down the tube we'd all be gassed, and the next day they said, "Sorry, we were only joking. Carry on going down the tube."'

'Rumpole! Do you take nothing seriously?'

'Some things,' I assured Soapy Sam. 'But not the government.'

'We are,' here Ballard ignored me as an apparently hopeless case, and addressed the meeting, 'especially vulnerable.'

'Why's that?' I was curious enough to ask.

'We represent the Law, Rumpole. The centre of a civilised society. Naturally we'd be high on their hit list.'

'You mean the Houses of Parliament, Buckingham Palace, and number 4 Equity Court? I wonder, you may be right.'

'I propose to appoint a small Chambers emergency committee consisting of myself, Claude Erskine-Brown, and Archie Prosser. Please report to one of us if you notice anything unusual or out of the ordinary. I assume you have nothing to report, Rumpole?'

'Nothing much. I did notice a chap on the tube. A fellow of Middle Eastern appearance wearing a turban and a beard and muttering into a Dictaphone. He got out at South Kensington. I don't suppose it's important.'

Just for a moment I thought, indeed I hoped, our Head of Chambers looked at me as though he believed what I had said, but then justifiable doubt overcame him.

'Very funny,' Ballard told the meeting. 'But then you can scarcely afford to be serious about the danger we're all in, can you Rumpole? Considering you're defending one of these maniacs.'

'Rumpole would defend anyone,' said Archie Prosser, the newest arrival in our chambers, who had an ill-deserved reputation as a wit.

'If you mean anyone who's put on trial and tells me they're innocent, then the answer is yes.'

Nothing alarming happened on the tube on my way home that evening, except for the fact that, owing to a 'work to rule' by the drivers, the train gave up work at Victoria and I had to walk the rest of the way home to Froxbury Mansions in the Gloucester Road. The shops and their windows were full of glitter, artificial snow, and wax models perched on sleighs wearing party dresses. Taped carols came tinkling out of Tesco's. The Chambers meeting had been the last of the term, and the Old Bailey had interrupted its business for the season of peace and goodwill.

There was very little of either in the case which I had been doing in front of the aptly named Mr Justice Graves. Mind you, I would have had a fairly rough ride before the most reasonable of judges. Even some compassionate old darlings like Mr Justice 'Pussy' Proudfoot might have regarded my client with something like horror and been tempted to dismiss my speech to the jury as a hopeless attempt to prevent a certain conviction and a probable sentence of not less than thirty years. The murder we had been considering, when we were interrupted by Christmas, had been cold-blooded and merciless, and there was clear evidence that it had been the work of a religious fanatic.

The victim, Honoria Glossop, Professor of Comparative Religions at William Morris University in east London, had been the author of a number of books, including her latest, and last, publication *Sanctified Killing – A History of Religious Warfare*. She had been severely critical of all acts of violence and aggression – including the Inquisition and the Crusades – committed in the name of God. She had also included a chapter on Islam which spoke scathingly of some Ayatollahs and the cruelties committed by Islamic fundamentalists.

It was this chapter which had caused my client, a young student of computer technology at William Morris named Hussein Khan, to issue a private fatwa. He composed, on one of the university computers, a letter to Professor Glossop announcing that her blasphemous references to the religious leaders of his country deserved nothing less than death – which would inevitably catch up with her. Then he left the letter in her pigeonhole.

It took very little time for the authorship of the letter to be discovered. Hussein Khan was sent down from William Morris and began spending time helping his family in the Star of Persia restaurant they ran in Golders Green. A week later, Professor Glossop, who had been working late in her office at the university, was found slumped across her desk, having been shot at close quarters by a bullet from a revolver of Czech origins, the sort of weapon which is readily and cheaply available in certain south London pubs. Beside her on the desk, now stained with her blood, was the letter containing the sentence of death.

Honoria and her husband Richard 'Ricky' Glossop lived in what the estate agents would describe as 'a three-million-pound townhouse in Boltons'. The professor had, it seemed, inherited a great deal of money from a family business in the Midlands which allowed her to pursue her academic career, and Ricky to devote his life to country sports, without the need for gainful employment. He was clearly, from his photograph in the papers, an outstandingly handsome figure, perhaps five or six years younger than his wife. After her murder, he received, and everyone felt deserved, huge public sympathy. He and Honoria had met when they were both guests on a yacht touring the Greek Islands, and she had chosen him and his good looks in preference to all the available professors and academic authors she knew. In spite of their differences in age and interest, they seemed to have lived happily together for ten years until, so the prosecution said, death overtook Honoria Glossop in the person of my now universally hated client.

Such was the case I was engaged in at the Old Bailey in the run-up to Christmas. There were no tidings of great joy to report. The cards were stacked dead against me, and at every stage it looked like I was losing, trumped by a judge who regarded defence barristers as flies on the tasty dish of justice.

Mr Justice Graves, known to me only as 'The Old Gravestone', had a deep, sepulchral voice and the general appearance of a man waking up with an upset stomach on a wet weekend. He had clearly come to the conclusion that the world was full of irredeemable sinners. The nearest thing to a smile I had seen on the face of The Old Gravestone was the look of grim delight he had displayed when, after a difficult case, the jury had come back with the guilty verdict he had clearly longed for.

So, as you can imagine, the atmosphere in Court One at the Old Bailey during the trial of the Queen against Hussein Khan was about as warm as the South Pole during a blizzard. The Queen may have adopted a fairly detached attitude towards my client, but the judge certainly hadn't.

The prosecution was in the not altogether capable hands of Soapy Sam Ballard, which was why he had practically named me as a founding member of Al-Qaeda at our chambers meeting. His junior was the newcomer Archie Prosser.

These two might not have been the most deadly optimists I had ever had to face during my long career at the bar, but a first-year law student with a lowish IQ would, I thought, have had little difficulty in securing a conviction against the young student who had managed to become one of the most hated men in England.

As he was brought up from the cells and placed in the dock between two prison officers, the jury took one brief, appalled look at him and then turned their eyes on what seemed to them to be the less offensive figure of Soapy Sam as he prepared to open his devastating case.

So I sat at my end of counsel's benches. The brief had been offered to several QCs (Queer Customers I always call them), but they had excused themselves as being too busy, or unwell, or going on holiday – any excuse to avoid being cast as leading counsel for the forces of evil. It was only, it seemed, Rumpole who stuck to the old-fashioned belief that the most outrageous sinner deserves to have his defence, if he had one, put fairly and squarely in front of a jury.

Mr Justice Gravestone didn't share my views. When Ballard rose he was greeted with something almost like a smile from the bench, and his most obvious comments were underlined by a judicious nod followed by a careful note underlined in the judicial notebook. Every time I rose to cross-examine a prosecution witness, however, Graves sighed heavily and laid down his pencil as though nothing of any significance was likely to come.

This happened when I had a few pertinent questions to ask the pathologist, my old friend Professor Arthur Ackerman, forensic scientist and master of the morgues. After he had given his evidence about the cause of death (pretty obvious), I started off.

'You say, Professor Ackerman, that the shot was fired at close quarters?'

'Yes, Mr Rumpole. Indeed it was.' Ackerman and I had been through so many bloodstained cases together that we chatted across the court like old friends.

'You told us,' I went on, 'that the bullet entered the deceased's neck – she was probably shot from behind – and that, among other things, the bullet severed an artery.'

'That is so.'

'So, as a result, blood spurted over the desk. We know it was on the letter. Would you have expected the person, whoever it was, who shot her at close quarters to have had some blood on his clothing?'

'I think that well may have happened.'

'Would you say it probably happened?'

'Probably. Yes.'

When I got this answer from the witness, I stood awhile in silence, looking at the motionless judge.

'Is that all you have to ask, Mr Rumpole?'

'No, my Lord. I'm waiting so your Lordship has time to make note of the evidence. I see your Lordship's pencil is taking a rest!'

'I'm sure the jury has heard your questions, Mr Rumpole. And the answers.'

'I'm sure they have and you will no doubt remind them of that during your summing up. So I'm sure your Lordship will wish to make a note.'

Gravestone, with an ill grace, picked up his pencil and made the shortest possible note. Then I asked Ackerman my last question.

'And I take it you know that the clothes my client wore that evening were minutely examined and no traces of any bloodstains were found?'

'My Lord, how can this witness know what was on Khan's clothing?' Soapy Sam objected.

'Quite right, Mr Ballard,' the judge was quick to agree. 'That was an outrageous question, Mr Rumpole. The jury will disregard it.'

It got no better. I rose, at the end of a long day in court, to cross-examine Superintendent Gregory, the perfectly decent officer in charge of the case.

'My client, Mr Khan, made no secret of the fact that he had written this threatening letter, did he, Superintendent Gregory?'

'He did not, my Lord,' Gregory answered with obvious satisfaction.

'In fact,' said Mr Justice Graves, searching among his notes, 'the witness Sadiq told us that your client boasted to him of the fact in the university canteen?'

There, at last, The Gravestone had overstepped the mark.

'He didn't say "boasted".'

Soapy Sam Ballard QC, the alleged Head of our Chambers, got up with his notebook at the ready.

'Sadiq said that Khan told him he had written the letter and, in answer to your Lordship, that "he seemed to feel no sort of guilt about it".'

'There you are Mr Rumpole.' Graves also seemed to feel no sort of guilt. 'Doesn't that come to exactly the same thing?'

'Certainly not, my Lord. The word "boasted" was never used.'

'The jury may come to the conclusion that it amounted to boasting.'

'They may indeed, my Lord. But that's for them to decide, without directions from your Lordship.'

'Mr Rumpole,' here the judge adopted an expression of lofty pity, 'I realise you have many difficulties in this case. But perhaps we may proceed without further argument. Have you any more questions for this officer?'

'Just one, my Lord.' I turned to the superintendent. 'This letter was traced to one of the university word processors.'

'That is so, yes.'

'You would agree that my client took no steps at all to cover up the fact that he was the author of this outrageous threat.'

'He seems to have been quite open about it, yes.'

'That's hardly consistent with the behaviour of someone about to commit a brutal murder is it?'

'I suppose it was a little surprising, yes,' Jack Gregory was fair enough to admit.

'Very surprising, isn't it? And of course by the time this murder took place, everyone knew he had written the letter. He'd been sent down for doing so.'

'That's right.'

The Gravestone intervened. 'Did it not occur to you, Superintendent Gregory, that being sent down might have provided an additional motive for the murder?' The judge clearly thought he was onto something, and was deeply gratified when the superintendent answered. 'That might have been so, my Lord.'

'That might have been so,' Graves dictated to himself as he wrote the answer down. Then he thought of another point that might be of use to the hardly struggling prosecution.

'Of course, if a man thinks he's justified, for religious or moral reasons, in killing someone, he might have no inhibitions about boasting of the fact?'

I knew it. Soapy Sam must have known it, and the jury had better be told it. The judge had gone too far. I rose to my feet, as quickly as my weight and the passage of the years would allow, and uttered a sharp protest.

'My Lord, the prosecution is in the able hands of Samuel Ballard QC. I'm sure he can manage to present the case against my client without your Lordship's continued help and encouragement.'

This was followed by a terrible silence, the sort of stillness that precedes a storm.

'Mr Rumpole.' His Lordship's words were as warm as hailstones. 'That was a most outrageous remark.'

'It was a point I felt I should make,' I told him, 'in fairness to my client.'

'As I have said, I realise you have an extremely difficult case to argue, Mr Rumpole.' Once more Graves was reminding the jury that I was on a certain loser. 'But I cannot overlook your inappropriate and disrespectful behaviour towards the court. I shall have to consider whether your conduct should be reported to the proper authority.'

After these dire remarks and a few more unimportant questions to the superintendent, Graves turned to the jury and reminded them that this no doubt painful and shocking case would be resumed after the Christmas break. He said this in the solemn and sympathetic tones of someone announcing the death of a dear friend or relative, then he wished them a 'Happy Christmas'.

The tube train for home was packed and I stood, swaying uneasily, sandwiched between an eighteen-stone man in a donkey jacket with a heavy cold, and an elderly woman with a pair of the sharpest elbows I have encountered on the Circle line.

No doubt all of the other passengers had hard, perhaps unrewarding lives, but they didn't have to spend their days acting as a sort of buffer between a possibly fatal fanatic and a hostile judge who certainly wanted to end the career of the inconveniently argumentative Rumpole. The train, apparently as exhausted as I felt, ground to a halt between Charing Cross and the Embankment and as the lights went out I'd almost decided to give up the bar. Then the lights glowed again faintly and the train jerked on. I supposed I would have to go on as well, wouldn't I, not being the sort of character who could retire to the country and plant strawberries.

When I reached the so-called 'Mansion Flat' in the Gloucester Road I was, I have to say, not a little surprised by the warmth of the reception I received. My formidable wife Hilda, known to me only as 'She Who Must be Obeyed' said, 'Sit down, Rumpole. You look tired out.' And she lit the gas fire. A few minutes later, she brought me a glass of my usual refreshment – the very ordinary claret available from Pommeroy's Wine Bar in Fleet Street, a vintage known to me as 'Château Thames Embankment'. I suspected that all this attention meant that she had some uncomfortable news to break and I was right.

'This year,' she told me, with the firmness of Old Gravestone pronouncing judgement, 'I'm not going to do Christmas. It's getting too much for me.'

Christmas was not usually much of a 'do' in the Rumpole household. There is the usual exchange of presents; I get a tie and Hilda receives the statutory bottle of lavender water, which seems to be for laying down rather than immediate use. She cooks the turkey and I open the Château Thames Embankment, and so our Saviour's birth is celebrated.

'I have booked us this year,' Hilda announced, 'into Cherry Picker's Hall. You look in need of a rest, Rumpole.'

What was this place she spoke of? A retirement home? Sheltered accommodation? 'I'm in the middle of an important murder case, I can't pack up and go into a home.'

'It's not a home, Rumpole. It's a country house hotel. In the

Cotswolds. They're doing a special offer – four nights with full board. A children's party. Christmas lunch with crackers and a dance on Christmas Eve. It'll be something to look forward to.'

'I don't really think so. We haven't got any children and I don't want to dance at Christmas. So shall we say no to the Cherry Picker's?'

'Whether you dance or not is entirely up to you, Rumpole. But you can't say no because I've already booked it and paid the deposit. And I've collected your old dinner jacket from the cleaners.'

So I was unusually silent. Not for nothing is my wife entitled 'She Who Must Be Obeyed'.

I was unusually silent on the way to the Cotswolds too, but as we approached this country house hotel, I felt that perhaps, after all, She Who Must Be Obeyed had made a wise decision and that the considerable financial outlay on the 'Budget Christmas Offer' might turn out, in spite of all my apprehension, to be justified. We took a taxi from the station. As we made our way down deep into the countryside, the sun was shining and the trees were throwing a dark pattern against a clear sky. We passed green fields where cows were munching and a stream trickling over the rocks. A stray dog crossed the road in front of us and a single kite (at least Hilda said it was a kite) wheeled across the sky. We had, it seemed, entered a better, more peaceful world far from the problem of terrorists, the bloodstained letter containing a sentence of death, the impossible client, and the no less difficult judge I struggled with down at the Old Bailey. In spite of all my troubles, I felt a kind of contentment stealing over me. Happily, the contentment only deepened as our taxi scrunched the gravel by the entrance of Cherry Picker's Hall. The old grey stones of the one-time manor house were gilded by the last of the winter sun. We were greeted warmly by a friendly manageress and our things were taken up to a comfortable room overlooking a wintry garden. Then, in no time at all, I was sitting by a blazing log fire in the residents' lounge, eating anchovy paste sandwiches with the prospect of a dark and alcoholic fruitcake to follow. Even my appalling client, Hussein Khan, might, I thought, if brought into such an environment, forget his calling as a messenger of terror and relax after dinner.

'It's wonderful to be away from the Old Bailey. I just had the most terrible quarrel with a particularly unlearned judge,' I told Hilda, who was reading a back number of *Country Life*.

'You keep quarrelling with judges, don't you? Why don't you take up fishing, Rumpole? Lazy days by a trout stream might help you forget all those squalid cases you do.' She had clearly got to the country sports section of the magazine.

'This quarrel went a bit further than usual. He threatened to report me for professional misconduct. I didn't like the way he kept telling the jury my client was guilty.'

'Well isn't he guilty, Rumpole?' In all innocence, Hilda had asked the awkward question.

'Well. Quite possibly. But that's for the jury of twelve honest citizens to decide. Not Mr Justice Gravestone.'

'Gravestone? Is that his name?'

'No. His name's Graves. I call him Gravestone.'

'You would, wouldn't you, Rumpole?'

'He speaks like a voice from the tomb. It's my personal belief that he urinates iced water!'

'Really, Rumpole. Do try not to be vulgar. So what did you say to Mr Justice Graves? You might as well tell me the truth.'

She was right, of course. The only way of appeasing She Who Must was to plead guilty and throw oneself on the mercy of the court. 'I told him to come down off the bench and join Soapy Sam Ballard on the prosecution team.'

'Rumpole, that was terribly rude of you.'

'Yes,' I said, with considerable satisfaction. 'It really was.'

'So no wonder he's cross with you.'

'Very cross indeed.' Once again I couldn't keep the note of triumph out of my voice.

'I should think he probably hates you, Rumpole.'

'I should think he probably does.'

'Well, you're safe here anyway. You can forget all about your precious Mr Justice Gravestone and just enjoy Christmas.'

She was, as usual, right. I stretched my legs towards the fire and took a gulp of Earl Grey and a large bite of rich, dark cake.

And then I heard a voice call out, a voice from the tomb.

'Rumpole!' it said. 'What an extraordinary coincidence. Are you here for Christmas? You and your good lady?'

I turned my head. I had not, alas, been mistaken. There he was, in person – Mr Justice Gravestone. He was wearing a tweed suit and some type of regimental or old school tie. His usually lugubrious features wore the sort of smile only previously stimulated by a long succession of guilty verdicts. And the next thing he said came as such a surprise that I almost choked on my slice of fruitcake.

'I say,' he said, and I promise you these were Gravestone's exact words, 'this is fun, isn't it?'

II

'I've often wondered what it would be like to be married to Rumpole.'

It was a lie, of course. I dare swear that The Honourable Gravestone never spent one minute of his time wondering what it would be like to be Mrs Rumpole. But there he was, having pulled up a chair, tucking in to our anchovy paste sandwiches and smiling at She Who Must Be Obeyed (my wife Hilda) with as much joy as if she had just returned twenty guilty verdicts – one of them being in the case of The Judge versus Rumpole.

'He can be a bit difficult at times, of course,' Hilda weighed in for the prosecution.

'A little difficult! That's putting it mildly, Mrs Rumpole. You can't imagine the trouble we have with him in court.'

To my considerable irritation, my wife and the judge were smiling together as though they were discussing, with tolerant amusement, the irrational behaviour of a difficult child.

'Of course we mustn't discuss the case before me at the moment,' Graves said.

'That ghastly terrorist.' Hilda had already reached a verdict.

'Exactly! We won't say a word about him.'

'Just as well,' Hilda agreed. 'We get far too much discussion of Rumpole's cases.'

'Really? Poor Mrs Rumpole.' The judge gave her a look of what I found to be quite sickening sympathy. 'Brings his work home with him, does he?'

'Oh, absolutely! He'll do anything in the world for some ghastly murder or other, but can I get him to help me redecorate the bathroom?'

'You redecorate bathrooms?' The judge looked at Hilda with admiration as though she had just admitted to sailing round the world in a hot air balloon. Then he turned to me.

'You're a lucky man, Rumpole!'

'He won't tell you that.' Hilda was clearly enjoying our Christmas break even more than she had expected. 'By the way I hope he wasn't too rude to you in court.'

'I thought we weren't meant to discuss the case.' I tried to make an objection, which was entirely disregarded by my wife and the unlearned judge.

'Oh, that wasn't only Rumpole being rude. It was Rumpole trying to impress his client by showing him how fearlessly he can stand up to judges. We're quite used to that.'

'He says,' Hilda still seemed to find the situation amusing, 'that you threatened to report him for professional misconduct. You really ought to be more careful, shouldn't you Rumpole?'

'Oh, I said that,' Graves had the audacity to admit, 'just to give your husband a bit of a shock. He did go a little green, I thought, when I made the suggestion.'

'I did not go green!' By now I was losing patience with the judge Hilda was treating like a long-lost friend. 'I made a perfectly reasonable protest against a flagrant act of premature adjudication! You had obviously decided that my client is guilty and you were going to let the jury know it.'

'But isn't he guilty, Rumpole? Isn't that obvious?'

'Of course he's not guilty. He's completely innocent. And will remain so until the jury come back into court and convict him. And that is to be their decision. And what the judge wants will have absolutely nothing to do with it!'

I may have gone too far, but I felt strongly on the subject. Judge Graves, however, seemed completely impervious to my attack. He stood, still smiling, warming his tweed-covered backside at the fire and repeated, 'We really mustn't discuss the case we're involved in at the moment. Let's remember, it is Christmas.'

'Yes, Rumpole. It is Christmas.' Hilda had cast herself, it seemed as Little Lady Echo to his Lordship.

'That's settled then. Look, why don't I book a table for three at dinner?' The judge was still smiling. 'Wouldn't that be tremendous fun?'

'What a perfectly charming man Judge Graves is.'

These were words I never expected to hear spoken, but they contained the considered verdict of She Who Must be Obeyed before we settled down for the first night of our Christmas holiday. The food at dinner had been simple but good. (The entrecôte steak had not been arranged in a little tower swamped by tomato coulis and there had been a complete absence of roquette and all the idiocy of smart restaurants.) The Gravestone was clearly on the most friendly of terms with 'Lorraine', the manageress, and he and Hilda enjoyed a lengthy conversation on the subject of fishing, which sport Graves practised and on which Hilda was expert after her study of the back number of *Country Life* in the residents' lounge.

Now and again I was asked why I didn't go out on a day's fishing with Hilda's newfound friend the judge, a question I found as easy to answer as 'Why don't you take part in the London Marathon wearing nothing but bikini bottoms and a wig?' For a greater part of the dinner I had sat, unusually silent, listening to the ceaseless chatter of the newfound friends, feeling as superfluous as a maiden aunt at a lovers' meeting. Soon after telling me how charming she had found The Gravestone, Hilda had sank into a deep and contented sleep. As the moonlight streamed in at the window and I heard the faraway hooting of an owl, I began to worry about the case we hadn't discussed at dinner.

I couldn't forget my first meeting in Brixton Prison with my client, Hussein Khan. Although undoubtedly the author of the fatal letter, he didn't seem, when I met him in the company of my faithful solicitor Bonny Bernard, to be the sort who would strike terror into the heart of anyone. He was short and unsmiling with soft brown eyes, a quiet monotonous voice, and unusually small hands. He wasn't only uncomplaining, he seemed to find it the most natural thing in the world that he should find himself locked up and facing the most serious of all charges. It was, he told us early in the interview, the will of Allah, and if Allah willed, who was he, a 22-year-old undergraduate in computer studies, to ask questions? I was, throughout the case, amazed at the combination, in my inexplicable client, of the most complicated knowledge of modern technology and the most primitive and merciless religious beliefs.

'I wrote the letter. Of course I did. It was not my decision that she should die. It was the will of God.'

'The will of God that a harmless woman should be shot for writing something critical in a book?'

'Die for blasphemy, yes.'

'And they say you were her executioner, that you carried out the sentence.'

'I didn't do that.' He was looking at me patiently, as though I still had much to learn about the faith of Hussein Khan. 'I knew that death would come to her in time. It came sooner than I had expected.'

So, was I defending a man who had issued a death threat which had then been obediently carried out by some person or persons unknown in the peaceful precincts of a south London university? It seemed an unlikely story, and I was not looking forward to the murder trial which had started at the Old Bailey during the run-up to Christmas.

At the heart of the case there was, I thought, a mystery. The letter, I knew, was clear evidence of Hussein's guilt, and yet there was no forensic evidence – no bloodstains on his clothing, no traces of his having fired a pistol with a silencer (there must have been a silencer, because no one in the building had heard a shot). This was evidence in Hussein's favour, but I had to remember that he had been in the university building when the murder had taken place, although he'd already been sent down for writing the letter.

As the owl hooted, Hilda breathed deeply. Sleep eluded me. I went through Hussein Khan's story again. He had gotten a phone call, he said, when he was at his parents' restaurant. (He had answered the phone himself, so there was no one to confirm the call.) It had been, it seemed, from a girl who said she was the senior tutor's secretary and that the tutor wanted to meet him in the university library at ten o'clock that evening to discuss his future.

He had got to the William Morris building at nine forty-five and had told Mr Luttrell, the man at the main reception area, that he was there to meet the senior tutor at the library. He said that when he had arrived at the library, the tutor wasn't there and that he had waited for over an hour and then went home, never going near Honoria Glossop's office.

Of course the senior tutor and his secretary denied that either had made such a telephone call. The implication was that Hussein was lying through his teeth and that he had gone to the university because he had known that Professor Glossop worked in her office until late at night and he had intended to kill her.

At last I fell into a restless sleep. In my dreams I saw myself being prosecuted by Soapy Sam Ballard who was wearing a long beard and arguing for my conviction under Sharia law.

I woke early to the first faint flush of daylight as a distant cock crowed. I got up, tiptoed across the room, and extracted from the bottom of my case the papers in *R v Khan*. I was looking for the answer to a problem as yet undefined, going through the prosecution statement again, and finding nothing very much.

I reminded myself that Mr Luttrell, at his reception desk, had seen Honoria and her husband arrive together and go to her office. Ricky Glossop had left not more than fifteen minutes later, and later still he had telephoned and couldn't get an answer from his wife. He had asked Luttrell to go to Honoria's office because she wasn't answering her phone. The receptionist had gone to her office and found her lying across her desk, her hand close to the bloodstained letter.

Next I read the statement from Honoria's secretary, Sue Blackmore, describing how she had found the letter in Honoria's university pigeonhole and taken it to Honoria at her home. On Honoria's reaction at receiving it, Ms Blackmore commented, 'She didn't take the note all that seriously and wouldn't even tell the police.' Ricky Glossop had finally rung the anti-terrorist department in Scotland Yard and showed them the letter.

None of this was new. There was only one piece of evidence which I might have overlooked.

In the senior tutor's statement he said he had spoken to Honoria on the morning of the day she had died. She had told him that she couldn't be at a seminar that afternoon because she had an urgent appointment with Tony Hawkin. Hawkin, as the senior tutor knew, was a solicitor who acted for the university, and had also acted for Honoria Glossop in a private capacity. The senior tutor had no idea why she had wanted to see her solicitor. He never saw his colleague alive again.

I was giving that last document some thought when Hilda stirred, opened an eye, and instructed me to ring for breakfast.

'You'll have to look after yourself today, Rumpole,' she told me. 'Gerald's going to take me fishing for grayling.'

'Gerald?' Was there some new man in Hilda's life who had turned up in the Cotswolds?

'You know. The charming judge you introduced me to last night.'

'You can't mean Gravestone?'

'Don't be ridiculous. Of course I mean Gerald Graves.'

'You're going fishing with him?'

'He's very kindly going to take me to a bit of river he shares with a friend.'

'How delightful.' I adopted the ironic tone. 'If you catch anything, bring it back for supper.'

'Oh, I'm not going to do any fishing. I'm simply going to watch Gerald from the bank. He's going to show me how he ties his flies.'

'How absolutely fascinating.'

She didn't seem to think she'd said anything at all amusing and she began to lever herself briskly out of bed.

'Do ring up about that breakfast, Rumpole!' she said. 'I've got to get ready for Gerald.'

He may be Gerald to you, I thought, but he will always be the Old Gravestone to me.

* * *

After Hilda had gone to meet her newfound friend, I finished the bacon and eggs with sausage and fried slice – which I had ordered as an organic, low calorie breakfast – and put a telephone call through to my faithful solicitor Bonny Bernard. I found him at his home talking over a background of shrill and excited children eager for the next morning and the well-filled stockings.

'Mr Rumpole!' The man sounded shocked by my call. 'Don't you ever take a day off? It's Christmas Eve!'

'I know it's Christmas Eve. I know that perfectly well,' I told him. 'And my wife has gone fishing with our sepulchral judge, whom she calls "Gerald". Meanwhile, have you got any close friends or associates working at Hawkin's, the solicitor?'

'Barry Tuck used to be our legal executive – moved there about three years ago.'

'A cooperative sort of character is he, Tuck?'

'We got on very well. Yes.'

'Then get him to find out why Honoria Glossop went to see Tony Hawkin the afternoon before she was shot. It must have been something fairly urgent. She missed a seminar in order to go.'

'Is it important?'

'Probably not, but it just might be something we ought to know.'

'I hope you're enjoying your Christmas break, Mr Rumpole.'

'Quite enjoying it. I'd like it better without a certain member of the judiciary. Oh, and I've got a hard time ahead.'

'Working?'

'No,' I told my patient solicitor gloomily. 'Dancing,'

'Quick, quick, slow, Rumpole. That's better. Now *chassé*. Don't you remember, Rumpole? This is where you *chassé*.'

The truth was that I remembered little about it. It had been so long ago. How many years could it have been since Hilda and I had trod across a dance floor? Yet here I was in a dinner jacket, which was now uncomfortably tight round the waist, doing my best to walk round this small area of polished parquet in time to the music with one arm round Hilda's satin-covered waist and my other hand gripping one of hers. Although for much of the time she was walking backwards, she was undoubtedly the one in command of the enterprise. I heard a voice singing, seemingly from far off, above the music of the five-piece band laid on for the hotel's dinner dance. It was a strange sound and one that I hadn't heard for what seemed many years – She Who Must be Obeyed was singing. I looked towards my table, rather as someone lost at sea might look towards a distant shore, and I saw Mr Justice Gravestone smiling at us with approval.

'Well done, Hilda! And you came through that quite creditably I thought, Rumpole. I mean, at least you managed to remain upright, although there were a few dodgy moments coming round that far corner.'

'That was when I told him *chassé*. Rumpole couldn't quite manage it.'

As they were both enjoying a laugh I realised that, during a long day by the river which had, it seemed, produced nothing more than two fish so small that they had had to be returned to their natural environment, Mrs Rumpole had become 'Hilda' to the judge, who had become 'Gerald'.

'You know, when you retire, Rumpole,' the judge was sounding sympathetic in the most irritating kind of way, 'you could take dancing lessons.'

'There's so much Rumpole could do *if* he retired. I keep telling him,' was Hilda's contribution. 'He could have wonderful days like we had, Gerald. Outdoors, close to nature and fishing.'

'Catching two small grayling you had to put back in the water?' I was bold enough to ask. 'It would've been easier to pay a quick visit to the fishmongers.'

'Catching fish is not the point of fishing,' Hilda told me. Before I could ask her what the point of it was, the judge came up with a suggestion.

'When you retire, I could teach you fishing, Rumpole. We could have a few days out together.'

'Now then. Isn't that kind of Gerald, Rumpole?' Hilda beamed and I had to mutter, 'Very kind,' although the judge's offer had made me more determined than ever to die with my wig on.

It was at this point that Lorraine the manageress came to the judge with a message. He read it quickly and then said, 'Poor old Leslie Mulliner. You know him, don't you, Rumpole? He sits in the chancery division.'

I had to confess I didn't know anyone who sat in the chancery division.

'He was going to join us here tomorrow but his wife's not well.'

'He said on the phone that you'd do the job for him tomorrow.' Lorraine seemed anxious.

'Yes, of course,' Graves hurried to reassure her. 'I'll stand in for him.'

Before I could get any further explanation of the 'job', the music had struck up a more contemporary note. Foxtrots were out, and with a cry of 'Come along Hilda,' Graves was strutting the dance floor, making curious rhythmic movements with his hands. And Hilda, walking free and unfastened from her partner, was also strutting and waving her arms, smiling with pleasure. It wasn't, I'm sure, the most up-to-date form of dancing, but it was, I suppose, a gesture from two sedate citizens who were doing their best to become, for a wine-filled moment on Christmas Eve, a couple of teenagers.

Christmas Day at Cherry Picker's Hall was uneventful. The judge suggested church, and I stood while he and Hilda bellowed out 'Come, all ye Faithful'. Then we sat among the faithful under the Norman arches, beside the plaques and monuments to so many vanished rectors and country squires, looking out upon the holly round the pulpit and the flowers on the altar. I tried to understand, not for the first time, how a religious belief could become so perverted as to lead to death threats, terror, and a harmless professor shot through the head.

We had lunch in a pub and then the judge announced he had work to do and left us.

After a long and satisfactory sleep, Hilda and I woke around teatime and went to the residents' lounge. Long before we got to the door, we could hear the excited cries of children, and when we went in we saw them crowded round the Christmas tree. And there, stooping among the presents, was the expected figure in a red dressing gown (trimmed with white fur), Wellington boots, a white beard, and a long red hat. As he picked up a present and turned towards us, I felt that fate had played the greatest practical joke it could have thought up to enliven the festive season.

Standing in for his friend Mulliner from the chancery division, the sepulchral, unforgiving, prosecution-minded Mr Justice Gravestone, my old enemy, had become Father Christmas.

On Boxing Day, I rang a persistent, dogged, ever useful private eye detective who, sickened by divorce, now specialised in the cleaner world of crime – Ferdinand Ian Gilmour Newton, known in legal circles as 'Fig Newton'. I told him that, as was the truth, my wife Hilda was planning a long country walk and lunch in a distant village with a judge whom I had spent a lifetime trying to avoid. And I asked him, if he had no previous engagements, if he'd like to sample the *table d'hôte* at Cherry Picker's Hall.

Fig Newton is a lugubrious character of indeterminate age, usually dressed in an old mackintosh and an even older hat, with a drip at the end of his nose caused by a seemingly perpetual cold – most likely caught while keeping observation in all weathers. But today he had shed his outer garments, his nose was dry, and he was tucking in to the lamb cutlets with something approaching enthusiasm. 'Bit of a step up from your usual pub lunch, this, isn't it Mr Rumpole?'

'It certainly is, Fig. We're splashing out this Christmas. Now this case I'm doing down the Bailey...'

'The terrorist?'

'Yes, the terrorist.'

'You're on to a loser with that one, Mr Rumpole.' Fig was gloomily relishing the fact.

'Most probably. All the same, there are a few stones I don't want to leave unturned.'

'Such as what?'

'Find out what you can about the Glossops.'

'The dead woman's family?'

'That's right. See what's known about their lives, hobbies, interests. That sort of thing, I need to get more of a picture of their lives together. Oh, and see if the senior tutor knows more about the Glossops. Pick up any gossip going round the university. I'll let you know if Bonny Bernard has found out why Honoria had a date with her solicitor.'

'So when do you want all this done by, Mr Rumpole?' Fig picked up a cutlet bone and chewed gloomily. 'Tomorrow morning, I suppose?'

'Oh, sooner than that if possible,' I told him.

It was not that I felt that the appalling Hussein Khan had a defence – in fact he might well turn out to have no defence at all. But something at the children's Christmas party had suggested a possibility to my mind.

That something was the sight of Mr Justice Graves standing in for someone else.

III

Christmas was over, and I wondered if the season of goodwill was over with it. The Christmas cards had left the mantelpiece, the holly and the mistletoe had been tidied away, we had exchanged green fields for Gloucester Road, and Cherry Picker's Hall was nothing but a memory. The judge was back on the bench to steer the case of *R v Khan* towards its inevitable guilty verdict.

The Christmas decorations were not all that had gone. Gerald the cheerful dinner guest, Gerald the energetic dancing partner of She Who Must be Obeyed, Gerald the fisherman, and, in particular, Gerald as Santa Claus had all gone as well, leaving behind only the old thin-lipped, unsmiling Mr Justice Gravestone with the voice of doom, determined to make a difficult case harder than ever.

All the same there was something of a spring in the Rumpole step. This was not only the result of the Christmas break but also due to a suspicion that the case *R v Khan* might not be quite as horrifyingly simple as it had appeared at first.

As I crossed the hall on my way to Court Number One, I saw Ricky Glossop – the dashingly handsome husband of the murdered professor – with a pretty blonde girl whom I took to be Sue Blackmore, Honoria's secretary, who was due to give evidence about her employer's reception of the fatal letter. She seemed, so far as I could tell from a passing examination, to be a girl on the verge of a nervous breakdown. She lit a cigarette with trembling fingers, then almost immediately stamped it out. She kept looking, with a kind of description, towards the door of the court, and then turning with a sob to Ricky Glossop and choking out what I took to be some sort of complaint. He had laid a consoling hand on hers and was talking in the sort of low, exaggeratedly calm tone that a dentist uses when he says, 'This isn't going to hurt'.

The medical and police evidence had been disposed of before Christmas and now, in the rather strange order adopted by Soapy Sam Ballard for the prosecution, the only witnesses left were Arthur Luttrell, who manned the reception desk, Ricky Glossop, and the nervous secretary.

Luttrell, the receptionist, was a smart, precise, self-important man with a sharp nose and a sandy moustache who clearly regarded his position as being at the centre of the university organisation. He remembered Hussein Khan coming at nine thirty that evening, saying he had an appointment with the senior tutor, and going up to the library. At quarter to ten the Glossops had arrived. Ricky had gone with his wife to her office, but had left about fifteen minutes later. 'He stopped to speak to me on the way,' Luttrell the receptionist told Soapy Sam, 'which is why I remembered it well.'

After that, the evening at William Morris University followed its horrible course. Around eleven o'clock, Hussein Khan left, complaining that he had wasted well over an hour, no senior tutor had come to him, and that he was going back to his parents' restaurant in Golders Green. After that Ricky telephoned the reception desk saying that he couldn't get any reply from his wife's office and would Mr Luttrell please go and make sure she was all right. As we all know, Mr Luttrell went to the office, knocked, opened the door, and was met by the ghastly spectacle which was to bring us all together in Court Number One at the Old Bailey.

'Mr Rumpole.' The judge's tone in calling my name was as aloofly disapproving as though Christmas had never happened. 'All this evidence is agreed, isn't it? I don't suppose you'll find it necessary to trouble Mr Luttrell with any questions.'

'Just one or two, my Lord.'

'Oh very well.' The judge sounded displeased. 'Just remember, we're under a public duty not to waste time.'

'I hope your Lordship isn't suggesting that an attempt to get to the truth is a waste of time.' And before the old Gravestone could launch a counterattack, I asked Mr Luttrell the first question.

'You say Mr Glossop spoke to you on the way out. Can you remember what he said?'

'I remember perfectly.' The receptionist looked personally insulted as though I doubted his word. 'He asked me if Hussein Khan was in the building.'

'He asked you that?'

'Yes, he did.'

'And what did you tell him?'

'I told him "yes". I said Khan was in the library where he had an appointment with the senior tutor.'

I allowed a pause for this curious piece of evidence to sink into the minds of the jury. Graves, of course, filled in the gap by asking if that was my only question.

'Just one more, my Lord.'

Here the judge sighed heavily, but I ignored that.

'Are you telling this jury, Mr Luttrell, that Glossop discovered that the man who had threatened his wife with death was in the building, then left without speaking to her again?'

I looked at the jury as I asked this and saw, for the first time in the trial, a few faces looking puzzled.

Mr Luttrell, however, sounded unfazed.

'I've told you what he said. I can't tell you anything more.'

'He can't tell us any more,' the judge repeated. 'So that would seem to be the end of the matter, wouldn't it, Mr Rumpole?'

'Not quite the end,' I told him. 'I don't think it's quite the end of the matter yet.'

This remark did nothing to improve my relations with his Lordship, who gave me a look from which all traces of the Christmas spirit had been drained.

The jury may have had a moment of doubt during the receptionist's evidence, but when Ricky Glossop was put in the witness box, their sympathy and concern for the good-looking, appealingly modest, and stricken husband was obvious. Graves supported him with enthusiasm.

'This is clearly going to be a terrible ordeal for you, Mr Glossop,' the judge said, looking at the witness with serious concern. 'Wouldn't you like to sit down?'

'No, thank you, my Lord. I prefer to stand,' Ricky said bravely. The judge gave him the sort of look a commanding officer might give to a young subaltern who'd volunteered to attack the enemy position single-handed. 'Just let me know,' Graves insisted, 'if you feel exhausted or overcome by any part of your evidence, and you shall sit down immediately.'

'Thank you very much, my Lord. That *is* very kind of your Lordship.'

So with formalities of mutual admiration over, Ricky Glossop began to tell his story.

He had met Honoria some ten years before when they were both cruising round the Greek Islands. 'She knew all the classical legends and the history of every place. I thought she'd never be bothered with an undereducated slob like me.' Here he smiled modestly, and the judge smiled back as a sign of disagreement. 'But luckily she put up with me. And, of course, I fell in love with her.'

'Of course?' Soapy Sam seemed to feel that this sentence called for some further explanation.

'She was extremely beautiful.'

'And she found you attractive?'

'She seemed to. God knows why.' This answer earned him smiles for his modesty.

'So you were married for ten years,' Ballard said. 'And you had no children.'

'No. Honoria couldn't have children. It was a great sadness to both of us.'

'And how would you describe your marriage up to the time your wife got this terrible letter?' Ballard was holding the letter out, at a distance, as though the paper itself might carry a fatal infection.

'We were very happy.'

'When she got the letter, how did she react to it?'

'She was very brave, my Lord,' Ricky told the judge. 'She said it had obviously been written by some nutcase and that she intended to ignore it.'

'She was extremely brave.' The judge spoke the words with admiration as he wrote them down.

So Ricky Glossop told his story. And when I, the representative, so it appeared, of his wife's murderer, rose to cross-examine, I felt a chill wind blowing through Number One Court.

'Mr Glossop, you said your marriage to your wife Honoria was a happy one?'

'As far as I was concerned it was very happy.' Here he smiled at the jury and some of them nodded back approvingly.

'Did you know that on the afternoon before she was murdered, your wife had consulted a solicitor, Mr Anthony Hawkin of Henshaw and Hawkin?'

'I didn't know that, no.'

'Can you guess why?'

'I'm afraid not. My wife had considerable financial interests under her father's will. It might have been about that.'

'You mean it might have been about the money?'

'Yes.'

'Did you know that Anthony Hawkin is well known as an expert on divorce and family law?'

'I didn't know that either.'

'And you didn't know that your wife was considering proceedings for divorce?'

'I certainly didn't.'

I looked at the jury. They were now, I thought, at least interested. I remembered the frightened blonde girl I had seen outside the court and the hand he had put on her as he had tried to comfort her.

'Was there any trouble between your wife and yourself because of her secretary, Sue Blackmore?'

'So far as I know, none whatever.'

'Mr Rumpole, I'm wondering, and I expect the jury may be wondering as well, what on earth these questions have to do with your client's trial for murder.'

'Then wonder on.' I might have quoted Shakespeare to Graves: 'Till truth makes all things plain.' But I did not do that. I merely said, 'I'm putting these questions to test the credibility of this witness, my Lord.'

'And why, Mr Rumpole, are you attacking his credibility? Which part of this gentleman's evidence are you disputing?'

'If I may be allowed to cross-examine in the usual way, I hope it may become clear,' I said, and then I'm afraid I also said, 'even to your Lordship.'

At this, Gravestone gave me the look that meant 'you just wait until we come to the summing up, and I'll tell the jury what I think of your attack on this charming husband', but for the moment he remained as silent as a block of ice, so I soldiered on.

'Mr Glossop. Your wife's secretary delivered this threatening letter to her.'

'Yes. Honoria was working at home and Sue brought it over from her pigeonhole at the university.'

'You've told us that she was very brave, of course. That she had said it was probably from some nutcase and that she intended to ignore it. But you insisted on taking the letter to the police.'

'An extremely wise decision, if I may say so,' Graves took it upon himself to note.

'And I think you gave the story to the Press Association so that this death threat received wide publicity.'

'I thought Honoria would be safer if it was all out in the open. People would be on their guard.'

'Another wise decision, the members of the jury might think.' Graves was making sure the jury thought it.

'And when the letter was traced to my client, everyone knew that it was Hussein Khan who was the author of the letter?'

'He was dismissed from the university, so I suppose a lot of people knew, yes.'

'So if anything were to have happened to your wife after that, if she were to have been attacked or killed, Hussein Khan would have been the most likely suspect?'

'I think that has been obvious throughout this trial.' Graves couldn't resist it.

'My Lord, I'd really much rather get the answers to my questions from the witness than receive them from your Lordship.' I went on quickly before the judge could get in his two pennies' worth. 'You took your wife to the university on that fatal night?'

'I often did. If I was going somewhere and she had work to do in her office, I'd drop her off and then collect her later on my way home.'

'But you didn't just drop her off, did you? You went inside the building with her. You took her up to her office?'

'Yes. We'd been talking about something in the car and we went on discussing it as I went up to her office with her.'

'He escorted her, Mr Rumpole,' the sepulchral voice boomed from the bench. 'A very gentlemanly thing to do.'

'Thank you, my Lord.' Ricky's smile was still full of charm. 'And what were you discussing?' I asked him. 'Was it divorce?'

'It certainly wasn't divorce. I can't remember what it was exactly.'

'Then perhaps you can remember this. How long did you stay in the office with your wife?'

'Perhaps five, maybe ten minutes. I can't remember exactly.'

'And when you left, was she still alive?'

There was a small silence.

The witness looked at me and seemed to catch his breath. Then he gave us the invariably charming smile.

'Of course she was.'

'You spoke to Mr Luttrell at the reception area on your way out?'

'I did, yes.'

'He says you asked him if Hussein Khan was in the building?'

'Yes, I did.'

'Why did you do that?'

'I suppose I'd heard from someone that he might have been there.'

'And what did Mr Luttrell tell you?'

'He said that Khan was in the building, yes.'

'You knew that Hussein Khan's presence in that building was a potential danger to your wife.'

'I suppose I knew. Yes.'

'I suppose you did. And yet you left and drove off in your car without warning her?'

There was a longer silence then and Ricky's smile seemed to droop.

'I didn't go back to the office. No,' was what the witness said.

'Why not, Mr Glossop? Why not warn her? Why didn't you see that Khan left before you went off?'

And then Ricky Glossop said something which changed the atmosphere in court in a moment, even silencing the judge.

'I suppose I was in a hurry. I was on my way to a party.'

After a suitable pause I asked, 'There was no lock on your wife's office door, was there?'

'There might have been. But she never locked it.'

'So you left her unprotected, with the man who had threatened her life still in the building, because you were on your way to a party?'

The smile came again, but it had no effect now on the jury.

'I think I heard he was with the senior tutor in the library. I suppose I thought that was safe.'

'Mr Glossop, were you not worried by the possibility that the senior tutor might leave first, leaving the man who threatened your wife still in the building with her?'

'I suppose I didn't think of that,' was all he could say.

I let the answer sink in and then turned to more dangerous and uncharted territory.

'I believe you're interested in various country sports.'

'That's right, my Lord.' The witness, seeming to feel the ground was now safer, smiled at the judge.

'You used to go shooting, I believe.'

'Well, I go shooting, Mr Rumpole.' A ghastly twitch of the lips was, from the bench, Graves' concession towards a smile. 'And I hope you're not accusing me of complicity in any sort of a crime?'

I let the jury have their sycophantic laugh, then went on to ask, 'Did you ever belong to a pistol shooting club, Mr Glossop?' Fig Newton, the private eye, had done his work well.

'When such clubs were legal, yes.'

'And do you still own a handgun?'

'Certainly not.' The witness seemed enraged. 'I wouldn't do anything that broke the law.'

I turned to look at the jury with my eyebrows raised, but for the moment the witness was saved by the bell as the judge announced that he could see by the clock that it was time we broke for lunch.

Before we parted, however, Soapy Sam got up to tell us that his next witness would be Mrs Glossop's secretary, Sue Blackmore, who would merely give evidence about the receipt of the letter and the deceased's reaction to it. Miss Blackmore was, apparently, likely to be a very nervous witness, and perhaps his learned friend Mr Rumpole would agree to her evidence being read.

Mr Rumpole did not agree. Mr Rumpole wanted Miss Sue Blackmore to be present in the flesh and he was ready to cross-examine her at length. And so we parted, expecting the trial of Hussein Khan for murder to start again at two o'clock.

But Khan's trial for murder didn't start again at two o'clock or at any other time. I was toying with a plate of steak and kidney pie and a pint of Guinness in the pub opposite the Old Bailey when I saw the furtive figure of Sam Ballard oozing through the crowd. He came to me obviously heavy with news.

'Rumpole! You don't drink at lunchtime, do you?'

'Yes. But not too much at. Can I buy you a pint of stout?'

'Certainly not, Rumpole. Mineral water, if you have to. And could we move to that little table in the corner? This is news for your ears alone.'

After I had transported my lunch to a more secluded spot and supplied our Head of Chambers with mineral water, he brought me up to date on that lunch hour's developments.

'It's Sue the secretary, Rumpole. When we told her that she'd have to go into the witness box, she panicked and asked to see Superintendent Gregory. By this time, she was in tears and, he told me, almost incomprehensible. However, Gregory managed to calm her down and she said she knew you'd get it out of her in the witness box, so she might as well confess that she was the one who had made the telephone call.'

'Which telephone call was that?' Soapy Sam was demonstrating his usual talent for making a simple statement of fact utterly confusing.

'The telephone call to your client. Telling him to go and meet the senior tutor.'

'You mean…?' The mists that had hung over the case of Khan the terrorist were beginning to clear. 'She pretended to be…'

'The senior tutor's secretary. Yes. The idea was to get Khan into the building whilst Glossop…'

'Murdered his wife?' I spoke the words that Ballard seemed reluctant to use.

'I think she's prepared to give evidence against him,' Soapy Sam said, looking thoughtfully towards future briefs. 'Well, she'll have to, unless she wants to go to prison as an accessory.'

'Has handsome Ricky heard the news yet?' I wondered.

'Mr Glossop has been detained. He's helping the police with their enquiries.'

So many people I know, who help the police with their enquiries, are in dire need of help themselves. 'So you'll agree to a verdict of not guilty of murder?' I asked Ballard, as though it was a request to pass the mustard.

'Perhaps. Eventually. And you'll agree to guilty of making death threats in a letter?'

'Oh, yes,' I admitted. 'We'll have to plead guilty to that.'

But there was no hurry. I could finish my steak and kidney and order another Guinness in peace.

'It started off,' I was telling Hilda over a glass of Château Thames Embankment that evening, 'as an act of terrorism, of mad, religious fanaticism, of what has become the new terror of our times. And it ends up as an old-fashioned murder by a man who wanted to dispose of his rich wife for her money and be free to marry a pretty young woman. It was a case, you might say, of Dr Crippen meeting Osama Bin Laden.'

'It's hard to say which is worse.' She Who Must be Obeyed was thoughtful.

'Both of them,' I told her. 'Both of them are worse. But I

suppose we understand Dr Crippen better. Only one thing we can be grateful for.'

'What's that, Rumpole?'

'The terrorist got a fair trial. And the whole truth came out in the end. The day when a suspected terrorist doesn't get a fair trial will be the day they've won the battle.'

I refilled our glasses, having delivered my own particular verdict on the terrible events of that night at William Morris University.

'Mind you,' I said, 'it was your friend Gerald Graves who put me onto the truth of the matter.'

'Oh really.' Hilda sounded unusually cool on the subject of the judge.

'It was when he was playing Father Christmas. He was standing in for someone else. And I thought, what if the real murderer thought he'd stand in for someone else. Hussein Khan had uttered the death threat and was there to take the blame. All Ricky had to do was to go to work quickly. So that's what he did – he committed murder in Hussein Khan's name. That death threat was a gift from heaven for him.'

One of our usual silences fell between us, and then Hilda said, 'I don't know why you call Mr Justice Graves my friend.'

'You got on so well at Christmas.'

'Well, yes we did. And then he said we must keep in touch. So I telephoned his clerk and the message came back that the judge was busy for months ahead but he hoped we might meet again eventually. I have to tell you, Rumpole, that precious judge of yours does not treat women well.'

I did my best. I tried to think of The Old Gravestone as a heartbreaker, a sort of Don Juan who picked women up and dropped them without mercy, but I failed miserably.

'I'm better off with you, Rumpole,' Hilda told me. 'I can always rely on you to be unreliable.'

Simon de Rougemont reined in his horse the better to gaze with pleasure upon his newly acquired domain. It was his reward for services rendered to William the Bastard. Every prospect pleased: the rich pastures, the wooded slopes teeming, no doubt, with game, and the glittering river promising fine fishing. And the settlement, of course. He sighed. Only man, in the form of his reluctant tenantry, was vile.

Beside him, Claude Villeneuve, the interpreter foisted on him by necessity, sniffed audibly. 'To think that they call this a village!' Claude's finger led his lord's eye to the cluster of low wooden huts, reed-thatched, from the roofs of which smoke meandered through more orifices than the builder had presumably intended. 'Animals!' the young man added tersely. 'In fact, worse than animals, which know no better.'

Simon raised a minatory hand. 'Only think how much greater will be the joys of civilising them. First of all, we will build a church worthy of the name of the Almighty. And then we will introduce them to a proper legal system —'

'Fortifying your castle is the best way of civilising those beasts.'

Simon chose to ignore the interruption. Somehow this invasion – no, this just retrieval of lands willed to William – had contrived to bring to the fore men who would never in earlier days have achieved any prominence. Some of his fellow barons were behaving in the most ungodly ways, in the interests, they insisted, of the rapid subjugation of their English cousins. To Simon's mind, they were little better – and sometimes regrettably worse – than the savage Saxons whose confiscated fiefdoms they had been granted.

'Not just wooden palisades,' Villeneuve continued. 'Good stone walls. The sort of building to show who's boss.' He dropped his whip ostentatiously. 'Oy! You. You there!' he slipped off his right glove to click his fingers.

A broad-shouldered man in his early twenties walked unsmilingly, and unhurriedly, towards them. He picked up the whip, reaching up to restore it to Villeneuve's grasp. If he did not expect largesse, he certainly would not have expected the vicious cut across the cheek to which Villeneuve treated him. But he neither flinched nor swore, merely stepping back a pace and regarding his assailant steadily, as if to fix Villeneuve's face in his memory.

'Enough of that,' Simon said sharply, as even their escort of soldiers shifted uneasily. 'Law enforcement is one thing, brutality another. We are here —'

'I know, to civilise and secure. But they're like dogs, my lord – they need to be shown who's in charge.'

'So you say. With undue frequency, if you will permit the observation.' Simon raised an acid eyebrow. He was Villeneuve's senior not just in rank but also in age: Why should the wretched man not show him due respect?

Villeneuve was unmoved. 'Now, how about that for a game piece?' He pointed with the offending whip at another villager.

'For God's sake, man, can you think with nothing but your fist or your pizzle?'

The young woman in question, though, like all the villagers, thin to the point of emaciation, was extremely pretty, and her shabby, shapeless gown couldn't conceal her magnificent breasts. But her occupation declared itself all too clearly as her charges trotted in front of her.

'You'll be forbidding access to the forest, no doubt, my lord?' Villeneuve suggested.

It would be pleasant to believe that Villeneuve had only good husbandry in mind.

'Only if my land agent recommends it. But there is nothing like pigs for keeping down undergrowth: I welcome them back in my estates in Beaune.' He almost expected Villeneuve to protest that those were French porkers, these merely swine. 'And remember the pig's nose for truffles.'

'I have a nose for something else,' Villeneuve declared, swinging down from the saddle, contriving, as he landed in the mud, not to hear his lord's rebuke. He set off briskly after the swineherd, slipping an arm round her to pull her face to his. His free hand was ready to pull her shift from her breast.

Simon swore in exasperation. There was no law to say a soldier couldn't kiss pretty damsels. Kiss and more. It was almost de rigueur. Young men had appetites. And many a girl had a gown to her back and food in her belly she'd have lacked but for the generosity of the man who'd bedded her. But Villeneuve, old enough at twenty-five to know better, didn't differentiate between a supposedly welcome frolic and what was seemly in the confines of the stockade, for example. At least in his lord's sober company, however, he must no doubt show a little restraint.

Simon swore again, but this time with anger. Restraint! Well, if Villeneuve didn't show it, at least the young woman did. Even from where he sat, Simon could see her pull back her hand to strike the face now so offensively close to hers, but hold off from the final blow. Not, Simon thought, from cowardice – though she could have been excused for fearing that she would not strike a conqueror with impunity – but, from the expression on her face, distaste at the prospect of having her wrist captured, as inevitably it would be. However thin and ragged the woman – and what Saxon after the long campaign would be sleek and smart? – and however lowly her function, she possessed a dignity that appealed to the older man, and he spurred his horse forward to deal with Villeneuve. But he was not the only one. One of the pigs, almost as if responding to the girl's choked cry, turned sharply and, head down, charged, its evil little eyes like blazing beads. Villeneuve was too absorbed in extracting a kiss to notice. But the young man who might have been expected to relish a terrible injury to the Norman stepped swiftly forward, bringing down the shaft of his axe hard enough to stun the pig in mid charge. It reeled drunkenly away. Simon dismounted, elbowing Villeneuve sharply back to his mount. He dipped into his purse. The coins he proffered needed no interpretation, nor did the silent doffing of the man's cap as he accepted them. But for all the goodwill in the world, Simon could not frame in the man's own tongue the words of gratitude he sought, and he was a man of few gestures. At last the young woman stepped forward, pointing at the pig and making from her own breasts to the bottom of her belly a sign they all understood – the pig was in fact a sow and was enceinte. She waved her hands vigorously from side to side, pointing back to the sow. This, she gave Simon clearly to understand, was not the moment to upset a female.

Villeneuve was, alas, too highly born for Simon to condemn him to a public beating for disobeying orders. But he had to endure a veritable tongue-lashing, and lost his privileges for many days. Simon would have sent him home in disgrace immediately had he not needed him so much: to discuss the plans for the improvement of the stockade, to find the best timber, locate the purest springs. And to recruit – if that was not too mealy-mouthed a term – the local workmen. Simon was entitled to enslave the entire populace and work it to death if so he wished. Many of his brother barons certainly did. But he was a soldier, not a slave master, and though he didn't think anyone had ever accused him of lax discipline, he preferred to temper force with fairness. And, like every good soldier, he prided himself on knowing not just every man in his command but also what that man's function was and where he might be found at any time.

Most of the men were serfs, unskilled men with little to commend them except their numbers and their – enforced – willingness. But others – the scaffolders, the carpenters – had an expertise that Simon found himself respecting. One of the latter was the young man who'd saved Villeneuve from the pig. They would greet each other with a silent nod. Simon had no desire to encourage insubordination; no doubt the carpenter – Beom – didn't want to toady. At least, however, it was a greeting. Perhaps, Simon reflected, it wasn't just his new hilltop castle that was being built, looming over the countryside with threatening grandeur. Perhaps a bridge was being slowly built between the rulers and the ruled.

Except that even as he turned to inspect the next section of bailey, he could see Villeneuve still going his best to chop the imaginary bridge off at the foundations, harrying, striking, cutting with his glove. Would he never learn?

'Enough!' Simon shouted. 'If you spent more time on your own function, less on interfering with others', I should be better satisfied. I said, enough! Present yourself to me tomorrow morning, after prayer.'

✳ ✳ ✳

The animals were hungry. Well, the people were hungry, and devoured scraps which would normally have been the swines' almost by right. So Aedburgha had let her charges wander deeper than usual into the forest, rooting through beech mast and snuffling for acorns. Aedburgha could still hear them, would be able to gather them together when dusk came. She sat against the south face of an oak tree, huddling in what little sun penetrated the gloom, and wished that there was more bread. Not that she was unhappy. She was handfasted to Beom, a good man seemingly well respected up at the castle. And now she was with child – her breasts and latterly her belly assured her this was so – they would soon be married. As for living – well, he would build them their own place as soon as he had the chance. And the few groats the Normans doled out would help.

Maybe if Beom spoke well of her, she might find work up there herself. But when she asked if he'd done so, he always found some excuse, and the village rumours suggested he was right. Better be poor with your pigs for company than poor with unruly hands to fend off. But there were other more welcome hands. She smiled to herself. It was about this time that Beom would be making his way back through the forest. He told his masters he was discussing with the forester which trees to fell next, which would season well. And because he was an honest man, she was sure he did. At the end of the day he would help her gather the swine together and herd them back to shelter. But between the forestry and his herding, there was time for the sort of moment that made her lean back against the tree, a smile softening her face.

She was waiting for him. Look at her: not so much waiting as positively inviting. Villeneuve's eyes relished her face as he imagined pushing apart those soft lips. But the lips weren't his target. Oh no. Much lower down. Which would he do? Take her by surprise? Or enjoy the thrill of the chase, see her eyes flare, see her run from him, falling as he caught her and watch her face contort as he took her? Some men said women liked force. Like it or not, that was what she was going to get.

He thought with his fist or his pizzle, did he? Well, as he slipped from his horse, he knew just what he was thinking with today.

No one up at the castle took much notice when Villeneuve was late for the evening meal. It wasn't the first time, probably wouldn't be the last. Not unless Simon chose to make a real example of him. Yes, this time he must. The man's swaggering insolence set a bad example to men all too ready to follow it. As for his fornication, the Lady Rosamunde, who would be joining Simon as soon as the living quarters were ready for feminine company, would demand an end to that. She'd been ready to embrace a contemplative life when her father had preferred a more earthly union for her, and she brought to Simon's circle an air of delicacy and refinement he could see was sadly lacking now. Tomorrow morning, then, Villeneuve would be flogged and sent on his way. If Simon himself still found it impossible to get his tongue around the agglomeration of alien diphthongs these Saxons insisted on calling a language, many of his men had devised a rough lingua franca which enabled them to communicate. Another interpreter they would surely need, but they could make shift – wasn't that the term he'd heard Beom using? – until the replacement arrived. Tomorrow. So be it.

How dare the wretched man disobey a direct order? There was no sign of him at the time Simon had appointed. When asked, his colleagues shuffled awkwardly. Perhaps he was dealing with a thick, mead-filled head? For whatever reason, he hadn't appeared in the chapel, nor had he broken his fast with the others, either in the hall or in the guardroom, where he was wont to boast of the previous night's amorous adventures. It wasn't the first time his servant had to admit that his master had not returned at all – perhaps he had found a congenial bed to wait in till curfew was lifted. Rutting when he should have been begging his lord for mercy? Simon slammed his fist into his palm with anger. When noon had come and gone, however, he despatched search parties. A Norman – even one intent on dalliance – did not go far without armour, but all Villeneuve had taken, his servant admitted, were his helm and his hauberk.

'Has his horse returned yet?' Simon demanded. Perhaps he was being unjust. The man might simply have taken a toss and be lying unconscious.

The answer was negative. But that was inconclusive, too: a foot in a rabbit hole could injure a horse as well as a man. More ominously, the ability of the Saxons to spirit away a valuable horse was legendary.

The search parties returned with nothing to report.

'No tracks? No signs of a scuffle?' he demanded. 'Did the dogs pick up no scent?'

'Only the smell of pigs, my lord. That young woman's let the damned animals range the whole forest.'

'Come, the man couldn't have vanished into thin air! Have you questioned the villagers?'

'Villeneuve was the only man who could talk to them,' came the predictable reply.

Simon knew what Villeneuve's counsel would have been. It was standard, if illegal, policy. They kill one of ours, we kill as many of theirs as we can lay hands on. But what was the point of such measures if those punished didn't know what they were being punished for? A baser thought struck him. Mass executions would delay the building of his private quarters, and the Lady Rosamunde was joining him on the understanding that the nearest he could achieve to civilisation was awaiting her. Damn Villeneuve: an irritation in life, and now irritation in what was almost certainly death.

There must be some in the team of workmen who spoke French well enough to assist him in the interrogations he knew he must carry out. He summoned Luc, his clerk of works, a man, like himself, of middle years.

'It's hard to tell, my lord. There's plenty that understand without wanting to let on, if you see what I mean. Sullen, some of them. But there's one that's grown into a sort of foreman – thickset man, early twenties. Listens more than he talks, it's true. But there's a look about his eyes, if you know what I mean – like a good alert dog.'

'And he speaks French?'

Luc shook his head. 'I don't say that. I do say he'll understand enough to find someone who does or just to get the whisper going round that you're going to torch the village if they don't come up with news of Villeneuve. That'll bring some action.'

'I don't like making threats I can't fulfil,' Simon said, almost to himself.

The clerk looked at him. 'Ah, you're the sort that'd rather build up than pull down! And…'

'Go on, man.'

To his astonishment, Luc blushed. 'I've – well, I've got my own reasons why I don't want the village destroyed.'

'The usual?' he asked tolerantly.

'She's what they call a comely wench, my lord.'

'So *you* can speak their tongue?'

'Who said anything about speaking, my lord? But we've got one on the way, and to my mind – well, isn't conquest by the cock kinder than conquest by the sword?'

'So it's a political bedding, is it?' Simon laughed. 'Go and fetch your foreman, Luc, and we'll see if we older ones can achieve what the younger ones can't.'

Within a few minutes a familiar figure bent a polite but not obsequious head. Beom. So that was the foreman. Simon wasn't surprised. Beom listened with an air of calm dignity, but, as Luc had predicted, gave little away. Little – apart, perhaps, from a tiny frisson of – of fear?

Surely not. Within the tiniest of moments, his face was phlegmatic again. Nodding, he listened to Simon, raising a hand to his ear when he wanted a phrase repeated.

'You know this knight of mine?' Simon asked at last.

Beom's features assumed a sneer, and he mimed the big-balls swagger of a man set on sexual conquest. Oh yes: He knew him, all right.

'And does he have enemies?'

Beom's disbelieving shrug would have put a Norman's to shame it was so expansive. Such a man undoubtedly had enemies. Beom even managed an ironic smile, pointing to the scar left by Villeneuve's whip.

'Did you kill him?'

Eyes meeting his lord's, Beom shook his head.

'Do you know the man who did?'

The same response.

'Tomorrow morning I shall question every man in the village, and you will tell me their answers. If the murderer confesses, I shall spare the rest of the village.'

Boem nodded. Simon waved him away. But he stood his ground, and for the first time spoke. He had to repeat what he said several times before Simon could understand him. At last it seemed to make sense: 'Have you found this man's body yet?'

Simon decided to treat the man honestly. He shook his head.

Was it relief that flashed across Beom's face? Ah, a man like him would know the law, wouldn't he? Wherever a Norman body was found, the nearest village would find itself paying a punitive fine.

Simon had no compunction in ousting what had been the thegn from his hut and appropriating his chair. The only chair. My God, no wonder these people shuffled round older than their years if they squatted all the time! He asked each villager, freeman or serf, the same questions, making them lay their hands on his Bible as they replied. And Simon, even without this, would have believed them. There was an air of bafflement about them, not to mention the terror of losing more of what little they had.

At the end of a tedious morning, Simon waved them all away. 'Beom, get them all back to work. My wife will be coming next week: everything must be ready for her.'

It was the sort of day that you wished you could cram into a flask and keep forever. The sun was warm on his back, the air full of birdcall. And the news, that the Lady Rosamunde had but this morning whispered that she was soon to offer him another pledge of her love for him, still sang in his ears. Simon rode gently down to the village. Another hut was being built: Beom had told him it was his and his new wife's. Aedburgha was nowhere to be seen. She must be near her time now. The squeals of her charges told him where he might find her, and he never had any objections to being smiled on by – what was the term? – a comely wench. He reeled in shock when he saw what she and another woman were doing to the young pigs they'd penned immovably in a tight wattle tunnel. It was all very swift, of course, but the very thought brought tears to his eyes.

If Beom was now speaking a little of his tongue, Aedburgha still relied on sign language. She pointed to the sows, the sleekest and best looking he'd seen since he'd come over from Beaune. Then there came piglets. She mimed a fierce boar, then a snip. She smiled, waving her hands to show all fierceness was over, and that the desexed animals would grow big and fat and healthy. Next came a fearsome pregnant sow. She gestured a slit: The female ones, untroubled by pregnancy, would do the same. Suddenly she reached for one and held it up, still bleeding after surgery. Heavens, she was giving him a pig.

He took it graciously, but handed it swiftly to the soldier escorting him. He hoped and he trusted that the villagers were coming to appreciate his humanity and realise they could get a man six times worse in his place, but he didn't take risks. This, however, must be the ultimate peace offering – a woman who had been insulted by one of his henchmen giving something she could ill afford. She waved away the coin he offered. A good woman. The sort who might attend the Lady Rosamunde when her time came.

'Pig?' he said carefully, pointing at the wriggling animal. No, it would be another word for the female. 'Sow?'

She shook her head. 'Gilt,' she said. She pointed to an animal which had not yet been on the receiving end of her ministrations. 'Sow.' Then she pointed to the one she'd given him. 'Gilt.'

Lords might do as they liked, and if Simon chose to visit a small wattle enclosure to check his animal's daily progress, there was no one with the temerity to laugh. In fact, it was while he was scratching her ears and speculating on the quality of the meat she would produce that Luc came up to him. One look at his face told Simon he'd rather not hear his news.

Luc produced from his tunic a ring. 'Found it when I was casting a line yesterday evening. Villeneuve's, isn't it, my lord?' He polished it before he handed it over. 'See – that's his crest.'

Simon took it. Yes, it looked like it, didn't it? 'The river you say?' He held Luc's gaze. 'The man must have dropped it and tried to save it. The water's very swift, and of course his helm and hauberk would weigh him down. Even Villeneuve wasn't so stupid as to go round without them. Drowned, swept away. Poor bastard. Still, it's good to have the mystery solved. I'll get the priest to write to his family. Thank you, Luc.'

Alone once more, Simon stared at the sow, currently tucking into scraps from last night's venison and some mouldy bread. Her little eyes were contented, almost benign. Not like those of the raging sow that had almost done for Villeneuve. The pregnant ones were dangerous under provocation. Aedburgha had shown him. He shivered. Provocation? What if Villeneuve had renewed his assault on Aedburgha? What if the sow —? Or, God help him, what if pregnant women were equally dangerous. God knew she'd been provoked...but sufficiently provoked to kill? There was no doubt how she'd have disposed of the body – her pigs would have fallen readily upon anything they thought edible.

He buried his face in his hands. He represented law and order and justice here. If there was a crime, it must be punished. But Beom had told him only two days before that he was now the proud father of a hopeful son, and Simon had offered to be a sponsor at the child's christening. In his mind's eye he could see the little family, the newborn suckling at its mother's breast – a breast that he'd hoped would nourish his and Rosamunde's own child when the time came. Could such a woman really have killed a man and fed his flesh to those remarkably healthy sows? If he ordered Beom's hut to be pulled down, would they find the contents of Villeneuve's purse buried under the foundations? He looked at the ring.

The armour! That would provide the answer.

But a woman who knew the forest as she did would have had no difficulty hiding a helm, even bulky chain mail – up one tree, inside another.

Simon looked across at the mass of green, pulsing in the gentle wind. The sky was blue again, with fluffy clouds. The pastures were dotted with sheep and cattle cropping their way to a prosperous future. Wheat and corn were greening the fields.

No, he told himself, there'd be no reopening of the inquiry. If wrong had been left unavenged in his life, the Almighty would deal with it in the next. And if he felt a tremor of remorse as he called for the priest to convey his condolences to the Villeneuve family, he knew he'd just have to endure it. He'd live with the guilt.

And with the gilt. He leant over and scratched her ear again.

'There is a window in your life. All you have to do is open it and let the sunshine in.'

Nikki listened, fascinated. She'd come here expecting a con, but the man spoke like a prophet. He had his audience enthralled. He was a brilliant speaker. Looks, perfect grooming, charisma. He had it all.

'How many times have I heard someone say, "You should have been here yesterday. It was glorious"?' He smiled. 'A comment on our English weather, but it sums up our attitude to life. "You should have been here yesterday." My friends, forget about yesterday. We are here today. Seize the day. Open that window and let the sunshine in.'

The applause was wild. He'd brought them to a pitch of excitement. And this wasn't evangelism. It was about being effective in business. The setting was Lucknam Park in Wiltshire, where the government held its think-tank sessions. Companies had paid big bucks to send their upcoming executives here. Lives were being changed forever. Not least, Nikki's.

This was her window of opportunity. She'd been sent here for the weekend by the theatrical agency to help with the role play. Inspired by what she had heard, she was about to act a role of her own. She stepped to the front, scythed a path through the admirers, and placed a hand over his arm. 'If you don't mind, Julian, there's someone you should meet upstairs, in your suite.'

To his adoring fans she said, 'He'll be back, I promise.'

It worked. In the lift, he said, 'Who is it?'

'Me.'

His amazing blue eyes widened. 'I don't understand.'

'I've seized the day.'

The moment he laughed, she knew she'd succeeded. He was still high on the reception he'd got. When they entered the suite, she put the Do Not Disturb sign over the doorknob. The sex was sensational.

* * *

They had a weekend in Paris and a Concorde trip to New York. Nikki found herself moving in circles she'd never experienced before. Royal Ascot. Henley. Her drama school training came in useful.

They married in the church in rural Dorset where her parents lived. She arrived with Daddy in a pony and trap and after the reception in Dorchester's best hotel, she and Julian were driven to the airport in a stretch limo. The honeymoon was in Bermuda. Julian paid for almost everything. Daddy couldn't have managed to spend on that scale.

'It's no problem,' Julian said. 'I'm ridiculously well-off. Well, *we* are now.'

'You deserve to be, my darling,' Nikki said. 'You've brought sunshine into so many lives.'

They bought a huge plot of land in Oxfordshire and had their house built to Julian's design. As well as the usual bedrooms and reception rooms, it had an office suite, gym, games room, and two pools, indoors and out. A tennis court, stables, and landscaped garden. 'I don't want you ever to be bored,' Julian said. 'There are times when I'll be away.'

Nikki was not bored. True, she'd given up her acting to devote more time to homemaking, but she could not have managed both. When Julian was at home, he was forever finding new windows of opportunity, days to seize. His energy never flagged. He got up at five thirty and swam a mile before breakfast and made sure she was up by seven. Even in her drama-school days she hadn't risen that early. Actors work to a different pattern.

He had each day worked out. 'We'll plant the new rockery this morning and clear the leaves out of the pool. This afternoon I'll need your help fitting the curtains in the fourth bedroom. This evening the Mountnessings are coming for dinner and I want to prepare an Italian meal, so we'll need to fit in some shopping.'

Nikki suggested more than once that most of these jobs could be done by staff. They could afford to get people in.

'That goes against my principles,' Julian said. 'There's immense satisfaction in doing the jobs ourselves.'

'One day I'd like to sit by the pool we keep so clean,' she said.

'Doing what, my love?'

'Just sitting – or better still, lying.'

He laughed. He thought she was joking.

In bed, he showed no sign of exhaustion. Nikki, twelve years younger than he, was finding it a trial to match his energy.

At such a pace, it didn't take long for the house to be in perfect shape, all the curtains and carpets fitted, the pictures hung. Nikki had looked forward to some time to herself when the jobs were done, but she hadn't reckoned on maintenance.

'Maintenance?'

'Keeping it up to the mark,' Julian explained. 'We don't let the grass grow under our feet.'

In the middle of their lovemaking the same night, the thought occurred to her that he regarded this, too, as maintenance. From that moment, the magic went out of their marriage.

What a relief when he went to America for a week on a lecture tour. He left her a maintenance list, but she ignored it and lounged by the pool every day watching the leaves settle on the surface and sink to the bottom.

When he returned he was energised as ever. Jet lag was unknown to Julian's metabolism. 'So much to attend to,' he said. 'If I didn't know better, I'd almost think you'd ignored that list I gave you.'

He was as active as usual in bed. And up before five next morning. He'd heard some house martins building a nest under the eaves above the bedroom window. They made an appalling mess if you didn't do something about it.

When Nikki drew back the bedroom curtains she saw his suntanned legs right outside. He'd brought out his lightweight, aluminium ladder. His feet, in gleaming white trainers and socks, were on one of the highest rungs. She had to push hard to open the window and force the ladder backwards, but she succeeded. And let the sunshine in.

Barbara Cleverly
Love-Lies-Bleeding

It had taken me two hours to get here. I swished my way, bouncing through the puddles in a haze of falling leaves up the long drive to Felthorpe Hall in north Norfolk. Now, Norfolk isn't Suffolk, and that's a fact. The skies are wider, the building flints are bigger, the distances greater, and the cry of the wheeling plover more forlorn. Only fifty miles from home, but Felthorpe Hall could never have been in Suffolk.

For the last half-hour of my journey through dripping lanes, the rain had eased off, the sun had come out, and the whole countryside had taken on a more cheerful cast. But it would still have to work a whole lot harder to please me, I thought resentfully. I drove carefully down the tree-lined carriage road to the Hall, eagerly awaiting my first sight of the ancient house, so praised in the architectural guide I had hastily referred to before I started out. I turned a corner and there it stood by the side of a dark, reed-fringed, and heron-haunted lake.

The front door was wide and welcoming, its brick dressings satisfyingly good-hearted, and the lowering sun, reflected from its many windows, spoke of ancient warmth, but as I got out of my car I paused and shivered.

'Keep off! Go away!' said the house to me.

'*Deus tute me spectas*,' said a stone inscription in the parapet. 'Thou, Lord, see'st me.'

All too likely, I thought.

I didn't want to be here. It wasn't my job. I paused for a moment to curse my boss, Charles Hastings. The words 'spoilt' and 'manipulative' were as closely associated with his name in my mind as were 'rosy' and 'fingered' with dawn in Homer's. I ought to have seen this coming. Well, the truth was – I had. So why had I gone along with it? For the joy of seeing a gem of a house I had never visited before and the satisfaction of arriving by myself and saying, 'Hello, I'm the architect, Eleanor Hardwick.' By myself, not scuttling in Charles's wake carrying the files and the hard hats and answering to the name of 'little Miss...er...'

We do a lot of work for the English Country Houses Trust. Of the grandees who run it, Charles appears to have been at school with the few to whom he is not related. And, as our region of East Anglia is thickly strewn with great houses, the practice is a busy one. It was one of the reasons – it was my main reason – for applying for the job of his architectural assistant. Charles calls his Trust work the office 'bread and butter'. I would call it the 'strawberry jam'. I'm mad about ancient buildings. I always have been. And if you're lucky enough to get a job working for an expert in this field and you're based between Cambridge and the North Sea, you've died and gone to heaven!

The lush, rolling countryside seamed with narrow overhung lanes is rich in ancient churches, cathedrals, and even a castle or two, as well as the old domestic buildings. Down one of the overhung lanes in the middle of the county of Suffolk is Charles's house, a wing of which masquerades as his office. Latin Hall is a fine though eccentric showcase for Charles's skills. For a start, it's thatched, and to go on, it was built in the late thirteen hundreds. Yes, *thirteen* hundreds. There was still a Roman emperor on the throne when the foundations were being dug, Charles told me at my interview. A rather debased emperor, perhaps, and ruling out of Constantinople, but it made a good story for the clients. They were intended to draw the inference 'If this bloke can keep this building standing, he might be able to do something for *mine.*'

My first autumn working at Latin Hall was miserable. The weather was exceptionally wet and the medieval house leaked badly. The rain-swollen doors stuck, the windows funnelled the icy draughts that knifed down from the Arctic. Charles laughed at my complaints. 'Keep you healthy, Ellie,' he'd said. 'Nothing like a low temperature and a constant air circulation to kill off the bugs! Much better for you to inhale air straight from Siberia than that pre-breathed rubbish they fill your lungs with in London.'

Rain fell in torrents, torrents were followed by gales, tarpaulins blew off roofs, and water rose in cellars as it never had before. Every time I looked out of the window thinking that the rain could get no heavier, it redoubled its maniacal and mindless persistence. But there was one source of cheerful amusement for me in all this gloom. Charles had caught a very bad cold! I came in one morning to find him hunched over his desk, clutching a box of tissues.

'For goodness' sake, Charles,' I said, 'go home! You don't have to stay here!' I pointed to the wall chart. 'You've got no meetings today or tomorrow and then it's the weekend. Go home, have a bath, find a good book, and go to bed. I'll man the main brace.'

He winced.

'Can't,' he said. 'Just had a call from the Trust. Felthorpe Hall. Main staircase. There's a problem. I've just been looking up my last quinquennial survey report.' He paused and pretended to run a critical eye over it. 'It's rather good, I think. Listen to this, Ellie, and mark the style.' He began to read:

'The condition of the main staircase has been mentioned in previous reports and its stability is now a matter of concern. A newel stair with four quarter-space landings, its strength is dependent on the support each flight derives from the flight below. Provided tenons are sound…' He droned on and I switched off. *'…is due to more than shrinking and old age.'*

'Well, what do you think?'

'I'd say you'd covered yourself pretty well, there, Charles…all those *provided-that's* and *suspicions-ofs*,' I began to say, but he interrupted.

'It is always my concern, Ellie, to have a care for the building as well as my own neck. I go on: *I would suggest that where shrinkage gaps are to be seen, small hardwood wedges be lightly inserted, and if the distortion referred to increases, these wedges will fall. Should this happen, further structural investigation would appear imperative.'*

'Don't tell me! Your wedges have fallen?'

'They have. Luckily, the house is closed to the public for end-of-season cleaning, but they've got some sort of anniversary shindig coming up at Christmas. So they ring me. "Is this staircase safe?" they want to know. What can I say? "Leave it to me. I'll come up and have a look."' He blew his nose dolefully once more, pushed his spectacles up onto his forehead, and rubbed his reddened eyes.

His partner was on holiday. There was only one thing I could say. 'Look, tell them you can't come until next week, or if there's a panic on, I'll go for you. Why not? I don't think you'll make much sense in your present condition.'

Charles blinked and shivered theatrically for a moment, looked doubtful, and then said, as though my offer was all so unexpected, 'Well, if you're sure, Ellie, that would be a godsend…and it's not as though you could do any real damage…I mean, I've laid on a carpenter – Johnny Bell will meet you there at half-past two. He's very experienced and —'

'Just give me the file, Charles! But – Felthorpe Hall? Where is it, incidentally?'

'Er…north Norfolk,' he had mumbled apologetically.

The house may not have welcomed me, but the carpenter, Johnny Bell, greeted me warmly enough in the hallway from which a fine newel stair climbed its way to a dim upper floor. I needn't have come, really. Mr Bell was perfectly capable of taking up a few boards, dismantling a few stair treads, and, indeed, diagnosing the problem and solving it. The architect is very often the third wheel on the bicycle. This was one of those occasions. He knew it, and so did I. But with kindly East Anglian courtesy he explained the situation and even managed to make it appear he was hanging on my words.

'Didn't like to start until you got here, Miss Hardwick. Thought if we took up a couple of treads here and a floorboard on the landing and perhaps the riser off the step up into the pass door, we ought to see what we're up to.'

I was about to say, 'Nails must be cut and punched…' but almost before I could speak he had slipped a hacksaw under the first stair tread and had started to cut the nails which held it in place, When he'd slipped the stair treads out of the strings, the risers followed with no more difficulty. We knelt together on the stairs and peered into the cavity we had created. I held the torch while Johnny Bell felt inside.

'Carriage has gone,' he said. 'It's supposed to be bird's-mouthed under the trimmer and…' feeling along the wall, 'the wall string's gone in the same place.'

I reached into the hole, broke off a section of timber, and brought it into the light.

'Deathwatch beetle,' I said.

'How do you know?' said a voice behind us.

I turned to confront a tall, stooping, birdlike figure peering over our shoulders. He reminded me of one of the bony herons I'd seen on arrival, hunched at the edge of the lake. This was Nicholas Wemyss, the curator, and introductions followed.

'How do you know?' he asked again.

'If the exit holes are big enough to let you poke a match head into them, it's deathwatch beetle. If they're only big enough for a pin, it's woodworm – furniture beetle, that is,' I said, as I'd been taught.

'Ah!' said Nicholas, looking impressed. 'Now I really appreciate a complicated technical explanation! But, Ellie, is this serious? Does it mean the stairs are unsafe?'

'Well, it shouldn't be left. Some of this bore dust,' I held out a sample, 'is quite fresh and, no, it probably isn't quite safe.' I looked at Johnny, who was nodding in agreement. 'Let's see if we can take up a board on the quarter landing. That'll tell us more.'

Once more the hacksaw blade disappeared under the stair nosing, and one by one the ancient nails were snipped through. The first mighty board came loose. Loose for the first time since some ancient carpenter had tapped it into place over three hundred years before. Johnny waggled it to and fro, inserted the end of a nail bar, and prised it upwards. 'Can't move it!' he said in surprise. 'That's stuck! There's something under there!'

He poked around with the end of a two-foot rule. 'Yes, bugger me – there's something under there!'

We watched in puzzlement as he took up a second board. With that obstruction gone, the first board came out more easily. But it was unnaturally heavy. It was as much as the two of us could lift and, as it came from its ancient seating, 'Corst blast!' said Johnny. 'There's a little old box fastened up to the bottom of that!'

'Little old box, nothing!' said Nicholas. 'No…that's a little old coffin!'

* * *

There was no mistaking it. The profile of a coffin lid is in some way branded on the memory. The eternal symbol of death and dissolution, an object of reasonless fear buried in the country memories of us all. It was tiny; not above two foot long. A whiff of profound grief and misery briefly embraced us all as the darkness deepened, the thunderous rain began to fall again, and the damp chill of the day sharpened to an icy coldness.

The carpenter ran a knowledgeable hand over the small structure. *Must have made hundreds of coffins in his time,* I thought.

'Oak boards. Nicely made,' he said, absently caressing the joints with a craggy thumb. 'That were tacked up from below.' He slipped the point of a chisel under the rim of the coffin and pressed upwards against the covering board. 'Lift it off, shall I?'

'No! Wait!' I heard my own voice call out. I didn't want him to take off the lid. I didn't want to see what the box held. 'Perhaps we should call the police? Isn't that what you do when you find a ...er...come across a burial?'

'If that's what it is, it's a very *ancient* burial,' said Nicholas gently. 'I don't think the police will be interested in something so old. Because it *is* very old, wouldn't you say?'

'It went in the same day as the staircase was put up,' said Johnny Bell firmly. 'The only way you could get it in with this construction.'

'So we have a date, then,' said Nicholas. 'Diana will know. My wife, Diana. She's somewhere about...'

'Sixteen sixty-two. That's the year it was put in.' A low clear voice called down to us from the upper floor. Diana came to join us, taking in the strange scene at a glance. 'Oh dear! How extraordinary! But how fascinating! Look, with the stairs in their present parlous state I think we should take whatever that is downstairs and put it on the big table in the yellow drawing room and decide what to do about it when we're in no danger of disappearing through a hole. Eleanor, is it? Eleanor Hardwick? I'm Diana Wemyss. I was just making you a cup of tea. Perhaps that can wait for a few minutes?'

I smiled as Diana's comforting presence chased away the chill foreboding. She couldn't have been more different from her gaunt husband. Short and rounded, with merry brown eyes, she had the cheerful and confident charm of a robin. We all made our way back down the stairs and into the drawing room and gathered around the little box waiting for Diana to tell us what to do next.

'We really have to open it,' she said. 'Too embarrassing if we hauled a busy constable all the way out from Norwich to witness us opening an empty container.'

Everyone nodded, and Johnny got to work again with his chisel. Hardly breathing, we all peered into the coffin as the lid rose.

'Ah,' said Diana in an unsteady voice. 'Nicholas, perhaps you'd better inform the constabulary? Just to be on the safe side.'

Two hours later, an inspector had called and viewed the pathetic contents of the box, and had taken brief statements. He agreed that the burial had been clandestine and there'd probably been dirty work at the crossroads back in the seventeenth century but, really, this was one for *Time Team*, not the Norfolk constabulary. He was quite happy to leave it, as he put it, 'in the hands of the experts'. That was us. We were on our own.

On a scatter of almost-fresh sawdust in the bottom of the box lay the yellowed bones of a very small infant. It lay on its side in a foetal position and, as far as our appalled and fleeting glances could determine, there was no obvious cause of death. There was no tattered winding sheet, no identifying bracelet. The only other thing the box contained was a slip of parchment. It had been glued inside the lid and so remained unaffected by the decay within the box. On it a neat hand had written, '*Deus tute eum spectas.*'

'Good heavens!' said Diana. 'What have we here? The lost heir of the Easton family?'

I remember even then, in the turmoil of mixed emotions I was feeling, that something was off-key. I felt sick and guilty that we had, however innocently, displaced and disturbed the little body after all those years. With uncomfortable sideways glances at each other, we had replaced the lid on the coffin, Johnny Bell solemnly making the sign of the cross before packing up his tools and leaving.

Gratefully I accepted Diana's invitation, in view of the late hour and the filthy weather, to stay the night in one of the guest rooms. While she put together a supper in their small flat on the second floor, Nicholas invited me to come round the house with him as he 'put it to bed'. I watched him set alarms and lock doors, the whole process taking about half an hour. As we wandered down through the dark house, our progress was much delayed by Nicholas's discursions as we passed one beautiful thing after another.

Pausing finally in the gallery which encircled the staircase at first-floor level, he drew my attention to a run of portraits. 'I'd like to haul this lot in for interrogation, Ellie,' he said. 'I bet one of *them* could tell us more about the contents of that box. The Easton family. They were all here the year the staircase was put in. They came up from their London home for the jollifications in sixteen sixty-two. The celebrations covered the restoration of the monarchy two years earlier, but also the marriage of the younger brother of the earl.'

He lifted the shade of a table lamp and held it upwards. 'Here he is, with his wife alongside. This is the chap whose anniversary we're celebrating this Christmas. Father of the dynasty. His descendants still live hereabouts – they gave the house to the Trust thirty years ago. Robert Easton. Took over when his elder brother died childless in sixteen seventy-two.'

I looked up at the handsome florid features of Robert Easton, Earl of Somersham. An impressive man in a shoulder-length curling brown wig, he wore a coat of dark-blue velvet with gold frogging over a ruched shirt of finest white linen, a lace jabot at his throat. The painter had conveyed his subject's confidence and pride by the seemingly casual placing of one elegant hand on his hip.

Nicholas for a moment dipped the lamp to illuminate the left-hand corner of the painting. I was impressed but not surprised to read: 'P Lely *pinxit*'.

'A Peter Lely!'

Nicholas smiled. 'Yes, the Dutchman who painted all those sumptuous portraits of Charles Stuart's mistresses. The Windsor beauties. All white bosoms, floating draperies, and slanting invitation in their sloe-black eyes. Hmmm...'

We looked together at the lady in this painting. She was young and fair and quite lovely, but here were no sloping shoulders, no flirtatious glance at the artist. Her gown was of chestnut silk, draped and shimmering, and the luscious autumnal colouring was all that you could have hoped for from Lely but worn with an unusual modesty, her only jewellery a simple pearl necklace. In her lap rested a basket overflowing with autumn fruits and flowers – a cornucopia. In the background leaves drifted down from stately parkland trees.

'Mary, Countess of Somersham. As she became on her husband's accession to the title. We assume this was a wedding portrait – it was certainly done in the year of their marriage when Robert was the younger brother-in-waiting. Not much of a catch for a girl, you might think, but he was – for *her*. She was no aristocrat. Mary was the daughter of a Quaker shipbuilder, but very rich, so they both got what they wanted from the marriage. An unusual match, but it turned out well.'

'And the cornucopia is a pointed reference to the wealth she was bringing to the Easton family?'

'That's right. After the lean years of the Commonwealth it was a miracle they had survived as a family at all, and they were certainly pleased to have her injection of cash. Bet if the truth were known she even paid for the staircase! She saved the whole dynasty. She was fruitful in other ways, too,' he added, showing me a further picture.

A charming portrait showed seven children gambolling in a landscape which was clearly Felthorpe Hall. Formally dressed miniatures of adults, they played with toys and small spaniels or clustered at the feet of their mother, an older and now matronly Mary. All here was sunshine striking satin, rounded pink cheeks, and laughing eyes. An idyllic scene. A perfect family. I said as much to Nicholas.

He grunted. 'Unfortunately, not perfect. These little poppets had the most appalling uncle. They only inherited because William, Robert's older brother, died an early death. A lethal combination of drink and the pox, it's said. He died abroad and spent very little time here at Felthorpe, which was held together by the efforts of Robert and his trusty steward.'

The light changed direction again and illuminated a third portrait.

A harsh white face in a black periwig. A diamond ring on a thin white hand lightly holding a small purple flower, a bunch of lace, lidded eyes. A clever face. A voluptuous face. I shivered.

'Wicked William Easton,' said Nicholas.

'Not by Lely, this one,' I said, peering more closely at the portrait. 'But a similar style, surely?'

'It's unsigned, and we have no record of the painter. A pupil of Lely? Could be. Skillfully done, though. Taken during William's youth, obviously, before he became dissolute.'

I shuddered. 'That man was born dissolute!'

I looked again at the hooded eyes and tried to read their expression. Dark and scornful, but there was more – they gleamed with unconcealed invitation. The full lips twisted with a humourless certitude. This man knew he could have anyone he wanted. After more than three centuries, he still had the power to make me look away, blushing, repelled and overwhelmed by the force of his flaunting sexuality.

Locking more doors, having first checked that all the rooms were empty, and turning off the last remaining lights, we returned to the landing.

'Hang on! Wait a minute!' I said. 'There's someone downstairs.'

'Can't be,' said Nicholas comfortably. 'There's no one in the house but ourselves.'

'Sorry. For a moment I thought I saw someone under the stairs. Where does that door lead to?'

'Doesn't lead anywhere. It's been blocked for over a hundred years.'

'Perhaps it was the moon?'

'That *would* be a miracle! No moon through all this cloud.'

We returned quickly to the cheerful, candlelit dining room under the roof.

It was midnight before, equipped with a spare toothbrush and an old pair of Diana's pyjamas, I was shown to a small spare room on the floor below.

'Hope you'll be all right in here. We'd better aim for eight o'clock breakfast. Suit you? Right then, sleep well!'

It had been a long day, and I had hardly been able to keep my eyes open for the last hour, but as soon as I reached this little room I knew I was in for a sleepless night. My mind went into unwelcome overdrive. Schemes for the repair of the stairs were uppermost, but speculation as to the possible history of the little box and its pathetic contents followed close behind. I got out of bed, drew the curtains, and looked out across the park. The moon appeared briefly through a rent in the cloud, and a flight of mallards slipped swiftly across this luminous patch.

'And there is nothing left remarkable beneath the visiting moon.'

I wasn't so sure about that!

I climbed back into bed and the unwelcome thought came to me that I needed to make a last dash to the bathroom. I made my reluctant way onto the landing trying to remember where on earth the bathroom was and thankful for the torch that Nicholas handed to me. On my return I was, still more reluctantly, drawn to peer down into the darkness below, prodded by a childish element of self-challenging bravado.

A door opened and shut and a dim figure on the floor below slipped under the stairs and out of sight.

'There *is* somebody down there! Somebody *has* got locked in. A cleaner perhaps? But surely the whole place is covered with movement detectors? Who the hell's that?'

My question was answered by a sigh from below and an indistinguishable gabble of words in a female voice. The words ended in a rack of sobbing and I was much afraid.

A shaft of light broke from a suddenly opened door on the floor above and the Wemysses peered down over the balustrade.

'Ellie?'

'Yes?'

'Did you hear that?'

'Yes. There's somebody down there. I thought there was.'

'Can't be,' said Nicholas. 'Can't be.'

They hurried down and joined me. I was very glad of their nearness. The house was desperately cold.

'We heard someone on the stairs,' said Diana.

'That was me going to the loo.'

'No, before that. Did it wake you up?'

'No, I wasn't asleep. But I saw someone just now... And there – look there!'

The tail of a shaft of passing moonlight seemed again to illuminate a dim figure and once again we heard that mutter of pathetic sobbing.

'Come on, Ellie,' said Nicholas. 'Let's go and look at this.'

'You're not leaving me up here by myself,' said Diana.

There was a hiss, a whirr, and a metallic click, and, after a moment of aged hesitation, an ancient clock struck one.

'If I might make rather a folksy suggestion,' I said, 'would we all like a cup of tea?'

'Now that's what I really appreciate,' said Nicholas. '*The sheeted dead did squeak and gibber in the Roman streets*, and the architect calls for a cup of tea!'

'What did Johnny Bell say?' asked Diana when we sat down in the kitchen, fragrant mugs of Earl Grey clutched in shaking hands. 'That the coffin must have been put in when the staircase was constructed? Sixteen sixty-two. Then perhaps Mr Stillingfleet can help us.'

'Mr Stillingfleet?' I asked. 'Who's he?'

'Was. Hugo Benedict Stillingfleet. Tutor to the little Easton boys.'

'Wicked Easton?'

'Yes, William and his brother Robert. He was also chaplain and finally steward. He lived here for about fifty years and kept the most wonderful account books – more like a diary, really. Every farthing that got spent, he recorded it. Everyone who was in the employ of the family and what they earned...family journeys, who came to stay and practically what they had for breakfast! If anything funny happened when the staircase was being installed, I bet Stillingfleet has recorded it. Nick, go and get Stillingfleet!'

'I'm not getting Stillingfleet at this time of night! Weighs about a ton and I'm not going down there to unlock the library! It'll keep until morning.'

'That coffin,' I said drowsily. 'That secret little box. Did we release something? Something very small. Something very sad. Did we call back somebody? Somebody who is distressed by the disturbance?'

'We'll ask Stillingfleet in the morning,' said Diana, and we finally went to bed.

It was a week before I could return to Felthorpe Hall. Johnny Bell was doing a beautiful job on the stairs, and it was nearing completion. The little box still stood safely on the table in the drawing room.

Diana and Nicholas were very subdued. 'We've had terrible nights,' they said. 'The same mutterings and sobbings every night since we disturbed that box! Haven't slept for a week. We don't know what to do. But we've a lot to tell you!'

They led me into the library where the central table was covered in page of notes and several leather-bound and ancient books. With barely suppressed excitement Diana went straight into the result of her researches. 'This is sixteen sixty-one,' she said, one finger on her notes and turning the ponderous pages of the Stillingfleet papers with the other hand. 'Here's the boss telling him to get estimates for "Ye newe westerne stair". And here's "Jas. Holbrooke, Master Carpenter", riding out from Norwich to give his estimate – £482.9.2d. Expensive!

'And here we are in sixteen sixty-two. A lot of comings and goings. The family were here for nearly all that year. Lots of company. Ate them out of house and home. Bills for barrels of oysters, anchovies, game birds by the dozen brace, cakes and sweetmeats, sacks of coffee... John Fox and his brother Will taken up for pilfering at the Lammas Fair and the good Stillingfleet goes over to the assizes to plead for them. Successfully, obviously, because they were back on the payroll the next month. And here's one Jayne Marston.'

Diana paused.

'Is she important?'

'Oh yes, we think so,' said Nicholas.

'Jayne Marston – "Miss Comfort's abigail".'

'Abigail? A lady's maid, you mean?'

'Yes, quite posh. Comes down from London and – note this – without her mistress. And that's odd. This was January. Season still in full swing in the capital. Miss Comfort wouldn't have sent her abigail down to the country for no good reason.'

'Does Stillingfleet give us a clue?'

'Sort of. He refers to her quite often and affectionately.' She quoted, '"Ye sorrowful Jayne...that forlorn wretch... That sweet slut in her sorrow..." Something wrong there, don't you think? And then the staircase gets under way. And in April they start getting ready for a party. Seems to be a belated celebration of the restoration of Charles the Second – the Eastons were all stout monarchists. Economically, they are planning to run it with the celebrations for Robert's engagements to Mary Chandler. Then, in June, two or three things happen – "Did wait on his Lordship under God's guidance and besought him to remember his Creator in the days of his youth, when the evil days come not."'

'That would be William he was beseeching. And did he remember his Creator? Did he do what Stillingfleet wanted?'

'It doesn't say, but one rather infers not. And then – dismay and disaster – on the fifteenth of June – "To me at dawn this day comes the swanward early. Jayne Marston, God receive her, found drowned in ye lake."'

Diana turned to me, wide-eyed. 'And she's not in the burial register! She's not buried in the churchyard!'

'Suicide, then? Denied a Christian burial.'

'Looks like it. And then William disappears.'

'Disappears?'

'Yes – "...raging to London", leaving poor old Stillingfleet to unscramble the party. Sounds as though there was the most almighty family row going on.'

'And the staircase?'

'Finished. Here – "Thanks be to God!" Then – and this is where the fun starts – "'Twas as though the Devil himself wailed about the house this night and these seven days past. God bless us all."'

'Is that what it's been like for *you*?'

'Yes. Sobs rather than wails, perhaps, but going on and on. Just the same for Stillingfleet. At the end of every day he wrote just two words – "No change" – until we get to: "All day working in pursuit of my resolve."'

'Working! Working at what, I wonder?'

'Well, in addition to his other accomplishments, Mr Stillingfleet was a carpenter and turner, and he made tables and chairs, and he was a bit of a scientist, too. He had a workshop. We think it was the little room at the end of the stillroom passage.'

'What do you think he was working at? The coffin?'

'Yes, that's what we think. A secret burial for a tiny child. A child who must have been illegitimate, inconvenient, disposable. Infanticide was sadly common in those days, and the rubbish heaps of London, certainly, were where the bodies ended up in large numbers, but this child was different. He was special to someone. Someone who was determined to grant him as decent a burial as was possible in adverse circumstances.'

'It's a long shot, and we'll never know for certain,' said Diana, 'but listen – Jayne Marston is sent down to the country estate from London without her mistress. Pregnant?'

'If this is her baby, and it was born in June,' I said, hurriedly calculating, 'she would have been three months gone in January and just beginning to show... Yes, the right moment to send her into obscurity. But is this consistent? Is that what the family would have done? Wouldn't they have just turned her out of the house?'

'I don't think so – not then. This wasn't the Protectorate, this was the Restoration. Cavalier politics and Cavalier morality. Cavalier kindness, if you like. And all the evidence from Stillingfleet is that the Eastons treated their servants with consideration. He was himself almost part of the family. They couldn't have functioned without him. But suppose I'm right. Suppose Jayne comes down to Norfolk because she's pregnant. Suppose Wicked William is the father. Suppose he comes down for the party and takes no notice of her, or spurns her, and perhaps that was what Stillingfleet was begging him to remember, begging him to do something for the wretched girl. Then the baby is born and is stillborn? Or dies, perhaps?'

'Dies? How? And where?'

'We'll never know,' said Diana slowly. 'Let's just say the baby dies. The body must have been hidden away. There is no recorded death of an infant at that time. Perhaps Jayne, at the death of her child, goes demented and throws herself into the lake?'

'Did she fall or was she pushed?'

'I'm sure Stillingfleet knew, but he's not saying. Loyalty to the family. It was only a servant involved, I know, but this was an isolated community where a scandal would have torn through the county, and don't forget that most people up here were still rigidly puritan in their outlook. William would have had a bad time of it if it had come out.'

'At any rate, there was no Christian burial for Jayne's child, no baptism even, and this would have been a horrifying thing for the mother. The child would have been condemned to eternal perdition.'

'And this is when the nightly wailing starts?'

'Yes. But Stillingfleet knows what to do. He makes a little coffin. He places the body inside with a copy of the words from the family motto…'

'Wait a minute, though – it's not quite the right wording, is it? Look at the third word. The motto is *Deus tute me spectas*. It should say "me". "Thou, Lord, see'st me", but this says "eum". "Him". God sees *him*. Who?'

'I thought it might mean "God watch over him" – the child, that is.'

'No. *Spectas*. It doesn't mean look out for in the sense of watching over, it means see, look at.'

'Well, I think this is as close as he dares get to an identification, a direct link with the Eastons. And one night, as the staircase is nearly finished, he fixes it up under a floorboard, replaces the floorboard, and says a burial service over it. It was the best he could do.'

'Any more from the diary?'

'Only this, but significantly – "Under the hand of God, I pray, I finish my work, and, all praise to Him, a quiet night at last."'

We sat for a moment in silence. 'I bet that was it, or something very like that,' I said. 'All quiet until I came along with a nail bar.

What do we do now?'

'I've been thinking about this,' said Diana. 'Look, Johnny is still here working on the stairs…do you think we could just put it back again? Say a few words, perhaps?'

'Yes, I'm sure we could do that,' I said.

We laid it back in its place and Johnny tapped nails back into position through the rim the thoughtful Hugo Stillingfleet had left for this purpose. The new nails sank in easily. We stood back and looked at each other uncertainly.

'May he rest in peace and light perpetual shine upon him,' said Diana quietly and clearly.

But something was worrying me. We had worked out a solution of sorts to an intriguing puzzle, but I hadn't heard that satisfying click as the last piece of the jigsaw falls into place. We had heard the truth, I was sure, from Stillingfleet, but had we heard the *whole* truth? I didn't think so.

I went to look again at the Easton portraits. I remembered Nicholas had said he would like to interrogate them. Well, why not? I thought I knew the right questions to ask, and I thought Peter Lely and his unknown pupil had given their subjects a voice which could still be heard over the years. I had released something which had lain dormant but only just contained through the years, and now I believed it was calling out for resolution and justice. The Norfolk police weren't interested in knowing who had committed infanticide and possibly a second murder all those years ago, but *I* was.

I managed to evade the hypnotic stare of Wicked William and concentrated first on the sunny opulence of the wedding portrait. Robert and Mary. Even the names were reassuringly solid. Following the painter's clues, I knew that this couple had married in the autumn; their betrothal, according to Stillingfleet, had been in the summer of 1662, and presumably Robert had been pursuing this heiress during the previous London season. At the very time Jayne Marston had been sent away to the country. Had he known the sorry story of his sister Comfort's maid? It was a family with a reputation for large-heartedness in its dealings with its retainers.

Yes, he would have known. He would have been concerned. But concerned, perhaps, for another reason.

Mary's fortune had saved the family and guaranteed his position in society. Robert would not have welcomed any breath of scandal to do with the family his golden goose was about to marry into. 'Of Quaker stock,' Nicholas had said. I looked again at the heart-shaped face, framed by wispy golden tendrils, the modest dress, the tightly pursed lips, and I wondered about Mary.

'Was it to avoid offending you?' I murmured, 'That Jayne and her child were done away with? Too inconvenient, too vocal. A servant, yes, but so intertwined with the family she had forgotten her place and was making herself a nuisance? Would it have ruined Robert's schemes if you'd discovered that his brother had seduced a family maid?'

I couldn't believe that.

'And why did you flee?' I asked, turning at last to William, 'Why didn't you just tough it out?' An earldom, the king's supporters back in power again – the future looked good for William Easton. What was he fleeing? Not a family scandal – there must have been something more.

The dark eyes taunted, enticed, seduced. I speculated again about the identity of the unknown painter and was struck by a devastating thought. A thought so obvious and yet so shocking I groped my way to a Chippendale chair and, against all the house rules, sat down on it. The painter's message now screamed out at me. How could I not have seen it before?

I heard Nicholas leaving the library and called out to him.

'Ellie? You OK?' He hurried to join me.

'We've got it all wrong, Nicholas!' I said. 'Come and have a look again at Wicked William. He's been wrongly accused! It couldn't have been him!'

I positioned Nicholas in front of the portrait. 'Now, imagine you're the painter. And that, of course, in the sixteen sixties, means you're a *man*. The sitter is reacting to *you*. What do you see?'

'Oh my God!' said Nicholas. 'I see it! And to think that all these years women have been averting their eyes thinking he was trying to seduce *them*. He wasn't at all, was he?'

'No. I'm not sure they had a word for it in Cavalier England, but this chap was gay and proud of it, as you'd say.'

'I'm certain they didn't have a word for it in north Norfolk! And it was a capital offence at the time. "Death without mercy", according to the Articles passed by Parliament in sixteen sixty-one. He could, technically, have been executed if discovered.'

'What if he *were* discovered?' I speculated. 'Caught *in flagrante* with a handsome young painter, let's say?'

'He'd have had to flee to somewhere more worldly – to France…to Italy… Poor old Stillingfleet, holding all this together! But this is just guesswork, Ellie.'

'Oh yes. But look at his hand, Nick! Do you see the flower he's holding?'

Nicholas peered at the tiny purple face.

'Always assumed it was a violet, but it's not, you know! It's heartsease. Common little English flower. It's got a lot of names – love-lies-bleeding, love-in-idleness, *la pensée* in French, wild pansy.'

'Exactly! Pansy! A badge. The seventeenth-century equivalent of a pink ribbon. That's what you'd call flaunting it! So how likely is it that he'd be spending time in London undoing a lady's maid? Possible, I suppose – but I can't see it! No. I think we've got to look elsewhere for the father of that little scrap in the coffin.'

Our eyes turned on Robert's handsome countenance. I waved a hand at his line of progeny. 'It's pretty obvious in which direction *his* preferences lay!' I said with more than a touch of bitterness. 'And he had such a lot to lose if his puritan bride-to-be were to catch him with his hand up a maid's skirt! Mary doesn't look the understanding kind to me!'

I looked at the pair in disgust. Their faces had taken on a cast of smug respectability. Their innocent children, healthy and happy, had thrived perhaps at the expense of that other unwanted child.

Suddenly I found myself playing the role of judge in this case that would never come to court and I knew what was required of me. I knew the formula that would ensure undisturbed nights for Diana and Nicholas.

I spoke aloud to the portrait and to anyone else who was

listening on the stairs. 'Robert Easton, I find you guilty of infanticide,' I said simply. 'May God have mercy on your soul.'

'*Deus tute eum spectas,*' said Diana, who had come silently to join us. 'God has seen him. God knows what he has done.'

A week later Charles waved a postcard at me.

'Not much in the post. It's for you from some boyfriend of yours in Norfolk. A picture of a bloke in a periwig and it says, "Thank God! At last a quiet night! Eternally grateful, love, Nicholas." What *did* you get up to in Norfolk, Ellie?'

Mr Edgerton was suffering from writer's block; it was, he quickly grew to realise, a most distressing complaint. A touch of influenza might lay a man up for a day or two, yet still his mind could continue its ruminations. Gout might leave him racked with pain, yet still his fingers could grasp a pen and turn pain to pennies. But this blockage, this barrier to all progress, had left Mr Edgerton a virtual cripple. His mind would not function, his hands would not write, and his bills would not be paid. In a career spanning the best part of two decades he had never before encountered such an obstacle to his vocation. He had, in that time, produced five moderately successful, if rather indifferent, novels; a book of memoirs that, in truth, owed more to invention than experience; and a collection of poetry that could most charitably be described as having stretched the capacities of free verse to the limits of their acceptability.

Mr Edgerton made his modest living from writing by the yard, based on the unstated belief that if he produced a sufficient quantity of material then something of quality was bound to creep in, if only in accordance with the law of averages. Journalism, ghostwriting, versifying, editorialising: nothing was beneath his limited capabilities.

Yet, for the past three months the closest he had come to a writing project was the construction of his weekly grocery list. A veritable tundra of empty white pages stretched before him, the gleaming nib of his pen poised above them like a reluctant explorer. His mind was a blank, the creative juices sapped from it, leaving behind only a dried husk of frustration and bewilderment. He began to fear his writing desk, once his beloved companion but now reduced to the status of a faithless lover, and it pained him to look upon it. Paper, ink, desk, imagination, all had betrayed him, leaving him lost and alone.

To further complicate matters, Mr Edgerton's wallet had begun to feel decidedly lightweight of late, and nothing will dampen a man's ardour for life more than an empty pocket. Like a rodent gripped in the coils of a great constricting snake, he found that the more he struggled against his situation, the tighter the pressure upon him grew. Necessity, wrote Ovid, is the mother of invention. For Mr Edgerton, desperation was proving to be the father of despair.

And so, once again, Mr Edgerton found himself wandering the streets of the city, vainly hunting for inspiration like a hungry leech seeking blood. In time, he came to Charing Cross Road, but the miles of shelved books only depressed him further, especially since he could find none of his own among their number. Head down, he cut through Cecil Court and made his way into Covent Garden in the faint hope that the vibrancy of the markets might spur his sluggish subconscious into action. He was almost at the Magistrates' Court when something caught his eye in the window of a small antique shop. There, partially hidden behind a framed portrait of General Gordon and a stuffed magpie, was a most remarkable inkpot.

It was silver, and about four inches tall, with a lacquered base adorned by Chinese characters. But what was most striking about it was the small, mummified monkey that perched upon its lid, its clawed toes clasped upon the rim and its dark eyes gleaming in the summer sunlight. It was obviously an infant of its species, perhaps even a foetus of some kind, for it was no more than three inches in height, and predominantly grey in colour, except for its face, which was blackened round the mouth as if the monkey had been sipping from its own inkpot. It really was a most ghastly creature, but Mr Edgerton had acquired the civilised man's taste for the grotesque and he quickly made his way into the darkened shop to enquire about the nature of the item in question.

The owner of the business proved to be almost as distasteful in appearance as the creature that had attracted Mr Edgerton's attention, as though the man were somehow father to the monkey. His teeth were too numerous for his mouth, his mouth too large for his face, and his head too great for his body. Combined with a pronounced stoop to his back, his aspect was that of one constantly on the verge of toppling over. He also smelled decidedly odd, and Mr Edgerton quickly concluded that he was probably in the habit of sleeping in his clothes, a deduction that briefly led the afflicted writer to an unwelcome speculation upon the nature of the body that lay concealed beneath the layers of unwashed clothing.

Nevertheless, the proprietor proved to be a veritable font of knowledge about the items in his possession, including the article that had brought Mr Edgerton into his presence. The mummified primate was, he informed the writer, an inkpot monkey, a creature of Chinese mythology. According to the myth, the monkey provided artistic inspiration in return for the residues of ink left in the bottom of the inkwell.

Mr Edgerton was a somewhat superstitious (and, it must be said, sentimental) man: he still wore, much to the amusement of his peers, his mother's old charm bracelet, a rag-tag bauble of dubious taste that she found one day while walking upon the seashore and had subsequently bequeathed to him upon her death, along with a set of antique combs, now pawned, and a small sum of money, now spent. Among the items dangling from its links was a small gold monkey. It had always fascinated him as a child, and the discovery of a similar relic in the window of the antique store seemed to him nothing less than a sign from the Divine. As a man who was profoundly in need of inspiration from any source, and who had recently been considering opium or cheap gin as possible catalysts, he required no further convincing. He paid over money he could ill afford for the faint hope of redemption offered by the curiosity, and made his way back to his small apartments with the inkpot and its monkey tucked beneath his arm in a cloak of brown paper.

Mr Edgerton occupied a set of rooms above a tobacconist's shop on Marylebone High Street, a recent development forced upon him by his straitened circumstances. Although Mr Edgerton did not himself partake of the noble weed, his walls were yellowed by the fumes that regularly wended their way between the cracks in the floorboards, and his clothing and furnishings reeked of assorted cigars, cigarettes, pipe tobaccos, and even the more eyewatering forms of snuff. His dwelling was, therefore, more than a little depressing, and would almost certainly have provided Mr

Edgerton with the impetus necessary to improve his finances were he not so troubled by the absence of his muse. Indeed, he had few distractions, for most of his writer friends had deserted him. They had silently, if reluctantly, tolerated his modest success. Now, with the taint of failure upon him, they relished his discomfort from a suitably discreet distance.

That evening, Mr Edgerton sat at his desk once again and stared at the paper before him. And stared. And stared. Before him, the inkpot monkey squatted impassively, its eyes reflecting the lamplight and lending its mummified form an intimation of life that was both distracting and unsettling. Mr Edgerton poked at it tentatively with his pen, leaving a small black mark on its chest. Like most writers, he had a shallow knowledge of a great many largely useless matters. Among these was anthropology, a consequence of one of his earlier works, an evolutionary fantasy entitled *The Monkey's Uncle*. (*The Times* had described it as 'largely adequate, if inconsequential'. Mr Edgerton, grateful to be reviewed at all, was rather pleased.) Yet, despite searching through three reference volumes, Mr Edgerton had been unable to identify the origins of the inkpot monkey and had begun to take this as a bad omen.

After another unproductive hour had gone by, its tedium broken only by the spread of an occasional ink blot upon the paper, Mr Edgerton rose and determined to amuse himself by emptying, and then refilling, his pen. Still devoid of inspiration, he wondered if there was some part of the arcane ritual of fuelling one's pen from the inkpot that he had somehow neglected to perform. He reached down and gently grasped the monkey in order to raise the lid, but something pricked his skin painfully. He drew back his hand immediately and examined the wounded digit. A small, deep cut lay across the pad of his index finger, and blood from the abrasion was running down the length of his pen and congregating at the nib, from which it dripped into the inkpot with soft, regular splashes. Mr Edgerton began to suck the offended member, meanwhile turning his attention to the monkey in an effort to ascertain the cause of his injury. The lamplight revealed a small raised ridge behind the creature's neck, where a section of curved spine had burst through its tattered fur. A little of Mr Edgerton's blood could be perceived on the yellowed pallor of the bone.

The unfortunate writer retrieved a small bandage from his medicine cabinet, then cleaned and bound his finger before resuming his seat at his desk. He regarded the monkey warily as he filled his pen, then put it to paper and began to write. At first, the familiarity of the act overcame any feelings of surprise at its sudden return, so that Mr Edgerton had dispensed with two pages of close script and was about to embark upon a third before he paused and looked in puzzlement first at his pen, then at the paper. He reread what he had written, the beginning of a tale of a man who sacrifices love at the altar of success, and found it more than satisfactory; it was, in fact, as fine as anything he had ever written, although he was baffled as to the source of his inspiration. Nevertheless, he shrugged and continued writing, grateful that his old talent had apparently woken from its torpor. He wrote long into the night, refilling his pen as required, and so bound up was he in his exertions that he failed entirely to notice that his wound had reopened and was dripping blood on to pen and page and, at those moments when he replenished his instrument, into the depths of the small Chinese inkpot.

Mr Edgerton slept late the following morning, and awoke to find himself weakened by his efforts of the night before. It was, he supposed, the consequence of months of inactivity, and after coffee and some hot buttered toast he felt much refreshed. He returned to his desk to find that the inkpot monkey had fallen from its perch and now lay on its back amid his pencils and pens. Gingerly, Mr Edgerton lifted it from the desk and found that it weighed considerably more than the inkpot itself and that physics, rather than any flaw in the inkpot's construction, had played its part in dislodging the monkey from its seat. He also noted that the creature's fur was far more lustrous than it had appeared in the window of the antique shop, and now shimmered healthily in the morning sunlight.

And then, quite suddenly, Mr Edgerton felt the monkey move. It stretched wearily, as though waking from some long slumber, and its mouth opened in a wide yawn, displaying small blunt teeth.

Alarmed, Mr Edgerton dropped the monkey and heard it emit a startled squeak as it landed on the desk. It lay there for a moment or two, then slowly raised itself on its haunches and regarded Mr Edgerton with a slightly hurt expression before ambling over to the inkpot and squatting down gently beside it. With its left hand, it raised the lid of the inkpot and waited patiently for Mr Edgerton to fill his pen. For a time, the bewildered writer was unable to move, so taken aback was he at this turn of events. Then, when it became clear that he had no other option but to begin writing or go mad, he reached for his pen and filled it from the well. The monkey watched him impassively until the reservoir was replenished and Mr Edgerton had begun to write, then promptly fell fast asleep.

Despite his unnerving encounter with the newly animated monkey, Mr Edgerton put in a most productive day and quickly found himself with the bulk of five chapters written, none of them requiring more than a cursory rewrite. It was only when the light had begun to fade and Mr Edgerton's arm had started to ache that the monkey awoke and padded softly across a virgin page to where Mr Edgerton's pen lay in his hand. The monkey grasped his index finger with its tiny hands, then placed its mouth against the cut and began to suck. It took Mr Edgerton a moment to realise what was occurring, at which point he rose with a shout and shook the monkey from his finger. It bounced against the inkpot, striking its head soundly upon its base, and lay unmoving upon a sheet of paper.

At once, Mr Edgerton reached for it and raised it in the palm of his left hand. The monkey was obviously stunned, for its eyes were now half-closed and it moved its head slowly from side to side as it tried to focus. Instantly, Mr Edgerton was seized with regret at his hasty action. He had endangered the monkey, which he now acknowledged to be the source of his new-found inspiration. Without it, he would be lost. Torn between fear and disgust, Mr Edgerton reluctantly made his decision: he squeezed together his thumb and forefinger, causing a droplet of blood to emerge from the cut and then, his gorge rising, allowed it to drip into the monkey's mouth.

The effect was instantaneous. The little mammal's eyes opened fully, it rose on to its haunches, and then reached for, and grasped, the wounded finger. There it suckled happily, undisturbed by the revolted Mr Edgerton, until it had taken its fill, whereupon it burped contentedly and resumed its slumbers. Mr Edgerton gently laid it beside the inkpot and then, taking up his pen, wrote another two chapters before retiring early to his bed.

Thus it continued. Each day Mr Edgerton rose, fed the monkey a little blood, wrote, fed the monkey once again in the evening, wrote some more, then went to bed and slept like a dead man. The monkey appeared to require little in the way of affection or attention beyond its regular feeds, although it would often touch fascinatedly the miniature of itself that dangled from Mr Edgerton's wrist. Mr Edgerton, in turn, decided to ignore the fact that the monkey was growing at quite an alarming rate, so that it was now obliged to sit beside him on a small chair while he worked and had taken to dozing on the sofa after its meals. In fact, Mr Edgerton wondered if it might not be possible to train the monkey to do some light household duties, thereby allowing him more time to write, although when he suggested this to the monkey through the use of primitive sign language it grew quite irate and locked itself in the bathroom for an entire afternoon.

In fact, it was not until Mr Edgerton returned home one afternoon from a visit to his publisher to find the inkpot monkey trying on one of his suits that he began to experience serious doubts about their relationship. He had noticed some new and especially disturbing changes in the monkey. It had started to moult, leaving clumps of unsightly grey hair on the carpets and exposing sections of pink-white skin. It had also lost some weight from its face; that, or its bone structure had begun to alter, for it now presented a more angular aspect than it had previously done. In addition, the monkey was now over four feet tall and Mr Edgerton had been forced to open veins in his wrists and legs in order to keep it sated. The more Mr Edgerton considered the matter, the more convinced he became that the creature was undergoing some significant transformation. Yet there were still chapters of the book to be completed, and the writer was reluctant to alienate his mascot. So he suffered in silence, sleeping now for much of the day and emerging only to write for increasingly short periods of time before returning to his bed and collapsing into a dreamless slumber.

On the 29th day of August, he delivered his completed manuscript to his publisher. On the 4th of September, which was Mr Edgerton's birthday, he was gratified to receive a most delightful communication from his editor, praising him as a genius and promising that this novel, long anticipated and at last delivered, would place Mr Edgerton in the pantheon of literary greats and assure him of a most comfortable and well-regarded old age.

That night, as Mr Edgerton prepared to drift off into contented sleep, he felt a tug at his wrist and looked down to see the inkpot monkey fastened upon it, its cheeks pulsing as it sucked away at the cut. Tomorrow, thought Mr Edgerton, tomorrow I will deal with it. Tomorrow I will have it taken to the zoo and our bargain will be concluded for ever. But as he grew weaker and his eyes closed, the inkpot monkey raised its head and Mr Edgerton realised at last that no zoo would ever take the inkpot monkey, for the inkpot monkey had become something very different indeed…

Mr Edgerton's book was published the following year, to universal acclaim. A reception was held in his honour by his grateful publishers, to which the brightest lights of London's literary community flocked to pay tribute. It would be Mr Edgerton's final public appearance. From that day forth, he was never again seen in London and retired to the small country estate that he purchased with the royalties from his great, valedictory work. Even his previous sentimentality appeared to be in the past, for his beloved charm bracelet could now be found in the window of a small antique shop in Covent Garden where, due to some imaginative pricing, it seemed destined to remain.

That night, speeches were made, and an indifferent poem recited by one of Mr Edgerton's new admirers, but the great man himself remained silent throughout. When called upon to give his speech, he replied simply with a small but polite bow to his guests, accepting their applause with a gracious smile, then returned to toying with the small gold monkey that hung from a chain around his neck.

And while all those around him drank the finest champagne and feasted on stuffed quail and smoked salmon, Mr Edgerton could be found sitting quietly in a corner, stroking some unruly hairs on his chest and munching contentedly on a single ripe banana.

Peter Tremayne
The Banshee

For three days the Banshee had been heard wailing outside his door at night. It was no surprise when his body was discovered. His time had come.

Sister Fidelma gazed at Brother Abán with surprise.

The elderly monk was sitting slightly forward on his chair, shivering a little although the day was not cold. His thin mouth trembled slightly; a fleck of spittle from one corner caught on the greying stubble of his unshaven chin. His pale eyes stood out in a bony, almost skeletal head over which the skin was stretched taut and parchment-like.

'He was fated to die,' repeated the old man, almost petulantly. 'You cannot deny the summons of the death wail.'

Fidelma realised that the old man was troubled and he spoke with deadly seriousness. 'Who heard this wailing?' she asked, trying to hide her natural scepticism.

The old man shivered. 'Glass, the miller, whose house is not far away. And Bláth has confirmed that she was disturbed by the sounds.'

Fidelma pursed her lips and expelled a little air through them in an almost soundless whistle. 'I will speak with them later. Tell me what you know about this matter, Brother Abán. Just those facts that are known to you.'

The early *religieux* sighed as if suppressing irritation. 'I thought that you knew them. Surely my message was clear?'

'I was told that a man had been found dead in suspicious circumstances. The messenger requested that the Chief Brehon of Cashel send a *dálaigh*, an officer of the court, to come and ascertain those circumstances. That is all I know so far, except that this man was named Ernán, that he was a farmer, and that he was found dead on the doorstep of his house with a jagged wound in his throat.'

Fidelma spoke without irritation but precisely.

Brother Abán was suddenly defensive. 'This is a peaceful spot. We are just a small farming community here by the banks of the Siúr River. Even nature bestows her blessings on us and that is why we call this place "The Field of Honey". Nothing like this has ever happened before.'

'It would help if I knew exactly what has happened,' murmured Fidelma. 'So, tell me what you know.'

'I am the only religious in this community,' went on Brother Abán, as if ignoring her request. 'I have been here forty years, tending to the spiritual needs of this little community. Never before…'

He fell silent a moment and Fidelma was forced to control her impatience and wait until the old man was ready to begin. 'The facts?' he suddenly asked, his bright eyes upon her. 'These are the facts. Yesterday morning I was at my morning prayers when Bláth came to my threshold, crying in a loud voice that Ernán had been found just outside the door of his house with his throat torn out. I went to his house and found this to be true. I then sent to Cashel for a *dálaigh*.'

'What was so suspicious about the circumstances that you needed to do so?'

Brother Abán nervously rubbed the stubble on his chin. 'Bláth told me…'

Fidelma held up a hand. 'First, tell me exactly who Ernán was.'

'Ernán was a young farmer who worked the lower fields along the riverbank. A handsome young man, married and without an enemy in the world. I knew his parents before they died. Good Christians leading blameless lives.'

'And Bláth? Was she his wife?'

Brother Abán shook his head. 'Ernán's wife was Blinne. Bláth is her sister. She lived with them. She helps about the farm. A good girl. She comes to sing the psalms in the chapel each week.'

'And where was Blinne at this time?'

'Distraught. Beside herself with grief. She loved her husband very much.'

'I see. And Bláth told you…what?'

'Bláth said that she had been awoken each of the last three nights hearing a terrible wailing outside the farmhouse.'

'Did she investigate the cause of this sound?'

The old monk laughed sarcastically. 'This is a rural community.

We live close to nature here. You do not go to investigate the wailing of a Banshee.'

'Surely the new Faith has taught us not to be fearful of Otherworld creatures? As a Christian, do you really accept that there is a woman of the hills, a wraith, who comes to the threshold of a person about to die and then wails and laments in the middle of the night?' demanded Fidelma.

'As a Christian, I must. Do not the Holy Scriptures talk of spirits and ghosts who serve both God and Satan? Who knows which the woman of the hills serves? In the old days, it was said that the Banshee was a goddess who cared for a specific noble family and when their time came to be reborn in the Otherworld, the spirit would cry to announce their impending death in this world.'

'I know the folklore,' Fidelma said quietly.

'It is not to be dismissed,' Brother Abán assured her earnestly. 'When I was a small boy I heard a story from a neighbour. It seems that the time had come for his father, an old man, to pass on. A plaintive wailing was heard within the vicinity of their dwelling. The son went out the next morning and found a strange comb, which he picked up and took into the house. The following night the wailing returned but this time the doors and windows rattled as if someone was trying to get in.

'Realising it was the Banshee, the man placed the comb in a pair of tongs and held it out the window. Unseen hands seized the comb, and the tongs were twisted and bent out of recognition. Had he handed the comb out through the window, his arm would have been wrenched off. This is the power of the Banshee.'

Fidelma dropped her gaze and tried to contain her smile. Obviously, Brother Abán was steeped in the old ways and superstitions. 'Let us return to the case of Ernán,' she suggested gently. 'Are you saying that his sister-in-law, Bláth, heard this wailing and did so on three consecutive nights?'

'The third night was when Ernán was found dead.'

'And Blinne had heard this wailing as well?'

'I only spoke to Glass the miller who confirmed that he had heard it also.'

'So you have not spoken to Blinne, Ernán's wife.'

'She has not been well enough to speak with me, as you can imagine.'

'Very well. Who discovered the body?'

'Bláth was up in the morning to milk the goats and found Ernán outside the house. He had been dead some hours. Bláth believes that —'

Fidelma held up her hand. 'I will see what she believes when I speak with her. At this point, she came to you?'

'That is right. I went to see the body while she went inside to comfort Blinne.'

'Where is the body now?'

'In the chapel. We shall bury it tonight.'

'I would like to examine this wound of which you speak.'

Brother Abán stirred uncomfortably. 'Is that necessary? After all, you are —'

'I am a *dálaigh* and used to such sights as the corpses of people who have died in violent ways.'

The old monk shrugged. 'It is not often that you would see the corpse of one who has been taken by the Banshee,' he muttered.

'Has there been much wolf activity in these parts recently?'

The question was innocent enough, but Brother Abán realised what she was implying and pulled a sour face. 'You will not be able to pass off this death as a wolf attack, Sister,' he said. 'I know the marks made by a wolf when it is driven to attack a human. A wolf rarely attacks a full-grown man, a strong and muscular man. And the wailing was certainly not that of a wolf. You will have to think again if you want to dismiss this death as having a rational cause.'

'I want to find the truth, that is all,' Fidelma replied evenly. 'Now let us inspect the corpse.'

The old monk had been right and Ernán had been young and handsome in life. He was obviously well muscled and strong. The only disfigurement on his body was the jagged wound beneath his chin, which severed his windpipe and arteries. Fidelma bent forward and saw immediately that no teeth marks could have made the wound. It had been made by something sharp, although it had been drawn across the throat, tearing the flesh rather than cutting cleanly.

She straightened up after her inspection.

'Well?' demanded the old man.

'Ernán was certainly attacked, but not by some Otherworld entity,' she said softly.

She led the way out of the small chapel and stood in the sunshine looking down through the collection of buildings to where the broad expanse of river was pushing sedately along, glistening and flickering in the bright light. There were several dwellings clustered around, including a blacksmith's forge and grain stores. The main part of the community dwelt in outlying farmsteads and would probably be in the fields at this time. However, there were a few people about. The blacksmith stood deep in conversation with someone who had in tow a thick-legged workhorse, and Fidelma could see a couple of people at the far end of the square just emerging around the corner of a storehouse. One was an attractive woman with auburn hair, young and pretty and slim. Her companion was a young man, long-faced, intense.

Fidelma's keen eyes deduced that neither was happy. The young man was stretching out a hand to the woman's arm in an almost imploring gesture. The woman seemed irritable and knocked the hand away, turning swiftly and striding towards the chapel. The young man gazed after her for a moment, then seemed to notice Fidelma and walked rapidly away, disappearing behind the far building.

'Interesting,' muttered Fidelma. 'Who are they? The woman seems to be coming here.'

Brother Abán, standing at her shoulder, whispered: 'This is Blinne the widow of Ernán.'

'And who was the young man with whom she seemed annoyed?'

'That was Tadhg. He is a…he is a bard.'

Fidelma's lower lip thrust out a moment in amusement at the disapproval in the old man's voice. 'That is appropriate.'

The name Tadhg meant 'poet'.

Brother Abán was already moving to greet the woman called Blinne.

'How are you, my child?'

'Only as can be expected,' Blinne replied shortly. Fidelma noticed that her face seemed an expressionless mask. Her lips were thinned in the set of her jaw. She had a tight control of her emotions. Her hazel eyes caught those of Sister Fidelma and her chin came up defiantly. 'I have come to see the body of Ernán one last time. And Bláth says that she will sing the *caoine,* the keening at the interment.'

'Of course, my child, of course,' muttered the old monk. Then he remembered his manners. 'This is Sister Fidelma from Cashel. She is —'

'I know who she is,' replied the young woman coldly. 'She is sister to our king as well as being a *dálaigh.*'

'She has come to inquire into the death of your husband.'

Was there a slight blush on Blinne's cheek?

'So I have heard. The news is all around the community.'

'I am sorry for your troubles, Blinne,' Fidelma greeted her softly. 'When you have finished.' She nodded imperceptibly to the chapel, 'I would like to ask you a few questions.'

'I understand.'

'I shall be at Brother Abán's dwelling.'

It was not long before Blinne came to Brother Abán's threshold. Fidelma bade her be seated and turned to the old monk. 'I think you said you had something to attend to in the chapel?' she suggested pointedly.

'No, I...' Brother Abán caught her gaze and then nodded swiftly. 'Of course. I shall be there if you need me.'

After he had left, Fidelma took her seat opposite the attractive young woman. 'This must be distasteful to you, but your husband has died in suspicious circumstances. The law dictates that I ask you certain questions.'

Blinne raised her chin defiantly. 'People are saying that he was taken by a Banshee.'

Fidelma regarded her thoughtfully. 'You sound as if you give that story no credence.'

'I have heard no wailing messengers of death. Ernán was killed, but not by a ghostly visitation.'

'Yet, as I understand it, the wailing on three separate nights thrice awakened your own sister, who dwells with you. This wailing was heard by one of your neighbours.'

'As I said, I did not hear it, nor was I awakened. If wailing there was, it was that of a wolf. He was killed by a wolf, that is obvious.'

Fidelma regarded her thoughtfully, then she said: 'If it was obvious, then there woul be no need for this inquiry. Tell me about Ernán. He was a farmer, handsome, and I am told he was well liked. Is that true?'

'True enough.'

'He had no enemies?'

Blinne shook her head but responded too quickly, so Fidelma thought. 'Are you sure about that?' she pressed.

'If you are trying to tell me that you suspect he was murdered, then I —'

'I am not trying, Blinne,' interrupted Fidelma firmly. 'I tell you facts. A wolf did not create the wound that caused his death. Now, are you saying that he had no enemies that you know of? Think carefully, think hard, before you reply.'

Blinne's face had become a tight mask. 'He had no enemies,' she said firmly.

Instinctively, Fidelma knew that she was lying. 'Did you love your husband?' she asked abruptly.

A red flush spread swiftly over the other woman's response.

'You had no problem between you? Nothing Ernán said that might have led you to think that he nurtured some problem and tried to hide it from you?'

Blinne was frowning suspiciously. 'It is the truth I tell you when I say that there were no problems between us and that I loved him very much. Are you accusing me of...of murdering my own husband?' Her voice rose sharply, vehemently.

Fidelma smiled disarmingly. 'Calm yourself. I am required to ask certain questions and must do so. It is facts that I am after, not accusations.'

Blinne's mouth formed a thin line and she still stared belligerently at Fidelma.

'So,' Fidelma continued after a moment or two of silence, 'you are telling me that he had no problems, no enemies, that your relationship was good.'

'I have said as much.'

'Tell me what happened on the night he died.'

Blinne shrugged. 'We went to bed as usual. When I woke it was dawn and I heard Bláth screaming outside the house. I think that was what actually awoke me. I rushed out and found Bláth crouching on the threshold with Ernán's body. I cannot remember much after that. Bláth went for Brother Abán, who is also the apothecary in the community. I know he came but could do nothing. It is all a blur.'

'Very well. Let me take you back to the time you went to bed. You say, "We went to bed"? Both of you at the same time?'

'Of course.'

'So, as far as you know, you both went to bed and fell asleep together?'

'I have said so.'

'You were not disturbed by Ernán getting up either in the night or at dawn?'

'I must have been very tired, for I remember that I had been feeling sleepy after the evening meal and was almost asleep by the time I reached the bed. I think we have been working hard on the farm in recent days, as I have been feeling increasingly tired.'

'You heard no disturbances during the night nor during the previous nights?'

'None.'

Fidelma paused thoughtfully. 'How was your sleep last night?'

Blinne was scornful. 'How do you think? My husband had been killed yesterday. Do you think I slept at all last night?'

'I can understand that,' agreed Fidelma. 'Perhaps you should have had Brother Abán mix you a sleeping draught.'

Blinne sniffed. 'If there was need for that, I would not have needed to bother him. My sister and I were raised knowing how to mix our herbal remedies.'

'Of course. How do you feel now? – physically, I mean.'

'As can be expected. I am not feeling well. I feel nauseous and have a headache.'

Fidelma smiled softly and rose. 'Then I have taxed you too long.'

Blinne followed her example.

'Where would I find your sister, Bláth?'

'I think she went to see Glass the miller.'

'Good, for I have need to see him as well.'

Blinne stood frowning at the door. 'You have been told that Glass is claiming he heard this wailing in the night?'

'I have been told.'

Blinne extended her front teeth over her lower lip for a moment, pressing down hard. 'I did not hear any noises in the night. But...'

Fidelma waited. Then she prompted: 'But...?'

'Could it be true? Bláth said...people believe...I...I don't know what to believe. Many people believe in the Banshee.'

Fidelma reached out a hand and laid it on the young woman's arm. 'If the wailing of the hills exists, it is said her task is to be the harbinger of death, lamenting the passing of a soul from his world to the Otherworld. The belief is that the Banshee merely warns; she is never the instrument of death. Whether you believe that is your own affair. Personally, I believe that the Banshee, indeed, all the ghostly visitations that I have encountered, are merely visible manifestations of our own fears, fears whose images we cannot contain within the boundaries of our dreams.'

'And yet —'

'I tell you this, Blinne,' Fidelma interrupted in a cold voice. 'Your husband was killed neither by a Banshee nor by animal agency... A human hand killed him. Before this day is out, the culprit will stand before me.'

Brother Abán had directed her along the path towards Glass's mill. The path ran alongside a small stream that twisted itself down to feed the broad river, the Siúr. As she followed the path through a copse of birch trees she heard a strong masculine voice. It was singing:

'No pleasure
that deed I did, tormenting her,
tormenting her I treasure...'

Fidelma came upon a young man sitting on a rock by the stream. He heard the snap of a twig beneath her feet and swung his face round, flushing crimson as if he had been caught in a guilty deed.

'Greetings, Tadhg,' Fidelma said, recognising him.

He frowned; the crimson on his cheeks deepened. 'You know me?'

Fidelma did not answer, for that much was obvious. 'I am Sister —'

'Fidelma,' broke in the young man. 'News of your arrival has spread. We are a small community.'

'Of course. How well did you know Ernán?' she went on without further preamble.

The young man hesitated. 'I knew him,' he said defensively.

'That's not what I asked. I said, how well? I already presume that everyone in this community knows each other.'

Tadhg shrugged indifferently. 'We grew up together until I went to the bardic school, which has now been displaced by the monastery founded by Finnan the Leper.'

'The place called Finnan's Height? I knew of the old school there. When did you return here?'

'About a year ago.'

'And presumably you renewed your friendship with Ernán then?'

'I did not say that I was his friend, only that we grew up together, as most people here of my age did.'

'Does that mean that you did not like him?' Fidelma asked.

'One does not have to like everyone one knows or grows up with.'

'There is truth in that. Why didn't you like him?'

The young man grimaced. 'He was arrogant and thought himself superior to...to...'

'A poet?' supplied Fidelma.

Tadhg looked at her and then lowered his eyes as if in agreement.

'He was a farmer and thought strength and looks were everything. He called me a weak parasite fit for nothing, not even to clean his pigsty. Most people knew how arrogant he was.'

'Yet I am told that Ernán was well liked and had no enemies in the world.'

'Then you were told wrong.'

'I was told by Blinne,'

'Blinne?' The young man's head jerked up and again came an uncontrollable rush of blood to his cheeks.

Fidelma made an intuitive leap forward.

'You like Blinne very much don't you?'

A slightly sullen expression now moulded the young poet's features.

'Did she tell you that? Well, we grew up together, too.'

'Nothing more than an old friendship?'

'What are you saying?'

'Saying? I am asking a question. If you disliked Ernán so much, you must surely not have approved of Blinne being married to him.'

'You would soon find that out from anyone in the community,' admitted Tadhg sullenly. 'I do not deny it. Poor Blinne. She did not have the courage to leave him. He dominated her.'

'Are you saying that she did not love him?'

'How could she? He was a brute.'

'If she disliked the marriage, there are nine reasons in law why she could have divorced him and more why she could have separated from him.'

'I tell you that she did not have the courage. He was a powerful, controlling man and it is poetic justice that he was taken by the Banshee, whether you call it Banshee or wolf. That he was a beast and the stronger beast of the night attacked him and tore out his throat was poetic justice.'

The young man finished his speech with defiance.

'Poetic?' Fidelma gazed thoughtfully at him. 'Where were you the night before last? Where were you when Ernán was killed?'

'In my house. Asleep.'

'Where is your house?'

'Up on that hillside.' He raised an arm to gesture in the direction.

'Was anyone with you?'

The young man looked outraged. 'Of course not!'

'A pity,' Fidelma said softly.

'What do you mean?' Tadhg blinked, disconcerted.

'Just that I would like to eliminate you from the vicinity of Ernán's farmstead. He was murdered, his throat cut, and you have just given me a very good reason why you might be suspected of it.'

Now Tadhg's face was suddenly drained of blood. 'I was told that he had his throat ripped out,' he said quietly. 'I presumed that it was by a wolf, although many superstitious people are talking about the Banshee.'

'Who told you that this was how he died?'

'It is common talk. You say he was murdered? How can you be so sure?'

Fidelma did not bother to answer.

'Well, I did not do it. I was in my bed, asleep.'

'If that is the truth, then you have presented me with another suspect,' she said reflectively. 'Blinne.'

Tadhg swallowed rapidly. 'She would never...that is not possible. She had not enough courage to divorce Ernán. She was too gentle to strike him down.'

'Human beings react in peculiar ways. If not Blinne, nor you, then who else had cause to hate Ernán, a man who was supposed to have no enemies?'

Tadhg raised his hands in a helpless, negative gesture.

'I will want to see you again later, Tadhg.'

Fidelma turned and resumed her progress along the path, her brow furrowed in thought.

Bláth had already left Glass's mill when Fidelma reached there.

The miller was a genial, round-faced man of middle age with twinkling grey-blue eyes, which might well have been the reason for his name, which indicated such a colouring. He was a stocky man, clad in a leather apron and open shirt, his muscles bulging as he heaved a sack of flour into a cart.

'A bad thing, Sister, a bad thing,' he said when Fidelma introduced herself.

'You were a close neighbour of Ernán, I believe.'

The miller turned and pointed. From where they stood the ground began to descend slightly towards the broad river across some fields to where an elm grove stood. 'That is Ernán's farmhouse, the building among those trees. We are scarcely ten minutes' walk away from each other.'

'And were you a friend of his?'

'I saw young Ernán grow to manhood. I was a friend of his father and mother. They were killed when Crundmáel of Laighin came raiding along the Siúr in his battle boats in search of booty. Only Ernán survived out of his entire family and so he took over the farm and continued to make it prosperous. Blinne, his wife, is my niece.' He grinned briefly. 'So is Bláth, of course.'

'And Ernán was well liked?'

'Not an enemy in the world,' Glass replied immediately.

'He and Blinne were happy?'

'Never happier.'

'And Bláth lived with them?'

'She could have come here to live, but Blinne and Bláth were always close. There is only a year between them and they are almost like twins. Blinne wanted her sister to be with her and Ernán did not mind, for she helped with the farm work. But why do you ask me these questions?'

Fidelma did not answer. 'Tell me about the Banshee,' she said.

Glass smiled briefly. 'I heard the sound only too well.'

'When did you first hear it?'

'I would not want to hear that sound more than once.'

Fidelma frowned. 'You heard it only once?'

'Yesterday morning about dawn.'

'Not before the morning Ernán was found dead?'

'No. Only that one morning. That was enough. It wailed like a soul in torment.'

'What did you do?'

'Do? Nothing at all.'

'You weren't curious?'

'Such curiosity about the Banshee can endanger your immortal soul,' replied Glass solemnly.

'When did you realise that Ernán was dead?'

'When Brother Abán came to tell me and asked me if I had heard anything in the night.'

'And you were able to tell him that you had?'

'Of course.'

'But only yesterday morning?'

Glass nodded.

'As a matter of interest, if Ernán was the only survivor of his family, I presume that his farm passes to Blinne?'

'Blinne is his heir in all things,' agreed Glass. His eyes suddenly flickered beyond her shoulder in the direction of what had been Ernán's farmstead. Fidelma turned and saw a figure that she initially thought was Blinne making her way up the hill. Then she realised it was a young woman who looked fairly similar.

'Bláth?'

Glass nodded.

'Then I shall go down to meet her, as I need to ask her some questions.'

Halfway down the path were some large stones which made a natural seat. Fidelma reached them at the same time as Bláth and greeted her.

'I was coming back to my uncle's mill, for Blinne told me that you had gone there in search of me. You are the *dálaigh* from Cashel, aren't you?'

'I am. There are a few questions that I must ask you. You see, Bláth, I am not satisfied about the circumstances of your brother-in-law's death.'

Bláth, who was a younger version of the attractive Blinne, pouted. 'There is no satisfaction to be had in any death, but a death that is encompassed by supernatural elements is beyond comprehension.'

'Are you sure we speak of supernatural elements?'

Bláth looked surprised. 'What else?'

'That is what I wish to determine. I am told that you heard the wailing of the Banshee for three nights?'

'That is so.'

'You awoke each night and investigated?'

'Investigated?' The girl laughed sharply. 'I know the old customs, and turned over and buried my head under the pillow to escape the wailing sound.'

'It was loud?'

'It was fearful.'

'Yet it did not wake your sister or your husband?'

'It was supernatural. Perhaps only certain people could hear it? Glass, my uncle, heard it.'

'But only once.'

'Once is enough.'

'Very well. Were your sister and Ernán happy?'

Fidelma saw the shadow pass across Bláth's face.

'Why, yes.'

There was hesitation enough and Fidelma sniffed in annoyance. 'I think that you are not being truthful. They were unhappy, weren't they?'

Bláth pressed her lips together and seemed about to deny it. Then she nodded. 'Blinne was trying to make the best of things. She was always like that. I would have divorced Ernán, but she was not like that.'

'Everyone says that she and Ernán were much in love and happy.'

'It was the image they presented to the village.' She shrugged. 'But what has this to do with the death of Ernán? The Banshee took him.'

Fidelma smiled thinly. 'Do you really believe that?'

'I heard —'

'Are you trying to protect Blinne?' Fidelma snapped.

Bláth flushed.

'Tell me about Tadhg,' Fidelma prompted, again sharply, so that the girl would not have time to collect her thoughts.

'You know…?' Bláth began and then snapped her mouth shut.

'Did this unhappiness begin when Tadhg returned to the village?'

Bláth hung her head. 'I believe that they were meeting regularly in the woods.'

'I think that you believe a little more than that,' Fidelma said dryly. 'You think that Tadhg and Blinne plotted to kill Ernán.'

'No!' Bláth's face was crimson. 'There was no reason. If things became so unbearable, Blinne could have sought a divorce.'

'True enough, but there was the farmstead. If Blinne divorced

Ernán, she would lose it.'

Bláth sniffed. 'You know the laws of inheritance as well as I do. Land cannot pass to a female heir if there are male heirs.'

'But in Ernán's case, there were no male heirs. The land, the farmstead, would go to the *banchomarba*, the female heir.'

Bláth suddenly gave a deep sigh of resignation. 'I suspected something like this might happen,' she confessed dolefully.

'And you invented the story of the Banshee to throw people off the scent?' queried Fidelma.

Bláth nodded. 'I love my sister.'

'Why not claim an attack by a wolf? That would be more feasible.'

'Anyone would realise the wound in Ernán's throat was not the bite of a wolf. Questions would be asked of Blinne and…'

'Questions are now being asked.'

'But only by you. Brother Abán was satisfied and people here would not question the old ways.'

'The old ways.' Fidelma echoed the words thoughtfully.

The girl looked nervously at Fidelma.

'I suppose that you intend to have Blinne and Tadhg arrested?'

'Tonight is the funeral of Ernán. We will see after that.'

'You have some doubts still?'

Fidelma smiled sadly. 'We will see,' she said. 'I would like a word alone with your sister.'

Bláth nodded towards the farmstead. 'I forgot something at my uncle's mill. You'll find Blinne at the farmhouse.'

The girl left Fidelma and continued up the path to the mill while Fidelma went on to the farmhouse. As she approached, she heard Blinne's voice raised in agitation.

'It's not true, I tell you. Why do you bother me so?'

Fidelma halted at the corner of a building. In the farmyard she saw Tadhg confronting the girl. Blinne looked distracted.

'The *dálaigh* already suspects,' Tadhg was saying.

'There is nothing to suspect.'

'It was obvious that Ernán was murdered, killed by a human hand. Obvious that Bláth was covering up with some story about a Banshee. It did not fool me, nor will it fool this woman. I know you hated Ernán. I know it is me that you really loved. But surely there was no need to kill him? We could have eloped and you could have divorced him.'

Blinne was shaking her head in bewilderment. 'I don't know what you are saying. How can you say this…?'

'I know. Do not try to fool me. I know how you felt. The important thing is to flee from this place before the *dálaigh* can find the evidence. I can forgive you because I have loved you since you were a child. Come, let us take the horses and go now. We can let Bláth know where we have gone later. She can send us some money afterwards. I am sure the *dálaigh* suspects and will be here soon enough.'

With a thin smile, Fidelma stepped from behind the building. 'Sooner than you think, Tadhg,' she said.

The young man wheeled round and his hand went to the knife at his belt.

'Don't make it worse for yourself than it already is,' snapped Fidelma.

Tadhg hesitated a fraction and let his hand drop, his shoulders slumping in resignation.

Blinne was gazing at them in bewilderment. 'I don't understand this.'

Fidelma glanced at her sadly and then at Tadhg. 'Perhaps we can illuminate the situation?'

Blinne's eyes suddenly widened. 'Tadhg claims that he has always loved me. When he came back from Finnan's Height he would waylay and annoy me like a sick dog, mooning after me. I told him that I didn't love him. Is it…it cannot be…did he…did he kill…?'

Tadhg looked at her in anguish. 'You cannot reject me so, Blinne. Don't try to lay the blame for Ernán's death on me. I know you pretended that you did not love me in public, but I had your messages. I know the truth. I told you to elope with me.' His voice rose like a wailing child.

Blinne turned to Fidelma. 'I have no idea what he is saying. Make him stop. I cannot stand it.'

Fidelma was looking at Tadhg. 'You say you had messages from

Blinne? Written messages?'

He shook his head. 'Verbal, but from an unimpeachable source. They were genuine, right enough, and now she denies me and tries to blame me for what has happened...'

Fidelma held up her hand to silence him. 'I think I know who gave you those messages,' she said.

After the burial of Ernán, Fidelma sat on the opposite side of the fire to Brother Abán in the tiny stone house next to the chapel. They were sipping mulled wine. 'A sad story,' sighed Brother Abán. 'When you have seen someone born and grow up, it is sad to see them take a human life for no better reason than greed and envy.'

'Yet greed and envy are among the great motivations for murder, Brother.'

'What made you suspect Bláth?'

'Had she said that she heard the Banshee wail once, it might have been more credible because she had a witness in her uncle who heard the wail. All those with whom I spoke, who had claimed to have heard it, said they heard it once, like Glass did, on the morning of Ernán's killing. The so-called Banshee only wailed once. It was an afterthought of Bláth's once she had killed her brother-in-law.'

'You mean that she was the one wailing?'

'I was sure of it when I heard hat she had a good voice and, moreover, knew the *caoine*, the keening, the lament for the dead. I have heard the *caoine* and know it would have been only a small step from producing that terrible sound to producing the wail associated with a Banshee.'

'But then she claimed she had done so to lay a false trail away from her sister. Why did you not believe that?'

'I had already been alerted that all was not well, for when I asked Blinne about her sleep, I found that she had not even awoken when Ernán rose in the morning. She slept oblivious to the world and woke in a befuddled state. She was nauseous and had a headache. Blinne admitted that both she and Bláth knew all about herbal remedies and could mix a potion to ensure sleep. Bláth had given her sister a strong sleeping draught so that she would not wake up.

Only on the third night did an opportunity present itself by which she killed Ernán.

'Her intention all along was to lay the blame at her sister's door, but she had to be very careful about it. She had been planning this for some time. She knew that Tadhg was besotted by Blinne. She began to tell Tadhg an invented story about how Blinne and Ernán did not get on. She told Tadhg that Blinne was really in love with him but could not admit it in public. She hoped that Tadhg would tell someone and thus sow the seeds about Blinne's possible motive for murder.'

Brother Abán shook his head sadly. 'You are describing a devious mind.'

'One must have a clever but disturbed mind to set out to paint another guilty for one's own acts. Bláth had both.'

'But what I do not understand is why – why did she do this?'

'The oldest motives in the world – as we have said – greed and envy.'

'How so?'

'She knew that Ernán had no male heirs and so on his death his land, under the law of the *banchomarba*, would go to to Blinne. And Bláth stood as Blinne's *banchomarba*. Once Blinne was convicted of her husband's death, she would lose that right and so the farm and land would come to Bláth, making her a rich woman.'

Fidelma put down her empty glass and rose.

'The moon is up. I shall use its light to return to Cashel.'

'You will not stay until dawn? Night is fraught with dangers.'

'Only of our making. Night is when things come alive; it is the mother of counsels. My mentor, Brehon Morann, says that the dead of night is when wisdom ascends with the stars to the zenith of thought and all things are seen. Night is the quiet time for contemplation.'

They stood on the threshold of Brother Abán's house. Fidelma's horse had been brought to the door. Just as Fidelma was about to mount, a strange, eerie wailing sound echoed out of the valley. It rose, shrill and clear against the night sky, rose and ended abruptly, rose again and this time died away. It was like the *caoine*.

Brother Abán crossed himself. 'The Banshee!' he whispered.

Fidelma smiled. 'To each their own interpretation. I hear only the lonely cry of a wolf searching for a mate. Yet I will concede that for each act there is a consequence. Bláth conjured the Banshee to cover her crime and perhaps the Banshee is having the last word.'

She mounted her horse, raised her hand in salute, and turned along the moonlit road towards Cashel.

Ken Bruen
Fade to…Brooklyn

Only the Dead Know Brooklyn.

Man, isn't that a hell of a title. I love that. Pity it's been used, it's a novel by Thomas Boyle. I read it years ago when the idea of moving to Brooklyn began to seriously appeal. Don't get me wrong, I'm going, got a Gladstone bag packed. Just the essentials, a few nice *shoirts*. See, I'm learning Brooklynese, and it's not as easy a language as the movies would lead you to believe. I've had this notion for so long now, it's an *idée fixe*. Like the touch of French? I'm no dumbass, I've learned stuff, not all of it kosher. I don't have a whole lot of the frog lingo, so I've got to like, spare it. Trot it out when the special occasion warrants. Say you want to impress a broad, you hit her with a flower and some shit in French, she's already got her knickers off. OK, that's a bit crude but you get the drift.

I'm hiding out in an apartment in Salthill. Yeah, yeah, you're thinking…but isn't that, like, in Galway, Ireland? I like a challenge.

Phew-oh, I got me one right here. If only I hadn't shot that Polack, but he got right in my face, you hear what I'm saying? So he wasn't Polish, but I want to accustom myself to speaking American and if I don't practise, I'm going to be in some Italian joint and sounding Mick. How the hell can you ask for linguini, fried calamari, cut spaghetti alla chitarra, ravioli, scallops with a heavy sauce, and my absolute favourite in terms of pronunciation, fresh gnocchi, in any accent other than Brooklyn? It wouldn't fly. The apartment is real fine, huge window looking out over Galway Bay, a storm is coming in from the east, and the waves are lashing over the prom. I love the ferocity, makes me yearn, makes me feel like I'm a player. I don't know how long this place is safe. Sean is due to call and put the heart crossways in me. I have the cell close by. We call them *mobiles* – doesn't, if you'll pardon the pun, have the same ring. And the Sig Sauer, nine mil, holds fifteen rounds. I jacked a fresh one in there first thing this morning and racked the slide, sounds like reassurance. I'm cranked, ready to rock 'n' roll. Sean is a header, a real headbanger. He's from South Armagh, they grow up shooting at helicopters, bandit country, and those fuckers are afraid of nothing. I mean, if you have the British Army kicking in your door at four in the morning and calling you a Fenian bastard, you grow up fast and you grow up fierce.

I was doing a stretch in Portlaoise, where they keep the Republican guys. They are seriously chilled. Even the wardens gave them space. And, of course, most of the wardens, they have Republican sympathies. I got to hang with them as I had a rep for armed robbery, not a very impressive rep or I wouldn't have been doing bird. Sean and I got tight and after release, he came to Galway for a break and he's been here two years. He is one crazy gumba. We had a sweetheart deal, no big design – like they say in twelve-step programs, we kept it simple. Post offices, that's what we hit. Not the major ones but the small outfits on the outskirts of town. Forget banks, they've got CCTV and worse, the army does guard detail. Who needs that heat?

Like this.

We'd drive to a village, put on the balaclavas, get the shooters out, and go in loud and lethal, shouting, 'Get the fuck down, this is a robbery, give us the fucking money!'

I let Sean do the shouting, as his Northern accent sent its own message. We'd be out of there in three minutes, tops. We never hit the payload, just nice, respectable, tidy sums, but you do enough of them, it begins to mount. We didn't flash the proceeds, kept a low profile. I was saving for Brooklyn, my new life, and Sean, well, he had commitments up north. I'd figured on another five jobs, I was outa there. Had my new ID secured, the money deposited in an English bank, and was working on my American.

Sean didn't get it, would say, 'I don't get it.'

He meant my whole American love affair. Especially Brooklyn. We'd been downing creamy pints one night, followed by shots of Bushmills, feeling mellow, and I told him of my grand design. We were in Oranmore, a small village outside Galway, lovely old pub, log fire and traditional music from a band in the corner, bodhrans, accordions, tin whistles, spoons and they were doing a set of jigs and reels that would put fire in the belly of a corpse. I'd a nice buzz building, we'd done a job three days before and it netted a solid result. I sank half my pint, wiped the froth off my lip, and said, 'Ah, man, Fulton Ferry District, the Brooklyn Bridge, Prospect Park, Cobble Hill, Park Slope, Bed-Stuy, Bensonhurst, Bay Ridge, Coney Island.'

These names were like a mantra to me, prayers I never tired of uttering, and I got carried away, let the sheer exuberance show. Big mistake, never let your wants out, especially to a Northerner, those mothers thrive on knowing where you're at. I should have heeded the signs – he'd gone quiet, and a quiet psycho is a fearsome animal. On I went like a dizzy teenager, saying, 'I figure I'll get me a place on Atlantic Avenue and, you know, blend.'

I was flying, seeing the dream, high on it, and he leaned over, said in a whisper, 'I never heard such bollix in me life.'

Like slapping me in the tush, cold water in my face. I knew he was heavy, meaning he was carrying, probably a Browning, his gun of choice, and that occurred to me as I registered the mania in his eyes. 'Course, Sean was always packing – when you were as paranoid as him, it came with the territory. He'd always said, 'I ain't doing no more time, the cunts will have to take me down.'

I believed him.

The band were doing that beautiful, 'O'Carolan's Lament'…the saddest music I know, and it seemed appropriate as he rubbished my dream, when he said, 'Cop on, see that band over there, that's your heritage, not some Yank bullshit. You can't turn your back on your birthright. I'd see you dead first, and hey, what's with this fucking Yank accent you trot out sometimes?'

I knew I'd probably have to kill the cocksucker, and the way I was feeling, it would be a goddamm pleasure.

Clip
Whack
Pop
Burn

All the great terms the Americans have for putting your lights out.

Sean ordered a fresh batch of drinks, pints and chasers, and the barman, bringing them over, said, 'A grand night for it.'

I thought, little do you know.

Sean, raising his glass, clinked mine, said, 'Forget that nonsense, we have a lot of work to do. There's going to be an escalation in our operation.'

I touched his glass, walloped in the Bush, felt it burn my stomach, and wanted to say, *'Boilermakers, that's what they call it. You get your shot, sink the glass in the beer, and put a Lucky in your mouth, crank it with a Zippo, one that has the logo, "First Airborne".'*

What I said was, 'God bless the work.'

And got the look from him, supposed to strike fear in my gut. He asked, 'You fucking with me, son?'

Son...the condescending prick, I was five years older, more probably. I raised my hands, palms out, said, 'Would I do that? I mean, come on.'

Sean had the appearance of a starved greyhound, all sinewy and furtive. He didn't take drugs, as the Organisation frowned on it, but man, he was wired, fuelled on a mix of hatred and ferocity. He belonged to the darkness and had lived there so long, he didn't even know light existed anymore. He was the personification of the maxim, *retaliate first*, always on the alert. His eyes bored into mine and he said, 'Just you remember that.'

Then he was up, asking the band for a request. I was pretty sure I could take him. As long as his back was turned and preferably if he was asleep. You don't ever want the likes of those to know you're coming. They live with the expectation of somebody coming every day, so I'd act the dumb fuck he was treating me as. The band launched into 'The Men Behind the Wire'. Sean came back, a shit-eating grin in place, and as the opening lines began, *'Armoured cars and tanks and guns...'* he joined with, *'Come and take away our sons...'* Leaned over, punched my shoulder, said, 'Come on, join me.'

I did, sounding almost like I meant it.

Maybe he's found out by now dat he'll neveh live long enough to know duh whole of Brooklyn. It'd take a lifetime to know Brooklyn t'roo an' t'roo. An' even den, yuh wouldn't know it at all.

Thomas Boyle said that in *Only the Dead Know Brooklyn.*

I'd never been out of Ireland but I was getting to know Brooklyn. I had a pretty good notion of it. In my bedroom there is a street map, place names heavily underlined in red. I've pored over it a hundred times, and with absolute joy. Using my finger, I'd take a few steps to the corner of Fulton and Flatbush, check the border between Downtown and Fort Greene, I'd glance at Brooklyn's tallest building, the Williamsburg Savings Bank, smile at the idea of taking it down, but I'd be a citizen then, running a small pastry shop, specialising in *babka*, the Polish cake. I learnt that from *Seinfeld*. Then maybe stroll on Nassau Street to McCarren Park, heading for the south end to the Russian Church of the Transfiguration, light a candle for the poor fucks whose money I stole.

As well as the books on Brooklyn, I managed to collect over a long period the movies. Got 'em all I think.

Whistling in Brooklyn
It Happened in Brooklyn
The Lords of Flatbush
Sophie's Choice
Moscow on the Hudson

Waited ages for the top two to come on TV, I mean those were made in 1944 and 1942.

Saturday Night Fever?... Bay Ridge, am I right or am I right? *Last Exit to Brooklyn*, book and movie, *yeah, got 'em*. Red Hook, a fairly barren place is...lemme see, give me a second here...Ah, that's easy, *On the Waterfront*.

Writers too, I've done my work.

Boerum Hill? Washington Irving and James Fenimore Cooper lived there. I'm on a roll here, ask me another. Who's buried in Greenwood Cemetery? Too easy, Mae West and Horace Greeley.

When I was in the joint, other guys did weights, did dope, did each other. Me, I read and reread, became a fixture in the library. I didn't get any grief from the other cons. Sean had my back, better than a Rottweiler. What happened was, he'd got in a beef with the guy running the cigarette gig, the most lucrative deal in the place. I heard the guy was carrying a shiv, fixing to gut Sean in the yard. I tipped off Sean only as this guy had come at me in my early days. He was trailer trash, a real bottom-feeder – if it wasn't for the cigs, he'd have been bottom of the food chain. Mainly I didn't like him, he was a nasty fuck, always whining, bitching, and moaning, bellyaching over some crap or other. I hate shivs, they're the weapon of the sneak who hasn't the *cojones* to front it. Sean hadn't said a whole lot when I told him. He nodded, said, 'OK.'

Effusive, yeah?

The shiv guy took a dive from the third tier, broke his back, and the cigarette cartel passed to Sean's crew. From then on, he walked point for me.

Back in the Eighties, a song 'Fade to Grey', blasted from every radio – it launched the movement, 'New Romantics', and guys got to wear eyeliner and shit. You know they always wanted to, but now they could call it art.

Gobshites.

But I liked the song, seemed to sum up my life, those days, everything down the crapper, a life of drab existence as grey as the granite on the bleak, blasted landscape of Connemara. That's when I met Maria.

Lemme tell you straight up, I'm no oil painting. My mother told me, 'Get a personality 'cos you're fairly ugly.'

I think she figured the 'fairly' softened the blow.

It didn't.

Nor was I what you'd call a people person. I didn't have a whole lot of them social skills.

I was at a dance in Seaport, the massive ballroom perched on the corner of the promenade, the Atlantic hurling at it with intent. Now, it's a bingo hall. That night, a showband, eight guys in red blazers, bad hairpieces, with three bugles, drums, trombone, and a whole lot of neck, were massacring 'Satisfaction'. They obviously hated the Stones. Those days, there was a sadistic practice known as 'ladies' choice'.

Jesus.

Pure hell. The guys used it to nip outside and get fortified with shots of Jameson. I was about to join them when I heard, 'Would you like to dance?'

A pretty face, gorgeous smile, and I looked behind me to see whom she meant. This girl gave a lovely laugh, said, 'I mean you.'

Hands down, that is the best second of my life. I haven't had a whole line of them, but it's the pinnacle, the moment when God relented, decided, *'Cut the sucker a little slack.'*

'Course, like all divine gifts, he only meant to fuck with me later. That's OK, I've lived that moment a thousand times. And yeah, you guessed it, she was American…from Brooklyn. I loved her accent, her spirit; hell, I loved *her.* Miracle two, she didn't bolt after the dance, stayed for the next one, 'Fade to Grey'. A slow number, I got to hold her, I was dizzy.

Walked her back to her hotel. I stood with her, trying to prolong the feeling, and she said, 'You're kinda cute.'

Put it on my headstone, it's all that counts. She kissed me briefly on the mouth and agreed to meet me at seven the next evening.

She didn't show.

At 10:30, I went into the hotel, heard she checked out that morning. The clerk, a guy I went to school with, told me her surname, Toscini, and that she was travelling with her mother.

I palmed him a few notes and he let me see the register – the only address was Fulton Street, Brooklyn, New York.

I wrote letter after letter, all came back with *'Return to sender, address unknown'.* Like that dire song.

I began to learn about Brooklyn. I'd find her. Her not showing or leaving a note, it was some awful misunderstanding. Her mother had suddenly decided they were leaving and Maria had no way to contact me. Yeah, had to be that. I made it so. Got to where I could see her pleading, crying with her mother, and being literally dragged away. Yes, like that, I *know.*

Mornings, like a vet, I'd come screaming, sweating outa sleep, going, 'Maria, hon, I'm on my way!'

Shit like that, get you killed in prison. They're not real understanding about screamers, though there's plenty of it.

No more than any other guilt-ridden Catholic Irish guy, I'm not superstitious. But I tell you, the omens, they're…like…there. You just gotta be open to them.

Listen to this: A while ago, there was a horse running at the Curragh. I'm not a gambler but read the sports pages, read them first to show I'm not gay. At 15/1, there was one, Coney Island Red. How could I not? Put a bundle on him, on the nose.

He lost.

See the omen? Maria wouldn't want me gambling, lest I blow the kids' college fund. Over the years, if I was asked about girlfriends, I'd say my girl was nursing in America, and came to believe it. She was caring and ideal for that. 'Course, when the kids arrive, she'll have to give up her career – I wouldn't want my wife working, it's the man's place to do the graft – I know they'll appreciate those old values in Brooklyn.

Sean came to see me about the new plan. He was wearing one of those long coats favoured by shoplifters or rock stars. The collar turned up to give him some edge. I made coffee and he said, 'Nice place you got here.' I sat opposite him and he launched: 'We're going to do the main post office.'

I didn't like the sound of that, said, 'Don't like the sound of that.'

He gave the grin, no relation to warmth or humour, and said, 'It's not about what you like or don't like, money is needed and a lot of it. This Thursday, there is going to be a massive sum there, something to do with the payment of pensions and the bonus due for Social Benefit. It's rare for them to handle such a large amount so we have to act now.'

I went along with it, there wasn't a whole lot of choice, he wasn't asking me, he was delivering orders.

We went in hard and it was playing out as usual, when I took my eye off the crowd, distracted for one second, and that's when the guy came at me, grabbed my gun, and it went off, taking half his face. Then we were out of there, running like demented things, got in the stolen car, then changed vehicles at Tuam and drove back into town, the exact opposite of what would be anticipated. Sean was breathing hard, said, 'You fucked up.'

'Hey, he came at me, it was an accident.'

He gritted his teeth, a raw sound like a nail on glass, said, 'This is going south.'

He was right. The dead man was a cop, in plain clothes, and the heat was on. Sean called me that evening, went, 'You wasted a fucking policeman, there's going to be serious repercussions. I've a meet with my superiors and I'll let you know what's going to happen.'

He slammed down the phone. So I waited, checking my travel arrangements. I'd fly from Shannon to New York and, hell, splurge a little, grab a cab all the way to Brighton Beach, because I liked the sound of it. Then I'd find Maria.

I'd already packed and was trying to decide what movies to bring, when Sean called. 'It's bad.'

'Tell me.'

'We can't have a cop-killer on our hands, the pressure is enormous.'

I took a deep breath, said, 'You've given me up.'

For the first time, he sounded nervous, then, 'I'm giving you a chance, I wasn't even supposed to call you.'

'You're all heart, Sean. So what's the bottom line?'

Deep breath, then, 'They're sending two guys to pick you up, they'll be there in twenty minutes, so get the fuck out and run like hell.'

Curious, I asked, 'And these guys, they're not bringing me to the authorities, are they?'

'You're wasting time, get moving.'

Click.

I've poured a Bush, opened a beer, and am going to have a boilermaker. The Sig is in my lap and I have that song playing, here comes my favourite riff: '*Fade...*'

Perhaps it was the glory of England returning after the grim days of the Great War. Or perhaps it would prove, after all, to be something quite otherwise. It was the day of the first post-war Eton and Harrow match, that annual event, more social than sporting, which in the years up to 1914 had brought together in one place, Lord's cricket ground, almost all the Upper Ten Thousand. There, on the excuse of watching the next generation bat and bowl, as many of them had themselves in past years generation after generation, they had come once more to parade themselves in the sunshine, to assert their status once again. And in the Pavilion and in beflagged tents, dark blue and light, to have luncheon.

Now at the beginning of a new decade all seemed to be as it once had been. Yet before a single ball had been bowled after the lunch interval, murder was to splatter an ugly blot on the fair surface of the day.

At the time that it took place none of the nine or ten thousand spectators, in whose ranks the late conflict had cut such a swathe, knew, of course, that it had happened. It was only in the days succeeding the match that the news of it came to dominate every conversation. During the interval they had, as was the custom in 'the old days', strolled about on the grass in front of the Pavilion, the gentlemen in tall shining silk hats, their womenfolk twirling bright parasols in dresses and hats as elaborate and striking as money could buy, if here and there could be seen a skirt that allowed stockinged calves to be fully in view.

'I had hoped,' the Bishop of Cirencester, the Right Reverend Dr Pelham Rossiter, remarked, catching sight of one young lady so dressed, 'that no such indication of the dreadful decline in the country's morality would be seen here today of all days. But it was, I fear, a hope destined to perish.'

'My dear bishop,' his companion, Wilfred Boultbee, the well-known City solicitor, replied, 'I can see the day when ladies without even hats will be admitted at Lord's, and heaven knows what depravities will go along with that.' His full grey moustache sank to an even lower angle than habitually.

The two of them wandered on, gently digesting their shares of the lobsters and pigeon pies, the salmon mayonnaise and tender lamb that had been provided after the long years of wartime deprivation in all the abundance of the milk-and-honey days of yore. The last bubbles of champagne gently eructated behind their firmly closed lips.

Just a few yards away a rather less elevated conversation was taking place between two other people soon to be caught up in the murder.

'God, what a fearful bore a day like this is,' Julia Hogsnorton, daughter of the Earl, exclaimed to the Hon. Peter Flaxman, immaculate in beautifully brushed tall hat, tailcoat fitted to the twentieth of an inch over broad shoulders, pale spats just visible at the ends of black-and-white striped trousers, thin dark moustache trimmed to a nicety. 'I can't imagine how you can stand it.'

'My dear girl, I stood it for four years before the war, and even enjoyed it then, in a way. Nice to show one is one of the world, you know. So I don't find it impossible to enjoy it all again today. Since the fools with money are prepared to lay it on for me, and those Jewish Scotsmen are prepared to provide me with some cash, I'm happy to take advantage of their kindness. It's better than Flanders fields.'

'Not that you spent much time slogging through the mud there, flinging yourself down in it each time a shell landed. Or not if what you told me one drunken evening was true. An ADC somewhere well behind the lines, wasn't it?'

'Fortunes of war, old girl. Fortunes of war. But, talking of drunken evneings shall we go back to the tent? I seem to remember unopened bottles lurking somewhere in the background.'

'Oh, all right. But it can't go on for ever, you know, this relying on the gods and the moneylenders. A lady begins sometimes to feel uncomfortable in circumstances like that.'

'Well, you'll have to put up with circumstances like that, unless you can suggest a way I can unclasp old Boultbee's tight fists.'

He walked on, at a slightly faster pace than before.

Unpleasant revelations were, too, manifesting themselves now to the older moral couple digesting their luncheon.

'Bishop, excuse me,' Wilfred Boultbee said abruptly. 'I think I really must – Well, I think I should return to the luncheon tent. My soda-mint lozenges. I had them on the table, preparatory to taking one as I customarily do after any meal, but somehow I failed to see them as I left. But now I feel the need, acutely. You know my weakness of old, since we were at school even. A digestion that – how shall I put it? – that frequently fails to digest.'

'I remember. Indeed I do. What was it we called you? Belcher Boultbee. Yes, that was it. Old Belcher Boultbee.'

His richly reverberant episcopal laugh rang out.

But Belcher Boultbee was immune to it. He had suddenly spotted something, or rather someone, yet more irritating to himself than a young woman showing her calves.

'Bishop,' he said, 'let's, for heaven's sake, step out. I see that French fellow's heading back to the tent, chap young Flaxman insisted on bringing to luncheon. I had hoped, once we'd eaten, he would have the decency to remove himself. It seems he has not.'

'I'll step out, if you want, though I must confess I found our foreign friend – What did Flaxman say he was called? The Comte de – de somewhere. I found him agreeable enough.'

'Oh, agreeable,' the City solicitor replied. 'Yes, he's all of that. It's what you might call his stock-in-trade. And, for all that title of his, trade is what he's about. I happen to know rather more about the fellow than he'd like to think I do.'

'Very well, let's get there before him. Perhaps he'll sheer off if he sees us. For myself perhaps I'll take just one more glass of champagne. And you can consume your soda-mint lozenge.'

A more modest version of the episcopal laugh could be heard as they hurried on.

Equally making their slow way towards the tent where they had lunched were the last two members of the party whom the murder was deeply to concern, Peter Flaxman's cousin, Captain Vyvyan Andrews – they were both distantly related to Bishop Rossiter, the host – with his wife, Mary. Their conversation, too, was not as placidly reminiscent of the past days of glory as it might have been.

But they had better reasons for lacking in *joie de vivre*.

'We should never have agreed to come,' Vyvyan Andrews, pale-faced to the point where his fair, once military moustache seemed almost to have vanished away, in his borrowed tailcoat and slightly stain-marked silk hat, was saying in a bitter undertone. 'Never, never. I told you. But you would do it.'

'But, darling, it was because – well, because I hoped it would do you good, cheer you up.'

'Cheer me up. You're pathetic, pathetic. How can you believe all I need is to be cheered up, as if I was having a bad cold, or a bit of a belly-ache? But I'm not sniffling and snuffling. I'm ill. Ill. My whole inside's been gassed out, and I'll never be the same again. Never.'

He came to an abrupt standstill, plunged his hand feverishly into the top pocket of the frayed and ancient tailcoat, pulled out, not a silver cigarette case, but a crumpled packet of gaspers, and fumbled one into his mouth.

His wife, ever alert, opened her handbag, extracted a box of matches, lit one and held it, in both hands for steadiness, to the up-and-down jiggling tip of the cheap cigarette.

Stolidly watching the little scene some dozen yards away, PC Williams thought enviously for a moment of the man who could light up whenever he wanted. On duty, keeping a benevolent eye – an eye, to tell the truth, a good deal more benevolent than that of the Bishop of Cirencester – on the nobility and the gentry strolling in the sunshine, no hope for him of the pleasure of tobacco for many hours to come. Especially since he was also keeping a less benevolent eye on the free seats not much further off where a small number of members of the proletariat, not top-hatted though equipped with squashy low-brimmed headwear, awaited the resumption of play.

But then, taking in how much that feverishly puffed-at cigarette must be meaning to a man with uncontrollably trembling hands and twitching facial muscles, PC Williams abruptly found envy was not at all what he was feeling.

'I can't even hold down a job,' he could make out Captain Andrews' raised voice saying. 'Not even when I manage to get one.

Having to depend on my wife going out to work. Yes, on you working, and working for a pittance. And you talk of cheering me up.'

'Darling, I don't mind going out to work. I'm only glad Mr Boultbee found me something to do in his office.'

'Yes, a piece of charity. From that tight-fisted monster who's our trustee. And what are you there? A filing clerk, a filing clerk, a filing clerk.'

'But, darling, Mr Boultbee – and I know he does treat the family trust as if it was his private fortune, not a penny to be spent from it except under duress – does need someone to file away the documents in that office, and it should be someone who's responsible enough to handle things which could be terribly important. So you can't really say I'm being paid out of charity. You know you can't.'

'All I know is that day after day I feel terrible. I wish to God Jerry had put me out once and for all. Yes, I do.'

He gave his wife, in her sad imitation of the de rigueur extravagant hats and dresses of the strolling ladies of the Upper Ten Thousand, a look that was not far short of being one of hatred.

'Darling,' she said, 'Let's go in and sit down. Perhaps some champagne...'

When PC Williams had safely seen Captain Andrews and his long-suffering wife, closely followed by the Hon. Peter Flaxman with his lady-of-the-moment and the dandified figure of the French count, enter the isolated little pavilion-like tent, from which earlier he had been able all too clearly to hear the clink of china, the popping of corks, he did not hear again, as he had expected, the murmur of smooth conversation and occasional discreet laughter. Instead, there was an ear-piercing shriek and then voices raised in sharp questioning.

A moment later he found himself summoned with a single imperious gesture by Peter Flaxman. And, still helmeted, as he stooped to enter the tent in his turn, he saw Wilfred Boultbee, City solicitor, trustee of the estates of a dozen of the noblest and richest families in Great Britain, frigid moralist, lying slumped across the long-ago cleared lunch table, his right hand clutching a large white table-napkin. At the solicitor's side there was standing, distraught and utterly unbishop-like for all his purple vest and immaculate dog-collar, the Right Reverend Dr Pelham Rossiter.

Williams immediately took charge. He noted names, even those of the caterers. He examined the scene, as much of it as there was to be examined, an empty round table with gilt chairs still more or less in their places, a side table on which there remained four or five bottles of champagne together with a dozen or so of wide-brimmed glasses. He ascertained that Wilfred Boultbee was indeed dead and that near the hand clutching, as he was to say later, 'with demonic strength' that napkin, there was a worn little tin in which there rested four flat white soda-mint lozenges. He suggested that Bishop Rossiter should sit in a chair in the corner.

'You'll be better off resting, your – your Grace,' he said, thereby showing he had taken in at a glance the purple vest. 'It must have come as a shock to you. Quite a shock.'

Then, looking at the deflated, trembling man, he decided that, if ever any evidence untainted by afterthoughts was to be obtained it had better be before the bishop was taken away to recover.

'Sir, your reverence, my lord, could you just tell me what happened? You'd not been in the tent here for as much as a minute – I happened to notice you arriving with – that is, I happened to notice you arriving – before I heard that loud cry, anguished it was, yes, anguished.'

'Very well, I – I'll try.'

He managed to look up.

'I – I – I – He took one of his lozenges, soda-mint lozenges. We'd come back for... Old Belcher for once forgot... He took one from – from that little – that tin he has. And – and – one crunch and – and he gave that terrible cry and was dead. I – I know very well when a soul has gone to the Great Father of us all. My sad task, clergyman... Often at the bedside...'

'Thank you, your Rev— Grace, my Lord. That was most helpful.'

PC Williams consulted the big silver watch from his pocket,

pulled out his notebook, wrote ponderously for a little. Then, stepping to the door of the tent, but not a foot further, he blew his whistle to call for assistance.

So it was that at noon next day Detective Inspector Thompson, shrewd-faced, grey-haired, upright, found himself standing in front of the Commissioner of the Metropolitan Police, summoned to give an account of his investigation of an affair all but dominating that morning's newspapers from the stately *Morning Post* down.

'I'm afraid it's going to be a nasty business, sir,' he said, 'Baffling, the *Daily Mail* called it.'

'I dare say it did, Inspector. But you're a Scotland Yard officer and we are not baffled at Scotland Yard. I require you to bring the matter to a conclusion in the shortest possible time. Damn it, man, from what I understand the possible suspects inside the locked gates of Lord's cricket ground comprise almost every member of the Upper Ten Thousand, Dukes and Earls and Cabinet Ministers among them. Unless – certainly the best possible outcome – you find your man is some disgruntled person from the free seats.'

'Not any chance of that, sir, I'm sorry to say. The luncheon tent in which the tragedy occurred was under the eye all morning of PC Williams, from the Albany Street station, a man I once had under my command. A thoroughly reliable fellow. If anyone unauthorised entered that tent at any time Williams will have seen them. I can promise you that.'

The commissioner puffed out a huge sigh of relief.

'Well, that would seem to eliminate the majority of the spectators,' he said. 'The Cabinet Ministers along with the riff-raff from the free seats.'

He sat in thought for a few moments. Then looked up, eyes bright with hope.

'The waiters,' he exclaimed. 'There'll have been two or three of them at least in that tent, and you get some pretty dubious characters among such people nowadays with so many unemployed about, a good many of them resentful and undisciplined.'

'Looking into them was one of my first tasks, sir. And I can say with assurance that both of them – they numbered only two, as a matter of fact – have been vouched for. Elderly men, in service with the catering firm in question from before the war and too old to have been called to the colours.'

The commissioner, who was in full uniform, picked up his leather-covered swagger-stick from the desk in front of him, appeared to give it a close scrutiny and then replaced it.

'Tell me, Inspector,' he said. 'Have I got the situation right? Mr Boultbee died as the result of – ha – ingesting what appeared to be a common soda-mint lozenge – good God, I take the things myself on occasion – but which had been treated with a poison. Do we yet know what particular substance it was? Eh?'

'No, sir, we don't. None of the four remaining mints in the tin have proved to be other than what they ought to be, and – and we shan't know precisely what was in the gentleman's stomach until further tests have been carried out. But, as you will know, sir, it is by no means impossible for a determined murderer to get hold of what they need. A visit to some chemist's shop at a distance, a false signature in the Poisons Book, it's altogether too easy.'

'Yes. Very well, Inspector. I suppose our man... Unless, by God, it's a woman. Poison's a woman's weapon, you know. There were ladies present, weren't there?'

'Yes, sir. Miss Julia Hogsnorton, younger daughter of Earl Hogsnorton —'

'Well, I don't believe... No, perhaps we should bear that young lady in mind. Now I come to think of it, I've heard she's rather wild like a lot of young women these days. What they're calling the post-war generation. But who was the other lady there?'

'Mrs Mary Andrews, sir, wife of Captain Vyvyan Andrews, who was also present of course.'

'Hm. Anything known, eh?'

'No, sir. A thoroughly respectable lady, sir. However, there is one circumstance that may be relevant.'

'Well, let's hear, man. Let's hear it.'

'Mrs Andrews is employed in the office of Mr Boultbee, sir. She works as a filing clerk. Something of a sinecure post, sir, I've gathered. Captain Andrews is one of the casualties of the War, sir, a victim, as I understand from his doctor, of neurasthenia arising from his experiences in the trenches and no man's land.'

'Hm. You seem to have covered a good deal of ground in the last twenty-four hours, Inspector.'

For a moment the Commissioner looked at his comparatively junior officer with an air of interest.

But it was for a moment only.

'Very well. So much for the female element. Species more deadly than the male, eh? Rudyard Kipling said that somewhere just last year. We shouldn't forget it. But who were the gentlemen present at the time?'

'Well, sir, there is, I suppose, the Bishop of Cirencester...'

'Ha. Bit of an awkward thing here. I know Rossiter pretty well. First met him, as a matter of fact, on the day of an Eton and Harrow match long ago. He was playing for Eton, a pretty fair bat, and I was, of course, an Harrovian. And, by golly, I took his wicket. Clean bowled him.'

Inspector Thompson watched the Commissioner of the Metropolitan Police chuckling.

'I think, sir,' he said eventually, 'that the Bishop can be safely discounted. He did, of course, according to PC Williams's very thorough evidence, go into the empty tent with Mr Boultbee. But it was apparent to Williams, from the loud cry of agony he heard from where he was stationed not far away, that the poisoning occurred almost as soon as the two of them had entered. And the Bishop was certainly in a state of almost total collapse when Williams saw him immediately afterwards.'

'Very well, I can take it then I shan't have to bowl him out again.'

'No, sir. I don't think we will need to interview him further. He returned, with his chaplain, to Cirencester, by the first possible train and there took to his bed at the palace.'

'Ha, poor old Rossy, bowled over if not bowled out, eh? But let's get on with it Inspector. Let's get on with it. We neither of us have time to spare today. So have you found out anything about the remaining gentlemen?'

'Yes, sir. I have. If we're to go by motive alone, there is a good deal of suspicion attaching to the Hon. Mr Peter Flaxman. And with the confusion there was in the tents as they all left after lunch, which my inquiries have shown must have been when the poisoned lozenge must have somehow been put there for Mr Boultbee to take, it looks as if we may well have to rely simply on what motives the – er – suspects might have.'

'Young Flaxman, eh? Then spit it out, Inspector, spit it out. May as well hear the worst.'

'Mr Flaxman is a gentleman of limited means, sir, but considerable expectations, as I learnt from the late Mr Boultbee's junior partner. It seems Mr Boultbee was one of the trustees of a considerable fund which will come to the two beneficiaries, the cousins Peter Flaxman and Vyvyan Andrews, only when they attain the age of thirty. Neither will, in fact, do that for some five years yet.'

'Ha, the root of all evil.'

'Yes, sir. So we are told. And at Mr Boultbee's office I managed to gather that both gentlemen have applied since the Armistice for advances on their expectations, something which their trustees are permitted to make. However, it seems the three other trustees relied entirely on the advice of the late Mr Boultbee. And that advice has consistently been that no disbursements should be made.'

'I hope, Inspector, that you brought no improper pressure on to Mr Boultbee's junior partner. You seem to have acquired a good deal of information which I should have thought was confidential.'

Inspector Thompson looked steadily at the Commissioner

'No, sir,' he said, 'there could, of course, be no question of that.'

'I'm glad to hear it. So we appear to have arrived at a point where two of the people, and perhaps their ladies, who could have placed a poisoned lozenge into the cachou-box in which Mr Boultbee kept his supply of soda-mints were —'

'Excuse me, sir,' Inspector Thompson broke in, with not a little daring, 'but it is as well perhaps to have things entirely clear. Mr Boultbee, so his partner happened to mention, lost several years ago the silver box he carried his lozenges in, and – his partner indicated that he had, what shall I say, a certain mean streak – he refused to replace it but used instead a battered little tobacconist's tin that had once contained snuff. My informant indicated that people used to joke about that.'

'Rather poor taste on his part, Inspector, if I may venture to say so.'

'Perhaps it was, sir. However, it may be helpful to know about it if it comes down to trying to discover exactly what happened at that table when the lunch party set off for a stroll.'

'No. No, wait, Inspector, you've forgotten something. Important, you know, to keep every thread in your hands.'

A little frown gave added force to the rebuke.

'The French gentleman, sir? The Conte de Charvey. I have made enquiries about him. It seems he was a slight acquaintance of Mr Flaxman's and had put him in the position of being unable to withhold an invitation to the match.'

'Had he indeed? A trifle suspicious that, eh? French fellow wanting to watch cricket. Unless, of course, he's one of those froggies who seem to think the game is one of the secrets of British power. As I suppose it is, come to think of it.'

'Yes, sir. However, I also learn from the late Mr Boultbee's partner that Mr Boultbee knew something to the Count's disadvantage. I have had a word with Fraud, and apparently they've been keeping a sharp eye on him.'

'Fraud, eh? Why haven't they informed me that a character of this sort has come to our shores? Eh? Eh?'

'I'm sure I couldn't say, sir.'

'No. I dare say not. But... But do you think the fellow may have needed to get rid of someone who had come to learn too much about some underhand business of his? That sort of thing?'

'It always could be, sir. But one ought perhaps to bear in mind that the murderer would need to have known Mr Boultbee's habit of taking one of those soda-mint lozenges shortly after his every meal. But while all of the other four persons under consideration might well have been aware of that, it's scarcely likely that a stranger such as the Count would be.'

'Yes. Yes, Inspector, I take your point. Good man, good man. Yet, let me remind you, we shouldn't put our French bad hat altogether out of the picture.'

'No, sir. No, of course not. I will bear him in mind throughout the investigation.'

'Hah. Yes. Yes, Inspector, you speak blithely enough of *throughout the investigation*, but let me tell you once again: this is a matter which has got to be cleared up in the very shortest of times. All right, this PC Wilkins, Watson, whatever, whom you seem to have such faith in, would appear, thank goodness, to have eliminated the hundreds of extremely distinguished persons who might conceivably have committed this appalling crime. But nevertheless the yellow press will, if they get half a chance, hope to draw public attention to – well, to even the highest in the land. So action, Inspector, action.'

'Yes, sir.'

When Inspector Thompson left the Commissioner's office he had little hope that any amount of action would see the case concluded quickly enough to suit his chief. But, in the end, action proved to be what was needed. Directed more or less to go back to Lord's, where by night and day a police watch had been kept, he made his way into the luncheon tent, everything there still preserved just as it had been when PC Williams had entered. Though convinced that it was only in the motives of the four people most likely to have committed the deed that the solution must lie, he nevertheless stood looking down at the stained white cloth of the table. A blank sheet.

Or was it?

Wasn't there something there that somehow differed from Williams' minutely accurate description?

For more than a few minutes he stood there puzzling. What was it that seemed somehow wrong?

Is it, he asked himself, the mere absence of that little tobacconist's snuff tin from which the one deadly lozenge had, by chance surely, been plucked by that tight-fisted City solicitor? Nothing more than that? The tin itself, of course, had been sent to the fingerprint bureau at the Yard, and within an hour a report had come back to say that someone had scrupulously wiped the little shabby article clean of any possible clue as to who had flipped it open, taken out one lozenge – Wilfred Boultbee, so careful of other people's money, was very likely to have kept count of his supply of the miraculous means of combating the intolerable pangs of indigestion – and added that one deadly other.

No help there.

And then... Then it came to him. What was missing from the scene as he looked at it now was an object PC Williams had described well, if with a touch of honest Welsh hyperbole. In the dead man's hand, he had said, there had been a soiled white table-napkin clutched *with demonic force*. It had been, almost certainly, taken away with the body when it had gone for medical examination. But why had it been there on the table at all? It must have been left when the guests had risen from their places to go and stroll outside.

But – could this be what had happened? – had someone still had it, perhaps in their hand, after all the debris had been cleared away by the waiters? And had they then let it fall on the table in such a way that it covered up Wilfred Boultbee's little battered old tobacconist's tin? That could, if what Williams quoted me from his notebook had it right, have accounted for the unusual circumstance of the dead man forgetting to take a lozenge immediately after eating.

But which of them was it? Who had picked up that napkin, dropped it so as to hide the little tin, and then, of course, subtly urged Wilfred Boultbee out of the tent before he had gathered himself together enough to remember he had not taken a lozenge?

Well, if that is what happened, one thing is clear. It's very unlikely to have been one of the women. I can hardly see either of them – I can hardly see any lady – taking that rigid man by the arm and laughingly leading him off. So it must come down to one of the two cousins, each with motive enough. Because, as I tried to make clear to the Commissioner, the French count, whatever he's up to in England, could not possibly have known about Wilfred Boultbee's poor digestion. So which of the two is it? Which?

Captain Andrews, the ruined man? The victim of the carnage which the civilised nations of the world have inflicted on one another? A man, you might say, with nothing to live for. Had he, as a last wild bid to acquire a decent income, murdered his tight-fisted, implacable trustee? A bid to free his wife from the daily toil of grubbing together enough to make their lives possible? Easy enough to feel sympathy for a man who had done more than give his life for his country, a soldier who had given all that made life bearable, had been left with the prospect of years ahead carrying round with him the body that the war had gassed out? Yet, if he has been driven to the last extreme of murder, he has to be brought to trial for it. Let judge and jury find what extenuating factors they can.

So, the Hon. Peter Flaxman? What about that typical example of the new, pleasure-devoted, careless world that seems to have come into being in the wake of all the horrors and deprivations of the years between 1914 and 1918? Is he a new breed, and a by no means pleasant one? A breed of self-seeking, hedonistic young people, uncaring of all below them in the social hierarchy? And is that, when you come down to it, what brought about the demise of a man altogether opposed to such a way of life? An old man who, you could say, represented all the virtues, all the strict morality, of an age on the verge of extinction?

Which of those two men is it – all but certain that one or the other of them put that deadly lozenge into Wilfred Boultbee's little tin – who in truth conceived that deadly scheme? Isn't the balance, however unfairly it might seem, equal between them? Each with the same obvious motive, each with opportunity enough, each offered the same easy means of finding a solution to their problems?

So which?

And only one answer. Startlingly plain, once one ceases to look at the human complexities and turns a steady gaze on the simple facts.

Captain Andrews, poor devil, has hands that constantly tremble, shake to the point, as Williams vividly recalled for me, of hardly being able even to hold a cigarette when he desperately wants to inhale the tranquillising smoke. I cannot for a moment see Captain Andrews carrying out that little necessary piece of legerdemain under the starched white table-napkin.

So, if it isn't the one, it must be the other. Simple. Appallingly simple.

Right, I'm off to see the Hon. Peter Flaxman in his rooms in the Albany.

Or do they insist you have to say just *Albany*?

Whichever. It's there that I'll arrest the murderer of Mr Wilfred Boultbee, City solicitor, repository of a thousand secrets and tight-fisted representative of an age that's going, going, gone.

John Harvey
Drummer Unknown

There's a photograph taken on stage at Club Eleven, early 1950 or perhaps late '49, the bare bulbs above the stage picking out the musicians' faces like a still from a movie. Ronnie Scott on tenor sax, sharp in white shirt and knotted tie; Dennis Rose with his trumpet aimed toward the floor, skinny, suited, a hurt sardonic look in his eyes; to the left of the picture, Spike Robinson, on shore leave from the US Navy, a kid of nineteen or twenty, plays a tarnished silver alto. Behind them Tommy Pollard's white shirt shines out from the piano, and Lennie Bush, staring into space, stands with his double bass. At the extreme right, the drummer has turned his head just as the photo has been taken, one half of his polka-dot bow tie in focus but the face lost in a blur of movement. The caption underneath, reads DRUMMER UNKNOWN.

That's me: drummer unknown.

Or was, back then.

In ten years a lot of things have changed. In the wake of a well-publicised drug raid, Club Eleven closed down; the only charges were for possession of cannabis, but already there was heroin, cocaine.

Ronnie Scott opened his own club in a basement in Chinatown; Spike Robinson sailed back across the ocean to a life as an engineer; and Dennis Rose sank deeper into the sidelines, an almost voluntary recluse. Then, of course, there was rock 'n' roll. Bill Haley's 'Rock Around the Clock' at number one for Christmas 1955, and the following year Tony Crombie, whose drum stool I'd been keeping warm that evening at Club Eleven, had kick-started the British bandwagon with his Rockets: grown men who certainly knew better cavorting on stage in blazers while shouting, 'I'm gonna teach you to rock,' to the accompaniment of a honking sax. Well, it paid the rent.

And me?

I forget now, did I mention heroin?

I'm not usually one to cast blame, but after the influx of Americans during the last years of the war, hard drugs were always part of the scene. Especially once trips to New York to see the greats on Fifty-Second Street had confirmed their widespread use.

Rumour had it that Bird and Diz and Monk changed the language of jazz the way they did – the complex chords, the flattened fifths, the extremes – to make it impossible for the average white musician to play. If that was true, well, after an apprenticeship in strict tempo palais bands and pickup groups that tinkered with Dixieland, they came close to succeeding where I was concerned. And it was true, the drugs – some drugs – helped: helped you to stay awake, alert, keep up. Helped you to play an array of shifting counter rhythms, left hand and both feet working independently, while the right hand drove the pulse along the top cymbal for all it was worth. Except that in my case, after a while, it wasn't the drumming that mattered. It was just the drugs.

In a matter of months I progressed, if that's the word, from chewing the inside of Benzedrine inhalers to injecting heroin into the vein. And for my education in this department I had Foxy Palmer to thank. Or blame.

I'd first met Foxy at the Bouillabaisse, a Soho drinking club frequented by mainly black US servicemen and newly resident West Indians, of whom Foxy was one. He was a short, stubby man with a potbelly beneath his extravagantly patterned shorts and a wisp of greying beard. His ears stuck out, foxlike, from the sides of his head. A scaled-down Foxy would have made the perfect garden gnome.

'Hey, white boy!' he hailed me from his seat near the piano. 'You here to play?'

'Maybe.'

'Forgot your horn?'

For an answer, I straightened my arm and let a pair of hickory drumsticks slide down into the palm of my hand.

A bunch of musicians, mostly refugees from some dance-band gig or other, were jamming their way through 'One O'clock Jump', but then a couple of younger guys arrived, and Foxy pulled my arm toward him with a grin and said, 'Here come the heebie-jeebie boys.'

In the shuffle that followed, Tony Crombie claimed his place behind the drums, and after listening to him firing 'I Got Rhythm' at a hundred miles an hour, I slipped my sticks back out of sight.

'So,' Foxy said, planting himself next to me in the gents, 'that Tony, what d'you think?'

'I'm thinking of cutting my arms off just above the wrist.'

Foxy smiled his foxy smile. 'You're interested, I got somethin' less extreme.'

At first I didn't know what he meant.

The Bouillabaisse closed down and reopened as the Fullado. Later there was the Modernaires in Old Compton Street, owned by the gangster Jack Spot. Along with half a hundred other out-of-work musicians, I stood around on Archer Street on Monday afternoons, eager to pick up whatever scraps might come my way: depping at the Orchid Ballroom, Purley, a one-night stand with Ambrose at the Samson and Hercules in Norwich. And later, after shooting up, no longer intimidated or afraid, I'd descend the steps into the smoke of Mac's Rehearsal Rooms where Club Eleven had its home and take my turn at sitting in.

For a time I made an effort to hide the track marks on my arms, but after that I didn't care.

Junkie – when did I first hear the word?

Applied to me, I mean.

It might have been at the Blue Posts, around the corner from the old Feldman Club, an argument with a US airman that began with a spilt pint of beer and escalated from there.

'Goddamn junkie, why the fuck aren't you in uniform?'

I didn't think he wanted to hear about the trumped-up nervous condition a well-paid GP had attested to, thus ensuring my call-up would be deferred. Instead, some pushing and shoving ensued, at the height of which a bottle was broken against the edge of the bar.

Blind luck enabled me to sway clear of the jagged glass as it swung toward my face; luck and sudden rage allowed me to land three punches out of four, the last dropping him to his knees before executing the *coup de grâce*, a swiftly raised knee that caught him underneath the chin and caused him to bite off a sliver of tongue before he slumped, briefly unconscious, to the floor.

As I made my exit, I noticed the thin-faced man sitting close by the door, time enough to think I recognised him from somewhere without being able to put a finger on where that was. Then I was out into the damp November air.

'I hear you takin' up the fight game,' Foxy said with glee, next time I bumped into him. And then: 'I believe you know a friend of mine. Arthur Neville, detective sergeant.'

The thin-faced man leaned forward and held out a hand. 'That little nonsense in the Blue Posts, I liked the way you handled yourself. Impressive.'

I nodded and left it at that.

In the cracked toilet mirror my skin looked like old wax.

'Your pal from CID,' I asked Foxy, 'he OK?'

'Arthur?' Doxy said with a laugh. 'Salt o' the earth, ain't that the truth.'

Probably not, I thought.

He was waiting for me outside, the grey of his raincoat just visible in the soft grey fog that had drifted up from the river. When I turned left he fell into step alongside me, two men taking an evening stroll. Innocent enough.

'Proposition,' Neville said.

I shook my head. 'Hear me out, at least.'

'Sorry, not interested.'

His hand tugged at my sleeve. 'You're carrying, right?'

'Wrong,' I lied.

'You just seen Foxy; you're carrying. No question.'

'So?' The H burning a hole in my inside pocket.

'So you don't want me to search you, haul you in for possession.'

Our voices were muffled by the fog. If Neville knew about Foxy but was allowing him to deal, Foxy had to be paying him off. If what he wanted from me was more back-handers, he had another thing coming.

'What do you want?' I asked.

A woman emerged from a doorway just ahead of us, took one look at Neville, and ducked back in.

'Information,' Neville said.

At the corner he stopped. The fog was thicker here, and I could barely see the far side of the street.

'What kind of information?'

'Musicians. In the clubs. The ones you hang around with. Of course, we know who's using. It would just be confirmation.'

'I'm sorry,' I said, 'you've got the wrong guy.'

Smuts were clinging to my face and hair, and not for the first time that evening I caught myself wondering where I'd left my hat.

Neville stared at me for a long moment, fixing me with gray-blue eyes; his mouth was drawn straight and thin. 'I don't think so,' he said.

I watched him walk, coat collar up, hat brim pulled down, until the fog swallowed him up.

'He's a nasty bastard.' The woman had reappeared and stepped up, almost silently, alongside me. Close to her, I could see she was little more than a girl. Sixteen, seventeen. Her eyes seemed to belong to someone else's face. 'Don't trust him,' she said and shivered. 'He'll hurt you if he can.'

Ethel, I found out her name was later, and she was, in fact, nineteen. She showed me the birth certificate as proof. Ethel Maude Rastrick, born St Pancras Hospital, March 17, 1937. She kept it with a handful of letters and photographs in an old stationery box hidden away inside the chest of drawers in her room. Not the room where she worked, but the room where she lived. I got to see both in time.

But after that first brief meeting in the fog, I didn't see her for several months. No more than I saw hide nor hair of Detective Sergeant Arthur Neville. I'd like to say I forgot them both, though in Neville's case that wouldn't be entirely true.

Somehow I'd talked myself into a gig with a ten-piece band on a tour of second-rank dance halls – Nuneaton, Llandudno, Wakefield, and the like – playing quicksteps and waltzes with the occasional hot number thrown in. The brass players were into booze, but two of the three reeds shared my predilection for something that worked faster on the pulse rate and the brain, and between us, we got by. As long as we turned up on time and played the notes, the leader cast a blind eye.

As a drummer, it was almost the last regular work I had. The same month Bulganin and Khrushchev visited Britain, the spring of '56.

On my second night back in the smoke, I met Ethel again.

I'd gone looking for Foxy, of course, looking to score, but to my bewilderment, Foxy hadn't been there. Nobody had seen him in a week or more. Flash Winston was playing piano at the Modernaires, and I sat around for a while until I'd managed to acquire some weed and then moved on.

Ethel's was a face at the window, pale despite the small red bulb and lampshade alongside.

I looked up, and she looked down.

NEW YOUNG MODEL read the card pinned by the door.

When she waved at me I shook my head and turned away.

Tapping on the window, she gestured for me to wait, and moments later I heard her feet upon the stairs. The light over the door was cruel to her face. In the fog I hadn't noticed what no amount of lipstick could hide, the result of an operation, partly successful, to remedy the fissure at the centre of her upper lip.

'Why don't you come up?' she said.

'I haven't got any money.'

'I don't mean business, I mean just, you know, talk.'

Now that I'd noticed, it was difficult not to stare at her mouth. She touched my hand. 'Come on,' she said.

An elderly woman in a floral-print overall sat like somebody's grandmother at the top of the first flight of stairs, and Ethel introduced her as the maid and told me to give her ten shillings.

The room was functional and small: bed, sink, bucket, bedside table. A narrow wardrobe with a mottled mirror stood against the side wall. Hard against the window was the straight-backed chair in which she sat, a copy of yesterday's *Evening News* on the floor nearby.

Now that I was there, she seemed nervous; her hands rose and fell from her sides.

'Have you got anything?' she said, and for an instant I thought she meant johnnies and wanted business after all, but then, when I saw the twitch in her eyes, I knew.

'Only some reefer,' I said.

'Is that all?'

'It was all I could get.'

She sat on the side of the bed, resigned, and I sat with her and rolled a cigarette, and after the first long drag, she relaxed and smiled, her hand moving instinctively to cover the lower half of her face.

'That plainclothes bloke,' I said. 'Neville. You said not to trust him.'

'Let's not talk about him,' she said. 'Let's talk about you.'

So I lay back with my head resting where so many other heads had rested, on the wall behind the bed, and told her about my mother who had run off with a salesman in home furnishings and started a new family in the Scottish borders, and my father who worked the halls for years as an illusionist and conjurer until he himself had disappeared. And about the moment when, age eleven, I knew I wanted to be a drummer: going to see my father on stage at Collins Music Hall and watching the comedian Max Bacon, previously a dance band drummer, topping the bill. He had this huge, to me, drum kit set up at the centre of the stage, all gold and glittering, and at the climax of his act, played a solo, all crash and rolling tom-toms, with the assistance of the band in the pit.

I loved it.

I wanted to be him.

Not the laughter and the jokes or the showy suit, and not fat like he was, certainly not that, but sitting there behind all those shimmering cymbals and drums, the centre of everything.

'Tell us about yourself, Ethel,' I said after a while.

'Oh,' she said, 'there's nothing to tell.' Her fair, mousy hair hung almost to her shoulders, and she sat with her head angled forward, chin tucked in.

'Aren't you going to get in trouble,' I said, 'spending all this time with me instead of a client?'

She looked toward the door. 'The maid goes home after twelve, and then there's nobody comes round till gone one, sometimes two.'

I presumed she meant her pimp, but I didn't ask.

'Besides,' she said, 'you saw what it's like. It's dead out there.'

She did tell me about her family then. Two sisters and three brothers, all scattered; she and one of her sisters had been fostered out when they were eleven and ten. Her mother worked in a laundry in Dalston, had periods in hospital, times when she couldn't cope. She didn't remember too much about her father, except that he had never held her, never looked at her with anything but distaste. When he was killed towards the end of the war, she'd cried without really knowing what for.

I felt a sort of affinity between us, and for one moment I thought I might reach out my hand, lean across, and kiss her, but I never did. Not then or later. Not even months down the line when she asked me back to the bed-sitter she had near Finsbury Park, a Baby Belling cooker behind a curtain in one corner and the bathroom down the hall. But I did take to stopping by between midnight and one and sharing a little of whatever I had, Ethel's eyes brightening like Christmas if ever it was cocaine.

Foxy was around again, but not as consistently as before. There'd been some falling-out with his suppliers, he implied; whatever arrangements he'd previously enjoyed had been thrown up in the air. And in general the atmosphere had changed: something was clearly going on. Whereas Jack Spot and Albert Dimes had more or less divided the West End between them, Spot lording it over Soho with a certain rough-hewn benevolence, now there were young pretenders coming out of the East End or from abroad, sleek, rapacious, unfeeling, fighting it out among themselves.

Rumour had it Arthur Neville had been demoted to a woodentop and forced to walk the beat in uniform, that he'd been shuffled north to patrol the leafy lanes of Totteridge and Whetstone. More likely, that he'd made detective inspector and was lording it in Brighton. Then one evening in the Blue Posts there he was, the same raincoat and trilby hat, same seat by the door. I'd been round the corner at 100 Oxford Street listening to the Lyttelton Band play 'Creole Serenade' and 'Bad Penny Blues'. Not my kind of thing, really, except he did have Bruce Turner on alto, and Turner had studied in the States with Lennie Tristano, which was more my scene.

I should have walked right on past him and out into the street.

'If you can find your way to the bar without getting into a fight,' he said, 'I could use another pint.'

A favourite refrain of my mother's came to mind: *What did your last servant die of?* I kept it to myself.

'Scotch ale,' Neville said, holding out his empty glass.

I bought a half of bitter for myself and shepherded the drinks back through the crowd.

'So,' Neville said, settling back, 'how's business?'

'Which business is that?'

'I thought you were in the bebop business.'

'Once in a while.'

'Lovely tune that.' Pleased with himself, Neville smiled his thin-lipped smile, then supped some ale. 'The Stardust, isn't it?' he said.

The Stardust had sprung up on the site of the old Cuba Club on Gerrard Street, and an old pal, Vic Farrell, who played piano there, had talked me into a job as doorman. I kept a snare drum and hi-hat behind the bar, and Tommy would let me sit in whenever my hands were steady enough. Which was actually most evenings now. I wasn't clean by a long chalk, but I had it pretty much under control.

'Oscar still running the place, is he?'

Neville had a liking for questions that didn't require an answer. 'What is with you and coons?' Neville said, 'Taste for the fucking exotic?'

Oscar was a half-caste Trinidadian with a bald head and a gold tooth and a jovial 'Hail fellow, well met' sort of manner. He was fronting the place for a couple of Maltese brothers, his name on the licence, their money. The place ran at a loss, it had to, but they were using it to feel their way in, mark out a little territory, stake a claim.

Neville leaned a shade nearer. 'You could do me a favour there. Comings and goings. Who's paying who. Keep me in the picture.'

I set my glass on the window ledge behind me half finished. 'Do your own dirty work,' I said. 'I told you before.'

I got to my feet, and as I did so Neville reached out and grabbed me by the balls and twisted hard. Tears sprang to my eyes.

'That ugly little tart of yours. She's come up light more'n a few times lately. Wouldn't want to see anything happen to her, would you?' He twisted again, and I thought I might faint. 'Would you?'

'No,' I said, not much above a whisper.

'Say what?'

'No.'

'Good boy.' Releasing me, he wiped his fingers down his trouser front. 'You can give her my love, Ethel, when you see her. Though how you can fuck it without a bag over its head beggars belief.'

So I started slipping him scraps of information, nothing serious, nothing I was close to certain he didn't already know. We'd meet in the Posts or the Two Brewers, sometimes Lyon's tea shop in Piccadilly. It kept him at bay for a while, but not for long.

'Stop pullin' my chains,' he said one fine morning, 'and give me something I can fuckin' use.' It was late summer and everything still shining and green.

I thought about it sitting on the steps at the foot of Lower Regent Street, a view clear across the Mall into St James's Park, Horse Guards Parade. Over the next few weeks I fed him rumours a big shipment of heroin would be passing through the club, smuggled in from the Continent. The Maltese brothers, I assured him, would there to supervise delivery.

Neville saw it as his chance for the spotlight. The raid was carried out by no less than a dozen plainclothes officers with as many as twenty uniforms in support. One of Neville's cronies, a crime reporter for the *Express*, was on hand to document proceedings.

Of course, the place was clean. I'd seen to that.

When the law burst through the door and down the stairs, Vic Farrell was playing 'Once in a While' in waltz time, and the atmosphere resembled nothing as much as a vicarage tea party, orderly and sedate.

'Don't say, you little arsewipe,' Neville spluttered, 'I didn't fuckin' warn you.'

For the next forty-eight hours I watched my back, double-checked the locks on the door to my room, took extra care each time I stepped off the kerb and into the street. And then I understood I wasn't the one at risk.

Wouldn't want to see anything happen to her, would you?

She was lying on her bed, wearing just a slip, a pair of slippers on her feet, and at first I thought she was asleep. And then, from the angle of her torso to her head, I realised someone had twisted her neck until it broke.

He'll hurt you if he can: just about the first words Ethel had said to me.

I looked at her for a long time, and then, daft as it sounds, I touched my fingers to her upper lip, surprised at how smooth and cold it felt.

And then I left.

Discreetly as I could, I asked around.

The maid had taken a couple of days off sick; only the usual slow but steady stream of punters had been seen entering the building. Up and down the street, nobody had noticed anything unusual.

SOHO VICE GIRL MURDERED, the headline read.

I traced Ethel's mother from one of her letters, and she promised to come to the funeral, but she never did. I stood alone in a little chapel in Kensal Green, fingers drumming a quiet farewell on the back of the pew. Outside, the first leaves were starting to fall. When it was over I took the tube back to Oxford Circus and met Tom Holland round the corner from the Palladium as arranged.

Holland was young for a detective inspector, no more than thirty-two or -three; something of a high flier, he'd recently transferred from the City of London police to run one of the CID squads at West End Central.

The year before, '55, the *Mail* had run a story about police corruption. Alleging many officers in the West End were on the take. The Met issued a bald denial. Everyone from the commissioner down denied the charge. What evidence existed was discredited or lost. No one was suspended, cautioned, even interviewed. Word was unofficially passed round: be less visible, less greedy.

Holland was the only officer I knew who wasn't snaffling bribes. According to rumour, when a brothel keeper slipped an envelope containing fifty in tens into his pocket, Holland shoved it down his throat and made him eat it.

He was just shy of six foot, I guessed, dark-haired and brown-eyed, and he sat at a table in the rear of the small Italian café, shirtsleeves rolled back, jacket draped across his chair. Early autumn, and it was still warm. The coffee came in those glass cups that were all the rage; three sips and it was gone.

I told him about Neville's involvement with pushers and prostitutes, the percentage he took for protection, for looking the other way. Told him my suspicions concerning Ethel's murder.

Holland listened as if it mattered, his gaze rarely leaving my face.

When I'd finished, he sat a full minute in silence, weighing things over.

'I can't do anything about the girl,' he said. 'Even if Neville did kill her or have her killed, we'd never get any proof. And let's be honest: where she's concerned, nobody gives a toss. But the other stuff, drugs especially. There might be something I can do.'

I thought if I went the right way about it, I could get Foxy to make some kind of statement, off the record, nothing that would come to court, not even close, but it would be a start. Place, times, amounts. And there were others who'd be glad to find a way of doing Neville down, repaying him for all the cash he'd pocketed, the petty cruelties he'd meted out.

'One month,' Holland said, 'then show me what you've got.'

When I held out my hand to shake his, his eyes fixed on my arm. 'And that habit of yours,' he said. 'Kick it now.'

A favourite trick of Neville's, whenever his men raided a club, was to take the musicians who'd been holding aside – and there were usually one or two – and feign sympathy. Working long hours, playing the way you do, stands to reason you need a little something extra, a little pick-me-up. Nudge, nudge, wink, wink. Men of the world. Just hand it over, and we'll say no more about it. Oh, and if you've got a little sweetener for the lads…lovely, lovely.

And ever after, if he walked into a club or bumped into them on the street, he would be into them for another fifty plus whatever they were carrying. Let anyone try saying no, and he was sorted good.

Inside a matter of weeks I talked with two pianists, a drummer, a guitarist, and three sax players – what is it with saxophonists? – who agreed to dish the dirt on Neville if it would get him off their backs. And finally, after a lot of arguing and pleading, I persuaded Foxy to sit down with Holland in an otherwise empty room, neutral territory, and tell him what he knew.

After that, carefully, Holland spoke to a few of Neville's team, officers who were already compromised and eager to protect themselves as best they could. From a distance, he watched Neville himself. Checked, double-checked.

The report he wrote was confidential, and he took it to the new deputy assistant commissioner, one of the few high-ranking bosses he thought he could trust.

It was agreed that going public would generate bad publicity for the force and that should be avoided at all costs. Neville was shunted sideways, somewhere safe, and after several months allowed to retire on a full pension for reasons of ill health.

One of his mutually beneficial contacts had been with a businessman from Nicosia, import and export, and that was where Neville hived off to, counting his money, licking his wounds.

I was at the airport to see him off.

Three and a bit years ago now.

I took Tom Holland's advice and cleaned up my act, the occasional drag at some weed aside. Tom, he's a detective chief inspector now and tipped for higher things. I don't play any more, rarely feel the need. There are a couple of bands I manage – groups, that's what they call them these days – one from Ilford, and one Palmers Green. And I keep myself fit, swim, work out in the gym. One thing a drummer has, even a second-rate ex-drummer like me, is strong wrists, strong hands.

I don't reckon Neville staying in Cyprus forever, can't see it somehow; he'll want to come back to the smoke. And when he does, I'll meet him. Maybe even treat him to a drink. Ask if he remembers Ethel, the way she lay back, twisted on the bed, her broken neck...

I

To Professor Moriarty, she is always *that bitch*.

Irene Adler arrived in our Conduit Street rooms shortly after I undertook to assist my fellow tenant in enterprises of which he was the pre-eminent London specialist. In short, sirrah, *crime*.

The old 'bread and honey' came into it, of course. The professor had me on an honorarium of six thousand pounds per annum. Scarcely enough to make *anyone* put up with Moriarty, actually, but it serviced my prediliction for pursuits the naïve refer to as 'games of chance'. Chronic cash shortage set in early, when *Pater* cut me off without a sou for an indiscretion involving a matched pair of Persian princesses. Libertinage on an heroic scale is my *other* expensive vice. However, I own that the *thrill* of do-baddery attracted me, that blood-running *whoosh* of fright and delight which comes from cocking repeated snooks at every plod, beak and turnkey in the land. When a hunting man has grown bored with bagging tigers, crime can still jangle the nerves and keep up the pecker. Moriarty, frankly bloodless, got *his* jollies in the abstract, plotting felony the way you might fill in a crossword puzzle. I've known him scorn an easy bank raid that would have netted millions and devote weeks to the filching of a tiny item of little worth that happened to be a more challenging snatch.

That morning, the professor was thinking through two problems simultaneously. A portion of his brain was calculating the timings of solar eclipses observable in far-flung regions. Superstitious natives can sometimes be persuaded a white man has power over the sun and needs to be given handy tribal treasures if *bwana sahib* promises to turn the light on again. Bloody good trick, if you can get away with it. The greater part of his attention, however, was devoted to the breeding of wasps.

'Your bee is a law-abiding soul,' he said, in his reedy lecturing voice, 'as reverent to their queen as the clods of England, dedicated to the production of honey for the betterment of all, buzzing about promiscuously pollinating to please addle-minded poets. They only defend themselves at the cost of their lives, for they sting but once. Volumes are devoted to the care of bees, and apiculture exists to exploit their good nature. Wasps do nothing but sting. Persistently venomous, they fly from one assault to the next. Unwelcome everywhere. Thoroughly nasty sorts. We are *not* bees, Moran.'

He smiled, a creepy thing for a man with lips as thin as his. His near-fleshless head moved from side to side. I was reminded of a cobra I chopped into three wriggling sections in the Hindu Kush. I couldn't follow Moriarty's drift, but that was usual. I nodded and hoped he would come eventually to a point. A schoolmaster before taking to villainy, his rambles tended to wind towards some inverted moral.

'Summer will be upon us soon,' he mused, 'the season for picnicking in the park, for tiny fat arms to go bare, for governesses to sit and gossip unveiled, for shopgirls and their beaux to spoon in public. This will be a bumper year for our yellow-and-black-striped friends. My first generation of *polistes pestilentialis* is hatching. The world is divided, Moran, between those who sting and those who are the stingees.'

'And you would be the sting-ers,' shrilled that *voice*.

The American Nightingale had been admitted by Mrs Halifax, the superannuated harlot who kept a brothel on the lower floors. Moriarty had persuaded Mrs H to let us have the flat rent-free. Following the interview at which this matter was arranged, she wore a bandage on her right hand. He acquired a neatly amputated little finger which, in a vial of brine, he used as a paperweight. In these rooms, the Consultantship of Moriarty and Moran received 'clients'.

'Miss Irene Adler,' acknowledged Moriarty. 'Your Lucia di Lammermoor was acceptable, your Maria Stuarda indifferent and you were perhaps the worst Emilia di Liverpool the stage has ever seen.'

'What a horrible man you are, James Moriarty!'

His lips split and sharp teeth showed.

'My business is being horrible, Miss Adler. I make no effort at sham or hypocrisy.'

'That, I must say, is a tonic.'

She smiled full-bore and arranged herself on a divan, prettily hiking her hemline up over well-turned ankles, shifting her decolletage in a manner calculated to set her swanny mams a-wobble. Even Moriarty was impressed, and he could keep up a lecture on the grades of paper used in the forgery of high-denomination Venezuelan banknotes while walking down the secret corridor with the row of one-way mirror windows into the private rooms where Mrs H's girls conducted spectacularly indecent business day and night.

I still maintain all would have been well if only I'd shown the Adler minx what was what straight off, tossed her skirts over her head, plonked her fizzog-down on the reception room rug (a tiger whose head snarled as if he still bore a grudge from that tricky shot I made bringing him down) and administered one of my famous 'Basher' Moran Specials. Had I but properly poked that Yankee popsy, she might have broken the habit which eventually set all manner of odd bods scurrying around trying to clear up her confounded messes.

Irene Adler had the face of an angel child, the body of a full-grown trollop and a voice like a steel needle slowly sliding into your brain. Even warbling to an audience of tone-deaf polacks, she hadn't lasted as *prima donna*. After her *Emilia* flopped so badly the artistic director of the Warsaw Opera had to blow his brains out, the company cut her adrift, leaving her on the loose in Europe to the disadvantage of several ruling houses.

And here she was on our settee.

'You are aware that the *services* I offer are somewhat unusual?'

She fixed Moriarty with a steely glint that cut through all the sugar.

'I am a soprano from New Jersey,' she began, pronouncing it 'Noo Joisey'. 'I know what a knob crook looks like. You can figure all the sums you like, *Professor*, but you're as much a *capo di cosa nostra* as the Moustache Petes in the back-room of the Burly-Cue. Which is dandy, because I have a job of burglary that needs doing urgently. *Capisce*?'

The professor nodded.

'Who's the military gent who hasn't taken his glims off my teats for the last minute and a half?'

'Colonel Sebastian Moran, the best heavy-game shot our Eastern Empire has ever produced.'

'Good with a gun, eh? Looks more like a shiv-man to me.'

She pointed her index fingers at her cleavage, which she thrust out, then angled her fingertips up to indicate her face.

'That's better. Look me in the lamps, Colonel.'

I harrumphed and paid attention. If she hadn't wanted fellows to ogle, she shouldn't have worn that dress. There's no reasoning with women.

'Here's the thing of it,' she said. 'Have you heard of the Duke of Strelsau?'

'Michael Elphberg, so-called "Black Michael", second in line to the throne of Ruritania.'

'That's the fellow, Prof. Things being slow this season, I've been knocking around a bit with Black Mike. They call him that because of his hair, which is dark where the rest of his family's is flame-red. He's a gloomy, glowering type as well so it suits him on temperamental grounds too. As it happens, photographs were taken of the two of us in the actual pursuit of knocking-around. Artistic Studies, you might say. Six plates. Full figures. Complete exposures. It would ruin my reputation should they come to light. You see, *I'm being blackmailed*!'

Her voice cracked. She raised a kerchief to her eye to quell a tear, then froze, a picture of slighted maidenhood. Moriarty shook his head. She stuffed the hankie back into her sleeve and snorted.

'Worth a try just to keep my hand in. I'm a better actress than critics say, don't you know? Obviously, I'm *not* being blackmailed. Like you said, there are stingers and stingees. We are stingers.'

'And the stingee?'

'Another bloody colonel. Colonel Sapt. Chief of the Ruritanian Secret Police. Which has been a dozy doddle for the last thirty years, since it's one of the most peaceable, least-insurrection-blighted spots on the map. Not so much as a whiff of dissent since '48. When, admittedly, the mob burned down the old White Palace. There are very scenic gardens on the site. Anyway, intrigue stirs. King

Rudolf is getting on, and two sons have claims to the throne. Rudolf the Red, the older, is set on shoring up his case by marrying his cousin, Princess Flavia. Where do they get these names? If you put them in an opera, you'd be laughed off stage. Sapt is loyal to Rudolf. Lord knows why, but there you are. Some people are like that. He's also a keen appreciator of the aesthetic worth of a fine photo.'

'I see,' I said, 'this Sapt thinks to blacken Michael's name – further blacken, I suppose – so the duke will never be king.'

Irene Adler looked at me with something like contemptuous pity.

'Gilbert the Filbert, Colonel of the Nuts, if those pics were seen, Black Mike'd be the envy of Europe. He'd be crowned in a wave of popularity. Everyone loves a randy royal. Look at Vicky's brood. No, Sapt wants the photographs *off* the market, so Mikey can be nagged into marriage by Antoinette de Mauban, his persistently pestering mistress. Which would scupper any chance he might have with Flavourless Flavia.'

'You said *Rudolf* was engaged to the princess?'

She made a gesture, suggesting the matter was in the balance. 'Whichever Elphberg marries Flavia is a cert to be king. Black Michael is scheming to cut his half-brother out. Are you following this?'

Moriarty acknowledged that he was.

'Why do you want those photographs?'

'Sentimental value. I come off especially well in Study No. 3, where the light catches the fall of my hair as I lower my... No? Not convinced? Rats, I must work on this acting lark. Obviously, I want to blackmail *everyone* – Colonel Sapt, Black Mike, Red Rudi, Mademoiselle Toni, Princess Lavatoria... With half Ruritania paying me to keep quiet and the other half to speak up, I should be able to milk the racket for a good few years – at least, until succession is settled – and secure my comfortable old age.'

She could not have been more than twenty-five.

'And where might these "artistic studies" be found?' Moriarty asked.

She dug into her reticule and produced a paper with a map drawn on it.

'The Ruritanian Embassy in Belgravia,' she said. 'I have a collector's interest in floor plans, schedules of guards, and the like.'

'What's this?' the professor indicated a detail marked with a red circle.

'A safe, hidden behind the portrait of Rudolf III, in the private office of Colonel Sapt. If I had the key, I wouldn't be here. I've been driven to associate with criminals by the need for skills in cracksmanship. You come highly recommended by Scotland Yard.'

Moriarty sniffed haughtily. 'Scotland Yard have never heard of Professor Moriarty, except in my capacity as a pure mathematician.'

'For someone as crooked as you, I call that a recommendation.'

Moriarty's head started bobbing again. He was thinking the thing through, which meant I had to look after practicalities.

'What's in it for us, missy?' I asked.

'A quarter of what I can screw from the Elphbergs.'

'Half.'

'That's extortion!'

'Yes,' I admitted with a wink. 'We're extortion men, you might say. Half.'

She had a little sulk, made a practised moue, shimmied her chest again, and bestowed a magnificent smile that warmed my insides. At some point in this business, I knew the old 'Basher' Moran Special would be required.

'Deal,' she said, sticking out a tiny paw to be shaken.

I should have shot her then and there.

II

The Ruritanian Embassy is a mansion in Boscobel Place. Belgravia fairly crawls with embassies, legates and consulates. The streets throng with gussied-up krauts strapped into fancy uniforms, tripping over swords they wouldn't know what to do with if a herd of buffalo charged them. I've no love for your average Johnny Native, but he bests any Frenchy, Sausage-Eater or Dutchman who ever drew breath. Never go into the jungle with a Belgian, that's my motto.

If Irene Adler had gone to a run-of-the-mill safe-breaker like that cricket-playing fathead, the caper would have run to after-midnight window-breakage and a spot of brace-and-bit boring, with perhaps a cosh to Colonel Sapt's dome as an added extra.

Moriarty scorned such methods as too obvious and not sufficiently destructive.

First, he wrote to the *Westminster Gazette*, which carried his angry letter in full. He harped on about the sufferings of the slum-dwellers of Strelsauer Altstadt some of which weren't even made up, which is where the clever part came in – and labeled Ruritania 'the secret shame of Europe'. More correspondence appeared, not all from the professor, chiming in with fresh tales of horrors carried on under the absolute monarchy of the Elphbergs. A long-nosed clergyman and an addle-pated countess formed a committee of busybodies to mount a solemn vigil in Boscobel Place. The protest was swollen by less-dignified malcontents – Ruritanian dissenters in exile, louts with nothing better to do, crooks in Moriarty's employ.

Hired ranters stirred passersby against the vile Ruritanian practice (invented by the professor) of cleaning the huge cannons of Zenda Castle by shoving little orphan girls into the barrels and prodding them with sticks until their wriggling wiped out the bore. A few of the Conduit Street Comanche – that tribe of junior beggars, whores, pickpockets and garotters whose loyalty the professor had bought – got themselves up as Zenda Cannon Girls, with soot on their faces and skirts, and threw dung at anyone who so much as dared step outside the Embassy.

After typical foreign bleating and whining, Scotland Yard sent two constables to Boscobel Place to rap truncheons against the railings and tell the crowd to move along quietly. To the Comanche, a bobby's helmet might as well have a target painted on it. And horse dung is easily come by on the streets of London.

So, within three days, there was the makings of a nice pitched battle outside the Embassy. Moriarty and I took the trouble to stroll by every now and then, to see how the pot was boiling.

Hawk-eyed, the professor spotted a face peering from a downstairs window.

'That's Sapt,' he said.

'I could pot him from here,' I volunteered. 'I've a revolver in my pocket. It'd be a dicey shot, but I've never missed yet.'

Moriarty's head wavered. He was calculating odds.

'He would only be replaced. We know who Sapt is. Another Secret Police Chief might not be such a public figure.'

My right hand was itching and I had a thrill in my water.

I had a notion to haul out and blast away, just for sport and hang the scheme. There were enough bearded anarchists about to take the blame. Sometimes an idea takes your fancy, and there's nothing to do but give in.

Moriarty's bony hand was on my wrist, squeezing. Hard.

His eyes shone. Cobra eyes.

'That would be a mistake, Moran.'

My wrist hurt. A lot. The professor knew where to squeeze. He could snap bones with what seemed like a pinch. He let me have my hand back.

Moriarty rarely smiled, and then usually to terrify some poor victim. The first time I heard him *laugh*, I thought he had been struck by deadly poison and the stutter escaping through his locked jaws was a death-rattle. That day's *Times* report from Ruritania solicited from him an unprecedented fit of shoulder-shaking giggles. He wound his fingers together like the claws of a praying mantis.

The prompt for this hilarity was Black Michael's vow to free the Zenda Cannon Girls!

'Let us wish him luck in finding them,' said the professor. 'How delicious that the duke should be our staunch ally in this enterprise. Then again, Queen Victoria has also expressed sympathy for our imaginary orphans.'

Flashes came from the Embassy. My hand was on my revolver.

'More photographs,' said the professor. 'Colonel Sapt's hobby.'

Sapt's face was gone, but a box-and-lens affair was pressed against the window. Moriarty and I had coats casually up over our faces, against the wind.

'The Secret Police Chief likes to know his enemies. A man in his position collects them.'

'Why's Sapt in London anyway? Shouldn't he be crackin' down on bomb-throwers on his home turf?'

Moriarty pondered the question.

'If we are to believe Miss Adler, Sapt can best serve his cause here.'

'His cause, Moriarty?'

'Up the Red, down the Black. But the Elphberg Brothers are halfway across Europe. So, Sapt's attention is directed here on subtler business.'

'The woman?'

Moriarty's shoulders lifted and dropped.

'The old goat probably hopes she'll give him a tumble to get her snaps back,' I suggested. 'I'll wager he pulls the pics out of the safe every night and gives 'em a proper lookin' over.'

'If that were the case, she wouldn't have engaged us. Miss Adler does not strike me as a lady who likes to share. Yet she has willed over half the earnings of a profitable enterprise to us.'

'No choice, Moriarty. Who else could get her what she wants?'

The professor tapped his teeth.

'No one but us, Moran. Evidently.'

Moriarty's fingers went to his watch-pocket. In my years of association with the professor, I never saw him pull out the timepiece I presume anchored the chain across his flat middle. Once an associate understood the import of timekeeping, everything went to schedule. Otherwise, there might have been *consequences*.

He had barely stroked his chain when Filthy Fanny dashed from the crowd and began kicking the police guard.

Fanny had been successfully presenting herself as a ten-year-old waif for a full two decades without anyone being the wiser. It was down to the proper application of dirt, which she arranged on her face with the skill other tarts devote to the use of paints and powder.

Now, Filth wore the sooty skirts of a Zenda Cannon Girl. And heavy shinkicking clogs.

She harangued in backslang ('Reggub the Esclop!') that sounded mighty like Ruritanian, or whatever heathen tongue they use.

After some painful toe-to-shin business, the plod got his truncheon out.

With a command of the dramatic that would put a Drury Lane tragedienne to shame, Filth tumbled down the Embassy steps, squirting tomato juice from a sponge clapped over her eye.

Moriarty handed me a cobblestone and pointed.

I threw the stone at the gawking copper, and fetched off his helmet. I'd once brought down a Bengal tiger with a cricket ball in exactly the same manner.

Then, the mob rose and rushed the Embassy. Moriarty hooked me with an umbrella handle and we milled in with the crowd.

The front doors caved, and the first rush of intruders slid about on the polished marble foyer floor like drunken skaters. Three guards tried to unscabbard sabres, but the Comanche set about stripping them – and the environs – of anything redeemable. Pawnshop windows would soon display cuirasses, plumed helms and other items stamped with the Elphberg Seal.

Sapt poked his head out of his door. Moriarty signalled. A couple of bruisers laid hands on the Secret Police Chief.

The professor sidled next to the anarchist with the biggest beard and suggested he draw up a list of demands, phrasing it so the fellow would think the whole thing was his idea.

Sapt looked about furiously, moustaches twitching. Dirty hands held him fast.

A bunch of keys rattled on Sapt's belt. Moriarty pointed them out, and an urchin brushed past, deftly relieving Sapt of the keys.

'Give him a taste of what the cannon girls get,' I shouted.

We left the mob happily shoving the Secret Policeman feet-first up the nearest chimney. The anarchist had posted lookouts at the doors, and was waving an ancient revolver at the still-surprised constables.

'You can't rush us,' said Comrade Beard. 'This Ruritanian territory is claimed by the Free Citizens' Committee of Strelsauer Altstadt. Any action against us will be interpreted as a British invasion.'

The average London crusher isn't qualified to cope with an argument like that. So they bullied someone into making them tea, and told the anarchist to hang fire until someone from the foreign office turned up. In return, Beard promised not to garotte any hostages just yet.

Sapt, it appeared, had got stuck.

With all this going on, it was a simple matter to slip into Sapt's private office, take down the portrait and open the safe. It contained a thick, sealed packet – and, disappointingly, no cash box or surplus crown jewels. Moriarty handed me the goods, and looked about, brows knit in mild puzzlement.

'What? Too easy?'

'No, Moran. It's just as I foresaw.'

He locked the safe again.

There was a clatter of carriages and boots outside. Boscobel Place was full of eager fellows in uniform.

'They've called out the troops.'

'Time to leave,' said the professor.

Back in the foyer, Moriarty gave the nod. Our Comanche confederates left off pilfering and detached themselves from those still intent on making a political point.

Sapt had fallen head-first out of the chimney, blacked like a minstrel. The professor arranged the surreptitious return of his keys.

We left the building as we came, through the front door.

The Comanche melted into another crowd.

I came smack face-to-face with a junior guards officer, who was about to set diplomacy aside and invade. I stiffened my neck and snapped off a salute, which was smartly returned. Once you've worn the colours, they never wear off.

'Carry on, lieutenant,' I said.

'Yes, sir,' he responded.

As so often, Moriarty had contrived not to be noticed. Like those lizards who can blend into greenery, he had the knack of seeming like a forgettable clergyman or a nondescript tutor, someone who has got off the omnibus two stops early and wandered into a bloodbath which was none of his doing.

We strolled away from the battle. Shouts, shots, thumps, crashes and bells sounded. Nothing to do with us.

A cab waited on the corner.

III

Moriarty was in a black thinking mood. He chewed little violet pastilles of his own concoction and paced his room, hands knotted in the small of his back, brow set in a crinkled frown.

I was still full of the thrill of jizzwhackery, and minded to pop downstairs to call on Flossie or Pussie or whatever the tiny blonde with the lazy eye said she was called. After the hunting grounds, the boudoir – I'd learned that in India, along with how to keep an eye on your wallet in the back of your trousers while they're draped over a chair.

But the professor was preoccupied.

The evening papers were in, along with tear-sheets of fuller reports that would be in tomorrow's editions. Sapt was claiming that dangerous Ruritanian revolutionary movements needed to be exterminated. He called upon Great Britain, Ruritania's ancient ally, to join the crusade against insurrection, alleging that the assault upon the Embassy (and his person) had been equally an insult to Victoria and Rudolf. Typical foreign sod, wanting us to fight his battles for him.

Back in Streslau, there had been street skirmishes between Michaelists and Rudolfites. Many arrests had been made, and Sapt was expected to return to his country with information which would lead to a complete sweep of the organised trouble-makers.

The packet of photographs lay on our bureau. It seemed that reclaiming this property of a lady had interesting side-effects – Moriarty's imaginary revolution had genuinely to be put down.

'I hope the blasted country don't go up in flames before Irene can cash these chips, Moriarty. She'll get no blackmail boodle out of 'em if they're hangin' from lamp posts in the public gardens.'

Moriarty growled. He left the room, and closeted himelf in the dark, buzzing space where he raised his wasps and plotted the courses of heavenly bodies.

Speaking of heavenly bodies, my eyes went to the packet.

The seal was nice and red and heavy and official.

I remembered the line of Irene Adler's throat, the trim of her calves under silk, the swell of...

No one had said anything about not examining the merchandise.

I listened out – Moriarty was whistling to his wasps, likely to be absorbed for hours; there was no tread on the stair and Mrs Halifax was ordered to keep all callers away. So, no chance of interruption.

I sat at the bureau, and turned up the gas-lamp to illuminate the blotter.

With a deft bit of penknifery, I lifted the seal intact so it could be re-attached with no one the wiser. My mouth was dry, as if I'd been in a hide for hours, watching a staked-out goat, awaiting the pad of a big cat. I poured a healthy snifter of brandy, an apt accompaniment to this pleasurable perusal.

With a warm pulse in my vitals, I slid the contents out of the packet.

It was like iced water tipped into my lap.

'Disgustin',' I blurted.

A sheet of paper was slipped into the sheaf of photographs.

MY DEAR COL. MORAN

I knew you'd not be able to resist a peek at these 'artistic studies'. Sorry for the disappointment.

For what it's worth, you may keep all monies which can be raised from them.

If b - - - - - - - -l proves unprofitable, I suggest you license them to a manufacturer of postcards.

My very best to the Prof. I knew I could rely on him to toss a pebble in the pond, sending out ripples enough to make a maelstrom. An ordinary workman would just have secured the package and been done with it. Only a genius on the level of a Buonaparte could turn a simple task into the prompt for turmoil raised across a whole continent.

Please convey the thanks of another colonel. Being Chief of Secret Police in 'one of the most peaceable, least-insurrection-blighted spots on the map' was not a career with a future. The

Elphbergs were intent on retiring him, but now – I fancy he'll be kept on with an increase in salary.

I expect you to retain the last figure for sentimental reasons, and I remain, dear Colonel Moran, very truly yours,

IRENE ADLER

I flipped through several more entirely innocent tourist photographs of picturesque Ruritania, until – at the bottom of the stack – I beheld the full face of the American Nightingale. In this final, studio-posed photograph she wore the low-cut bodice she'd affected on her visit to Conduit Street, somewhat loosened and lowered, though – dash it! – artistic fogging around the edges of the portrait prevented complete immodesty. Through the fog was scrawled her spidery autograph, 'as ever, Irene'. Even thus frozen, she looked like the sort who would be much improved by a 'Basher' Moran Special. I gulped the brandy, and chewed my moustache for a few moments, contemplating this turn of events.

Behind me, a door opened.

I swivelled in the chair. Moriarty looked at me, eyes shining – he had thought it through, and was unhappy. When the professor was unhappy, other creatures – animals, children, even full-grown men – tended to learn of it in extreme and uncomfortable manners.

'Moriarty,' I began, 'I'm afraid we've been stung.'

I held up Irene's photograph.

He spat out a word.

And that was how a great shambles broke out in Belgravia, shaking the far-off kingdom of Ruritania, and how the worst plans of Professor Moriarty were exploited by a woman's treachery. When he speaks of Irene Adler, or when he refers to her photograph, it is always as *that bitch*.

They smash through my front door at three in the morning. Two of them, dressed in black. The first – Patrick – is carrying a council kerbstone he probably found lying around somewhere, and which he uses to tap the lock out of the frame. He uses his other hand to turn on the lights and throw a small side-table along the hall. He does things like that to show how big and strong he is. People rarely argue with him.

The second man is tall, slim and black as night, with shiny dreadlocks hanging around his shoulders. He has a blowtorch in one hand and a Bic lighter in the other. Hooper. He strides cat-like to the foot of my bed and thumbs the lighter. The flame snaps the blowtorch into a steady, icy-blue tongue of fire which hisses like a dragon in the silence. I can feel the heat from six feet away. Hooper smiles.

I hope it's a social call. Hooper is so far off the wall even the Yardies threw him out for being too violent. Now here he is in my bedroom.

'I suppose knocking's too fucking much to ask?' I say. I don't know these two all that well, but I've heard it's best not to back down too quick. They respect that, for some insane reason.

Patrick drops the kerbstone on the bed and jerks a massive thumb towards the door.

'The Chairman wants to see you.'

'It's three in the morning,' I point out.

The flame comes nearer as Hooper advances round the bed.

'I'll get dressed.'

I hop around looking for socks and stuff while Patrick watches and Hooper plays the flame of his toy across a glass-fronted picture of a Paris street scene. It was a present from a former girlfriend who thought I needed cultural improvement. For some reason she thought I was artistically bland. She didn't last long after that, but the picture stayed. I like it, actually. Very...moody.

The glass pops and cracks while I pull on my shoes, and I figure

I'll get Hooper back for that. One day when he isn't looking.

'What does he want?' I ask conversationally, as we drive west towards The Chairman's office. We're in a black Toyota Land Cruiser, which is inappropriate for the city, but Patrick needs a big vehicle otherwise he'd have nowhere to keep his collection of kerbstones.

'He's got a job for you.' Hooper turns round in the passenger seat and stares at me. 'Gainful employment.' The words come out slow and singsong, and a gold tooth glints in his mouth, reflecting the streetlights. I reckon he's pissed I didn't put up a fight.

'I've already got a job,' I tell him. I do, too. I deliver things for people. Small packages, mostly; papers, diskettes, certificates, contracts, that sort of thing. Anything small, light and of high-value importance. You want it there, I'm your man. Guaranteed. Not drugs, though. I don't touch drugs. I'm old-fashioned about wanting to keep my freedom.

Hooper sneers. 'Courier shit, man? Don't make me laugh. That's for pussies.'

I debate shoving Hooper's gold tooth down his throat, but decide it will keep. Patrick would probably take a spare kerbstone out of his top pocket and cuff me with it.

Instead I sit back and ignore them both, and consider what I'm about to get into.

The Chairman – if he has a real name nobody uses it – is a fat slug who runs a business and criminal empire said to stretch across half Europe. Some say he's Dutch, and was kicked out of Rotterdam because he gave the local crims a bad name. He set himself up in London instead and proceeded to knock out every other syndicate in the place, allowing only a tiny network of small-time gangs to remain. It was a clever move; in return for letting them be, he allows them to tender for doing his dirty work. He has a small group of direct employees, three people like Hooper and Patrick, to protect his back from anyone who thinks he might be easy meat but other than that, he believes in lean and mean. Especially mean.

Like I say, clever move. He controls the whole criminal shebang, while letting some of the dumber members think they're important. It's a franchise, only the penalties for infringing the rules are more permanent.

I've done a couple of jobs for The Chairman before, but only out of desperation. They were simple fetch and carry assignments, the main risk being if I failed to deliver. I didn't enjoy them because I didn't feel clean afterwards, and the last time he'd called, which was about a month ago, I'd declined. Politely.

I wish I had Malcolm with me.

Malcolm's my little brother. I use the word little only in the age sense; he's three years younger than me, but way, way bigger. He caught our grandfather's bit of the gene pool, while I've been blessed with Grandma's. Granddad – a rough, tough stevedore back in the days when they still had them – was apparently a shade under six-ten, with shoulders and hands to match, while Grandma was normal.

At six-eight, and weighing in at seventeen stone, Malcolm can pick me up with one hand. He's also good-looking, with twin rows of pearly-white teeth, naturally swarthy skin and eyes which can bore right through you. Apparently it works wonders with the girls and means he never gets to go home alone.

The downside is, he's disturbingly honest and has never been known to tell a lie or get in a fight. At school he was left well alone from an early age, especially when they saw how much he could lift with one hand. And if anyone gave me grief, all I had to do was mention his name and I got swift apologies and a promise of immunity from the scummies who liked to prey on smaller kids for their lunch money. Not great for my self-esteem, but if you went to the sort of school I went to, you used whatever means you had to keep afloat, even if it was your kid brother.

As the Americans say, go figure.

The Chairman's office is in a smart, glass-fronted block in the West End, rubbing shoulders with a team of showbiz lawyers on one side and a well-known film company on the other. Like many top crims, The Chairman believes respectability comes from who you know, not what you do.

We troop upstairs with me sandwiched in the middle, through a set of armoured glass doors into a plush foyer with carpets like a grass savannah. An office at one end has the lights on and the door open.

'Ah, there you are, Stephen,' The Chairman says, like we're old buddies. His English is faultless. He's studying some spreadsheets under a desk-lamp and hitting the keyboard of a Compaq with quick fingers like the accountant he's rumoured to have been before he went sly. 'Sit down. Coffee?'

The offer and the first name familiarity are all part of the game of being in charge. Patrick pours me a coffee from a jug in one corner and hands me a cup. It looks like a thimble in his hand.

'I'd prefer to be home in bed,' I say tiredly. 'Without the kerbstone for company.'

The Chairman looks up from his figures and seeks out Patrick with a look of reproof. 'Say what? Have you been using those things again? Patrick, didn't I tell you, there are people you don't need them for. Mr Connelly, here, is one of them.' He shakes his head like you would with a small child. 'You'd better get the door repaired.'

'OK,' Patrick mutters, totally unconcerned. 'I'll do it tomorrow.'

'No, you'll do it now. Wake someone.' He says it nice and soft, while tapping away on the keyboard once more, but there's suddenly a chill in the air.

Patrick lumbers out, leaving Hooper to watch over me.

'How's that's nice brother of yours?' The Chairman sits back and smiles. Like he cares. If he ever met Malcolm, it must have been by accident.

'He's fine,' I say, and wonder where this is leading. Malcolm doesn't approve of my life, other than agreeing to the occasional meal round my flat when he's up in London. He thinks all criminals should be locked up, sometimes me included. It's not that I do anything overtly illegal, but he thinks anyone who doesn't use Her Majesty's Post Office to send letters and stuff must be pulling some serious strokes, and by association, I'm tainted by their guilt.

'Good. And your Auntie Ellen. How's her husband – is he any better?'

Now I'm seriously worried. Nobody knows about Auntie Ellen or Uncle Howard, for the simple reason that they live down in Devon and I don't talk about them. A nicer pair of old folks you'll never meet and I owe them a lot. They were instrumental in our upbringing after our parents died when Malcolm and I were kids.

'Say again?'

'Oh, come now.' The Chairman picks up a photo from his desk and shows it to me. It's a shot of a familiar white-haired old lady in her garden, innocently pruning her roses. In the background, made fuzzy by the distance but still recognisable, is the gangly figure of Uncle Howard. I can't see what he's doing but it looks like he's talking to himself. He does a lot of that, bless him. Early Alzheimer's, according to the doctors. 'I know all about your family, Stephen. Your aunt and your loopy uncle. I make it my business, you know that. It gives me leverage. If I need it.'

The last four words are uttered with meaning, and there's no misunderstanding; he needs leverage now. It's still in me to try, though.

'And if I don't want the job?'

He shrugs and drops the photo in the bin. 'Then you're short one aunt and uncle and the county of Devon is a sadder place.' He picks up a large manila envelope and flicks it across the desk. 'I want that to arrive in Brussels first flight this morning. Kill another passenger for their seat if you have to, but get it there.'

'Why not use Hooper or Patrick?'

He winces with impatience and I get a cool chill across my shoulders. 'If I could use them I would,' he says, like he's talking to a particularly dumb child. 'I'm using you.'

'For a simple delivery? What's inside – pictures of the Prime Minister? Funny money?'

He leans forward into the lamplight and I can see he's got a bead of sweat across his brow. Only I don't think it's the heat. 'You refused me once before, Stephen. I don't like that; it undermines my reputation. You understand about reputations, don't you?' He sits back, suddenly aware that Hooper's watching him now, not me. Men like Hooper are always on the lookout for chinks in the armour, and there's no bigger chink than a boss who shows signs of letting a minor problem get under his skin. Loyalty in his world is a commodity, and can be sold. 'There's a rumour going round that you won't work for me.' He waves a dismissive hand. 'Frankly, I don't care if it's true or not, and in any case, as you can see, it's both false and at the same time, useful.' He smiles coldly. 'Ring me the moment you complete. Be back here afterwards to collect a payment. No hand-over or no return here by three at the latest and Hooper gets to play with his blowtorch in sunny Devon.'

I pick up the envelope as The Chairman goes back to his computer, and turn to find Hooper watching me with dangerous intensity. He's hoping I'll fail.

Outside I breathe deeply and search for a cab. Eventually I pick up one going my way and get back long enough to have a shower, make one important phone call, throw on some respectable clothes and dig out my passport. Then it's off to the airport to wait for a plane and blag a ticket.

Brussels airport is all aluminium and zero atmosphere, and there are few people at Arrivals save for a couple of cleaners, a man with a bunch of flowers, and a fat, sweaty individual in a green suit. This last one is carrying a section of brown cardboard with the name Bouillon scrawled across it in large, black letters, and is staring at me with a look of deep melancholy.

I check my instructions and the name matches. When I look up, he's waddling away fast, his green jacket flapping in the breeze like an elephant's ears.

'Hey —' I go after him, but the man has a head start and leaves me behind, in spite of his size. What the hell is this?

It's only when I get a prickly feeling in the back of my neck and turn round that I realise I'm being followed by two men. One of them is the man with the flowers.

Shit, as we say in the courier business. This doesn't look good.

I stuff the envelope in my pocket and go after Green Suit. I don't know what his problem is, or what the envelope holds which is so important he's being tagged by two men. But I really don't want to get left holding it and have Hooper go after Auntie Ellen just because of some local territorial disagreement by a bunch of Walloons.

Running is out of the question; nobody runs in airports anymore, not unless they want to be brought down by a burly security guard and have a Heckler & Koch stuck in their ear.

I settle for a fast walk, with occasional snatches at my watch, like I'm late for a meeting. Behind me, the two men have split up and veered off at angles, no doubt so as not to appear on the same security monitors as me. One man hurrying, fine; three men hurrying, cause for alarm.

I end up out by the taxi rank, and catch a glimpse of Green Suit across the road, panting his way up the stairs to the upper levels of the multi-storey. The place is bedlam as usual, with taxis and cars streaking by without paying too much attention to the pedestrian crossing, but I risk it and race across after him. I leave a trail of burnt rubber and angry horn blasts in my wake, but at least I make it.

I hit the top level to find him about to squeeze his way into a tan Mercedes.

'What,' I gasp, throat dry, 'is your flicking problem?'

For some reason he looks puzzled, then scared. 'OK,' he hisses. 'Give it to me!'

OK? Like I'm doing him a favour? Now there are certain formalities we go through in this business, like exchanging IDs. It's not been unknown to have someone turn up for a collection who shouldn't, if you know what I mean. And with Hooper and Patrick waiting to take a trip to Devon and perform industrial injury on two lovely old people, there's no way I'm handing over this envelope to an unknown, two others in hot pursuit or not.

He huffs and puffs but hands over a business card. It confirms his name and I give him the envelope. Moments later he's heading for the down ramp.

As I walk back down the stairs, I get out my mobile and dial a number.

'Yes?' It's The Chairman. There are voices and the sound of glasses clinking in the background. Must be a breakfast meeting in gangland.

'Delivered,' I tell him. Then I see the two men at the bottom of the stairs. I show them my empty hands and they turn away as if deciding to cut their losses. 'There seems to be some local interest, though.'

'Local interest?' The Chairman sounds bored. 'What sort of interest?'

I tell him about the two men, and the enraged bellow begins to build the moment I say I handed the envelope to Green Suit. 'You what?' he snarls. 'Bouillon's tall and thin, you idiot! That was the wrong man! You've just handed over some priceless documents to the wrong person!'

There's more along those lines, but I'm no longer listening. Something doesn't sound right. *How did he know my Bouillon wasn't tall and thin? I hadn't mentioned it.*

Then it hits me. I've been set up. No wonder Bouillon was puzzled; I wasn't *supposed* to catch him. And the other two were merely for show. It means The Chairman hasn't forgotten my first refusal; in fact, he's found a way to use me as an example to others and salvage his dented pride. There was no handover, and I'm willing to bet his tirade just now was within earshot of some influential people he was looking to impress. Or frighten.

I dial another number. Malcolm answers.

'They OK?' I ask him.

'Fine,' he replies. 'We're having breakfast. Nice hotel in —'

'Don't tell me,' I instruct him. 'Walls have ears.'

Malcolm laughs. It's a game to him; a silly, ludicrous game in which he's indulging me. He doesn't know The Chairman like I do. I'd asked him to take Aunt Ellen and Uncle Howard out for the day, starting with an early breakfast somewhere swish and booking them into a nice, quiet hotel away from home. At short notice it was the only thing I could think of.

I travel back to London with a feeling of dread. If I call Malcolm again and warn him that Hooper and Patrick could be on their way down, he'll either think I'm lying, or panic and call the cops. To him, the seamier side of life is what you read about in the papers. The best I can do is hope he keeps their heads down, wherever they are.

I'm halfway back to London along the M4 when he rings me. He doesn't sound happy.

'It's Uncle Howard,' he says. 'He's gone for a walk.'

'Great,' I tell him. 'Get him back.' Then I realise what he's saying. Uncle Howard has reached the stage where he's virtually forgotten everyone he knows and where he lives, and 'going for a walk' means he's wandered off. He could be anywhere.

'Shit, Malc,' I shout. 'How the hell did you let that happen?'

'He went to the loo. I thought it was OK – he's done it OK before and always come back. This time he didn't. The hotel receptionist said she saw him walking towards Piccadilly.'

I feel a set of cold fingers clutch my guts. 'You said where?'

'Piccadilly, in London. You said take them out, so I thought a day in London...'

I want to shout and scream at him, and tell him what a stupid, naïve great pillock he is. But it's no use. It's not his fault – it's mine. Then I consider it. There's as much chance of them hiding successfully in the Smoke as anywhere else. Better, in fact. Just as long as they don't happen to walk past a certain office block in the West End just as The Chairman comes out.

'OK,' I say calmly. 'You did good, Malc. Can you leave Ellen there and go look for him? I'll be with you as soon as I can.'

He gives me the name of the hotel and I cut the connection. I have to get to The Chairman and get him to pull his dogs off. I don't know what I'll have to do, but there must be a way.

The Chairman is out and his secretary doesn't know when he'll be back. She won't ring him, either. There's no sign of Hooper or Patrick.

I drive along to Piccadilly and find the hotel where Malcolm has holed up with Aunt Ellen. It's small and posh and they'll have thought it beats the Savoy hands down.

Aunt Ellen answers when I call on the house phone. Malcolm has just called to say he's found Uncle Howard and they're on their way back to the hotel. I breathe a sigh of relief and tell her to stay where she is, then go downstairs to meet them.

Hooper is standing on the pavement, flicking his cigarette lighter.

He looks totally incongruous in that setting, and the hotel doorman is eyeing him with definite concern.

The Land Cruiser is at the kerb behind him, with Patrick in the driving seat. In the back sits the crumpled figure of Uncle Howard. Alongside him, Malcolm fills the other seat, looking drawn and pale and seemingly asleep.

'Hey, man,' says Hooper, grinning, his speech a deliberate Caribbean drawl. He normally talks straight London. 'Guess who we foun' walkin' long the street jus' now. I say to Patrick, I say, "Man, doesn't that look like Mr Connelly's big brother and his daffy uncle?" An' sure enough, it is.'

As I begin to move, he steps in my way, a hand on my chest. In the car, Patrick is leaning back, his hand alarmingly close to Uncle Howard's windpipe. He could snap it in an instant, the move says.

'What say we go for a ride?' says Hooper, dropping the drawl. He stands aside and I climb in alongside Patrick. Hooper slides in next to Uncle Howard, who smiles in a friendly, vague manner and doesn't know me from a tent peg. To him, it's all part of another day. Malcolm is breathing heavily and has a large bruise on the side of his handsome face.

The Land Cruiser blasts off and we twist and turn through the streets towards Paddington. In minutes we're running alongside some railway arches and pull up at one with large double doors. The rest of the street is deserted save for a mangy dog and two kids on bikes. At a look from Hooper, all three disappear.

We're bundled inside and the doors close. We're in some sort of workshop, the air thick with the smell of oil, grease and burned metal, the floor littered with scrap paper, fags ends and small twists of shaved metal, iron filings, the lot. On one wall is a storage rack full of lengths of steel, like giant knitting needles, and around the other walls is a collection of benches and machines, the use of which I can only guess at. Metalwork wasn't really my subject at school.

Hooper produces a blowtorch and fires it up, while Patrick looks on, holding a length of half-inch steel rod.

Uncle Howard is staring at everyone in turn, not alarmed, merely curious. His gentle eyes alight on a metal lathe in one corner, and he smiles in vague recognition. He used to work in a factory years before. He probably feels comfortable in this sort of place.

I look at Malcolm slumped against one wall, wishing him awake. If there's anyone who can help us it's Malcolm, with his enormous shoulders and powerful hands. Only I know he won't. Big as he is, he's got as much aggression in him as a cotton bud.

Hooper steps across to Uncle Howard and shows him the blowtorch. The old man looks at the cold, blue flame hissing away in front of him with a half-frown, and I wonder if the confused and tangled brain cells inside his head can still recognise danger.

I'm standing alongside a workbench. It's clear apart from one of those old pump-handled oil cans with a long nozzle. I reach out and bang my hand on the pump. Nothing. Hooper laughs and Patrick looks at me in disgust, like he'd expected it. He starts towards me with his steel rod, and I guess he's been waiting for something like this so he can have some fun.

I pump again and a jet of oil spits out and catches Hooper square in the face. It slicks across his cheeks, a thick, glutinous stain, and enters his eyes. He blinks, or tries to. Then he swears ferociously and tries to wipe it away. It just makes things worse.

By now Patrick is building up speed, the steel rod whistling through the air towards me. Only he's forgotten what workshops are like. He's forgotten the electric chain pulley for lifting the metal into position at the machines; he's forgotten the power lines that scatter the air in a tangle above our heads.

The tip of the rod is supposed to connect to my head. Instead, it hits the engine casing of the chain pulley with a dull, heavy thud, and travelling with the full force of Patrick's shoulder. The shock goes up the rod and into his arm, and pain registers on his face. Nerveless fingers can't hold onto the weapon, and it falls to the ground.

I don't waste time scooping it up; I grab the nearest piece of hanging chain and throw my body to one side, using my weight to pull as hard as I can. For a nanosecond the chain pulley doesn't want to move. Then it goes and gathers momentum and rumbles along its greased track above me. I can feel the weight carrying it along as I let go of the chain, the heavy links clanking together as they swing through the air. On the end of the chain is a giant, steel hook which gets momentarily left behind.

Hooper is too busy swearing and trying to scrape oil out of his eyes to notice what I've done, and looks for Uncle Howard, the blowtorch coming round.

But Uncle Howard isn't there. Somewhere deep in the recesses of his damaged brain is a reflex which tells him from his years in a factory that he has to move; that with heavy machinery in a noisy workshop, not all warnings can be heard and you have to have eyes in the back of your head. In spite of his age and condition, his upper body sways like a boxer, moving just enough to avoid the deadly sling-shot rush of the heavy hook as it tries to catch up with the engine block.

It swishes harmlessly past him and hits Hooper dead square. In the split second before impact, the Yardie's eyes seem to clear of oil and he sees what is about to hit him. But it's too late and he's gone, swept aside with a brief, soggy smack and tossed lifeless into a corner.

Patrick is snarling, trying to ignore the pain of his nerveless fingers. He picks up the steel rod with his other hand.

But this time there's an added complication: Malcolm has finally come to, and he rises up and stands in front of him like his own reflection. For the first time Patrick seems to realise he isn't the only big man in the world.

He whips the rod round in a scything arc, and I wait and wonder, because Malcolm has never had a fight in his life. He's never had to and he doesn't know how. For him, fighting is pointless.

But maybe he inherited something else from our stevedore grandfather. Like instinct. With no more effort than catching a fly, he opens his hand and takes the rod, the sound a dull smack in the silence. Patrick looks stunned and tries to pull it clear. Malcolm pulls back, only harder. As Patrick hurls towards him, my big brother steps forward and puts out his elbow, catching him under the chin with a dull crack. Patrick flies backwards then stands still, eyes filling with what looks like unimaginable pain and surprise.

When he doesn't move after that, and his head droops forward over his chest, I go for a look-see. Patrick is impaled on a length of mild steel sticking out of the storage rack. I turn to look at Malcolm, but he's fainted dead away, unaware of what he's done.

Later that night, I open the door to The Chairman's office. The building is deserted and I've got Patrick's keys to let me in. I'm wearing gloves and a floppy hat pulled over my face just in case the security cameras are loaded.

He's sitting at his desk, pounding keys. He's like a fat spider, counting his worth, and I know that what he wanted his men to do to me and Uncle Howard was no more than another accounting principle, a book-keeping procedure. It's not personal, because I don't think revenge is a concept he knows. I turned him down, which offended him, and had to be seen to suffer the consequences. To him it's part of the business.

And that's why I can't let this go. Because when he finds out about Patrick and Hooper, and how they failed to punish one old man or one old lady, he won't stop. It won't be because of his men – he doesn't see them as anything more than tools. But because of his twisted sense of pride, he'll simply order someone else – most likely one of the gangs, who I don't know – to complete the job instead. Procedure.

I snick the door shut and leave the building. Behind me The Chairman has hosted his last meeting. He's sitting at his desk, and clutched in his pudgy fingers is a small twist of dark, shiny dreadlock. It's not much, but sufficient to show signs of a struggle.

They won't find Hooper, of course. Well, not for a while, anyway. And when they do, they'll find Patrick, his fingerprints on the hook which killed his Yardie colleague. The scattering of white powder and money on the floor will do the rest.

As for Malcolm, he'll forget about it in time. There was a scrap, he intervened, and we left. Who knows what happened to the bad men?

After all, thieves fall out. They're known for it.

Auguste Didier stared gloomily at the eggs awaiting his pleasure for boiling. He had none to offer, although he admitted that his ill-humour had nothing to do with them. Still in its shell, one egg looked much like another, but today they provided an unfortunate reminder that he must choose which of two young gentlemen was the bad egg. They could not both be the missing heir to Lord Luckens.

Not that his lordship was dead. On the contrary, when last week he had brazenly staggered into the kitchens of Plum's Club for Gentlemen, over which Auguste presided as maître chef, he was very much alive. The staggering was not so much due to age or the excellent club wine cellars as to his gait which suggested his life was spent perpetually astride a horse, and his feet a mere aberration of nature to be ignored.

'Ha!'

The grey moustache had bristled, and keen eyes shot a triumphant look, as though Auguste were a fox planning a speedy exit from this world. 'You the detective fellow?'

'The chef fellow, your lordship,' Auguste murmured patiently, casting a despairing glance at his hollandaise sauce, which had been delighted at this opportunity to curdle. His detective work had come about by chance, and was not an art in which he could lay claim to perfection, as were his culinary skills.

Lord Luckens ignored his remark. 'Splendid. Here's what I need you to do. I want you to cook a dinner for me at Luckens Place. Know the old ruin, do you? You can cook what you like.'

Auguste relaxed. He must have misheard mention of detection work, for this assignment presented no such problem. Indeed, the idea was an attractive one, for he had heard that Luckens Place in Sussex, far from being an old ruin, was a magnificent Elizabethan mansion with its own ornate banqueting house in the grounds, and a splendid towered gatehouse with a bedroom where Good Queen Bess herself was said to have slept. He might even cook an Elizabethan dinner, and suggest they follow the old custom of walking to the banqueting house for sweetmeats and desserts. He warmed to Lord Luckens immediately.

'You cook it,' Lord Luckens boomed on, 'and then supervise the dinner in the Great Chamber, where it's to be served.'

'You wish me to act as butler too?' Professional etiquette rose up in protest.

'No, no.' An impatient hand flailed at this stupidity. 'Just stand there like a blasted maître d'.'

Auguste gaped at him, wondering just what his lordship's butler would have to say about this irregular suggestion.

'It's like this. I'm getting on in life. Time to think of wills,' Lord Luckens trumpeted. 'Only had one son, George, and he flounced out in 1867, thirty years ago, when he was twenty-one. Never bothered to keep in touch, never made the fortune he reckoned on. I had one of those Pinkertons' detective fellows track him down a few years back, and they told me George died in Leadville, Colorado, in '79.'

'I'm sorry to hear that, sir.' Auguste received a glare in thanks for his concern.

'Never understood the fellow. Took after his mother. Bookish. Not the sort to marry. Understand me?'

'Yes, sir.'

'Seems I was wrong.' Apparently this did not often occur, since Lord Luckens admitted it with great reluctance. 'Pinkertons found out he left a widow, but she moved away and vanished. I'd no interest in her, so I called off the hounds. My solicitor fellow in London, Jenkins, said where there were widows there might also be sons, so he advertised. Every good-for-nothing in the States claimed to be my son, but old Jenkins is a wily old bird, and he's whittled them down to two. He's crawled over the evidence, and is convinced it's one of them, but he can't blasted well decide which. One's a silver miner in Leadville, the other's a New York businessman, and both are flourishing birth certificates saying their father's George Luckens. They can't be brothers. Born within four months of each other, and even George with his saintly ideas couldn't achieve that. Thought you might like a crack at it, eh?'

'Me?' Auguste's heart sank, even as his mind began to fill with the delights of experimenting with suckets, leaches, possets and marigold tarts.

He had not surrendered easily, however. 'Who would inherit, sir, if no claimant can be found to satisfy you and your solicitors?'

'Knew you'd ask that,' Lord Luckens replied darkly. 'I had a brother once, Horatio. Couldn't stand the fellow. He couldn't stand me either. Died years ago, but he left a blasted son, as priggish and self-righteous as his blasted father. And a bachelor in his fifties. Another of those blasted nancies. Sort of fellow who given his way would see this country go to the dogs. Not content with sitting in the Commons, he's all for sitting in the Lords and putting a spoke in the wheel there too. With my title. He's got wind of this dinner and is insisting on his right to attend. Lady Luckens said it's fair enough and will save trouble later. Suppose she's right, damn it. His name's Jonathan Luckens – heard of him?'

Auguste most certainly had. You could hardly live in England and not have heard of him. A member of Keir Hardie's burgeoning Labour party, he seemed unlikely to be enthusiastic about inheriting a title, yet Auguste could well understand why he and Lord Luckens did not see eye to eye. He was, if Auguste remembered correctly, a vehement supporter of the rights of women to vote, which was not a policy Lord Luckens would be likely to endorse. Despite his reluctance, the case began to intrigue him – and besides, he'd always wanted to cook an Elizabethan banquet…

Auguste fidgeted nervously in the Great Chamber, under the frosty eye of the butler, who obviously suspected Auguste's presence as chef was a ruse to disguise the fact he was being assessed to replace him. He must be nearly eighty, so this would not be surprising, but Auguste could do without heavy disapproval at his elbow this evening.

At any moment the double doors would be thrown open by the footmen, and the guests enter. He glanced round at the awaiting banquet, or such of it as had already made its appearance. The spit-roasted carp stuffed with dried fruit and spices would appear shortly, the goose and sorrel sauce, a pie of Paris, two large chickens to masquerade as peacocks, complete with fanned-out tail feathers, the samphire salad, lemon salad; his mind flitted over merely some of the wonders he had prepared all for the sake of a handful of diners whose concentration would be on fraud not food.

The doors opened at last to reveal the six diners. On Lord Luckens' arm was a severe-looking lady in her middle years, dressed in grey, with only a cameo brooch as adornment. She, Auguste had gathered from the butler, was Miss Twistleden, Lady Luckens' companion. At the rear of the short procession of six was Lady Luckens, a sweet-faced, grey-haired old lady. She was clinging to the arm of Jonathan Luckens, whom Auguste recognised from sketches in the *Illustrated London News*. Thin, and gimlet-eyed, his immaculately trimmed beard quivering at the ready for any chance to demolish his rivals, he looked to Auguste a formidable opponent. He wouldn't care to be in the false claimant's shoes (or boots), or, come to that, in the true claimant's either. Sandwiched between these two couples must be the two claimants, Red and William, both allegedly surnamed Luckens. They were not arm in arm. Far from it.

'Pa!'

There was an immediate and simultaneous howl from both of them as their eyes fell on the portrait of George Luckens aged twenty-two, which was hung on the far wall facing them as they entered the Great Chamber.

'Gee, that's how I remember the old son of a gun,' one of them shouted. No doubt who he was, Auguste decided: the Colorado claimant. Red Luckens, towering over his companion, was dressed more like one of Buffalo Bill's cowboy riders than for an English evening dinner party. Only the hat was missing to complete his ensemble of high boots, sturdy brown trousers and jacket, yellow shirt and huge buckle belt. The holster slung at his side was empty, to Auguste's relief.

Auguste had met many Americans in the course of his employment, Americans in Paris, Americans in London, Americans in the depth of the English countryside, rich Americans and poor Americans, and they had ranged, as do most nations, from the highly civilised, down through the ranks of the vulgar wealthy and back up again to the straightforwardly unassuming. Never, however, had he seen (or heard) two American gentlemen of such disparity as these two.

Red's rival claimant William Luckens was hardly less ostentatious than Red, in that although clad in conventional evening dress, he wore the new tuxedo dinner jacket so popular in the United States and still so incorrect here. He might be shorter than Red but his pugnacious chin and sturdy build suggested he would meet punch for punch.

'That's how Red Luckens remembers the old guy. Like me, he was a humble but happy silver miner. Yes sirree, Grandpappy.' Red, seated at the table, gazed in rapt devotion at the portrait.

Auguste shuddered. Such an endearment was hardly furthering Claimant No. 1's cause with Lord Luckens.

'That's *my* pa.' William had a New York accent, and a quieter voice. 'It sure chokes me up seeing the old fellow up there.' His unctuous soulful glance at Lord Luckens was even harder to stomach than Red's brashness.

'What splendid memories both you gentlemen have,' Jonathan sneered, 'considering you were only seven when my cousin George died.'

'Sure do, Cousin Jonathan,' Red replied cheerfully. 'Why, I remember him kissing my ma as though it were yesterday.'

'Tell me about her,' Lord Luckens said grimly.

'Why, she was the purtiest little thing, a dancer she was.'

William interrupted angrily. '*My* mother, your daughter-in-law, sir, was a lady. Pa met her in Colorado. A schoolteacher. Dancer, my foot. Whoever your parents were, cowboy, your ma most likely came from the whorehouse.'

'Say that again!' Red leapt up from the table, overturning his chair in the process, and towering over William who continued eating his carp imperturbably, to Auguste's full approval.

'You don't look like George,' Lady Luckens observed plaintively to both of them. She had the vacant stare of the elderly who have chosen to let the world pass by them, but this might be deceptive, Auguste thought.

'No,' barked Miss Twistleden, defensive of her mistress.

'I agree, Aunt Viola,' Jonathan said superciliously. 'Nor like Uncle Alfred here. But then that's hardly surprising, since it's quite clear neither of you is my esteemed uncle's grandson.'

'Quite clear, eh, blast your eyes, Jonathan?' Lord Luckens growled. 'Not to me. Any some proof of that statement, have you?'

'No, but it will emerge soon enough.'

'I take after ma, ma'am.' Red casually threw a chicken bone over his shoulder, to the horror of the butler and Auguste alike. What would the courteous host do in such circumstances, he wondered. Proceed to throw his own over his shoulder, or ignore the faux pas? Lord Luckens didn't appear to notice and it was left to William to place his delicately and with much show on the dish provided for the purpose.

'See here, mister,' Red continued earnestly to Jonathan, 'I've a photograph here of my old man not long before he died. We moved to Leadville, Colorado in '77 from California, and here's the proof of *that*.' He produced a dog-eared faded photograph of a group of miners outside Billy Nye's Saloon. 'I was just five years old when this was taken.'

'Why, that's no proof at all. You can't tell one face from another,' William cried in triumph, seizing it from him. 'Now, just you look at this *carte de visite* I got here. Signed on the back: Yr affectionate George.' He tossed it onto the table and Jonathan and Red immediately made a grab for it. Red won.

'Mind letting me see a pic of my own son, Red?' Lord Luckens growled.

'That stuffed shirt's not my pa! He was a silver miner,' roared Red, reluctantly handing it over.

'Who struck it rich just before he died, enabling my mother to bring me to New York to start a new life,' William capped him triumphantly.

'Oh yeah?' Red sneered. 'What do you say, Grandpappy?'

Grandpappy wasn't saying anything, but his glare should have been sufficient an answer for most people.

'I know what *I* say.' Jonathan smirked. 'If that's all the proof you've got, I rather think I'd win in any contest at law.'

'Oh, they've got better proof than this, Jonathan. I explained that to you.' Lord Luckens recovered his good humour. 'Too much to be faulted. That's why we're here. Two impeccable birth certificates, duly registered in their birth town and in the State registries, one for a child to Mollie Luckens, née Huggett, dancer, on 20 April '72 in San Francisco, one to Amelia Luckens, schoolteacher, née Bruart, on 13 August '72 in Denver, Colorado.'

'I guess that makes me elder brother and the future Lord Luckens, if it comes to our splitting it, Will,' Red spluttered into his wine.

'I'll expose you for the bunco-artist you are, long before it comes to that,' snarled William. 'You're no good even as a professional fraud.'

'I'll expose the pair of you even sooner. We in the Labour party believe in justice for all,' Jonathan sneered. 'The courts will make short work of both you incompetent bunglers.'

'Not me, my friend,' William rejoined. 'Concentrate on Mr Wyatt Earp here.'

'I prefer to concentrate on this excellent beef. Most interesting flavour to it.' Jonathan momentarily won Auguste's approval.

'Call this beef stew?' growled Red, elegantly holding a piece of meat up with two fingers.

Auguste in fact called it a beef hare, a dish whose spicings of onion, clove and nutmeg appealed to him.

'Any Leadville chef would get booted out of town for this,' Red continued in disgust.

Auguste made an instant decision never to visit Leadville, but refrained from active interference in the conversation in the interests of earning his fee. So far his betting was even on the two rivals, and if there was any tripping up to be done Jonathan Luckens was more than capable of doing it.

'In New York, fortunately, we can appreciate the finer blessings of life.' One point to William!

'Including money, I've no doubt,' Jonathan quipped. 'Although both of you have quite an interest in that, don't you?'

'Pa,' Red looked soulfully up at the painting, 'I'm here to get

acquainted with my old Grandpappy while there's still time.'
Minus one to him.

Auguste had been so entranced by the battle, he realised he had
forgotten to worry about whether the potatoes were cooked as the
Elizabethan court would have enjoyed this newly discovered
delicacy.

Old Grandpappy growled something Auguste failed to catch,
but William and Jonathan both looked pleased. What he did hear
was Lord Luckens' next order: 'Show them the letters, William.'

William needed no urging, and produced a small bundle of letters
tied with tape. He extracted one, and leaned forward to pass it to
Jonathan, but Red was too quick for him and tore it from his hands.

'Can you even read it?' William asked politely.

'Sure can, when old Red smells a rotten fish. When was this
written, yesterday?' he snorted, waving it in the air.

'Read it out, Red,' Lord Luckens commanded.

Red obliged, albeit slowly. 'My darling Amelia, Denver is just
dandy. Wait till you see it. Our claim is sold, and we'll be rich, just
like I promised you. You'll be strolling along the New York streets
before the fall. I'll be back in Leadville to sort things out, and then
we'll be clip-clopping our way to happiness. Your loving George.'

'My little George.' Lady Luckens looked pleased. 'He always
had a poetical streak in him. How sad he never reached New York.'

'Sad,' echoed Miss Twistleden.

'No, ma'am,' Red hooted with glee, 'but he never reached it
because he never intended to go at all. He remained in Leadville,
married to my ma, *Mollie*, until he got run down by that darned
wagon.'

'Then how could he have written this letter?' Miss Twistleden
was emboldened to ask.

'Ma'am, he didn't. Our William here wrote it and the rest.'

'For once I agree with you, Red,' Jonathan sniggered. 'It's a
most interesting letter in many ways.' He picked it up from the
table where Red had let it fall, and looked at it with an air of faint
amusement.

'Forgive me,' Lord Luckens said heavily, 'but I should, I
suppose, recognise my own son's writing?'

'You'd be only too eager to do so, I'm sure,' Jonathan agreed sweetly.

Lord Luckens looked at him sharply. 'My solicitor's checked it out with a handwriting authority.'

'Then why this charade?' Jonathan asked politely. 'Unless —'

'Yes, mister, I got letters too,' Red drawled. 'Not so many, 'cos Pa and Ma were never separated more than the once, when he comes to Leadville from San Francisco in '77, and she followed a month later. Pa wasn't one for writing much – guess he'd have written you more, Grandpappy, if he had been. Look at this.' He tossed a scrap of yellowing paper onto the table, narrowly avoiding his beer glass (a refinement demanded of the butler, to Auguste's combined horror and amusement).

Jonathan picked it up: 'Moll, miss you, sweetheart. Come to me March. George,' he read out.

'How thoughtful.' Lady Luckens' eyes filled with tears at which her husband growled:

'Time to move, Viola.'

'What the heck for?' Red demanded. 'This your quaint English custom of getting rid of the ladies?'

'No, sir,' Jonathan chortled. 'An even quainter custom of repairing to the banqueting house for our dessert.'

'In Chuck's Diner you get the food brought to you.' Red snapped his fingers at Auguste and the butler. 'Maybe you fellows could learn a thing or two.'

'Perhaps you could learn even more, Red,' William said disdainfully. 'Good manners, perhaps?'

The banqueting house at Luckens Place was a separate building about two hundred yards from the main house, with one large room, a serving area, and a retiring room. Luckens ancestors stared down in beneficent envy of their descendants' banquets of elaborate sweetmeats and jellies. Auguste had contented himself for this small gathering with orangeflower and rosewater creams, lettuce suckets, two leaches, candied marigolds, and apricots, raspberry cakes, some preserves and a moulded and iced marchpane centrepiece of the Luckens arms.

He cast an anxious eye over his work. At least here with a more informal atmosphere he could pass among the guests and keep an eye both on his culinary work and on the two claimants. He was puzzled about the latter, who at the moment seemed to have forgotten their differences, as they demolished his Elizabethan delights with great gusto. No doubt their animated tête-à-tête was comparing them favourably with home fare.

'Blasted titbits,' Lord Luckens commented on a plate of kissing comfits, presented to him by Auguste. 'Nothing like a savoury to end a meal.'

Auguste agreed. It was revolting, in his view, to kill the pleasant afterglow of a meal with strong anchovies or cooked cheese, or kidneys.

'Ever tried hominy grits?' Red asked, strolling up to them, with one hand busy feeding a slice of the Luckens arms into his mouth. 'I'll sure miss it when I get to come here for good.'

'Don't concern yourself, Red.' William was following hard on his heels. 'You'll be on grits for the rest of your life.'

'Don't be too sure of that, pal.' Red helped himself to a candied marigold, then elegantly spat it out into his empty glass, which he handed to Auguste.

'I think you *both* can be sure of it,' Jonathan remarked complacently. 'I shall be the next Lord Luckens.'

'How about waiting till I'm dead?' his present lordship shouted furiously at his guests.

Lady Luckens' brow was clouded as she added her own contribution to the conversation. 'I am a great admirer of our dear Queen, especially in her Jubilee year, but I feel she has enough palaces already. And there's Osborne, of course.'

'Don't follow you, Grandmammy.' Red looked puzzled.

'I believe my aunt refers to the fact that I myself have no heirs and if no others can be traced the estate is likely to revert to the Crown after my death,' Jonathan explained kindly.

'Over my dead body,' William declared.

'Dear Victoria,' Lady Luckens said brightly. 'How she loves the Isle of Wight. We took our honeymoon there, do you remember, Alfred? We walked to Alum Bay, visited Carisbrooke Castle – ah, the peace. I don't wonder our dear Queen loves it so.'

'Grandma, I can assure you the Queen will not be the recipient of this estate *ever*. I myself am married, with a son,' William said earnestly. 'Little Jefferson is your great-grandson.'

'Bunkum,' Red yelled. '*I'm* your grandson, and I can tell you Red Luckens is gonna sire a whole wagonload of kids. No nancies here.' He smirked at Jonathan. 'No wife, no heirs, eh?'

'But after meeting you two gentlemen this evening, I am quite sure – forgive me, Uncle – who will be wearing the coronet next,' Jonathan retorted quietly. 'I should like a word with you both later.'

'And I'd like a word with you *now*, Didier.' Lord Luckens stomped over to him, and drew a reluctant Auguste aside from the marvels of his banquet. 'That blasted nephew of mine seems to have made his mind up. Have *you* found out which one's my grandson yet?'

Auguste hedged. 'I'm still assembling ingredients, sir.'

'Eh?' Lord Luckens had no time for metaphor. 'I've told Red and William we'll sleep on it. That all right with you?'

'Yes, sir.' Auguste was only too grateful. Such suspicions as he had as to whom was the impostor were vague, swimming around like unwelcome lumps in a béchamel sauce. A night's sleep would smooth out his thinking, leaving the paste smooth.

'I've told Jonathan what you're here for. Know what he replied?' Lord Luckens guffawed. 'I hope his detection is better than his cooking, he said. The beef was surprisingly good, but he'd seldom tasted a worse pie. Don't worry yourself, Didier. Everyone makes mistakes.'

Auguste Didier seethed. *He* never did.

Auguste woke up suddenly to find firstly that it was still the middle of the night, and secondly that he would not be able to sleep again without paying attention to the demands of nature. He had been pleasantly surprised to find his room was on the guest floor, and not in the servants' quarters, but he was not so impressed with the chamber pot under his bed. Lord Luckens did not go in for modern inventions like bathrooms, or apparently indoor privies. Somewhere, he decided, one must surely exist, and he went out to prowl in search of it.

So far as Auguste could tell, there had been little opportunity for Jonathan to beard his elected impostor during the remaining time the gathering had stayed in the banqueting house, and he presumed that Jonathan too had decided to postpone any confrontation until morning. As he walked along the corridor, Auguste was uncomfortably aware of his squeaking footsteps, and the guest rooms were so far from the Queen's Chamber where Jonathan was sleeping that Auguste wondered whether Red and William had been assigned these rooms deliberately, so that the floorboards would give warning of visitors. There was no sound from either of their rooms, however.

Reaching a closed door across the corridor without succeeding in his quest, Auguste realised he had reached one of the towers flanking the Queen's Chamber. Perhaps even now Jonathan was having his 'word'. Who could tell behind these thick walls? Between Auguste and the chamber lay a six-foot tower room, and any sound would be muffled.

He took the staircase down to the entrance hall, and here at the foot of the tower his search was rewarded. Nevertheless, a vague anxiety hovered inside him, as, primary mission accomplished in what must surely be the *original* scorned water closet invented by Sir John Harington for Queen Elizabeth, Auguste returned to bed.

He awoke hours later to the sounds of disturbance outside his room which reached a crescendo as pounding footsteps passed his door. Perhaps, he told himself hopefully, the housemaid had dropped the water ewer. He snuggled down once more under the inviting blankets, for there was no sign of a housemaid's ministrations to light a fire in the grate, where last night's ashes still presented a melancholy picture.

Then his door flew open, and his host, fully-dressed, stood on the threshold, gibbering: 'Didier, blasted man's dead.'

'Dead? Who?' Auguste sat up in bed. 'How?' Auguste's first thought that adulterated food might well come out of Lord Luckens' kitchen was dismissed. Yesterday it had been supervised by *him*.

'Shot.'

Auguste stared at him. 'But who?'

'My blasted sodomite nephew or that's what he calls himself. I told him he was no part of the Luckens family; lets the side down. He can get up to what he likes in his bed, but women with the vote indeed. Next thing we know there'll be women in parliament.'

Lord Luckens brooded on this potential catastrophe for a moment before returning to his present one. 'Might have killed himself, of course,' he said hopefully. 'Just like him, to choose my house.' He ruminated, then sighed. 'Unlikely, I grant you. Which one of those two did it? Which one's the fraud, Didier? This is going to mean having police barging around, and I want to know what's what before they get here.'

Auguste leapt from his bed to find his dressing robe. 'Where was Mr Luckens found?'

'In his bedroom. Where else? If that's your standard of detection —'

Auguste did not wait for him to finish his tirade, but followed by his lordship, hurried to the Queen's Chamber. News had spread quickly, for William and Red were already there, standing one each side of the body.

'Move aside, if you please, gentlemen,' Auguste said, steeling himself for the ordeal and glad that he had not yet had breakfast.

Jonathan Luckens, still fully dressed in his evening clothes, lay on his back on the rug by his bed, sightless eyes staring upwards, shot through the temple. One hand hung limply down and on the rug at his side was the gun, a Smith and Wesson. Auguste confirmed the obvious, then turned to his lordship.

'You were right, sir,' he said. 'It's murder. There are no powder burns round the wound or on the hand, as there would be if he had shot himself. In my opinion, he was shot from some feet away.'

'Murder?' William squeaked in horror.

Red seemed equally appalled. 'See here,' he began.

'Did any of you hear anything?' Auguste asked.

'Thick walls,' Lord Luckens said complacently, taking the credit for his ancestors' masonry.

'A risk though.' Auguste frowned. 'Suppose someone *had* heard; there's only one passage, and the murderer would have been trapped.'

'Window's open,' Lord Luckens snorted. 'Plenty of footholds on the ivy.'

Auguste went to look. 'It is certainly possible, but —' He broke off, collecting his thoughts as he looked round the room. There seemed nothing unusual, until he opened a bedside drawer. Inside was a pistol.

'What the devil's that doing there?' Lord Luckens glared. 'I don't leave guns around for my guests to play with. It's mine all right, but he must have taken it from the gunroom. With good reason, I'd say.'

'*Messieurs*,' Auguste said quietly, not commenting on the 'good reason', 'I suggest that we all retire from this room and that it is locked until the police arrive.'

William and Red were only too happy to agree, and after some demur Lord Luckens escorted them to the morning room. Heavily panelled in dark wood with only narrow windows and sombre furnishings, this gloomy chamber did little to dispel their sombreness. Even Red was subdued.

'Who do you reckon did it?' William asked quietly.

'A hobo?' Red offered feebly. 'What you folks call a tramp?'

Lord Luckens snorted. 'Not blasted likely. Jonathan had discovered which of you is the false claimant to the estate, and he was about to expose you. Took the gun to defend himself when he tackled you. Instead you walked in and shot him. Quite obvious, isn't it? A child of ten could see that.'

'Not so obvious,' William retorted, though not so fiercely as usual. 'Why should he expose one of us? If one of us is knocked from the running, the other one is thereby proven as the true heir. Of course, my hot-headed friend here could well have lost his temper with Jonathan last night.'

Red did not reply immediately and, when he did, like William his heart did not seem to be in his protestations. 'Listen, pal, if I wanted to kill a man, I'd do it honestly. With the fists I was given to fight with, man to man. How would I get a firearm in this country anyway? This here holster came over empty and it's stayed empty.'

'Smith and Wessons are American,' William snapped back.

'Sure, and it's the right of every American citizen, including you, bucko, to carry one.'

'In defence of others, I believe,' Auguste intervened, 'not in defence of his entitlement to a title and money. I have one question to ask both of you before I make my report to the police, and it's this: which of you did Jonathan Luckens ask to see first last night? There wasn't an opportunity in the banqueting house, so it must have been here, in his room.'

'Not me,' William came in promptly.

'Nor me,' Red said earnestly.

'Suppose they both went,' Lord Luckens growled. 'Thought of that?'

'We didn't, Grandpappy,' Red assured him. 'Why, speaking for myself, I slept like a babby all night.'

'Says you,' William snarled.

Auguste was puzzled. This was all very odd. After the police had been notified, he left them to return to the kitchen, for he needed room to think and breakfast. Both were possible since the servants taking theirs in the servants' hall. What should he have? All he could face was a drink of soothing chocolate. Then his eye fell on the humble egg. An egg!

One could always rely on an egg. Unassuming, nutritious, the self-sacrificing base of the most perfect dishes in the world. Who thought of the egg while a bavarois was in one's mouth? Who thought of the egg while a sauce hollandaise eased itself into one's stomach? Yes, he would boil himself an egg, plain and unadorned, perhaps with soldiers, as in the English fashion, crustless buttered bread cut into strips.

Eagerly, Auguste placed the egg in the boiling water, turned the ornamental egg timer, from Alum Bay no doubt, upside down for the coloured sands to run through, and prepared lovingly to watch the cooking of his breakfast.

Coloured sands? Alum Bay? Queen Victoria? *Egg timer*? He stared at it hypnotised, as first the solution of the case of the missing heir and then that of the murder of Jonathan Luckens clarified in his mind like heated butter. It was as plain as a boiled egg.

* * *

'Well?' Lord Luckens demanded, after Auguste had requested a private interview.

'Which of them did it?'

'I prefer to tell you which is the impostor.'

'Same thing.'

'Not necessarily.'

'Have it your own blasted way then. Just tell me.'

'Red Luckens is a fraud. I am convinced he has never been near a silver mine in his life, for hominy grits is a southern dish and Colorado is not in the south of the United States. Also, he is, like a neatly trimmed poached egg, too good to be naturally true.'

'So William's my grandson then,' Lord Luckens said glumly. 'Pity. Red has more spunk in him. Still, it's better than the estate going to Queen Victoria, God bless her. And Red killed Jonathan. Might have guessed it.'

'No, sir.'

'So it was William shot him,' Lord Luckens said immediately. 'He knew Jonathan had got it the wrong way round, and wasn't going to risk his precious inheritance vanishing.'

'No, sir. William as well as Red is an impostor. That letter must surely have been forged, for he wrote, "Wait till you see Denver", as though it would be his wife's first visit. In fact, William purports to have been born there, so that is impossible. I was puzzled by their apparently amicable private conversation at the banquet, and suspect they were discussing their spoils.'

'You're raving, Didier. How can both of them be impostors? There wouldn't be any spoils to discuss.'

'I refer to the spoils they have or will shortly receive from you, Lord Luckens.'

'What the devil do you mean?' he shouted, red in the face with anger.

'I looked at this case the wrong way up. It took an egg timer to understand that I needed to stand it on its head and let the sand trickle through. When I did so it was quite obvious that neither of these gentlemen could be your missing heir. That in any case was always a possibility, but the egg timer caused me to realise that it was you who had planned the whole thing, hired their services, forged the so-called evidence and falsely claimed to them and probably your solicitor that Pinkertons had checked out the birth certificates in the States.'

'Think I'm out of my mind, do you? I'd have to adopt one of them to keep Jonathan out of it. Why the devil should I adopt a stranger?'

'Because you hated your brother and then his son so much.'

'Enough to adopt an out-of-work actor and a smooth-talking rogue? That's who they are and that I can prove. How could I have known one of them was going to shoot the fellow to make sure of his inheritance?'

'You couldn't. You hated your nephew so much, you'd prefer the Queen to have the estate. With Jonathan dead you would later find proof that neither Red nor William is your missing heir. There is in fact no missing heir. It was a plot to rid yourself of Jonathan by murder. You shot him, Lord Luckens, in the expectation one of them would be blamed.'

To Auguste's surprise, Lord Luckens did not treat him to an outburst of abuse. Instead, he gave a bark of laughter.

'You're clever for a Frenchie, Didier. Not clever enough, though. If I were a murderer, I'd be unmasked the minute those two rabbits blabbed to the police. No, I'll tell you what really happened. I hired them all right. The mistake I made was to make it a gamble for them. Whichever you unmasked as the impostor would get nothing but his expenses; the one you decided was my grandson would get £5,000. Tidy sum, eh? Worth killing for. Hadn't foreseen that. Whichever Jonathan picked on as the impostor had good reason to stop him talking. With two such prime suspects, the police aren't going to suspect me just because I didn't like the fellow, no matter what beans they spilled about my hiring them.'

'Would the police not believe it a little strange that you were willing to pay so much money merely for the pleasure of seeing your nephew's ambitions temporarily thwarted? You could hardly explain that you knew in advance of hiring Red and William that Jonathan would no longer be alive when you disclosed the truth about them.'

Lord Luckens gave a gargoyle grin of pure evil. 'They'll

understand why I hired them, Didier. I'm a poor old man of eighty, and can't hang around for ever. Devoted to Lady Luckens, tears in her eyes, not too bright in the head, loving husband wants to make her happy. What better than that her beloved grandson's returned to her? Worth any price, that. Might even adopt one of them – which do you fancy, Didier? Money no object to make her ladyship happy. They'll believe me, not a blasted chef.'

'They will when they hear what I have to say.'

His lordship snorted. 'You stick to cooking, Didier. Blasted sugared lettuce stalks.'

With some effort Auguste ignored the insult to his suckets. 'I asked myself why Jonathan should have armed himself with a pistol to defend himself and then left it in a drawer when a night-time visitor arrived. If he were expecting Red or William, or if the visit were unannounced, the pistol would be within easy reach; if he knew the caller was you, however, he would hardly have felt fear for his life. I believe that you told him you were coming, giving the excuse that at such a time and in such a place you could not be overheard if Jonathan were to tell you whom he suspected of being the impostor. Or perhaps he suspected them both. You, Lord Luckens, were the only person who need not fear the gunshot being overheard. What's more natural than that the host, who sleeps nearby and who has placed his guests' bedrooms far away from the Queen's Chamber, should be first on the scene to find the cause of the alarm?'

'Poppycock,' Lord Luckens snorted, with less conviction.

'I think not. Had you hired only one impostor, you might well have succeeded. Your mistake, Lord Luckens, was to over-egg the pudding by hiring two, to try to make your story more convincing.'

Through the window Auguste could see the police arriving.

'*You* were the bad egg,' he continued. 'Your mistake was that you asked me, a master chef, to cook it.'

The man enjoyed the work. He always did. Just he and his dog and a summer's morning. It was 'their time' – his feet crumbling the loose gravel on the towpath as the last of the haze rose from the canal and his dog twisting and turning, now ahead of him, now beside him, now behind him, now ahead of him, now beside him, now behind him, now ahead of him again. They rounded the bend of the canal and entered the phase of the walk that the man loved most of all, where thick vegetation grew at either side of the canal and reached out over the water, so that in summer especially, when the foliage was at its most lush, this part of the canal resembled a walk in a tunnel. It was in this section of the York canal that the man saw the greatest incidence of wildlife, the moorhens, kingfishers, stoats, and water rats. The latter he minded not, for like all creatures, they had a place in the scheme of things. Here they were wild, not scavengers living off the debris of humankind, and he chose to accept them as beasts in their own place. And he also saw insects, dragonflies, butterflies, spiders. At the end of the 'tunnel' ahead of him, he could see the black-and-white gates of the 'Larkfield Three-Rise', a tier of three locks which lifted the canal up a full thirty feet to its next section, which took it across the Wold towards Hull and the seaport there. Or lowered it for the final stretch into York, depending upon which way the barge, now a pleasure craft rather than a working boat, was travelling. The man walked slowly, savouring the walk, just he and his best friend. An onlooker would see a man in his sixties, plus fours, stout shoes, a tweed jacket, and a white Norfolk hat, and with him, a confident chocolate-brown Labrador. The man left the shade of the 'tunnel' and put himself at the inclined path which ran alongside the three-rise until he stood at the top. These days he was finding the incline difficult…even a short incline such as this he found hard. He could, he felt, walk forever upon the flat, but inclines were proving difficult. He paused at the top of the incline and pondered the next section of the walk, another six hundred yards of canal towpath and then he'd turn into the wood and begin the sweep back towards home. He expected to be home by nine-thirty...in time for *Morning Service* on the BBC. It was a good walk, about three hours long, and he and his friend did it together twice a week, in all but the most extreme weather conditions.

Then he saw a shiny black object in the canal, and tutted at folk who thought nothing of throwing their refuse into the water. With a jolt, he realised that he wasn't looking at a black bin liner containing domestic rubbish, he was looking at oily water shimmering on a leather jacket which encased a human body, floating face down in the water.

The body was that of a female. The first police officer to attend waded into the canal and was eventually forced to swim the last few feet, the water being just too deep for a tall man to wade. He reached the body, gasping at the chill of the water despite it being high summer, and rolled it face up, just in case there was still time, but the pale and bloated, macerated skin said that all hope had gone. He swam sideways, dragging the body with him back to the towpath, where he and his colleague together hauled the body out of the water. Closer examination showed her to be a woman of middle years and possibly, probably, of privileged living. The leather jacket was not inexpensive, neither was the watch, nor the jewellery, nor the skirt, nor the shoes, which had remained on her feet, held firmly as the body expanded.

One of the police officers, the one who remained dry, stayed with the corpse. The other, saturated and chilled, walked to where they had parked the area car. He called Friargate police station, requested the police surgeon and CID attendance. He added that the death was probably suspicious, if only because middle-aged, middle-class women do not walk along canal towpaths alone at night. They just don't.

When, thirty minutes later, the police surgeon arrived, he noticed a blue-and-white police tape around the body, which by then lay under a black plastic sheet. He noted a member of the public being told firmly but politely that he couldn't walk along the canal despite the fact that he did that each morning. The police surgeon approached the tape, knelt by the body, lifted the plastic sheet, and let it fall reverently back in place as the member of the public turned and walked sullenly away.

'I can confirm life extinct.' The police surgeon stood. 'At nine-ten a.m.'

'Nine-ten a.m., sir?' the police constable repeated and noted in his notebook. He glanced up and noted two figures walking towards them along the towpath. 'CID here now, sir.'

'Good...I think they'll be needed.' He turned and glanced and nodded at the approaching figures, one a white male, the other a black female. Both tall, both slim, walking easily in each other's company, occasionally rubbing shoulders; two people who like each other. 'Dr Truelove,' he said when the officers were close enough.

'DCs Pharoah and Markov.' The woman spoke. 'I'm Pharoah.'

'We haven't met. Not local, are you, by your accent?'

'St Kitts, via Stoke Newington, London.' Carmen Pharoah smiled.

'Pleased to meet you. Well, to the matter in hand.' Truelove turned to the body. 'I think you'll be needing a pathologist. The police constable who phoned it in was correct to assume suspicious circumstances. She didn't drown, you see. I can tell that virtually at a glance. Eyes closed, you see. She was either unconscious or deceased before she entered the water. But that's really the territory of the Home Office pathologist, not I.'

'I see,' Carmen Pharoah said. 'Pathologist, as you say.'

'I've pronounced life extinct at nine-ten, this day. It's really up to the pathologist now.'

'Wonder where she came into the canal?' Carmen Pharoah said, more to herself than anyone around her. 'No sign of a struggle here that I can see.'

'Up there.' The constable spoke. He pointed along the canal, away from the locks, towards Hull and the coast. 'She would have drifted down overnight. Canals have currents, like rivers.'

'I didn't know that.' Markov spoke.

'It's true, sir.' The police constable spoke confidently. 'All canals are the same. They benefit from rainwater which runs off the land into the canal, but each canal has a river or a stream or a lake close to the highest point and they flow down from there. This part of the canal drains into the Ouse at York.' He turned. 'In that direction. So she would have drifted down from the opposite direction until she reached the locks, where she was caught.'

'Makes sense.' Markov nodded. 'We'll take a walk up there.' Carmen Pharoah pressed the Send button on her radio and called Friargate police station, requesting the pathologist and the mortuary van. She and Markov walked eastwards along the towpath in the opposite direction of the current. As she walked, she had to concede that this really was a very, very attractive part of England, lush fields and a flat landscape. She thought that she might settle here after all. She knew that she couldn't go back to London...horror of horrors...the commuting...and while St Kitts would always be 'home', to return there was not an option. But York, and North Yorkshire...an ancient city...affordable housing...vast skies produced by a flat landscape.

There are worse places.

Every few hundred yards along the York and Hull canal, as with all British canals, there are stone ramps which lead from the towpath into the water, the ramps being inclined towards each other with a gap of about six feet between them. Their purpose was to enable a horse to be recovered from the canal, so that should a horse that was pulling a barge slip into the canal, it could be unhitched from the barge and worked along the canal, through the water, until a ramp was reached where it could easily walk back up to the towpath, and be returned and rehitched to the barge. Diesel engines have rendered such ramps redundant, but they remain, and the six-foot gap between each ramp tends to be a collection point for floating debris. It was between two such ramps that Simon Markov noticed a handbag, black leather, floating among the plastic bags and bottles. He knelt down and fished it out of the water.

The handbag, by its contents, belonged to one Sadie Winner. The driving licence in that name gave an address of Dovecote Cottage, Lesser Listlea, North Yorkshire.

'I wonder what sort of car she drove?' Markov pondered. 'She wasn't without money. Lesser Listlea is a wealthy village, it's not far from here...and this handbag alone...'

'She drove a Beemer,' said Carmen Pharoah.

Markov smiled at her. 'How do you know that?'

'Ah…' Pharoah grinned. 'And I also know the colour. It's silver. German racing silver, as you'd expect of a BMW.'

'How —?'

'Because it's there.' She pointed to a road bridge over the canal about fifty yards away. The car was not fully visible, just the roof, but sufficient to be able to identify it. A BMW in German racing silver. Stationary, where a car would not be parked.

Markov placed the handbag in the self-sealing production bag and he and Carmen Pharoah walked yet further along the canal, to the bridge, to the steps from the towpath to the road. They examined the car. The doors were not locked, the keys were still in the ignition.

'The only reason this is still here is that its location was not known to the car thieves,' Markov said softly, more to himself than to Carmen Pharoah. 'So, did she fall or was she pushed?'

'Oh, pushed, I expect,' Pharoah replied matter-of-factly, but with tongue in cheek.

'I expect so as well.' He reached for his radio and pressed the Send button. He reported the location of the car and its possible relevance to the incident, requesting a constable and a roll of blue and white police tape. 'She didn't commit suicide… The police surgeon believes that she was not breathing when she went into the water. It's not a suicide spot anyway… So if she was attacked, the attacker had no interest in her possessions…the motive wasn't robbery. Her handbag, her jewellery say so.'

'Didn't want the car, either,' added Pharoah. 'He or she or they had to have had a personal motive, unless it was a random attack.'

'It's not the place for a random attack,' Markov said. 'On the one hand it's isolated, but on the other, there's quite a lot of traffic down the road. My money is on a personal motive.'

Leaving a constable on duty by the BMW, which had blue and white police tape fastened round it, Markov and Pharoah drove to Dovecote Cottage, Lesser Listlea. They found that Dovecote Cottage was a cottage in the same sense that the chapel at Kings

College, Cambridge, is a 'chapel' despite being as large as a small cathedral; and in the same sense that York is a city despite the fact that in terms of its area, it could fit within the confines of a housing estate in a major city. Dovecote Cottage revealed itself to be a half-timbered Elizabethan manor house, built in an L shape in front of a gravelled courtyard in the middle of which stood a stone fountain belonging to a later, possibly Victorian era... So thought Markov as he slowed the car to a halt beside the Bentley which stood near the front door. The door of the house opened as Markov and Pharoah stepped out of their car.

'Yes?' The man was well built, fifty-something. A dark-blue towelling dressing gown covered silk pyjamas.

'Police.'

'Yes?'

'Mr Winner?' Markov approached and showed his ID.

''Tis I.'

'We have a few questions...'

'You'd better come in.'

Winner received the police in the hallway of his house, where they sat opposite each other on benches which stood alongside walls of ancient beams.

'Oh my,' he said when Markov revealed the reason for their visit. 'Oh my...'

'Do you know what her car would be doing on the bridge over the canal?'

'The bridge in question...it's on the route that she favours to get from the village to York. She drives it daily. I prefer the main road, but she likes the rural route. But I've no idea why she should have stopped where she did. Which way was the car pointing?'

'Towards the village.'

'So she was coming home. She was very cautious...she wouldn't have stopped, not unless it was because she knew someone...someone she recognised.'

'What time did you expect your wife to return home?'

'Last night? About nine-thirty, ten. She went to visit her sister, she lives in York. The two of them, once they get their heads together, at my expense...calling up all my past misdeeds and indiscretions. She was about to take me to the cleaner's... They would have spent the evening planning my ruin.'

'So, you'd benefit from your wife's death?'

'Oh yes... In fact, I'm just beginning to realise just what a great weight might have been lifted from my shoulders...just what a shadow I am escaping from, if it is my wife.'

'We'll have to ask you to accompany us to York District Hospital to identify the body...if you can.'

'The car, the handbag, the clothing you describe – it'll be her all right. But yes, formality has to be observed.'

'Before we go, could you tell us where you were at about nine-thirty last night?'

'Here.'

'Alone?'

'Alone. I was working. The industry is in a bad state at the moment.'

'The industry?'

'Electronics. I am the Winner of Winner Electronics, the factory on the industrial estate.'

'Ah yes,' Markov nodded.

'I'm asking my managers to put in unpaid overtime to avert collapse. I can't do that if I'm not prepared to do the same.'

'Of course.'

'I made a few phone calls...sent a few faxes... They could be confirmed. I have itemised bills. The people to whom I spoke will be able to confirm that 'twas I who spoke.'

'This was at nine-thirty?'

'No... No, earlier. I was reading reports at about that time...then I went outside. I enjoy the dusk at this time of year – that would have been about nine-thirty, ten, just outside in the garden – but I was alone.'

'Your wife, was she depressed of late?'

'No... Just the opposite, in fact. She was enthusiastic in a vindictive sort of way...burning up with determination to fleece me in a divorce settlement.'

'But she was living here?'

'All part of the Great Plan to ruin me. Can't bring a lady friend home while she's in the house, can I? And she knows it. We sleep separately, but it's still the one roof... Makes things very difficult for me.'

'Not the sort of person to take her own life, then?'

'Hardly.' Winner smiled. 'My wife take her own life, I hardly think so... No...not a chance. She had everything to live for, i.e, my total ruin. She was poised to take half of what I possess, plus a massive amount of maintenance. She had a lot to live for. She and her sister had their knives out for me.'

'So you really have benefited from her death? If it is she?'

'Oh yes, only the collapse of my business empire to worry about now. A minor headache by comparison. I make no secret of it. I have no feelings for my wife now. I haven't for a long time. I was angry about the possible divorce settlement because she wasn't very supportive of me while I was building up...more of a hindrance. I really did it despite her, not because of her.'

'So, it's not true that behind every successful man there is a good woman?'

'Not in my case, it's not. Just isn't. I certainly could have used such a female in my life, but it wasn't my lot. I'd come home each day to a wife screaming for new clothes and no food. She would say that if I was hungry I could send out for a pizza. I went for her looks and found them skin-deep and that the skin was covering a very ugly personality. I should have listened to my grandmother when she told me to shut my eyes and listen to the voice. "Do your courting on the telephone," she'd say. I should have listened.'

'She sounds like a sensible woman.'

'She was. She's still alive but her mind is away. I visit her when I can, but it's difficult to sit with a woman who once was full of such horse sense and wisdom who now thinks she's a little girl and doesn't recognise me. Keeps asking me if her daddy's going to come home from the war. Anyway, I'll claw my kit on, go and see the corpse. Never done this before...' Winner stood.

'It's not like what you may have seen in the films... She won't be pulled out of a drawer, you'll see her from behind a glass screen.'

'It will be as if she is floating,' added Pharoah.

It was in fact just as Carmen Pharoah had described. The woman floating on a bed, tightly tucked up. 'It is she,' said Max Winner. 'That's my wife, Sadie Winner, aged forty-five years. Quite frankly, I don't know which one of us rests in peace.'

Bill Hatch stood – a short, balding, rotund man with stubby fingers. He was the sort of man who would be found in a pigeon loft lovingly stroking his beloved birds, or perhaps reading a tabloid newspaper on the top deck of a bus, or downing pints of mild and bitter in a smoky pub. But he was, in fact, a Home Office pathologist. He examined the corpse of Sadie Winner in the pathology laboratory of the York District Hospital and said, 'The police surgeon is quite correct. Even before I make the first and even slightest incision, I can tell you that she didn't drown.'

'No?' Carmen Pharoah responded from the corner of the room from where she was observing the post-mortem for the police.

'No.' He ran his hands through Sadie Winner's scalp hair. 'No, she was hit over the head. A single blow, feels like from behind... We'll see.' He took a scalpel and made an incision round the perimeter of the skull above the level of the ears and then peeled the scalp back and revealed the skull. 'Yes...fractured skull...bleeding was internal...subdural haematoma...a single blow with a blunt object...caused a starlike fracturing. She also had a very thin skull. A person with a thicker skull might have survived this blow, but in her case, death would have been instantaneous.'

Carmen Pharoah met Simon Markov, as arranged, for lunch in the town. Later they walked the walls back towards Friargate, the ancient city spreading out at either side beneath them. They walked in silence, enjoying each other's company, then Carmen Pharoah said, 'If you had battered someone over the head, what would you do with the murder weapon?'

'Get rid of it.'

'In the first conventional place?'

'Yes.'

'Such as a canal, for instance?'

Markov smiled at her. 'Yes, such as a canal, for instance?'

'A job for the frog boys. We'll ask Ken Menninot to authorise it. Meanwhile, to matters of greater import.' She slid her arm into his. 'Tonight I thought we'd eat Chinese.'

'Can do, if you wish. In fact…' Markov paused and halted. 'Look.' He indicated towards the railway station below and across the road from where they stood on the battlements. 'Isn't that Max Winner?'

'It is.'

The two cops watched as Max Winner stood talking with a woman many, many years his junior. She was slender, ginger-haired, casually dressed. The woman suddenly stepped forwards and kissed him. Max Winner responded by holding her upper arms, but perfunctorily so. She was more interested in him than he was in her. Their body language said so.

Ken Menninot, Sergeant, CID, listened to Pharoah's feedback on the PM and her theory about the discarding of the murder weapon. He authorised a small team of divers to search the canal beneath the bridge on which Sadie Winner's car had been located. The murder weapon revealed itself to have been a smooth rock, large enough to just fit in one hand, inside a woollen hiking sock. When swung, it would have made quite an impact, especially on an unusually thin skull.

Pharoah and Markov drove out to Winner's house.

'I thought I'd see you again,' he said pleasantly. 'Only not quite so soon.' He stood at the entrance of his house. As he and the cops stood there, a woman bundled out of the house, elbowing him aside, carrying a cardboard box with her.

The woman stopped at the sight of Pharoah and Markov, both in plain clothes but both with the unmistakable stamp of police officers about them. She turned and yelled 'Murderer!' at Winner. Then she stamped off to a small car and drove angrily away.

'My sister-in-law,' Winner explained apologetically. 'Won't you come in? Please.'

On this occasion Winner received Pharoah and Markov in the sitting room of his house. The cops, reading the room, noted he had a taste for antiques – furniture, china, paintings. 'The distress you just witnessed,' he said, settling into a chair, 'is due in part, I believe, to the fact that my ex-wife's sister believed that her money troubles would have been solved upon our divorce. My ex-wife's sister and her husband live a very hand-to-mouth existence. The car she had… I've never seen it before. She must have borrowed it. She certainly doesn't own one.'

'I see.'

'Tell you the truth, your arrival rescued me. But she'll be back, collecting Sadie's possessions and anything of mine I may be foolish enough to leave behind. In fact, she didn't make an attempt to remove all Sadie's possessions, gives her the excuse to come back.'

'You could leave them at the door.'

'I could, couldn't I? That hadn't occurred to me.' Winner smiled. 'It is my house, after all, isn't it?'

'Mr Winner,' Markov said, 'that young woman that you were speaking to outside the railway station this lunchtime —

'You saw us?'

'We were up on the walls.'

'I see. Yes…that was Julia. Another bane of my life. I don't really have a great deal of success with women – my ex…now Julia. Julia really was the start of all my troubles ten years ago now.'

'Ten years?'

'Julia's older than she looks. She's in her late twenties.'

'Really?'

'She acts and dresses like a teenager. I confess I worry about her, psychologically speaking. She's just not with us, it's as if she's on another planet.'

'How did you meet?'

'She was an employee at the factory. A low-skilled job…a secretarial job, but she seemed to latch herself onto me…speak to me on any pretext…sending notes to my wife. Telling Sadie that she, Julia, and I were to be married. Really set the cat among the pigeons. My ex – my wife – call her my ex, but we were not divorced. I'll have to start calling her my late wife now – anyway, Sadie. Once that seed of suspicion grew, it grew to something mammoth. A bit like a mustard tree. A small seed grows into a huge tree. So we drifted apart and I had my affairs, but definitely not with little Miss Julia Patton, though she continued to shadow me.'

'Do you know where she lives?'

'Tang Hall Estate, Two Cheviot Avenue. Seen the address often enough on the letters she has sent to me. Sorry, you are…?'

'DCs Pharoah and Markov. In case you should want to contact us – you may need a contact person – we're working the six a.m. until two p.m. shift this week.'

'Overtime, then.' Winner glanced at the grandfather clock. It was two-thirty p.m.

'Par for the course,' Markov said, smiling.

Pharoah and Markov drove back to York, through the city centre and out to Tang Hall: low-rise, unkempt gardens, houses with boarded-up windows, motorcycles fastened to lamp posts with massive chains and padlocks, cars in driveways being 'done up' prior to resale for a modest profit. Number 2 Cheviot Avenue fitted into the surrounding area, an overgrown garden and a pile of uncollected domestic refuse by the side door. The cops knocked at the front door. The sound of the knocker echoed within.

'I don't know why we are here,' said Pharoah.

'Because we are,' Markov replied. 'We're here to find what we shall find, if anything.'

The door was flung open and a woman with ginger hair and glazed blue eyes stood on the threshold. 'Yes?'

'Julia Patton?'

'Aye.' At close hand she did indeed look older than she did from a distance.

'Police.'

An intake of breath. 'Yes?'

'We understand that you know Mr Winner? Mr Max Winner?'

'Aye.' She smiled. The name clearly triggered something and she said, 'Winner by name, winner by nature.'

'You know him well?'

'Very. Very well indeed.'

'Where were you last night?'

'Here,' she said. 'At home.'

'All night?'

'Yes.'

'Alone?'

'Yes.' She adopted a more aggressive stance. 'You can ask my neighbours. They'll tell you my light was on all night, go and ask them.'

'You'll know Mrs Winner?'

'The cow. Of course I know her. She tried to stop me and Max...but she couldn't. True love will find a way.'

'You and Mr Winner are in a relationship?'

'Yes...for years now.'

'Do you hike?'

'What?'

'Walking...long walks in the country, do you do it?'

'No.'

'You wouldn't have any hiking socks, then?'

Julia Patton blushed a deep red but recovered quickly and said, 'No.'

'Do you mind if we come in?'

'Why? There's nothing to see.'

'Nothing to hide then, have you?' The cops stepped outside.

Julia Patton's house was threadbare and basic. Very basic. Worn-out chairs, no floor covering, and even at that time of the year, it had a chill about it. In the hallway Markov noted a pair of boots. Not hiking boots, but working boots, the sort that would have to be worn with thick socks over ordinary socks. He said, 'I've got a pair of boots like that. Use them for gardening.'

'Oh.'

'Have to wear hiking socks with them.'

'I do, too. They wore out. I threw them out.'

'They'll be in the refuse by the door.'

'No. Threw them out a long time ago.'

Markov picked up one of the boots and examined the sole. The soil trapped on the side was slightly damp. 'They've been worn recently?'

'Just in the garden. Don't need thick socks to go into the garden. Will that be all?'

Markov replaced the boot. 'Yes. For now.'

'Good. I've got plans to make.'

'For?'

'My marriage. Max and I are getting married. Nothing to stop us now she's dead. Heard it on the lunchtime news. Haven't felt better for years.'

That evening went as planned for Carmen Pharoah and Simon Markov; one recently arrived in York, the other settled but recently divorced, and now having found each other. They met outside the Minster and went on a Ghost Walk to satisfy Carmen Pharoah's curiosity, she having often seen such walks advertised. They joined a crowd of about fifty who were led around the city by an actor in Victorian dress who took them down the narrow, one-person-at-a-time snickleways, a street pattern within a street pattern, and who showed them the tall house where a hundred years previously a little girl had fallen to her death within, down the stairwell from the upper floor to the cellar, and who can sometimes be seen as she ascends the stairs for the last time. And they were shown the window where the most recently seen ghost in all England – about twenty sightings a year – is to be viewed; a little girl sobbing at the window. The story being that during the Black Death her parents noticed she had the symptoms of the plague and so locked her in her room and fled, not just the house, which they locked and left with the sign of the plague on the door, but York itself. Leaving their daughter to succumb to thirst, or starvation, or the plague. And they viewed the house where once a man had seen a column of Roman soldiers who were marching, as if on their knees, along the hallway of the house. Excavation revealed the house had been built on the site of a Roman road, the surface of which was two feet beneath the floor of the house.

'Lost something by doing the walk in summer,' Markov said as he glanced at the menu in the Green Jade restaurant.

'We could do it again,' replied Carmen, whose eye was caught by the chicken chow mein. 'A blustery winter's night, or Halloween. That would be fun.'

They spent the night at her house, where she was still living largely out of bin liners and cardboard boxes. She had bought 'within the walls', having been told that she would never have a problem selling her house if she bought 'within the walls' and that night they lay together listening to the Minster bells chime midnight.

Max Winner woke early the next morning, as he did during the summer months, but he remained long in bed, still feeling a sense of whirring confusion in his head. The sense of weight having been lifted from his life was tangible…but yet, strangely, there was a loss, too. He was now finally alone in his house. She was no longer in her room. He didn't miss her, not at all, but there was a space, a hole where previously there was no hole. He didn't think her loss would have had such an effect on him, and it surprised him that it did.

He heard the doorbell ring. He levered himself out of bed, wound into his dressing gown, and went down the ancient creaking staircase and answered the door. He gasped in surprise and astonishment.

'Morning, Max,' beamed Julia Patton. 'Did you miss me?' She stood with two suitcases at her feet. 'Nothing to stop us now, is there, Max?'

'No – no —' He said 'no' because he didn't know what else to say. 'Won't you come in?'

They sat in the sitting room where the day previously he had received Carmen Pharoah and Simon Markov. 'I don't know what to say,' he said.

'I knew you'd be pleased. I used to watch the house almost every evening…got to know her movements… Waited for her on the bridge. I knew she'd stop and give me a mouthful…and she did. Then when she turned away to go back to her car, I hit her over the head. I had a rock inside a sock. She went down slowly. I tried to lift her over the parapet, but I couldn't, so I dragged her down some steps and put her in the water, face down, dropped her handbag in after her and chucked the rock and sock in the water as well. So we can be together now, Max, I can be lady of this house.'

'Yes...' He smiled. 'Yes...have you breakfasted yet?'

'No. I came straight here. The police called yesterday but I got rid of them, they won't be back. Just you and me now, Max.'

Max Winner stood. 'Well, look, why don't you make yourself at home.'

'At home,' she echoed.

'I'll go and get my clothes on and I'll make us both something to eat.' He left the room and walked back up the stairs to his bedroom. He closed the door behind him and picked up the telephone by his bed. 'DC Pharoah or Markov,' he said when his call was answered. 'Either will do.'

One of the most baffling crimes Detective Inspector Jeremy Faro ever faced had nothing to do with murder, but quite a lot to do with buying presents for his mother and two small daughters. Birthdays were difficult enough for a widower, but Christmas presents were worse, especially when Rose, aged eight, took one look at the familiar oblong cardboard box and cried out reproachfully: 'Oh Papa, not another doll.'

Had his normal powers of deduction been functioning Inspector Faro might have found the vital clue in her younger sister Emily's letter, that she 'liked the dolly's frocks, but not very much'.

Birthdays were inevitable but by the 1870s the fashion set by Her Majesty and the late Prince Consort had been eagerly followed and the Christmas craze had spread to Edinburgh. Now a middle class, once content with the annual Hogmanay debauch, demanded turkey, plum pudding, a tree in the window and the unsteady march of Christmas cards across the mantelpiece. In mainly candlelit rooms this also had the city's fire engines on constant alert.

Nor were fires the only hazard in the homes of the well-to-do. A rash of Yuletide parties and conviviality, with a regrettable slackening of the tough moral fibre of Calvinism, was regarded as a positive enticement to sneak thieves. As a consequence this quite unnecessary season of peace and goodwill was greeted with less than enthusiasm by the Edinburgh City Police.

Advertisements like that of Jenners in Princes Street, offering customers a chance to inspect valuable seasonal items, had been viewed by the criminal element as an open invitation to more splendid opportunities of breaking and entering in a spate of daring robberies.

As Faro's young stepson Dr Vincent Laurie studied his sister's letter, he said:

'Now what do you think of that? I imagined that all little girls liked dolls.'

'They do indeed, Stepfather, but not every Christmas and birthday. Ever since our mama died —' he added sadly. 'Don't you see —'

Faro tried but failed. 'You wouldn't – I suppose —' he said wistfully.

'No, I certainly wouldn't,' was the stern reply. 'The very idea! I find it hard enough getting suitable presents for my own list.'

Vince could be notoriously unsympathetic sometimes but seeing his stepfather's anguished expression, he said: 'What about a piece of jewellery then? Small girls like lockets and bangles.' And warming to the idea. 'And a brooch for Step-grandma —'

'You really think so...'

'I do indeed. And what's more there's a splendid new jeweller's shop opened in South Clerk Street, just a step away. Foreign chap. Did an excellent repair on my pocket watch – a wizard with clocks, I understand – highly recommended.'

'In the circumstances – would you?'

'No, I wouldn't.' said Vince crossly. 'The experience will do you good.'

Rose and Emily had lived with their grandmama in Orkney for the past two years, and as the last date for posting parcels grew nearer, so too did Inspector Faro's frowns grow deeper and darker with the preoccupation of choosing suitable presents. Finally, with all the anticipatory joy of a man presenting himself for the extraction of a particularly sensitive tooth, he stared glumly into the jeweller's window, feeling utterly helpless faced with such a bewildering and dazzling selection.

If only he enjoyed shopping. He had relied on his dear Lizzie to keep his wardrobe up to the mark. His indifference to sartorial elegance was well known at the Central Office of the Edinburgh City Police. As long as garments were comfortable and covered him in modest decency, he did not care a fig for fashion. The reflection of his greatcoat in the window glass jolted him a little, but closing his eyes, he took a deep breath and entered the shop where a loud bell noisily proclaimed his presence.

Taking stock of his surroundings as he waited for the jeweller to appear, the shop was small, dark and depressing, a complete contrast to the brilliant sunshine of a winter afternoon settling into a rosy sunset sharp with frost.

A closer look at the owner, who entered through the curtain and bowed gravely, told a delighted Faro that he might have modelled Mr Dickens's Fagin but for those gentle eyes and dignified bearing.

Indicating a tray of brooches he found Mr Jacob most helpful. Was the recipient a young lady?

Faro shook his head. 'No, it is for my mother.' He was both delighted and relieved when Mr Jacob after careful deliberation pointed to the very one he had in mind. 'Yes, indeed, that is perfect,' said Faro. 'I will take it.'

'Is there anything else I might interest you in, sir?'

When Faro asked to see lockets, the jeweller beamed.

'For your lady wife, sir.'

'Actually for my two small daughters. I am a widower.'

Mr Jacob sighed. 'I also. I have a daughter to look after me.'

Choosing two identical gold lockets, Faro asked. 'Forgive my curiosity. I realise you are a newcomer to Edinburgh. May I ask what brought you here?'

'I have been here since May. As to what brought me here, sir, I will be frank with you. Persecution – yes, persecution. We have been dogged by utmost misfortunes and we are still wanderers. But Edinburgh gave us hope for a home and a future. Here it seemed that our race was tolerated and even encouraged to settle, to live and die in peace.'

Faro suspected that Mr Jacob had been lured by the fact that sixty years ago in the early years of the century, Edinburgh had seen the establishment of the first Jewish cemetery in Scotland, a stone's throw from his shop.

A sign of tolerance, generous but sadly misleading. Faro was well aware that to the ordinary Edinburgh citizen, a minority racial group was something to be jeered at, despised, and that any success in business by honest dealings and honest sweat, was treated with the darkest suspicion.

* * *

Mr Jacob was fitting the gifts into velvet boxes. When Faro said they were to be posted, a sturdy brown envelope was produced.

'Perhaps you would write on the address, sir. I have a card to enclose with your message.'

'That is most thoughtful of you, Mr Jacob.'

The jeweller studied the name and address. 'Faro – you are the Inspector – Inspector Faro?'

'I am,' said Faro, surprised and flattered to find himself famous.

'You must forgive me, sir, I did not recognise you again.'

'Again?' queried Faro.

'Yes, sir. I have the ring ready for you —'

'The ring – what ring?'

It was the jeweller's turn to look astonished. 'Why, sir, the valuable brooch you left.' And unlocking a drawer behind the counter Mr Jacob produced an emerald and diamond ring.

Faro was taken aback. Although no connoisseur of precious gems, he would have hazarded a rough guess that it was worth at least ten times his annual salary with Edinburgh City Police.

He also knew that he had never set eyes on it before.

Mr Jacob watching him intently mistook his expression as one of disapproval and said anxiously: 'I hope it is correct, sir. I tried to follow your instructions exactly.'

'My instructions?'

The jeweller nodded vigorously. 'Indeed, sir. I was to change the order of the diamonds and make the original brooch into a ring setting suitable for a lady,' he said slowly then frowning: 'There is some mistake?'

With a shake of his head, Faro replied: 'There is indeed. This piece of jewellery is not mine.'

'But you are Inspector Faro? Is that not so?' and Mr Jacob consulted his ledger. 'Here is the entry. This brooch was handed in two days ago by Inspector Faro. See for yourself.'

Now examining the ring thoughtfully, Faro said slowly: 'I didn't by any chance tell you how I had come by it, did I?'

Mr Jacob's bafflement equalled Faro's own. 'Come by it? What is that? I do not understand.'

'Did your customer tell you that he had inherited the brooch by any chance?'

'It was my daughter you – Inspector Faro – spoke to.'

Ah, and that explains the case of mistaken identity, thought Faro, as Mr Jacob darted behind the screen to reappear with a gazelle-eyed beauty.

Nadia was very young, so nervous as to be almost inarticulate in her forest-creature manner, but in a few years, Faro guessed, there would be few in Edinburgh to rival her exotic looks.

And Faro smiled to himself remembering a Bible picture from his childhood. If her father could have modelled a benign Fagin, then Nadia might well have been the lass setting the baby Moses adrift among the reeds.

Her father's admonishing tones in their own language made her wild-eyed and tearful. Trembling, she would have disappeared behind the curtain screen but for his restraining hand.

Urging her towards the inspector, Mr Jacob's voice was stern indeed. At last with downcast head, she began an unintelligible explanation.

'In English, daughter,' thundered her father.

Slowly she raised her eyes to Faro. 'He came in and asked for my father. I told him my father was not here. He did not want to leave the brooch but he was in a great hurry.'

'How did you know that?' asked Faro gently.

'He went often to the door and looked up and down the street as if expecting my father to come.'

Your father – or the people who were chasing him, thought Faro grimly, having now deduced the reason for the bogus inspector's anxiety and the urgent necessity of having the brooch transformed into a ring.

'He saw someone in the street,' said Nadia. 'He seemed anxious and thrust the brooch into my hand. My father was to have it ready for him today without fail.'

'Today – you are sure of that?' said Faro.

Nadia looked at her father. 'That is what he said.'

'He? He! Be polite, daughter, that is no way to address the

inspector.' And bowing. 'Her English – I apologise.'

'Allow her to explain in her own time,' said Faro with a smile.

In reply, Nadia touched her father's sleeve, whispered and then turning to Faro, Mr Jacob said, 'She thinks you are not the same man.'

'Ah,' said Faro. 'Now we are getting somewhere. Your exact words, Mr Jacob, if I recall them correctly were that you did not recognise me again. Your daughter's information confirms that I have never set foot in your shop before this afternoon.'

'But – but, sir,' Mr Jacob interrupted, 'it was the day you arrested the holy man, the one who was trying to steal from my shop.'

'A moment, if you please. A holy man stealing from you – and I was arresting him. Sir, you must be dreaming.'

'If it was a dream,' said the jeweller ruefully, 'then it was a costly one. I lost much money.'

'I presume you have reported this theft to the police.'

Father and daughter exchanged anxious looks and shook their heads.

'No? then I think you had better tell me exactly what happened.'

'You – the er, other inspector – were in a policeman's uniform that first time.'

Mr Jacob shrugged, 'It makes a man look different.'

'Describe this uniform, if you please.'

What Mr Jacob described was worn by police constables. Detective Inspectors, however, were allowed the privilege of plain clothes, if they wished. The experience of twenty years had led Faro to appreciate the advantages of anonymity in his line of enquiries, where an approach by an officer of the law was a hindrance rather than a help. Innocent as well as guilty were apt to become somewhat reticent when faced with an intimidating uniform.

'May we go right back to the beginning, if you please?' asked Faro.

At his stern expression, Mr Jacob sighed. 'Very well. Nadia will look after the shop while we talk inside.'

In the screened-off living quarters, domesticity was provided by a curtained bed in the wall for the father and a tiny room no larger than a cupboard for his daughter. From every corner stuffed animals glared at them yellow-eyed and fierce. A tray of dismembered clocks and watches ticked furiously as if in a constant state of anxiety at the close proximity of soldering iron and Bunsen burner.

Inviting Faro to a seat by the fire, the jeweller began his strange story.

'A few days ago, a customer, a holy man – of your faith – wished to buy a diamond ring for his wife —'

'Ah, you must mean a minister,' interrupted Faro and when Mr Jacob looked even more confused, he added, 'We call them "reverends".'

Mr Jacob nodded. 'I understand. This reverend selected a ring priced at forty pounds and offered to pay with a hundred-pound banknote.'

Fraud. Such was Faro's immediate reaction considering the few hundred-pound banknotes printed and in circulation. Only a foreigner would be taken in by such audacity.

'I see that you too are doubtful, sir, as I was. And so was this reverend. He said, "As I am a complete stranger you must be wondering if this note is real. I noticed a bank just across the road there. Would you care to ask the cashier to verify that this is a genuine banknote?"'

'Ah,' said Faro. 'How very convenient. You go across the road and leave him in the shop. And when you return —' He shrugged, said sadly: 'My dear fellow, this is a very old trick.'

'I am not stupid, Inspector. When I suggested that my daughter go to the bank instead, the reverend was not in the least dismayed. I was watching him intently and he was most complimentary about her. He talked – much as you have done, sir, curious about my reasons for coming to Scotland.

'Nadia came back and told us that both the bank cashier and the manager himself had assured her that the banknote was indeed genuine. I put the diamond ring into a box and from the safe – in the wall over there,' he pointed, 'and I gave the reverend his sixty pounds change.'

Mr Jacob sighed and shook his head. 'He seemed such a kindly man, but just as he was leaving the shop, you – I mean, the policeman – entered, seized him and said to me: "I am a police inspector and I have to tell you that this man is a thief, well known to us. He has already been in prison three times."'

Faro was puzzled. A trickster like the minister who had been jailed three times, yet he had never heard of him.

Mr Jacob continued: 'I am an honest man, sir, and I had to protest that this time no fraud was involved for the bank had examined the hundred-pound note and declared it genuine. You – er, this inspector, then asked me to show it to him. "Ah," he said, "as I suspected, like many other shopkeepers and bank cashiers, you have been tricked by a brilliant forgery. This is a master craftsman and I am arresting him. I shall have to take the fake banknote which will be required as evidence later."

'When he brought out the handcuffs, the reverend said to him: "They will not be necessary, Inspector. You have my word as a gentleman that I will come with you quietly."

'But the inspector just laughed at him and I felt sorry for the reverend. He did seem like a real gentleman who had fallen on hard times. Who knows what sorrows and misfortunes had driven him to a life of crime.'

Faro was curious about the man's identity. 'Can you describe him for me?'

'Garbed all in black, he was. Tall, pale-skinned, light-eyed...'

Mr Jacob ended with an embarrassed shrug for the description also fitted the man who was now questioning him.

Faro suppressed a smile. Did all Gentiles look alike to the jeweller?

'The reverend then began to plead. "There are hiring carriages outside. I will pay for one, Inspector. Please allow me this last indulgence." It was a wild day,' Mr Jacob continued, 'a blizzard blowing, so the inspector gave in.'

'And you were sent for a carriage and you watched the inspector hand his prisoner in and drive away,' said Faro. 'Is that so?'

Mr Jacob looked puzzled and then he sighed. 'You smile, sir? I expect you know what happened next,' he added glumly.

'When you came back into the shop you realised that your sixty pounds change had not been returned to you and that your fake minister had also carried off the diamond ring.'

The jeweller nodded sadly. 'I realised there had been a mistake. When I closed the shop I went at once to the police station. But do you know, Inspector, no one would believe a word of my story. They pretended that no inspector of theirs had brought in a holy man. When I protested that I was telling the truth they became very suspicious and asked a lot of questions while another policeman wrote it all down. Where are your papers, they kept shouting. What about this shop of yours? How did you pay for it?'

He spread his hands wide. 'I was so ashamed and upset, Inspector, and very afraid. This was the kind of life I had escaped from when I fled to Scotland. Was I to go through it all over again? Fortunately, for me, that is, there was a disturbance. A bad woman – from the streets – was brought in drunk and fighting. So I took my chance and ran away as quickly as I could.'

Faro shook his head aware that would make the Central Office even more suspicious. He knew his men. Edinburgh was full of people who came in with wild stories and tried to obtain compensation for imagined frauds. They would jump to the obvious conclusion that they were dealing with another criminal – or a madman. And they got plenty of both kinds in a day's work.

'After that I was afraid to go back again,' Mr Jacob continued. 'I know I should not have rushed out like that, but you see no one, not even a policeman, wishes to believe that a foreigner is telling the truth. I could see it in their eyes as they listened to me. An expression I have reason to know very well. Suspicion and something worse – hatred.'

Again the jeweller spread his hands in that despairing gesture. 'Like eager hungry dogs waiting for the chance to leap on their quarry,' he added in a horrified whisper.

Faro protested with some soothing platitudes regarding the law and justice, which he knew were untrue. His words rang hollow, for Mr Jacob was correct in his assumptions and Faro was well aware of strong anti-Semitic feelings.

Even those with skins the same colour and speaking the same language, Irish and English, and their own countrymen from the Highlands were abused. To the struggling teeming mass of Edinburgh poor, signs of affluence in any 'foreigner' however hard won, were a subject of the most bitter hostility.

And now Faro was faced with the hardest part of all, to tell the jeweller what was patently obvious.

'The police inspector who made the arrest, Mr Jacob. Well, I am afraid he was not a real policeman.'

'Not real? But how could one doubt it? He was wearing a uniform.'

'Alas, that is no criterion of honesty. He had probably stolen it.'

Mr Jacob looked at him wide-eyed. 'What are you trying to tell me, sir?'

'That your police inspector and the minister were both criminals, in league together, planning to steal a diamond ring and sixty pounds from you.'

'But the hundred-pound note —'

'Oh yes, that banknote was genuine enough. And a very necessary part of their trick to defraud shopkeepers who would be – as you were – immediately suspicious of such a large denomination, rarely exhibited in public and even more rarely handed across shop counters.'

As he spoke Faro realised that the jeweller must have seemed the perfect foil for the crooks. The success of this trick depended on the ignorance of new shopkeepers. Particularly foreigners who might have their own reasons, nothing to do with fraud, but a lot to do with past unhappy experiences of political persecution, which made them wary about any involvement with the law.

Mr Jacob continued to look astonished and Faro repeated. 'Please believe me, there was no inspector, no minister. You must understand that both men were thieves who had set out to rob you.'

'Ah, Inspector, in that you are mistaken,' said Mr Jacob stubbornly. 'There was no crime since the very day after I went to the police station the inspector came back – to return the diamond ring with many apologies. It had been found on the reverend's person when he was searched. He also returned my sixty pounds,' he added triumphantly. 'Now that is not the action of a thief.'

And leaning across the counter, he said, 'What I still fail to understand is why he gave your name.'

But Faro had already worked out that ingenious part of the fraud. The first episode with the minister and the diamond ring, his dramatic arrest by the bogus inspector and the subsequent return of both ring and sixty pounds were elaborate overtures to secure the jeweller's confidence.

As for the bogus inspector, Faro guessed that he was a seasoned criminal and that perhaps their paths had already crossed. There was a certain grim humour in claiming to be Inspector Faro in the very neighbourhood where he lived and was a familiar sight.

Faro saw something else, too. That this was merely the beginning, carefully planned with intended results far beyond the remodelling of an emerald brooch into a ring.

Of one thing he was absolutely certain, the emerald brooch had been stolen. No doubt when he returned to the Central Office it would be listed as one of the missing jewels from the recent robbery at Jenners.

Mr Jacob had to be unwittingly drawn into the thieves' kitchen. The most invaluable and hardest accessory to find was a skilled craftsman who would be adept at totally altering the appearance of stolen gems, and melting down gold.

Once the jeweller was committed to them, then there was no escape for him. The gang would make sure of that and their threats would be most effective, especially since the police would be ready to suspect an alien. Mr Jacob's visit to the Central Office with his disastrous and wild-seeming accusations written down and filed as possible evidence had landed him further into the net.

Faro knew that if the jeweller was to be saved and danger averted there was only one way. The bogus inspector must be seized when he came to reclaim the brooch. But when might that be?

He stared out of the window. At three o'clock on a December afternoon, there was little light outside, the street already almost deserted.

He could hardly stand guard for an indefinite period although most of his success in a long career owed much to that element of patient waiting. However, he had given up hope by the time the street lamps were lit and the smoking chimneys of Edinburgh that Robert Burns called 'Auld Reekie' added their acrid stench to the freezing fog.

A thin stream of customers had long since gone. Not one resembled the bogus inspector and Mr Jacob exchanged a despairing glance with Faro.

The plan had failed. Faro shook his head. Criminals, he knew, also have their intuitive moments. Perhaps the thief had already approached the vicinity of the shop in the dim light and, suspicions aroused, had decided that in his business, discretion was always the better part of valour.

Mr Jacob went around the counter and was rolling down the door blind, when a rap on the outside announced a last customer.

Concealed by the kitchen curtain, Faro observed a young woman. He groaned. His last hope had expired.

But wait – what was she asking?

'I have come from Inspector Faro – to collect my emerald ring. I am the inspector's sister and here is the note he asked me to give you.'

As Mr Jacob put on his spectacles and read the note slowly and carefully, Faro pushed aside the kitchen curtain. 'Hello, my dear. I thought you were never coming. I've been expecting you for some time. What kept you?'

The young woman was clearly taken aback and would have bolted had he not stood firmly between her and the door.

Looking round desperately she stammered: 'But – but —'

Taking the woman's arm firmly, Faro said: 'I have already collected the ring for you and outside I think you'll see a carriage awaits. Thank you, Mr Jacob, you have been most kind.'

And Faro marched her out of the shop to the police carriage he had summoned earlier which had been lurking discreetly out of sight round the corner. It approached rapidly and at the same time, another carriage bowled down the road.

A man stared out and, seeing that the woman had been taken

and that several constables were erupting from all directions, he leapt down, took to his heels and bolted down one of the closes.

'Bastard!' shrieked the woman after him. 'Bastard!' Her screams and bad language as two uniformed constables restrained her caused a few passersby to blanch. One elderly woman was so overcome by this display of unseemly emotions that she swooned on the spot.

As for Faro, he was already in hot pursuit of the bogus inspector who had discovered too late that his headlong flight carried him down a cul-de-sac.

The struggle was short and swift, since Faro's early training had included lessons in self-defence from a retired pugilist. The constables who had followed, truncheons at the ready, were not needed.

Handcuffing the man, who was tall and fair like himself but considerably younger, Faro said: 'You had better start talking, or it'll be the worse for you. I dare say your doxy is already telling them all she knows.'

And one look at the woman's scared face, the way she cursed and spat as her confederate was hustled into the police carriage, obviously convinced him that he need expect neither discretion nor mercy from that quarter.

'All right, Inspector bloody Faro, you've won this time...'

As Faro suspected the bogus inspector and the minister were mere links in an organised gang of jewel thieves.

Most of the missing gems from the haul at Jenners were recovered.

But that is another story.

'Ah!' said Mr Septimus Coram, surveying the large plate of eggs, bacon, pork sausages, tomatoes, mushrooms, and – his particular favourite – blood pudding. 'Gives you an appetite, my job, that nobody can deny.'

It was something he said on all such occasions, accompanying it with a deep swig from the pewter beer mug that he always used at such late breakfasts.

'Brute!' mouthed his daughter Esther. It was something *she* said on all such occasions, but only silently.

'He went quiet, did he?' asked his wife. It wasn't that she wanted to know, merely that the neighbours would ask.

'Didn't have no option. One brawny warder on one side of him, and another brawny warder on the other side. Not that I couldn't have coped on my own if need be.'

Mr Coram had all his life been wiry rather than heavy in frame, though a lifetime's addiction to massive fried meals and beer had given him an unattractive potbelly. His droopy moustache, pince-nez spectacles, and protruding ears produced a facial effect that was far from alluring.

'People like to know,' murmured his wife.

'Don't I know it! And haven't I had hundreds of good pints on the strength of it. He went quiet – more depressed than anything else. None of this shouting that he was innocent all the way, though they say he was protesting it even as they served him his breakfast. Innocent!'

He laughed heartily and speared a sausage.

'They said at the trial there was doubt,' said his wife.

'Said at the trial!' said her husband contemptuously, but not interrupting his chewing. '*Who* said it at the trial? The counsel for the bleeding Defence, that's who said it. It's his job. Beats me why they bother with one. No one believes a word they say. The police don't make mistakes, and Her Majesty Queen Victoria's judiciary don't make them, either. *Innocent?* Innocent men don't get hanged. And you can take that from me, who knows.'

'Fool!' mouthed his daughter, looking at her father closely as he finished the first tomato and sliced into the second.

'Well, I'll be off to the shops,' said Mrs Coram. 'And I'll go along to see Bessy Rowlands afterwards. She's poorly.'

'Suit yourself,' said her husband. 'I'll be having a kip. But mind you're back to cook me my dinner.'

Since Mary Coram had cooked her husband his dinner every day of her married life except the day they went to Brighton and the day Esther had been born (and *hadn't* he sworn on that occasion!), Mrs Coram didn't feel any need to reply. As she banged the front door that led directly from the Corams' parlour onto the street, Septimus put down his knife and fork.

'A meal like that crowns the day, puts a seal on a job well done,' he said. His daughter merely gave a sceptical grunt. 'It's like God giving me a nice pat on the back.'

'Must be nice to think that God takes such a special interest in you,' said Esther Coram. Her father stared at her suspiciously, but decided to ignore the note of satire in her voice.

'It is, my girl. But it's nothing to be surprised at. "Vengeance is mine, saith the Lord, and I will repay." I'm the instrument of the Lord's wrath with evildoers. It's natural He should take a special interest.'

'I see. And He would protect the innocent, to prevent any possible wrong being done?'

'Of course He would. But He doesn't need to in this country. We have our constitution and our free judiciary to protect the innocent.'

'And so if the courts say a man killed his wife, he killed her?'

'Still harping on about handsome Mr Critchley? Didn't look so handsome after the drop.' He chuckled. 'Yes – the court said he done it, and he did.'

'In spite of the lack of evidence?'

'Lack of evidence? The man works in a chemist's. She dies of arsenical poisoning. It stands to reason.'

'I'd have thought it stood to reason that if a worker in a chemist's wanted to kill his wife he wouldn't use poison.'

Mr Coram's disgust was manifest.

'That's the trouble with you, my girl. Too clever by half. The man had a girlfriend in the background to boot.'

'Name unknown, nature of relationship unknown.'

'He was loyal to her, I'll give him that.'

'And there was someone in the wife's life as well. Also identity unknown.'

'She wasn't in a position to tell us who it was, was she?' Septimus Coram added, 'Poor cow!' without a trace of compassion.

'She didn't sound like a very pleasant person to me.'

'A very pleasant person!' said Septimus, imitating her fastidious distaste. 'You'd believe anything the Defence told you, wouldn't you? Even if it was that the moon was made of blue cheese. What he said about the wife was just what Evan Critchley told *him*: that she made his life miserable by nagging. Well, he would say that, wouldn't he?'

'Not necessarily, if his defence was that he hadn't done it.'

'Hmm. Just trying to get the sympathy vote when he was found guilty... Ooh, that breakfast's sitting heavy.'

'That's the trouble with good food, isn't it, Dad? It has that built-in disadvantage.'

Coram's only response was another 'Ooh!'

'So the situation was this, then: Evan Critchley had got a girlfriend, and in order to marry her he needed to be rid of his wife, divorce being too expensive for the likes of him and us.'

'Quite right, too. Where would this country be if every Tom, Dick and Harry – not to say Henrietta – could get a divorce at the click of a finger? Morality would fly out the window.'

'And his wife, meanwhile – in the name of morality, no doubt – was enjoying a flirtation, or something stronger than that.'

'We don't know, do we? We just know that's what your Mr Critchley said.'

'There was a neighbour said she was often away from home for long periods during the day.'

'Yah! What does that amount to? There were no kiddies for her to look after. Why don't you mention the neighbour who said she talked of having bad stomach pains in the last weeks of her life?'

A grimace of agony passed over his face, and he let out another heartfelt groan.

'Not surprising she complained of pain. She was being poisoned, wasn't she? No one denies that. The question is, who was slipping her the arsenic?'

'Well, who more likely than her hubby?'

'That could be what the murderer banked on: that the police would settle on the obvious solution and the easiest suspect, and not look any further.'

'Well, why should they, when young Evan Critchley had the means, the opportunity and the motive?'

'But what the police hadn't got was *evidence*.'

'They had enough for the judge, enough for the jury.'

'The jury! People who believe what they read in the *Daily Mail* every day,' said his daughter contemptuously.

'And why shouldn't they read the *Mail*? It brings to light a lot of scandalous goings-on that oughtn't to be hid.'

'With about as much evidence as the Prosecution had in this case. If Isabella Critchley was being fed arsenic, why shouldn't it be by the lover who's tired of her?'

Mr Coram's eyes popped out with simulated outrage.

'Hark at her! A daughter of mine, sitting calmly in the parlour talking of women with lovers! A girl who goes out to work scrubbing floors instead of looking for a husband who'll give her a good home! Next thing you know, she'll be wanting to train as a doctor or a solicitor!'

'I'd aim higher than solicitor,' said Esther stoutly. 'Nothing less than a lawyer for me. And why not? It'll come in time, and better sooner than later.'

'A woman's mind's not suited to logic and reason. It's all emotion. Look at you! You start by demanding evidence, then you make accusations against this woman's lover with not a shred of evidence – no evidence, in fact, that there was one.'

'Oh, there was a lover,' said Esther Coram quietly. Her father's attention was distracted by a tremendous upheaval in his stomach. When it had settled down he looked at his daughter suspiciously.

'What do you know about her lover?'

'I know there was one.'

'How would *you* know?' he jeered.

Esther said quietly 'I have a life beyond this prison of a house.'

Her father made a feeble gesture, threatening her, but it petered out. 'You say I go out cleaning. In fact, I act as cook and lady's maid in the house where I work. I am in a position of trust. Almost a companion.'

'Almost a companion!' he sneered. A thought struck him. 'Why are you telling me this? Who is this woman who employs you? Was she his mistress? Or was she the wife of Mrs Critchley's lover? You imply there was a connection with the lover.'

Esther thought before she spoke.

'Mrs Critchley visited there. I overheard things.'

'No doubt!' he hectored her. 'You, in a position of trust, *would* hear things – by accident, of course. And I suppose you never passed them on to the police.'

'No, I never passed them on to the police. Mrs Critchley was a woman I greatly disliked: rude, offhand, a real little dictator when she felt like it.'

'So it was all right to murder her?'

'It was understandable... She and my mistress had known each other very well in the past.' Her father grunted. 'Very well indeed.'

'What's up with the girl?' Septimus demanded of the far wall. 'Speaks in riddles.'

'My mistress's secrets were Mrs Critchley's secrets. She could have done her a lot of harm.'

'Hmm,' said Septimus sceptically.

'My mistress is prominent in the suffragette movement. She could have ruined her, and ruined the movement.'

'More power to her – oh! OH! – to her elbow then.'

'So you see,' said Esther, relaxing momentarily, 'there's more than one suspect. And blackmailers don't normally have just one iron in the fire. There could have been people all over London whom Isabella knew dangerous things about.'

'What are you saying? That she was a madam? A brothel keeper? If she was, the police would have known.'

'I'm sure they would. Very interested in brothels, the police.

Either they want to use them or to shut them down.'

'Wash your mouth out, girl. Police wouldn't.'

'Police are men, just like soldiers and sailors. But I'm not saying she was a brothel keeper. She was a blackmailer. How she got her secrets doesn't concern you. I do know that my mistress was going to go to see her, to offer her a big payment to make an end of it.'

'Are you accusing her of murder?'

'I'm saying that a police force that knew what it was doing would have made her a suspect. But there's this difficulty about blackmailers: they're not looking for a quick fortune. They're looking for an income.'

'You're right there, for once, girl.'

'A steady drip of money's what they find useful. And that suits their sense of power, too. They love nothing so much as having someone in their power, gradually turning the screw. In any case, there was nothing that Mrs Critchley could hand over to my mistress and say: 'There's an end of it.' She didn't have any *thing*. What she had was knowledge. In her brain. And dying with her.'

She was interrupted by a great roar from her father.

'Doctor! Get a doctor!'

Esther remained as composed as a steel girder.

'A doctor, Dad? Not for a spot of indigestion, surely.'

'This isn't indi—' He sat forward in his seat, clutching his stomach.

'Have you realised that at last?' said Esther. 'No, it isn't indigestion. I'll tell you what it is, Dad. It's hyoscine, in your beer. You've been having small quantities for quite a while now. It all mounts up. I found out about it by reading all the stuff in the newspapers about the trial of Mr Critchley. They went mad about poisons, and I didn't think I should use the same thing. So here I am, you see, one more suspect: I could have read up about poison months ago. I could have decided to do my mistress a service and kill her tormentor for her.'

Again the groan, again the heaving sounds from the stomach, again the plea: 'A doctor!'

'Oh no, Dad,' said Esther, shaking her head. 'I'm going out, but not to fetch a doctor. I'm walking out of this room, locking the door, and I'm going to put this place behind me. See that bag behind the sofa? That contains everything I want to keep from my old life. Not much, is it?'

An expletive came from the floor, as Septimus slid down ungracefully from his chair. Esther stood up.

'I'm going to go now and fetch Mum from Bessy Rowlands'. I'm going to take her up to the West End, show her the sights, treat her to a meal at Lyons. I'll tell her I left your meal ready. And while we're eating I'll tell her I'm going to live with my mistress. And that's true, too. We're starting a new life in Manchester. That's one of the centres of the suffragette movement. So today is an end for you, and an end for me here. I'll be better off with my mistress.' She knelt down and hissed into his ear: 'That's what she is, Dad. My mistress. My lover.' There was an outraged grunt, and some slurred word that sounded like 'impossible'. She shook her head. 'Oh no, it's not impossible, Dad. That's what Mrs Critchley held over her – and over some other prominent women. They'd been lovers years before. Oh, there should have been a lot of suspects in the Isabella Critchley murder case, Dad. The police picked on the one nearest to hand, and you've just hanged him.'

Again the strangled syllables, words that sounded like 'right man'.

She knelt down and whispered straight into his protuberant ear.

'Oh no, you didn't hang the right man, Dad. I killed her myself. Not because I was involved with her husband. Men don't attract me. Not as a service to my mistress, though I'm fond of her, and was glad to be of help. I killed her because I'm your daughter. There is something in me that wants to kill, and gets pleasure from killing when the time comes. It's in the blood, Dad. I have an appetite for killing. I get it from you.'

When the young French doctor returned, Albert Potter thought he looked agitated. Noticing the Englishman's stare, he begged his guest to excuse his state of mind.

'You will have to forgive me, Monsieur Potter. I was attending to a patient. He gets a little…agitated when the wind howls in the trees. He thinks it is the Devil come to take him away. I have given him a sedative, and he will sleep now.'

Dr Gaston was a young man in his twenties – too young, Albert Potter thought, to be in charge of even a French lunatic asylum. But then who, with a reputation already earned, or a family to keep, would be prepared to hide himself away in this crumbling mausoleum of a place in the middle of nowhere? The good doctor, on the other hand, seemed to find his charges fascinating, and had explained he was writing a thesis on the causes of neurasthenia and dementia praecox.

'Now, please, tell me about this man you are seeking.'

Uneasy at the predatory glitter in the doctor's eyes, Potter tried to pull together in his mind all the events of the last few days. His own actions of the last few hours had not been all that rational, and he did not wish to seem entirely mad. After all, he was supposed to have been making sense of Louis Le Prince's actions. Potter realised at that very moment that, though he had traced the man's last journey meticulously, he had not sufficiently researched his habits and peculiarities. Nor his extraordinary invention, and the possible enemies it had created.

His mind drifted back to the meeting that had brought him to this remote asylum on the edge of a village that didn't even merit a stop on the main steam-train line between Dijon and Paris…

Albert Potter had been recommended to Mrs Le Prince as a young man of good character, forceful manner, and dogged determination who would find her husband if he was to be found. But more important to Potter than all those encomiums was the undisclosed reason for his proposed services – the state of his pocket. He was in dire need of funds. His remuneration as a clerk at the Colonial Office was satisfactory for a single man such as he was at present. But Albert had other ambitions, and they chiefly concerned the beautiful and well-connected Rosalind Wells.

Of course, he was no fool. He knew he was short and ungainly, with a head too big for his body. Indeed he had winced when once he had accidentally overheard Rosalind referring to him, to one of her friends, as 'that tadpole of a man'. But his ego was as large as his body was small, and when he set his mind to something, he usually got what he wanted. And Rosalind Wells was what he wanted.

So now he found himself in need of funds, and when someone told him of Mrs Le Prince and her search for her missing husband, he had travelled immediately up to Leeds. Private investigation had always piqued his curiosity, and the opportunity for travel this matter afforded was alluring. Besides, Rosalind Wells was in Leeds talking to trade-union organisers for the Fabian Society. Later, he would surprise her with his presence, but first he had to address the matter in hand.

'You say your husband simply disappeared while on the Dijon-to-Paris train, Madame Le Prince?'

'I am as English as you are, Mr Potter, so it's Mrs Le Prince, please. Or indeed, Elizabeth, if you prefer.'

Potter beamed at the presumed widow, detecting in her voice something of a northern accent. 'A native of these parts, then?'

Elizabeth Le Prince smiled coyly and fidgeted a little with the beaded reticule on her lap. She wore a fashionable cream blouse and full skirt of deepest pink, edged in white lace, with a matching bolero jacket. Potter guessed that her dress was a statement of her belief that her husband still lived. No widow's weeds for this woman. Potter reassured her that it was possible her missing husband was still alive. But his private opinion was that, after six months, perhaps Le Prince, even alive, had no wish to return to his wife. Other attractions, principally female, must have been the cause of his disappearance. Elizabeth Le Prince seemed to read Potter's mind.

'I am certain that my husband hasn't left me for another woman, Mr Potter.'

'Albert, please'

'He was – is – entirely faithful to me, Albert. I would know if he had not been.'

Potter wondered how many women had said that of secretly philandering husbands just before the bombshell landed. But he shelved that line of enquiry for the moment in deference to the woman's feelings.

'You say that Mr Le Prince was in France on family business? What was that exactly?'

'He was collecting his share of a small inheritance, I believe.'

So he was not short of cash, and dodging creditors by hiding away somewhere. Quite the opposite – he was a good mark for a robbery, in fact. But if he had been murdered during a robbery, then where was his body, and his baggage? The man had apparently disappeared into the blue – lock, stock and barrel. The Great Maskelyne could not have performed better in his magic act on the stage of the Leeds Hippodrome.

'What was Mr Le Prince working on when he left you...for France, that is? I understand he was a photographer.'

The woman smiled in a proprietorial manner.

'My husband was...*is* a genius, Mr Potter. He was making moving pictures.'

Potter didn't fancy becoming Dr Gaston's next guinea pig. Therefore, so as not to be thought mad, he did not tell this doctor of lunatics of Le Prince's secret work with moving pictures. Until a few days ago, he would have thought anyone mad who had claimed to have seen what he then had with his own eyes.

In fact, two matters had disturbed Albert Potter about his trip to Leeds. One was that he had missed his surprise rendezvous with Rosalind Wells. She had apparently cut her business short and disappeared God knows where – he hoped not as finally as had Le Prince. And the other – and a much more powerful one, he had to admit – was that of the remarkable images he had watched in the darkened room that had been Louis Le Prince's workshop. Like any red-blooded male, Potter had seen the jerky simulation of movement that presented itself down the periscope of a hand-cranked machine on the end of Southend Pier. But those flickering cards that always ended frustratingly before the lady had fully disrobed (he guessed because the attendant had removed the last cards of the sequence for his own delectation) – those simulacra were as nothing to the image that Mrs Le Prince had projected onto the wall of the curtained room.

It had been as though a window had suddenly opened onto the street beyond the blank wall, cleaving it apart. A foggy, greyish window, but a window nonetheless. And Potter sat dumbfounded as the mundane street scene of horse-drawn trams and people – real people scurried across the wall. They moved in a perfect imitation of reality, then jerked back to where they had been and scurried again, following the self-same route as before. Mesmerised, he watched them repeat their passage through time again and again, asking Mrs Le Prince, like some all-powerful God, to cause their movements to be repeated innumerable times until she was afraid the reel of collodion-sensitive paper would buckle and catch fire.

Sunk in thought as he recalled this phenomenon, Potter picked at the remains of the cold collation that a surly servant had brought him at Dr Gaston's behest. He left it to the doctor to break the silence.

'You say you followed in the unfortunate Monsieur Le Prince's footsteps, and they brought you here to my…institution?'

Potter nodded, and began to explain that he had started by traveling to Dijon, and speaking to the last man known to have seen Louis Le Prince alive. His brother.

As Albert Potter shook M. Le Prince's hand at the Dijon station, he was aware of just how uncanny it was to be so exactly repeating the actions of the man he sought. Le Prince's brother, who coincidentally was named Albert, too, but pronounced in the Continental way, now stood before him seeing him off on the Paris-bound train. He had not been able to help Potter much at all, merely confirming that Louis had been a little nervous and overexcited.

'But I put that down to the, er…camera device he was carrying with him.'

'Camera device?'

Albert Le Prince grimaced, the wrinkling of his nose conveying the condescension with which he clearly viewed his sibling. Potter had been painfully aware of this enmity from the moment he met Le Prince's brother. Indeed, it had crossed his mind that Albert Le Prince could be considered a suspect in the possible murder. He would need to check out further whether Louis Le Prince did indeed receive the inheritance he had travelled to Dijon to collect. He turned no more than a polite ear to the man's prattling.

'My brother was...obsessed with photography. He had a perfectly good job working for his brother-in-law's engineering firm. They manufactured wallpaper, you know. But he immersed himself in his...hobby of taking pictures. Quite literally immersed more often than not he was up to his elbows in all sorts of smelly and dangerous chemicals. His latest tomfoolery was to do with making these photographs move, like some...peep show.'

Potter refrained from telling the brother that it was not tomfoolery – he had seen the magic performed himself. He was reminded of the continuous loop that was the film he had watched with Mrs Le Prince. Her husband had trapped a moment in time which could be repeated over and over again, making each action on the screen susceptible to being studied from different angles until every iota of information was drained from it. It would have made his detecting job so much easier if he could have done the same with Le Prince's disappearance. If someone had been standing at the station, as Potter was now, six months on, at 2.42 p.m. on the sixteenth of September, 1890, taking a moving picture of Le Prince shaking his brother's hand – as Potter was now – matters might have been different.

'And you think this camera was for taking moving pictures?'

M. Le Prince snorted. 'You have not been taken in by my brother's trickery as well, have you? Of course it could not take moving pictures. You might as well suggest the Mona Lisa could rise from her chair and depart the frame in which she sits. He said there was just one more problem to solve before it worked properly.'

A supercilious sneer contorted Le Prince's face, and he tapped the side of his nose conspiratorially.

'There was always just one more problem for Louis to solve. I doubt that this one was the last, though he claimed to have come to a solution.'

The clanking giant steamed into the station, and for a while the noise of the massive engine's passing prevented any form of conversation between the two men. Then Albert Le Prince was all hustle and bustle, apparently all too eager to get rid of the meddling Englishman. Should he be added to Potter's extremely short list of suspects? As he climbed on board the train, Potter felt a hand placed lightly on his arm. He turned to look back, hoping for a last-minute revelation.

Le Prince grinned fatuously at him. 'Please try not to disappear like Louis.'

Potter hung off the rear of the carriage as the train pulled away, irritated by the man's flippancy. After all, his brother's body might still be lying unburied by the trackside even now. A final thought occurred to him, and he called out to the receding figure.

'What was the problem he claimed to have solved? Did Louis say?'

He could barely make out what Albert Le Prince was saying through the echoes of the engine in the cavernous station.

'Yes…new medium…celluloid…from Dr Marey, in Paris.'

At the time this meant nothing to Potter, and he settled in his seat, trying to put himself inside the mind of Le Prince.

He knew he was being followed from the moment he boarded the 2.42 p.m. train for Paris. He fingered his stiff celluloid collar, feeling the dampness of his fear. The station at Dijon was bustling with people, and everyone seemed engrossed in their own business. The accidental intersection of all their lives held no significance for anyone. But there was one particular fellow traveller – a tall, thin man enveloped in a long Inverness-cape coat – who was always hovering just on the limits of his vision. He could see the man over his brother's shoulder, as he shook his hand in farewell. Then, as he made his way to the platform, there was the man again; lurking behind the line of pillars that supported the ornate station roof. As if to confirm his fears, the man turned away just as he fixed him with a stare, tipping his felt bowler over his angular features.

Then, in a cloud of hissing steam, the engine pulled in, and doors were flung open as the train began to disgorge its passengers. For a moment he lost sight of the man in the milling crowd, and he waved to his brother, then concentrated on seeking out a free seat. He passed his bag to the porter on the steps of the nearest carriage, and pulled himself up on the handrail, keeping the box he was carrying to himself for safety. He suddenly had a sense of being watched, and looked along the length of the train uneasily. Several people were mounting the steps up to the other carriages, rushing now to escape a sudden flurry of rain. There was no sign of the tall, thin man. Then, leaning out of the nearest window, he spotted a flapping cape through the clouds of steam. The man was making a decisive move down the platform in order to get in the same carriage that he himself had chosen. He hugged the exquisitely carpentered box closer to his chest, feeling the metal mount of the lens pressing into him. He hunched his shoulders as he moved along the carriage, trying in vain to hide, for he stood well over six feet.

The porter was already stowing his other hand baggage – a well-worn carpetbag valise that had survived the rough handling of careless North American porters – on the luggage rack above an empty seat. He didn't want to sit down – he felt more like getting off the train and running for his life. The porter looked at him curiously, and waved an officious hand at the vacant seat. He recognised the imperious nature of all petty officials from this the country of his birth, and knew he would have to comply. Reluctantly, he sat down, reaching into his pocket for some money – a tip being the inevitable next part of the joint conspiracy. Pleased at his control of the passenger, the porter took the proffered coin and turned his officious attentions to the other sheeplike passengers.

For a moment he fidgeted nervously, rubbing the irritating open sore on his left hand, making it bleed again. Then he steeled himself to look up from his studious examination of his rain-spattered shoes. The tall, thin man, who had run the length of the platform to get in the same coach, was now sitting himself down right across from him! The *man was brushing the rain from the shoulders of his cape, and smiled as their eyes met. And what a smile! Disdain, complicity, pity – all epithets seemed inadequate to describe it. He struggled to find the right word, and eventually settled on the right one.*

Predatory.

The man's hook of a nose reminded him of the buzzards that drifted on the updrafts over the Yorkshire crags, looking for easy pickings. He hunched in on himself and racked his brain for what his next move should be.

Despite all his attempts at entering the mind of the man he sought, Albert kept drifting off to his amatory campaign concerning Rosalind Wells. Potter had come across her at a meeting of the Fabians three years earlier, and had been bowled over by her imperious manner. And her shapely figure and big brown eyes. She was somewhat German-looking – a trait that was fashionable amongst the intellectuals with whom Albert fancied he belonged. So Potter had pressed his suit in his usual blunt way. He was at first mortified that she professed not to be aware of this, but that had not deterred him, nor blunted the ardour of his campaign. He had known from the start that he was the perfect match for her – it would just take some time to convince her of the fact. What the eye saw was not always the full picture.

He gazed admiringly at his own reflection in the window, only half noticing the build-up of dark, heavy clouds outside the carriage. His rather short torso and legs obscured, the image that stared back was of a man with a thick mane of hair and luxuriant moustache and goatee beard. He preened a little, then began to doze off in the stuffy carriage.

He was beginning to sweat heavily, and his head pounded in rhythm with the thump of the train's motion along the track. His persecutor sat diagonally opposite him, mocking him with a leer every time he looked up. The sharp-faced man had not removed his curly-brimmed bowler, and a shadow hung over his brow. But it did not conceal the man's eyes. They glowed like red-hot coals at the fiery base of a furnace.

He clutched his stiff collar, trying to loosen it as his breathing became more and more difficult. His heart pounded faster in his chest, and his lungs strained to draw in the suddenly thick, clammy air of the railway carriage. He was suffocating – why did the other passengers not feel the same? Everyone else in the carriage seemed oblivious to his condition. In fact, he realised they were blurring out of focus as if seen through a badly adjusted camera lens. He blinked his eyes trying to clear his vision, but it was no use. The only face he could see clearly was that of the tall, thin man opposite as he leaned forward and said something to him. The words were lost in their own echoes, and he squeezed his eyes shut to close out the man's mocking face. A series of juddering crashes jarred through his body, and he almost cried out loud in fear.

His eyes flew open.

Then he realised the commotion was merely the train crossing the familiar set of junctions in the outer suburbs of Dijon. Almost at once the train settled to a more soothing rhythm, and he composed himself. He told himself he was being foolish – it was mere coincidence that this innocent man had seemed to dog his footsteps around the station. Like him, the man had been waiting for the Paris train, so it was only reasonable to assume they would have both been in the same places at the same time. Even the man's dash for the very carriage he had chosen could be explained by his wish to avoid the downpour which had suddenly swept the uncovered platform further up the stationary train.

No, he was imagining things, without a doubt.

In an effort to normalise the situation, he even forced himself to look directly at the man and squeeze a smile onto his parched, dry lips. The man spoke, but again the words did not register:

'I beg your pardon?'

'I was saying, you look a little pale, a little sickly. Perhaps that box on your lap is restricting your circulation. It does look very heavy. Here, let me take it from you.'

His loud protests, as he clutched the box even more tightly to his chest, keeping it from the outstretched hands of the man, cut through the other passengers' indifference. Now everyone in the carriage was giving him a curious and pitying look. His moment of calm was shattered, and he pressed as far back in his seat as possible, wishing for *it to swallow him up. His mind raced once more as he plotted a possible escape from the tall, thin man, who was firmly fixed once again in his mind as the destroyer of all his dreams, the thief of all his hopes.*

Potter woke with a start as the train rumbled over a set of points. He had been dreaming, and couldn't shake off the image of Le Prince being pursued by someone. A man who wanted Le Prince's invention. If Le Prince had truly created a moving-picture camera, and solved the problem of the medium on which to fix the images, then there would be those who wanted it. Either to claim it as their own, or to stifle it and promote their own invention. Mrs Le Prince had said the American inventor Edison was working in the same field as her husband.

If Potter was to solve this riddle, though, he had to work out how Le Prince, or his supposed assailant, come to that, had disappeared into thin air. Potter had got off the train at every station on the way down from Paris to Dijon, and spoken briefly with each stationmaster. Every one had been certain – as they had during the police enquiry only weeks after the disappearance – that no one resembling Louis Le Prince had alighted at their station. Now Potter was travelling back along the same line, no wiser after his interview with Albert Le Prince than he had been at the start of it all.

As the train rumbled through the peaceful countryside, he felt more and more agitated. The carriage was gradually emptying, as at each station the train stopped, and people got up and left. Soon, he would be left alone with the tall, thin man in his voluminous cape. And he could not begin to imagine what was on the man's mind, for his dark, glowing eyes betrayed nothing but emptiness. He felt pinned to his seat by their steely gaze, and when the train slowed for the next station, and their final two travelling companions rose to leave, he could do nothing. He wanted to leap up, grasp the elderly couple's arms, and convince them to stay. Perhaps he could suggest they alter their plans to get out at…where was it? He spotted the station sign as the train juddered to a halt.

Sens. They were halfway to Paris already. Why didn't they stay with him and enjoy the pleasures of the capital? If they stayed on with him to the terminus, he would treat them to a meal at Maxim's. And pay for a stay in a luxurious hotel for the night, if only they would stay on the train. Who wanted to finish their day in dreary old Sens? He would even offer to take their picture with his new camera – immortalise them on Dr Marey's new celluloid film. His pleas boiled in his brain, but remained unspoken, and the elderly couple descended slowly from the carriage, and were gone. The heavy camera box felt like an unbearable burden on his lap.

But their departure left him with an idea – a final defence. He surreptitiously turned the camera around on his lap until the two lenses in the front of the box pointed across the carriage at his tormentor. Though the stock inside the box was brittle, unlike the new celluloid, he had to hope it might work. He peered in the viewfinder set in the top, looking steadily at the image inverted in the little brass frame. Strangely, the intervention of the lenses between him and the man calmed him, as though the lens had captured and reduced the man to manageable proportions. He was able for the first time to look directly at him. No longer were his eyes so demonic, his posture so threatening. He was simply a tall, nondescript man sitting on a train, bored by the long journey, and anxious to return to his family in Paris.

Boldly, he began to turn the brass handle set in the side of the oak box.

The carriage was gradually emptying, as at each station the train stopped and people got up and left. He spoke to as many of his fellow passengers as possible within the limitations of his schoolboy French, and their reticence. Some of the people he spoke to travelled on the line regularly, but none could recall Le Prince as he described him – a tall, dark man with luxuriant Dundreary whiskers carrying a large box with brass fittings.

'*Six mois auparavant? Non, c'est impossible.* There are times I cannot even recall my own wife's name. Though that can be an advantage sometimes. Eh, monsieur?'

Potter was glad when the toothless and odorous peasant who wished to regale him with his amatory exploits on market days finally reached his stop. He looked out at the station, wondering if Le Prince had got this far.

Sens. An elegantly dressed man got on and sat opposite him.

The rain was teeming down now, and heavy droplets of water tracked slowly across the window. First they ran diagonally, driven by the forward motion of the train. He was only half aware of them out of the corner of his eye, for his gaze was still mainly on the inverted image in the viewfinder. He cranked the handle knowing that the film would soon be finished, fearing that the spell might then be broken. There was a burning sensation in his mouth and throat, and he craved a drink to soothe it. His heart was pounding once again in his chest, and he felt faint. He glanced up, and the man's eyes once again glowed murderously. He had to avert his gaze, and saw that the gobs of rainwater on the window were tracking almost vertically.

The train was coming to a halt.

The binding of the brakes woke Albert Potter from a doze, and he grasped the moquette-covered arm of his seat tightly as the carriage juddered to a halt. The elegant man opposite pitched forwards involuntarily.

He held his arm protectively round his moving-picture camera as the train lurched to a stop. And in the viewfinder he saw the tall, thin man leaping towards him across the carriage, his Inverness cape flapping like the wings of a bat. There was only one more thing he could do.

Potter looked out of the window onto darkness, seeing nothing more than his own reflection. On this occasion the image was of perplexity.

'Monsieur. Please, why have we stopped? There is no station.'

The elegantly dressed Parisian opposite, who had nearly been thrown into Potter's lap by the motion of the train, brushed off the dust that had settled on his grey, fur-trimmed pilot coat from the rack above his head and smiled wearily. He explained with a resigned nod of his coiffured head that the train always stopped here.

'It is for another train – where the lines cross. The driver knows he must stop, but it seems the signal always comes as a surprise to him. Hence the...'

A vague Gallic wave of his wrist finished the sentence, describing with a twirl of the fingers the abrupt stop to which they had come. Potter could well imagine that it would have thrown an unwary passenger facing the rear of the train out of his seat. He was glad his fellow traveller had braced himself, and done nothing more than steady himself with a hand on Potter's knee.

It was as he settled back in his seat that he realised the Frenchman had said something quite important. Potter lunged for his travelling bag, and staggered to his feet just as he felt the train start up again. Under the astonished gaze of the man, he flung open the carriage door and dropped down into the darkness.

He stumbled as he fell down onto the trackside, twisting his ankle. It buckled under him, and both his carpetbag and camera flew from his grasp, and disappeared into the darkness. He continued to tumble head over heels down the slippery embankment, bushes tearing at his clothes. His fall was broken by his landing on something soft in the damp gully at the bottom of the slope. It was his own bag, which had burst open to disgorge his clothes into the gully. A dress shirt drifted away from him on the rising water in the muddy channel. He sat up, wiped the rain out of his eyes, and watched the lights of the train gliding away from him. He was now committed to his course of action.

Potter picked himself up out of the muddy ditch, and realised what a mad thing he had done. But he still reckoned it could be no less than Le Prince had done six months before. If the police had not been able to find any trace of him getting off at the stations down the line between Dijon and Paris, it stood to reason that this must have been the only possible place that Le Prince could have alighted. The elegant Parisian had said the train always stopped here. While it had stood waiting in the dark for the passage of another train on the down line, Le Prince must have, for whatever reason, jumped down from the carriage with his bag and moving-picture camera. Had he been fleeing from someone, and what had been his pursuer's motive?

Potter turned up the collar of his muddied overcoat, hefted his bag, and clambered out of the gully. He found himself on a rutted, country road, and stood at the roadside, debating which way to follow it. Where would Le Prince have gone? While he stood considering this dilemma, he was aware of a glimmer of light flickering through the trees to his left, and thought at first it was a carriage coming his way. He determined to hail it, and hoped the driver would stop for a mud-covered madman who had just jumped off the Paris train in the middle of nowhere. Then he realised the apparent movement of the light was caused by the swaying of trees, whipped back and forth by the driving wind. The yellowish light was coming from the windows of a large house set far back in thick woodland.

He decided he needed to get out of the pouring rain, and walked along the road a few hundred yards until he found the driveway to the house. Two crumbling pillars loomed out of the darkness, both leaning at too precarious an angle to support the wrought-iron gates properly. These hung open, their bottom edges dug deep into the weed-covered driveway, clearly not having been moved for years. There was no indication on the pillars as to the name of the house, nor its owners. Potter hoped that, whoever they were, they would take pity on a damp and hungry traveller.

The driveway was as unkempt as the gateway, and Potter's only hope that the place was actually inhabited rested on the fact that he had seen lights in the upper rooms from the road. And as he approached the gloomy facade of the edifice, he was relieved to see at least one light still shining from one of the windows above the main portico. He was not so sure about wanting to place himself at the mercy of the inhabitants when he heard an unearthly scream emanating from the darkness above him.

When Potter had asked Doctor Gaston whether a tall, dark-haired man had appeared on the doorstep of his asylum six months ago, much in the same way he had done this night, Gaston had stared pensively into space for a long time. His eyes, when they had returned to stare at Potter, glittered darkly.

'I am afraid not. People very rarely choose to visit us voluntarily, you understand.' He had smiled knowingly, and by way of further explanation waved his hand to take in the dark, desolate chateau. 'The relatives of those patients who…' He strove to find a suitable word, one not tainted with the stain of incarceration, '…those patients…residing with us, pay as much as they can. But the upkeep of the chateau is so crippling that it is difficult to maintain it to the standards of its former residents…'

Potter, almost dozing off at the drone of Gaston's monologue on the causes of madness, suddenly realised the doctor was making a suggestion about his search for Le Prince.

'You know, it is no surprise to me that this man you are seeking…'

'Le Prince.'

'…Le Prince, disappeared. Little is known about the effects of cyanide on those who indulge in the science of photography.'

Potter frowned.

'What has cyanide to do with this case, doctor? Are you suggesting that Le Prince had been poisoned?'

Doctor Gaston smiled. 'Let me explain. About forty years ago, a man called Archer discovered that a substance called collodion made an excellent surface for photographic images. In order to fix this image, a solution was required, and most photographers used a weak solution of cyanide of potassium, silver nitrate, and water. Unfortunately, this solution is highly poisonous, and should not be allowed to touch broken skin, nor should the fumes be inhaled. Many people have died as a result of their interest in taking photographs.'

Potter remembered Albert Le Prince's comment about his brother's use of collodion, and being immersed in chemicals.

'What are the symptoms of cyanide poisoning?'

'Initially, headaches, faintness, anxiety. Often the sufferer has a burning sensation in his mouth. Later, he will suffer attacks of excitement, anxiety, and increased heart rate.'

'And finally?'

'Coma, convulsions, paralysis…and death. Inevitably – death.'

'You seem to know a lot about the subject.'

'Oh yes. I have been making a study of the progression of the symptoms, and have observed several research subjects in this very house.'

Potter shuddered at the apparent callousness of the doctor, and his reference to the demented, poisoned souls as simply subjects for his research.

'Then, if he did jump from the train that day, what were his chances?'

The doctor sighed.

'If he tried to hide somewhere, and the later stages of cyanide poisoning took effect – heart arrhythmia, respiratory depression – then he undoubtedly would have died a lonely and painful death.'

'And I am wasting my time. Fancy imagining him pursued and murdered by rivals, when in fact he was simply being persecuted by his own deranged imagination.'

'Not in the least. Our chance meeting has provided you with the most likely fate for the unfortunate Monsieur Le Prince. Break it to his wife gently.' He leaned back in his chair. 'Please, there is a village a kilometre down the road, Monsieur Potter – Pont-sur-Vanne – I will arrange for my assistant to take you there in the carriage.'

When Potter made a token protest at the inconvenience, Dr Gaston brushed it aside.

'It is better you do not stay here tonight. My patients can be…unsettled by strangers.'

So it was that Potter readily agreed to the doctor's offer of transport as he now felt his search was over. He thought it likely that Le Prince, doped with accidental cyanide poisoning, had fallen from the train and been killed. At the very least, he would have been seriously injured, and perhaps had crawled away into the woods only to succumb to cyanide and the elements soon afterwards. He shivered at the thought that Le Prince's fate could easily have been his own.

It was thus with some relief that he took his leave of the doctor and his forbidding residence, looking back only briefly to see the man standing in front of the portico, lit by the flickering lantern he held above his head. Then Potter sighed and settled back in his seat, looking forward to finding a warm dry hotel in the nearby village.

Dr Gaston, lantern in hand, waved goodbye to the Englishman, then mounted the steps back into his domain. He closed the creaky front door of the asylum against the elements. Taking a bunch of keys from his pocket, he carefully locked the door, turned, and crossed the vast, echoing hallway. The darkness hung heavy, like the cobwebs that adorned the upper of the high ceiling, but the lantern cast enough light for the doctor to see his way. Besides, he knew the house like the back of his hand now. To one side of the still imposing staircase that curved up into the darkness of the upper floors there was a secret door made to resemble the wall in which it was cut. He fumbled another key on the ring into the lock and stepped through the door, closing it behind him.

He heard a very familiar shriek. Descending the stairs that took him down to part of the warren of cellars under the chateau, he stopped at another locked door. The moaning came from behind this door. There was a shutter in the upper part of the door, and he slid it gently back. He looked at his latest research subject, and felt firm in his resolution to harbour the secret of his existence. The worth to science, and to Gaston's reputation, would be inestimable. He watched as the lunatic repeated his strange compulsion over and over again.

The man with the bushy Dundreary whiskers, now somewhat obscured by the full growth of beard on his chin, stared wide-eyed in terror at the illuminated square cast on the wall of his cell. He appeared transfixed by what he saw. In the corner of the room lay an oak box, bound with brass. Unfortunately, the brass had not saved the contents of the box from destruction in some sort of accident. One that Gaston now knew as the man's leap from the Paris train. The box rattled when shaken, but the man refused to relinquish it.

The occupant of the room screamed, and the doctor slid the shutter closed. He knew the cycle was now going to be repeated over again. And he longed to know what the man saw on the wall, where there was only a feeble square of light cast by the lamp he insisted on keeping burning all hours of the day and night. A blank patch of yellow light that terrified him. The doctor shook his head in bewilderment.

Louis sat mesmerised by the projected image of his persecutor on the wall. It was as real as reality itself. Like so many times before, the tall, thin man in the Inverness cape was sitting opposite him on the train, fixing him with his steely eyes. They were alone in the carriage. Slowly, that eternal, predatory leer formed on his face, and his silent lips formed the words, 'Give me the camera, Monsieur Le Prince.' Louis's heart sank. He could not take his eyes off the man, trying as he had done so many times to fix the man's features with his gaze. But the image was blurred, and lost in shadow, like a poorly developed photograph, sitting hopelessly in a tray of fixative. The only hope was to add more cyanide of potassium to it. He stared, knowing what was coming next, anticipating the inevitable.

The image shook, just as the camera had when the train had braked sharply, and the tall, thin man threw himself at Louis. The man's face filled the screen as Louis swung the camera at his head, a sickening crunch jarring him to the elbow. Then the image shifted jerkily to a shot of the carriage door, swinging open, and he was enveloped in the flapping wings of the man's cape. Under the dead weight of the body, Le Prince plunged into the darkness. He screamed.

I should stop smoking. I'm sure I should. I know I should. Smoking is bad. And it can lead to bad things.

On the other hand, there is a good side to smoking, especially these days. It's a social thing. And that's it. Smoking is social, and I don't just mean lighting up and sharing a cig after you-know-what.

Smoking has always been social, associated with parties, drinking, fun. But these days there's a new dimension. I'm talking about the way all us smokers gather in doorways outside office buildings and factories, the places where we're sent now we're banned from the insides. So those of us who persist, who resist, who continue, we're all bound to bond. When you're huddling together from the cold, you make friends.

And together we have common cause to complain. Fat people aren't sent out to eat. Idiots don't have to go make their dumb mistakes in the rain. Parents aren't sent to the bike shed with the bore-the-knickers-off-you pictures of their bloody children. I've known people who *pretended* to be smokers just to get away from all that.

Yeah, we're social on the doorstep, in ways the people left inside just aren't. That's what I find. I mean, I haven't done, like, the kind of research you read about in the papers, but it's my experience, and I'm not special or different. I'm just ordinary. So I bet it's true.

There's other things that follow from us being on the doorsteps. I mean, we're out there at times when before everybody – us included – was inside. I won't go so far as to say I think we're healthier than our workmates because of the fresh air we get, but if some clever clogs did research that said so, it wouldn't knock me down with a feather. And another thing is we see things that didn't used to get seen, you know? We're bound to, aren't we? Being as how we're out there looking around when nobody used to. So that's the thing with smoking, there's cons but there's also pros.

I work at Evening Eye, a fair size factory for the Marston Trading Estate – we have thirty-eight of us on the production side.

I don't know what 'Evening Eye' made when Jake, the owner, first picked the name. That was back when the factory was in the town centre, and before my time. But you have to be flexible to keep a business above water these days, what with the market ups and downs and all the new technological stuff. You have to be ready to respond to the market. Jake says so, and it makes sense. Whatever he made back then, now we make handbags. Not lumpy everyday bags a housewife will chuck all and sundry into. We're up-market, us. We make evening accessories for the posh and famous. Not Posh herself, yet, but lots of other rich people, some of them so posh I've never even heard of them.

Our bags are finest quality made from the best materials. A third of our output is filling special orders, but we do bread-and-butter top gear too, sold in high-tone catalogues and in places like Harrods. Not like Harrods. In Harrods. Well, you know what I mean.

All of it, even the catalogue stuff, is handcrafted. It sells for a bomb. We're in the *haute* fashion industry, so it ought to.

Evie says back when we were in town Jake didn't let us smoke on the factory floor either, because of the combustibility of stuff like the silks and velvets. But back then you could smoke in the canteen, no problem. Out here he doesn't even have a canteen. A sandwich wagon parks down the street every day in front of the double-glazing place. If you don't bring your own, that's where you get your grub. Unless you're one of them that goes off-site for lunch every day. I say them, but I mean only the one who does that on a regular basis, from the thirty-eight of us on the floor.

Evie says Jake moved the business during really hard years when lots of companies were going under. He survived by selling up the town site, moving to the unit in the trading estate, and using the cash difference to retool. Committed to Evening Eye, is Jake. It's his life and soul, anybody can see that. It doesn't make him likeable, but we respect him for it. And the business is still here, even if the thirty-eight of us used to be ninety-six of us when he was in town, according to Evie.

Evie used to be a smoker, like me. She tried to stop half a dozen times, and then all of a sudden it worked. She doesn't know why.

There aren't nearly so many smokers now as there used to be, only three now, among the thirty-eight. But we three nowadays get together on the doorstep with the mattress-makers from across the road and the double-glazing people and the carpets man and the something-to-do-with-cars people. All the smokers of this section of the estate smoke together. And we have a good laugh. As I said, in some ways it's more social than it's ever been.

Which is just as well, because back inside, at work, it's less social than it used to be. Jake has never been an easy-going guy, but now he's being monster-boss. That's because he's discovered that somebody's nicking.

What's missing is from our catalogue bags. I don't have the list of what's gone, but I've seen Jake wave it around. It seems the thieving began when he went on holiday last June. That's four – no, I tell a lie – that's three and a half months ago. Not many bags – we don't mass produce them – but enough to notice, obviously. Not enough to make a serious dent in profits, but enough to make a serious dent in Jake's mood. He's been on a rampage all week. Eight days. Eight work days. Since he discovered it.

Now, this week, he's put in a new policy. Each day when we leave work we're all going to be searched. Someone will look in our bags – a bit ironic that – and even check our persons. Evie's in charge. She's been around so long, Jake trusts her.

Not all the girls do, mind. 'Who's going to search Evie?' one of them asked when Jake announced the new policy last Friday so we'd have the weekend to think about it. But she didn't ask very loud and Jake didn't answer. That was Sandra who asked. Bit of a rebel, Sandra. She's one of the ones they suspect, I think.

I don't mind if Evie searches me. She can pat me down all she likes, so long as she doesn't tickle.

Sandra is not the number one suspect, though. The girls have another prime candidate. Linda. And the reason is that Linda is the one who goes off-site for lunch every day. Well, almost every day. You can tell ahead which days, because ahead of time – when we break for elevenses – Linda calls for a cab.

Yep, a cab. You see her make the call on her mobile. And then you see the cab pull up at one. And then a couple of minutes to two she's back – by cab again. Where does she go? some ask. How can she afford it? most ask.

Especially now. Now somebody's nicking.

They also don't like Linda much because she isn't social. She's not a smoker – that goes without saying – but she doesn't mix much over coffees and teas either. Keeps herself to herself. Hasn't been here all that long. All Evie knows about her is that she's married to a tarmac layer and they have a kiddie at school. Even when she doesn't go off on her taxi ride at lunch time she doesn't hang out with the girls. Keeps herself to herself. Reads. Books. Well, no wonder they're suspicious of her.

I reckon – though Evie's never said it – I reckon that the whole search thing at the end of the day is just a way to justify searching Linda's bag – and her person, if necessary. I think they have to search everybody in order to search the one they suspect.

Poor cow, Linda, I don't think she even knows they suspect her. She does her job, keeps herself to herself, thinks she's all right. Lost in her own world. Doesn't notice anything she doesn't have to notice, you know the type. She's not *social*. If you're social, you're interested in what your workmates are up to. OK, maybe not to the extent of keeping track of every new tooth of every baby in every family – especially if you're not lumbered with kids yourself and have no bloody plans to be. Gee, who could I be describing here?

And I also think that Jake and Evie figure that even if they don't catch anybody in *flagrante delicto*, at least the searches will put an end to the nicking.

I'm sure Jake would sorely love to catch somebody – I know men like Jake. Well, he is a man, so he's like the others, isn't he? He hates the idea that somebody's putting something over on him. He *says* it's because he thinks of us as one big family at Evening Eye. He *says* anybody robbing him is robbing us all. But the truth is he doesn't like some woman – because it's all women here, except for him – he doesn't like the idea of some woman cocking two fingers at him.

They're all the same, these guys. Guys in charge of women. I ought to know. I've known enough.

And I know something else. Jake is not going to catch Linda out. He can wait all day to pounce, search her big pouchy bag and her bouncy bra. Even look inside one of her books to see if the pages have been carved out.

Do you know why?

It's because what they think is the evidence against her isn't. They ask, how can she afford all those cabs? She must go off in the taxi three, four times a week, and then back again. Who on earth in Evening Eye has money for that? And if she does, where does she get it from?

I wouldn't put it past Jake to follow Linda around out of hours, to try to find where she sells the bags she supposedly nicks. Try to catch her going to a market and approaching a fashion trader who'll give her a tenth what they retail for in Harrods, and she'll be grateful for it.

But he can't follow her all day and all night.

If he wants to know about Linda, what he ought to do is take up smoking. He ought to come out on the doorstep where I go and see what I see while I'm out there.

I told you, smokers these days, we see things that other people don't. If Jake was to come out with me on the doorstep, and pay attention, he'd see Linda come out there or four times a week to her waiting taxi. And he'd see her arrive back at work at two minutes to two. Regular as clockwork.

But what he'd also see is that it's always the same taxi. Linda's shagging the taxi driver. Obvious. To anybody who cares to look. If any money's changing hands, it isn't coming out of Linda's purse. That's what Jake would see if he came out to socialise with the smokers.

But I very much hope he doesn't. If he was to start hanging out with us smokers it would put a serious cramp in my style. That's because it's me who is taking the occasional bag, and passing it over to Molly from the double-glazing at break times for her to sell to her mate on the market.

She gets a tenth what they sell for in Harrods. So I get a twentieth. But that's fine with me. Every little bit helps. Not least because they're bloody expensive these days, cigarettes.

I have faced the cavalry of Ayub Khan and ridden a war pony stolen from the Pashtu, as its owner swept down a rocky gully behind me, brandishing a rifle. I rode with Karim Bey across the Wild Pass in the Serbian rebellion of seventy-eight. I have seen a major in the Bengal Lancers take a wild pig through the fundament, only to have his spear bury itself into sun-baked mud beneath.

Good days. I miss them.

My name is Colonel John Hamish Watson, late of the Bombay Sappers and Miners. I know the weight behind a charging horse. I have faced it and lived. Four fine horses harnessed to a carriage whipped by one of the Queen's own coachmen carries enough force to smash a stone wall. So you will understand why I had little hope for the fool who stepped into my path on the high road through Kingston upon Thames.

There was, of course, little reason for my coachman to be whipping his horses so fast but I like to make my journeys at speed; the empire is large, the number of us who play the game surprisingly small and the rules complex, as you will realise from the fact I fought at Stara Planina with Karim Bey rather than the Serbs.

The first I knew of disaster was a shout from Hunter, followed by the frantic neighing of his horses and a thud. Something heavy catapulted across the roof of the carriage and tore varnished canvas above my head. A woman shouted, and the carriage tipped sideways.

We travelled maybe five paces before the first of the horses went down, tripping that behind. The scream of a wounded animal is something one never loses. It was such a scream, heard in the hills behind Kandahar, which convinced me Mr Darwin was correct and we did not, after all, rank between the angels and the animals. A man with his leg badly broken sounds little different to a horse in similar straits.

Using a window, which now showed only clouds, weak sunlight and the grey of an English sky, I crawled from the carriage, to find

Hunter already knelt beside the head of a magnificent grey, tears in his eyes.

'Done for,' Hunter said. 'Legs, ribs... All broken.' For Hunter this was almost a speech.

'Bad luck,' I said. Undoing my loden coat, I loosened a holster that kept a Bulldog in place. 'Here.'

Taking my proffered revolver in silence, the coachman put its blunt muzzle to the side of his horse's head.

'At the back,' I suggested, 'or directly from the front. I can do it if you'd rather.'

Hunter stared at me, although it's unlikely he saw much.

'Let me,' I said, and when he looked doubtful, in as much as a face carved from Irish oak can carry that expression, I admitted something few people know about me. 'I have a fine understanding of anatomy.'

'You, sir?'

'I used to be a surgeon.'

There are advantages in my world to being seen as a cold-blooded killer, and to admit to saving as many as I had killed. Such admissions can do harm. Although the truth is far stranger, because I have killed fewer people than most believe and saved many more than I am prepared to admit.

Taking the revolver from Hunter, I clicked back the hammer and clambered across a broken shaft to reach the animal's head. Speak kindly and most people will give you their trust. The same applies to animals. With one hand I stroked the dying animal and with the other I put my revolver between its eyes and pulled the trigger. It died with a kick and a spasm, but the fact its skull contained myriad cavities did much to baffle the sound and gave me an idea for later.

'Thank you, sir,' Hunter said, thus using up another week's worth of words.

It was only then I remembered the unfortunate cause of our crash. I could see where he lay by the interest his agony attracted. A smaller crowd had come together around my wrecked carriage, drawn by its quality, but a far larger crowd was gathered a dozen paces behind this, and it was here the human cause and casualty of our accident lay.

They grew quiet at my approach, the crowd. Men fell back and women looked away, averting their eyes. A small girl burst into tears and a youth old enough to know better stared openly into my face. That was when I realised it was my revolver which earned their silence.

'You have killed me...' The voice was high, slightly strange and the man who spoke indeed looked on the edge of death, which was an improvement on what I had been expecting.

'It is always a bad idea to step in front of a moving carriage,' I replied, unwilling to have him meet God believing the fault mine.

'Please,' he said, 'fetch me a doctor...'

He had the hollow face of a classics master and the fingers of a second violinist, somewhat bitten around the nails. Behind me, I could hear muttering and a woman bustled forward, mouth already opening to share her news. 'A doctor recently took residence in a street behind.' Several of the crowd began to agree, and one, a clerk from his dress, which was careful if none too clean, crouched beside me and offered to fetch this man.

I am a...

I almost said those words aloud, but instead I gave the clerk a guinea, to show the doctor his fee would be paid and told the man to run as swiftly as possible. Had I done what first occurred to me and announced myself a medical man, my coming retirement might have been very different.

'Tell your doctor to hurry,' I said. 'This patient needs urgent attention.'

A man running is always a ridiculous sight and the clerk confirmed this fact, his feet slapping cold cobbles and his elbows flexing like the wings of a game bird. A handful of seconds after he started, he disappeared down a narrow alley in a sideways skid that almost had him on his back. With nothing else to occupy the seconds, I sat back and waited.

Close examination of human blood has taught me three things. It is as thick as paint, it is surprisingly nutritious and, finally, like excreta, we do not find that our own excites a reflex of disgust.

The man lying on cobbles kept gagging at the taste of the watery red liquid which dribbled from his lips, and it was this that gave him away. A sponge, I guessed, hidden in the corner of his mouth and worked by his tongue. Chicken's blood, most probably, it looked too thin for pig.

His legs lay at strange angles, no bones visible through the cheap tweed of his trousers but obviously broken, at least, obviously broken to those who did not know how such breaks looked in real life.

If the clerk had looked ridiculous, the doctor was even more so, his short legs pumping and his face as red at that of a Sioux brave. He wore a frock coat that had seen better days and once belonged to someone else; unless our man had shrunk several inches in height as he filled out around his waist.

'Stand back,' he demanded. 'Stand back.'

Those around the injured man did as they were told.

'Ahh,' said the doctor, seeing me stand alone. 'You must be the unfortunate owner of that unhappy...' Shrewd eyes flicked from my carriage, which had him frowning, to my clothes, which seemed to put his mind at ease.

'A shocking accident,' he said, 'most shocking.' A refrain quickly taken up by a woman in the crowd and then by several people around her.

Kneeling, the doctor touched his hand to the victim's throat in a manner that would have been entirely convincing had be been checking a body for a pulse. Since the patient's eyes could be seen fluttering in his head such checking seemed entirely redundant.

Next the doctor reached inside the thin man's coat to feel for his heart, and when the doctor took his hand away, his fingers were red with blood. This was enough to make a woman faint. Needless to say, it was the woman who'd first taken up his refrain and as she fell, she twisted to land elegantly, revealing rather more ankle than was seemly.

This seemed to make the doctor angry.

'Hysteria,' he announced. 'Not helpful.' The fat little man eyed me grimly. 'All the same, not surprising. Such a shocking accident...' His smelling salts left the woman with tears running down her face.

An attempt to straighten the injured man's leg produced a

shriek of such pitch that it unsettled one of the horses now being cut from its harness. I knew this because Hunter swore, despite the tender sex of many of those around him and swore almost as loudly as the man had screamed.

The fat little doctor stood, shook his head and turned towards me. 'If we could talk...?' he said, taking my elbow.

We walked together towards the bridge, while those around us fell back as if afraid of the weight of guilt they believed I carried. The sky was still grey, the river little brighter than the surface of a rusty sword. A chill wind swept along its surface, and although this was nothing to the winds which blow so fierce in the Hindu Kush that they carve rock before one's eyes, it was in keeping with the drabness of a drab town. In England, bless it, everything works on a smaller scale.

'You are a gentleman,' he said.

When a man says that he means he considers you his equal. I found this idea amusing, although I was careful to keep that from reaching my face. As a young man I walked through the aftermath of the massacre of Meerut, my skin stained with walnut juice and let not a single sight disturb the calm that carried me through crowds of rioting sepoys.

'Indeed,' I said. 'A gentleman and a soldier.'

'And a man of comfortable means.'

I was about to object but saw his eyes slide across my loaden coat, which was lined with green silk. So instead of objecting, I muttered something non-committal, quintessentially English.

'This is difficult,' he said. 'Very delicate.'

At that point, I was meant to ask why it was difficult. He waited and I waited some more.

'Very difficult,' he added, as we turned back towards the press of people. 'I'll be blunt. You're a gentleman and this is a dreadful accident. It is my best opinion that this man will die. I am sure someone has already sent for the police.'

This I privately doubted, since the crowd were far too busy being shocked to do anything that useful.

'I can ease things,' he said. 'Let the patient be moved to my surgery. I will undertake to treat him.'

'But he will still die?'

'Oh yes,' said the fat little man. 'Nothing I can do will stop that.' He paused, with the manner of someone considering how far to risk his reputation. 'I can, however, delay slightly in announcing his death. I will mention complications, the poorness of his constitution, perhaps even suggest a certain unsoundness in his mode of life.'

'A more deserving man would have lived?'

'Indeed.' The little man nodded, delighted at my quickness of wit. 'There will be costs,' he said. 'Minor outlays. I can see the poor wretch's family on your behalf, maybe give his wife a few guineas towards a Christian burial and the keep of her children. My own fees will be modest.'

Raising my eyebrows, I waited.

The sum he named would have bought a town in Odessa.

'All in,' he added hastily. 'As would include my fees, outlay for his widow, a burial... Such a tragic accident,' he repeated, shaking his head. For one hideous moment I feared the man was about to begin his spiel all over again, for we were nearing the crowd and the last thing I wanted was to waste more time on fainting women and chicken's blood sponges.

'Let me examine the patient,' I said.

'You?' he said, sounding altogether less certain.

Put me in the path of danger and I will swear in the ripest Hindi. The man in front of me said his single word in an accent that spoke of education and birth. At times of great stress we all revert to the accents of our childhood. It seemed he was a rogue from choice rather than necessity.

'Did I not mention I was a surgeon?' Opening my coat further, to reveal the gun beneath, I began to push my way through the crowd.

'Look at me,' I demanded of the groaning man, and he opened his eyes with a great deal of fluttering and a dying fall of sobs, all the more convincing for being slight.

'Now focus on my finger.'

I moved this digit and watched his eyes trail after, delayed by a single second and inclined to roll back in his head. Mind you, good at acting or not, I could always use any man prepared to step in front of charging horses, catapult himself above a carriage and dislocate his own leg on landing.

Gripping that leg, I put my other hand to his knee and pulled, twisted and pushed almost simultaneously. The wretch gave a hideous shriek, more from shock I suspect than anything else and forgot to keep his eyes half focused.

'See,' I said, 'good as new.' To make my point, I worked his knee as one might work the leg of a horse. In the crowd someone began to clap.

'Those ribs,' I added. 'How are they feeling?'

He cast his eyes behind me to the fat man who hovered anxiously at my shoulder. Whatever passed between them, the wretch now sprawled on the ground sighed, his face already resigned.

'Better,' he said.

'Let me.' His ribs were fine, the sponge actually a bladder sewn into the side of his shirt and worked by pressure. Our man with the narrow face and darting eyes was so busy worrying that I might identify the object beneath my fingers, that he entirely failed to notice when I lifted his wallet.

'Nasty swelling,' I said, pocketing that object as I wiped my fingers on the side of my own trousers. 'Otherwise, just a graze.' Helping the man to his feet, I held him steady as he found his balance. It was a nice touch.

'Your name, sir?'

The man looked at me. 'Sigerson,' he admitted finally. 'Professor Sigerson.'

'Professor?'

'An American university. In San Francisco. A thoroughly modern institution.' He managed to imbue this description with a level of approval which would have been missing had the words come from my mouth.

'And your friend?'

'My brother,' he corrected.

Had someone told me those two men were picked at random from a thousand such, rounded up off the streets of London I would have believed him. The idea that they shared the same blood was an altogether stranger proposition. One man was fat and small eyed, the other tall and beak nosed, with eyes that belonged to an Ottoman potentate.

'Professor Sigerson,' I said, offering my hand. 'Pray let me call on you to confirm your recovery...'

Needless to say, the address given me was as fake as the name. The house in which this man really resided was behind the new railway station. A shiny brass plate by the gate announced it as the residence of Professor Sigerson, thinker & Dr Sigerson, general physician.

The screws holding this unlikely announcement were new, but a hundred tiny scratches at the four corners spoke of other walls and hurried exits. At least, so Hunter told me when he returned, following them being the task I gave him while I found a blacksmith to repair the broken rim of our wheel.

So, it was entirely my fault the two Sigersons had vanished by the time I presented myself at their door. Stripped bare, their rooms echoed to the sound of my search, even the carpets having been spirited away. A very agitated landlady, who had appeared out of breath, shortly after I had Hunter break down the door, kept demanding of me what kind of fiends stole everything.

'Efficient ones,' I told her, although I fear she did not entirely understand my joke. The constable who'd accompanied the landlady began to make notes and, as I listened, her list of items grew longer and ever more valuable.

'I will never get them back,' she wailed.

'On the contrary,' I said, 'you can have them this very afternoon with almost no effort...'

It never ceases to sadden me the things that amaze closed minds. The sun setting over the Hindu Kush, with wild dogs circling the last flames of a fire destined to die before dawn; waves deep enough to swallow St Paul's in one watery gulp; the innocence of a Nepalese child goddess so beautiful grown Generals cry in her presence, such things are put on this earth to stun us. To be amazed by anything less seems an insult to intelligence.

As I suspected, my comment that her goods would be returned

proved enough to silence the landlady. Although I then had to explain to the constable that my certainty the carpets could be found at the nearest pawnbroker was more to do with common sense, than any intimate, not to say inside, knowledge of the crime.

'We must be off,' I said.

The constable looked as if he might object but changed his mind at a glance from Hunter, who wore the badge of a Queen's Messenger beneath his coat. There my day might have ended, with an interesting meeting and my giving Inspector Lestrade descriptions of the two rogues and an order that I be notified when they were found. And so it would have ended, if Hunter and I had not proved woefully incapable of paying the blacksmith for his work on the wheel.

'Sir?'

I fumbled at the pig-skin bag in my hand and then stopped, angrily. I am not a man who fumbles. In it I felt a map of the empire painted onto silk, my cigars, which actually broke open to reveal sticks of hashish, which the dear Queen herself uses for pain, a little opium, a throwing knife, a set of prayer beads given me by Kais Bey.

Everything was where it should be, except my reward for work well done, the bag of gold I'd gone to Windsor to collect. Apparently, while I was first curing our accident victim, the fat little doctor had come to take a look at my carriage. This, it appeared, was not all he took.

'Sir?' said the blacksmith.

'Here,' I replied, impatience winning. With a flick of my wrist, I took the throwing knife and slashed open the bag's handle, revealing a dozen half-sovereigns sewn into a sealed silk tube. I took three coins, more than his work was worth and gave them to the man. 'That also buys your silence,' I told him, nodding towards the ruined bag.

He left without another word.

It was then I turned to the rogue's wallet and found my first real clue and proof of his name. The clue came in the form of a train timetable and the name from a scrap of newspaper. Sherlock Holmes, younger brother to Mycroft and pupil of Professor James

Moriarty. Almost every detail in the report was wrong – the events described took place at St Jean, not Pau, in August '71, not March '72 – but the scribbler was right about one thing, there had been a scandal.

When I put my mind to things I can make them happen quickly. So it proved in engineering my next meeting with the elusive Mr Holmes. The man had money, my money, he had no need to visit the town underlined in his railway timetable, but he would visit it just the same. I'd felt his heart beneath his shirt and it had been racing. He lived for the challenge. No man is so poor he has to jump in front of four galloping horses.

I would have taken Hunter with me, for he is a coachman beyond the ordinary. But the moment Hunter finally realised the crash on the road through Kingston upon Thames had not been an accident, and one of his best greys had been struck down in the course of a simple confidence trick, he vowed to hunt and kill the men responsible. He did so with such barbarity that I cannot even bring myself to put his threats down upon the page.

Choosing Edwards instead, I took a two-seater Hansom drawn by a single horse and a huge cloak in which to disguise myself. I chose an open-top carriage, because I was interested to see how Mr Holmes would handle his fall with no roof on which to somersault.

The city to which we travelled was barely more than a Hampshire town with pretensions to history. It was, however, well chosen. Winchester High Street is long and sloping and overlooked by a grain merchants and a general store, both busy with yeoman farmers, plump wives and red-faced gentlemen, the kind of people one expects to see in such a place.

We wasted a morning hunting for the brass plate, newly put up on the pillar of a narrow house in St Peter's Street, and the afternoon checking that both rogues were in the city and then Edwards spent his evening in the kind of tavern used by coachmen and servants. I was French, apparently, he was pleased with that touch, newly arrived from Paris and I spoke little English and greatly valued my privacy. Small wonder the brothers Holmes found us impossible to resist.

They took it in turns to watch my hotel for the rest of that night, only abandoning their watch when Edwards strode from his nearby lodgings to prepare my coach.

'*Vite, vite.*'

As instructed, he conveyed me down the High Street slightly faster than was decent and, as we passed the Buttercross, with its collection of ragged urchins seated around the base, a man stepped absent-mindedly into the road in front of us and was sent flying.

A woman screamed and Edwards began to apply the brake. A farmer stepped into the road to make sure we did not try to escape and then stepped back quickly, when Edwards took his hand from the lever for a few seconds. This time round the horse was unhurt and my carriage still whole. Which meant that all of the crowd's attention could be concentrated on the fallen man.

'He needs a doctor,' said a woman. 'Such a terrible accident. He needs...'

'Madame,' I said, clambering down. 'I am a doctor. And, as it happens, I am familiar with such accidents, having seen one almost identical only last week.' This time, when she fainted it was with no elegant twist or display of ankle, she merely crumpled and hit her head upon the kerb hard enough to make her nose bleed.

'Mr Holmes, allow me.' Taking Sherlock's leg, I pulled, twisted and pushed it until I felt the bones slot back into place. Someone in the crowd nodded in approval and allowed that I would make a good vet.

As Edwards carried the unconscious woman to safety, I turned my attention to the man on the ground. In the few seconds it had taken me to adjust his leg, I had watched Mr Holmes check all four exits from the Buttercross and realise, instantly, that these were closed. He'd noted Edwards carry the woman toward a waiting police van and seen his brother appear and disappear at the sight of trouble; not that this would be a problem. Lestrade had made a call to the Chief Constable of Hampshire, one of the few men in the county to possess a telephone. All the help I needed was available. I had no doubt that Mycroft Holmes was already in captivity.

'You have three choices,' I told his brother.

Since this was two better than Sherlock had imagined, I had his full attention. 'You can be arrested and hope you die in prison...'

'I doubt,' he said, 'that I should ever hope this.'

'How old are you?'

'Twenty-six,' he admitted.

'Hunter is thirty,' I told him. 'He is the coachman whose horse you killed in Kingston. He comes from a family that never forgets and has little interest in forgiveness.'

'My other alternatives?'

'Try to escape and be shot down.'

'By you?'

I nodded. 'By me, by my coachman, by that good detective standing over by the van. Does it make a difference?'

He allowed that it did not. 'And my last choice?'

'Work for me. I need a man who can throw himself in front of carriages, think on his feet, lie when necessary and hold up a mirror to dazzle the public. The work will be hard and dangerous, it will require levels of intelligence few men possess. You will have no official standing. In return, you will be provided with a pardon, lodgings, a housekeeper, funds, access to any delicate information you need, and an assistant.'

'My brother?'

'I have other plans for Mycroft.'

'Then who?'

'Me,' I told him. 'Your assistant will be me.'

'What about Hunter?'

'You will be working for me. I work for the Queen. Hunter is the Queen's favourite coachman. He will growl at you and I will take care not to introduce the two of you before time, but he will respect your position.'

'Which is what?' Few of the crowd remained to see Sherlock Holmes pull himself to his feet, glance quickly around to check the alleys were still blocked and turn back to me. He checked from habit only, his decision already made, there are some things one can see in a man's eyes. 'What am I to be called?'

I shrugged. 'Whatever is appropriate. Do you have something in mind?'

'Consulting Genius,' he suggested, with no appearance of shame.

I smiled, amused by his vanity. 'I will put that to the Queen,' I promised. 'Although you might have to settle for a little less.'

From her viewpoint high above street level Carol can see St George's Hall. Undergoing renovation, it is swathed in plastic, a colonnaded monument in bubblewrap. To her right, the sun sinks low and golden over the Mersey tunnel entrance. She loves the broad sweep of steps down from the Greco-Roman façade of the museum. She walks slowly, taking her time, head up, shoulders back; it makes her feel grand, like a movie star. She wears a trouser suit – a good linen mix in pale green. Her hair, ice blond and fine as spun silk, lifts in a faint breeze and she enjoys a moment of blessed coolness.

Carol has been working late on a new coleopteran exhibition. Her favourites are the iridescent types; they shimmer with false light – purple and green and electric blue – oil on water, prisms in sunlight. She checks her watch. Eight-thirty. Not too late to chance crossing the cobbled street into St John's Gardens.

The borders are planted with blue violas and pink biennial dianthus; warmed by the sun and enclosed within the walls of the old churchyard of St John's, the scent of violets and cloves is almost hypnotic. Laughter carries from one of the lawns to her right and she glances without turning her head. A group of students, talking, flirting, testing their knowledge of their current reading on their friends. Harmless.

She passes them unnoticed. She has learned the art of invisibility: walk confidently but without show; look like you know where you're headed, stare straight through a crowd, as though you can see your goal unimpeded by the crush – as though *they* are invisible. Never meet the eye of a stranger.

Traffic is heavy, belching hot exhaust fumes into the already hot and exhausted air. Too early for the clubs, but too hot to wait indoors for dark, the streets are already thronged with youths in white shirts, eager for the rut, eyeing the tanned girls who flaunt their toned midriffs and thighs. Liverpool city centre swelters in a brown heat haze, the crowds irascible and uncomfortable in their own skins: the heat has taken the fun out of the game.

Central station is empty. She walks invisible past the guard at the ticket barrier. She hears voices raised, laughter; it echoes, reminding her of swimming baths, caves. Cavemen. The constant scream of a faulty escalator handrail, rubber on metal, sets her teeth on edge, but it is cooler underground, and she is grateful for this.

The voices grow louder, nearer. She sees them without looking, using her peripheral vision. An untaught skill, urban survival. Three boys – only three. They hoot and howl, pounding the air with their shouts. The space – the emptiness of the platform – lends them size and significance. She keeps her gaze steady and flat, moves to the shelter of one of the massive square pillars to escape notice.

A faint whine and a puff of warm air announces the approach of a train. She hangs back, waiting to see what the boys will do. The vibration passes down the line like a series of whip-cracks, then the first glimpse: twin aspects, insectile, emerging from the dark. The train slows and stops with an electrical sigh.

The boys jostle each other into a carriage to her left. She steps into the next. Four or five others sit at discreet distances, respecting each other's space, taking care to avoid eye contact as they plunge into the tunnels and deep cuts on the edge of the city centre. Two disembark at Brunswick. Then she sees the three boys at the link doors; they peer into her carriage, grinning, making animal noises. She looks out of the window. They come in and she looks up again, alarmed, catches the eye of the man in the seat diagonally opposite. She sees him sometimes when she works late. Grey suit, tie loosened, respectable, early forties. He smiles and she is reassured. It's OK.

The boys sit at the far end of the carriage, out of sight, but she can hear them; their laughter, their sniggers. A whiff of solvent and the squeak of a marker pen on glass – they're vandalising the windows. She won't look. A woman gets off at St Michael's; their mutual vulnerability allows a brief moment of contact. Carol sees her own fear reflected in the woman's eyes.

The boys get up – she sees them ghosted in the window – it's almost night and the steep embankments on either side of the track draw darkness down into the carriage. Two tall lads, one who looks younger, nervous. They are dressed in the uniform of sports gear, trainers, baseball caps. She takes her paperback from her shoulder bag and pretends to read. The largest of the three walks down the car and sits opposite, staring at her until she is forced to look up. He has short brown hair and grey hate-filled eyes. His mouth is twisted with fury – against what? She knows the standards: society, authority, the self but looking into this boy's eyes she sees his hatred is directed at her. *You don't know me*, she wants to say, but the words won't come. He continues staring and she looks away again. Her invisibility has failed her.

A man gets out at St Michael's. She wants to get out with him, to stay close, to ask for his protection, but her legs won't carry her and she focuses instead on her book and prays the boy will go away.

Now it's just her and the three boys and the man in the suit. She wants to be home, to be out of the heat, drinking chilled wine, listening to the blackbird in her hawthorn tree improvising a tune in the last glimmer of dusk. She wants to be left alone.

The other two have been loitering at the far end of the carriage, but now one of them comes forward and kneels on the seat behind the tall youth, peering through the gap between the headrests. He has jug ears and a snub nose, which make him seem childlike – monstrous.

'D'you wanna come for a drink with us?' The first boy asks. His breath is thick with beer and vomit.

'I think you've had enough already, don't you?' Carol says.

The other boys laugh. 'Boz is getting his arse kicked by a *girl*!' the second boy says.

Boz. Carol memorises the name.

Boz leans so close that she can't see her novel when she looks down at it. His hair gel smells of coconut oil. His hooded jacket is open, showing off his six-pack. *This is not a boy you want to humiliate, Carol*, she told herself. *He's vain, and vanity does not forgive criticism.*

'D'you wanna bevvy or what?'

'No,' she says, pleased that her voice is so steady. 'Thanks.'

The second boy sobs theatrically. 'She's breaking his heart!'

Boz grabs his crotch. 'I might *fuck* it, but I'm not in *love* with it.' He lets his eyes drift to the top of her legs, the crease of her trousers. 'You a natural blonde?' he asks.

The skin on her scalp tingles and her heart flutters in her chest like a trapped bird. The man in the suit is reading his paper. *Is he deaf?* She wonders. *Can't he hear what's going on?*

Boz blows in her face and she flinches as if he has hit her. 'Look at me when I'm talking to you, *bitch.*'

He is smirking, enjoying her humiliation, and a tiny spark of anger flares in her gut.

'Sod off,' she says, but too tentatively.

He mimics her; he's a good mimic, he captures her accent, her voice, the note of fear she cannot hide.

'I mean it,' Carol says. 'Back off or I'll call the guard.'

His eyebrows lift. 'Yeah? How you gonna do that? ESP?'

The emergency cord is six feet away, above the door. It might as well be six miles. She glances around the carriage for security cameras, but can't see any.

She stands. The boy stands with her. She moves left. He mirrors the movement.

The man in the suit is still reading his paper. *Bastard.*

'Excuse me,' she says, her voice is weak, frightened. The man doesn't respond and the boy's eyes flicker greedily over her body. His sickly-sweet breath in her nostrils is an intrusion, a violation.

Why are you being so bloody polite?

'Hey!' she shouts.

Boz jerks back, startled.

The anger feels good. 'HEY, YOU!' she shouts again, louder this time.

The man flicks down a corner of his newspaper. He seems irritated.

'Are you going to help me?' The way she asks, it's a clear accusation.

The boys watch, curious to see what he will do.

She sees a muscle jump in the man's jaw, then he exhales through his nose as if he has been asked to perform some irksome task.

He folds his paper neatly and places it on the seat beside him. The train slows and the recorded announcement tells them they are approaching Cressington. *Thank God* – her stop.

'That's us, Boz.' The youngest boy has appeared suddenly by the door. He sounds troubled, unhappy.

The man stands in a smooth, easy movement. He's taller than they expected, more athletic, and the boy says again, the tremor in his voice accentuated by the rattle of the train, 'Our stop, man.'

Boz keeps his eyes on Carol, but she notices the tension in his shoulders, the bunching of his fists. He gives her one last disparaging look.

'What – did you think it was grab-a-granny night?' He jabs a thumb towards the youngest boy, standing anxiously in the doorway. 'I wouldn't even touch you with *his* dick.'

The doors open and they're off, onto the platform, whooping and laughing, making barking noises at her. They swarm up the steep stone steps; she hears their footsteps echoing all the way through the Victorian station house. She looks at the man and he raises a shoulder, a slight smile on his face – embarrassment or amusement? She can't tell. Doesn't care.

Her stop. She steps out onto the platform. Seized by dread certainty, she stares wide-eyed at the stairwell. What if they're waiting for her outside the station? The narrow muddy short cut she usually takes to Broughton Drive is dark and poorly lit, and even on the roadway there are places they might hide: behind skips outside the house refurbs, in the shop doorways on the main road. *To hell with it*, she'll go on to Garston, get a taxi home.

The warning buzzer sounds that the doors are about to close. She wheels round as they begin sliding shut, jumps back on the train. One of the doors slams into her shoulder and she is caught off-balance. She grabs the handrail and steadies herself. The man in the suit is watching her.

He sighs and smiles in resignation and welcome. He smells the fear on her. Exciting, raw, unrestrained. It smells of warmth. Of woman. Of pain. Of sex.

'It was a young woman who found him,' the village constable said. 'Molly Davitt, the blacksmith's daughter. She thought he was having a conversation on the telephone. After a while when he didn't move she decided something might be wrong.'

'After how long, exactly?' the inspector asked. He was a city man and disliked vagueness.

'Half an hour or so, Molly says. Could be longer.'

'You mean to tell me this young woman stood watching a man in a telephone box for half an hour or more?'

'There's not much happens round here. And the fact is, Molly's been fascinated with that telephone box from the time they put it up.'

It was the spring of 1924 when they came to install the telephone box in Tadley Gate. Nobody was quite sure why. The men from the Post Office travelled from Hereford, seventeen miles away as the pigeon flew and half as much again by winding country road. All they knew was that they'd been instructed to erect the standard model Kiosk One, designed to be especially suitable for rural areas, on the edge of the common, in between the old pump and the new war memorial. It was made of reinforced concrete slabs with a red painted wooden door and large windows in the door and sides. In a touch of Post Office swagger, a decorative curlicue of wrought iron crowned it, finishing in a spike that some people assumed was an essential part of the mechanism. Nobody in Tadley Gate (pop. 227) had asked for a telephone kiosk and very few had ever used a telephone. Still, they were pleased. The coming of the kiosk was an event at least, which made two events in eighteen months, counting back to the other new arrival, the petrol pump. The petrol pump belonged to Davy Davitt, Molly's father. A third-generation blacksmith by trade, he'd had more than enough of horses and fallen in love with cars. The sign over his workshop said 'Blacksmith and Farrier' in the curly old-fashioned letters that had been good enough for his grandfather. Underneath he'd painted, stark and white, 'Motor Vehicle Repairs Undertaken'. The fact that the parish included thirty-three horses and ponies and only one motor car limited his scope but he was a resourceful man. Long negotiations with a distant petrol company ended with the arrival of a tank and a pump. The pump was red like the phone kiosk door, topped by a globe of frosted glass with a cockleshell and 'Sealed Shell' on it in black letters. The tank below it held 500 gallons of petrol, delivered by motor tanker. In the first year Davy's only sales were five gallons every other week to the colonel from the big house who drove a Hillman Peace model very cautiously, so at that rate it would be nearly four years before the tanker needed to come with another delivery. But as Davey told anybody who'd listen in the Duke of Wellington, that was only the start. He was looking ahead to the arrival of the motor tourer. It stood to reason that as more people bought cars and the cars became more reliable, they'd drive for the pleasure far away from cities and into the countryside. It didn't matter the only motor tourist Tadley Gate had ever seen was somebody who'd got badly confused on the way to Shrewsbury and didn't want to be there.

Davy believed in the petrol pump the way an Indian believed in his totem pole. He was even inclined to credit it with attracting the telephone kiosk to the village. He reasoned that now, properly equipped with both telephone and petrol pump, Tadley Gate was ready to unglue itself from the mud and enter the age of speed. Only the age of speed seemed to be taking its time about getting there.

Molly had no strong feelings about the petrol pump. She didn't like the smell much, but petrol was no worse than the throat-grabbing whiff of burning horn when her father fitted red-hot shoes to horses' hooves. On the other hand, the phone-box enchanted her from the day it arrived. She was twenty then and single, having just broken her engagement to a local farmer's son. The second broken engagement, as it happened, and more than enough to get her a reputation as a jilt. She honestly regretted that. She'd quite liked the farmer's son, as she'd quite liked the young grain merchant before him, but shied away from marriage because they were both of them firmly tied by work and family to the country around Tadley Gate.

If she married either of them she'd have had to stay there for life and she knew – with the instinct that tells a buried bulb which way is upwards – that staying at Tadley Gate wasn't the way things were meant to be. She'd been away from the village once, for a family wedding in Birmingham where she'd been a bridesmaid. In the days before and after the ceremony she'd gone with her cousins to the cinema, bought underwear in a department store, read the *Daily Mail* and seen advertisements in magazines of sleek women poised on diving boards, leaning against the bonnets of cars, dancing quick-time foxtrot in little pointed shoes with men in evening dress. At the end of the visit, she'd gone quietly back to Tadley Gate with a new shorter hairstyle that nobody commented on, an unused lipstick tucked into her skirt pocket and a conviction as deep as her father's belief in his petrol pump that the world must somehow find itself her way. The men who came to set up the telephone kiosk, pleased to find an unexpectedly beautiful girl in such an out of the way place, had been only too pleased as they worked to answer the questions she put to them in her soft local accent.

'So who can you talk to from here?' (She had the idea that a telephone had a predetermined number of lines, each one to a different and single other telephone.)

'Anyone,' they said.

The elder and more serious of the two explained that when she went to the kiosk and picked up the receiver, a buzzer would sound in the telephone exchange. Then, in exchange for coins in the slot, the operator would connect her with anybody she wanted, anywhere in the country.

'But how would she know? How would the operator know where to find them?'

'Everybody has their own number,' the older man explained. 'they're written down on a list.'

'So if you had a particular friend,' the younger man said, risking a wink at her, 'he'd give you his exchange and number and you'd give that to the operator, then you could talk to him even if he was hundreds of miles away.'

'So I could stand here and talk to somebody in Birmingham or London?'

'As long as your pennies lasted,' the other man said.

At lunchtime she brought them out bread and cheese and cups of tea. At the end of the afternoon as they packed up their tools, the younger man explained about police calls.

'You don't have to put any money in. Just tell the operator you want police and she puts you straight through.'

'To Constable Price?'

He was their local man, operating from his police house in a larger village three miles away.

'Or any policeman. Just run to the box, pick up the telephone and they'll come racing along as if they was at Brooklands.'

Constable Price only had a bicycle. She assumed a telephone call would bring a faster kind of police altogether. It all added to the glamour of the phone kiosk. When the men had gone she stood looking at it for a long time, went in and touched the receiver gently and reverently. It was inert on its cradle and yet she felt it buzzing with the potential of a whole world. Every day her errands around the village would take her past it. She'd slow down, touch the kiosk, sometimes go inside and touch the receiver itself, trying to find the courage to pick it up. One autumn day, she managed it. The woman's voice at the other end, bright and metallic as a new sixpence, said 'Hello. What number please?' She dropped the receiver back on the cradle, heart thumping. She didn't know anybody's number, nobody's in the world. But in her dreams, one day a number would come into her head and she'd say it. Then the operator would say 'Certainly, madam,' the way they did in the department stores in Birmingham, the phone would click and buzz and there would be somebody on the other end – London, Worcester, anywhere – who'd say how nice to hear from her and he could tell from her voice that he'd like her no end, so why didn't he come in a car or even an aeroplane and whisk her away to a place where she could quick-time foxtrot in little pointed shoes and drink from a triangular glass under a striped umbrella? What was the point of telephones, after all, if they couldn't do magic? So like her father with his petrol pump she waited patiently for it to happen.

* * *

'So,' the inspector said, 'Miss Davitt decided after half an hour or possibly longer that all might not be well with our man in the kiosk. So she looks more closely and finds Tod Barker with the back of his head cracked open the way you'd take a spoon to your breakfast egg.'

Constable Price thought inappropriately of the good brown eggs his hens laid in their run at the back of his police house.

'Yes, sir. Only she didn't know it was Tod Barker, of course. She'd never seen the man before.'

'Which isn't surprising, because as we know the only times you'd find Tod Barker outside the East End was when he was on a racecourse or in prison. And unless I'm misinformed, there aren't any prisons or racecourses in this neck of the woods.'

'No, sir. He had quite a record, didn't he? Three burglaries, two assaults, two robberies with violence and four convictions for off-course betting.'

This feat of memory from the documents he'd read earned him an approving look from the inspector. But Constable Price reminded himself that a village bobby who wanted to keep his job shouldn't be too clever.

'Those are just the ones they managed to make stick in court,' the inspector said. 'Plenty of enemies in the underworld too. Our colleagues in London weren't surprised to hear that somebody had given Tod Barker a cranial massage with an iron bar.'

'An iron bar, was it?'

'So the laboratory men say. Flakes of rust in the wound.'

'And nobody surprised?'

'Not that he was dead, no. Not even that he was dead in a phone box. In the betting trade I gather they spend half their lives on the telephone.'

'And we know he'd made a call from that box earlier in the day.'

'Yes, and since they keep a record at the exchange of the numbers, we know the call was to the bookmaker he works for back in London. So no surprise there either. In fact, you might say there's only one surprise in the whole business.'

The inspector waited for a response. Constable Price realised that he was in danger of overplaying rural slowness.

'Why here, you mean, sir?'

'Exactly, constable. Why – when Tod Barker regarded the countryside as something you drove through as quickly as possible to get to the next race meeting – should he be killed somewhere at the back of beyond like Tadley Gate?'

'There's the petrol pump, of course.' Constable Price said it almost to himself. 'Does that mean you get a lot of cars here?'

'No, sir. We had two of them here on the day he was killed and I'd say two cars in one day was a record for Tadley Gate.'

When the first of the cars arrived, around midday on a fine Thursday in hay-making time, Molly was sitting at the parlour table with the accounts book open in front of her, getting on with her task of sending out bills to her father's customers. Men's voices came from outside and the sound of slow pneumatic wheels on the road. She jumped up, glad to be distracted, and looked out of the window. Advancing into their yard came an open-topped four-seater, sleek and green. A man with brown hair and very broad shoulders sat in the driving seat. It moved with funereal slowness because the engine wasn't running at all. Its motive power came from two men pushing from the back. One of them was plump, middle-aged and red-faced. The other – bent over with his shoulder against the car – happened to glance up as Molly looked out of the window. He smiled when he saw her and her heart did such a jolt of shock and unbelief that it felt like a metal plate with her father's biggest hammer coming down on it.

She thought, 'Did I really telephone for him after all?'

Then, because she was essentially a good and practical girl, she told herself not to be a mardy ha'porth, of course she hadn't, so stop daydreaming and get on with it. Her father hadn't heard or seen the car because he was hammering a damaged coulter in his forge out the back. It was up to her to get into the yard and see what they wanted. As she stepped outside the two men stopped pushing and let the car come to a halt not far from the petrol pump.

'Is there a mechanic here? Call him quickly, would you.'

It was the older, red-faced man who spoke, in a south Wales

accent. The other man, the one she'd have called on the telephone if she knew he existed and had his number, straightened up and smiled at her again, rubbing his back with both hands. He was pretending that pushing the car had exhausted him but Molly knew at once from the smile and the exaggeration of his movements that he wasn't exhausted at all, was just making a pantomime of it for her amusement. She smiled back at him. He was taller than average and maybe five years or so older than she was, with black hair, very white teeth and dark eyes that seemed more alive to her than any she'd seen before. And the smiles they exchanged were like two people saying the same thing at once. 'Well, fancy somebody like you being here.' But she had to turn away because the red-faced man was repeating his question loudly and urgently.

'I'll get my dad,' she said, whirled away into the shadowy forge and shouted to him over he hammer blows. Davy Davitt followed her into the sunshine, still wearing his thick leather farrier's apron and when he saw the motor car by his petrol pump his face lit up.

'Twelve horse power, Rover, nice cars, six hundred pounds new,' he murmured to himself. Then aloud, 'What's the trouble then, sir?'

'Blessed axle gone,' the red-faced man said. 'These roads are an insult to motor cars, not a yard of tarmac in the last twenty miles.'

'Come far, gave you?'

'Far enough,' said the tall young man. 'We started from Pontypridd.'

His voice was Welsh too, bright and dancing. The red-faced man gave him a hard look.

'Doesn't matter to him where we started, Sonny. Question is, can he do something so we can get where we're going to?'

'Where's that then?' Davy asked.

'London. And we're in a hurry.'

Even though the red-faced man's voice was impatient, they were some of the sweetest words in the language to Davy. In seconds he was horizontal under the car, with the man bending himself double to try to see what was happening. Nobody was paying much attention to the other young man who'd been in the driving seat. He'd got out and was sitting, calm and contented in the sunshine, on the low stone wall between the house and the yard, looking at Molly. And Molly was staring enchanted at the man called Sonny because she'd just heard from his lips some of the sweetest words in the language to her.

'Would there be anywhere here with a telephone I could use?'

Proudly she led him to the kiosk and sat on the step of the war memorial to watch. She always liked to watch, on the very rare occasions when people used the telephone, grieved by their hesitations and fumblings. Sonny was different. He didn't pause to read the card of instructions, or drop coins on the concrete floor or fidget with doubt or embarrassment. He simply picked up the receiver and spoke into it as if it were a thing he did every day, easy as washing your hands. She saw a smile on his face and his lips moving and knew he must be giving a number to the distant operator then he must have been connected to his number because his lips were moving again though she couldn't hear what he was saying.

'Blessed car's broken down, back of beyond. No sign of them though. Didn't guess we'd be going this way.'

He was speaking to his father, who ran a boxers' training gymnasium in Pontypridd.

'That's where you're wrong, boy. They're right behind you. Left Cardiff early this morning in a black Austin 20, heading same way as you.'

'How did they know, then?'

'Never mind that. Fact is, they do know. Tell Enoch. You at a garage?'

'Blacksmith's with a petrol pump.'

'Can't miss you then, can they?'

'They can't do anything to him, not in broad daylight.'

'Only takes a little nudge, you know that. Elbow in wrong place, oh dear so sorry, damage done.'

'Enoch and me wouldn't let a flea's elbow near him, let alone theirs.'

'You look after our boy.'

Molly watched as he came out of the kiosk looking worried.

'Have you had bad news?'

It didn't strike her that she had no right to ask this of a stranger. He answered her with another question.

'Your father good with cars, is he?'

'Very good.'

'We need to be moving, see? Quicker than I thought.'

She caught his urgency and they practically ran back to the yard. By then her father was out from under the car and delivering his verdict. Beam axle gone and rear axle just holding together but wouldn't make it to London. Both of them would need unbolting and welding.

'How long?' the red-faced man asked.

'Two or three hours, with luck.'

'Make it two hours or less and, whatever your bill is, I'll give you ten pounds on top of it.'

Davy's jaw dropped at the prospect of more money in two hours than he usually earned in a week. Then he went under the car with a spanner and Sonny, in his good suit and shiny shoes, went under too. Davy called out to Molly to go and tell Tick to make sure the fire in the forge was hot as he could make it. Tick was the apprentice, a large and powerful sixteen-year-old. Molly found him in the forge along with the other young man who'd been in the driving seat of the car and for an angry moment thought the two of them were fighting. Then she saw it was no more than play, the man dodging and dancing on the trodden earth floor among the scraps of metal and old horse-shoes, feet moving no more than an inch or two at a time, but enough to avoid the light punches Tick was aiming at him. A furious bellow came from behind them.

'Rooster, are you bloody mad, boy? Come away from there.'

It was the red-faced man.

'Sorry, Uncle Enoch.'

Obediently, the young man followed him out to the yard. Molly tried to give Tick her father's instructions but could hardly get the boy to listen. His face was shiny with excitement.

'Did you hear what he called him? I thought he might be, then I said to myself it couldn't be. I'd only see'd him from a good way off and he looks different in his clothes. So I put my fists up, joking like, and he...'

'What are you saying, Tick boy?'

'The Rhondda Rooster, that's all. He's only the Rhondda Rooster!'

'What's that?'

'Only the next British middleweight champion, that's all. He'll be fighting for the title in London the day after tomorrow and the money's on him to win it.'

'A boxer?'

'Then he'll take on the Empire champion after that. Could be world champion. When I see'd him at Cardiff he won by a knock-out in three rounds against a heavier man even though there was so much blood pouring down his face he could only see from one eye.'

Molly was a country girl, not squeamish.

'If he's as good as you say, how come he'd got so much blood on him?'

'He's got a glass eyebrow.'

'A what?'

'That's what they call a weak spot. Hard as iron all the rest of him, only he's got an old cut over his left eyebrow and if that opens up it pours with blood so the referee would have had to stop the fight if he hadn't knocked the other chap out first.'

It turned out that her father had heard of the Rhondda Rooster too because he got his head out from under the car just long enough to tell Molly to make the gentlemen comfortable in the front parlour and get something to eat. She rushed round making tea in the good china pot, putting bread, cheese and cold beef on the best tablecloth. Sonny had come out from under the car by then and she was conscious all the time of his eyes on her. The Rooster's eyes were just as admiring if she'd noticed, but he was nothing beside Sonny – shoulders and chest too broad for the cut of his suit, one ear a bit skew-whiff, big hands that he kept bunching and flexing all the time they weren't occupied with knife and fork. Under the stern eye of the red-faced man, Uncle Enoch, he had the clumsy good manners of a schoolboy, while Sonny seemed a man of the great world. Occupied with serving them, she missed another milestone in the speeding up of life in Tadley Gate. Another stranger went into the phone kiosk and picked up the receiver. It was the first time since the kiosk was built that it had been used more than once in a day.

The new stranger was small, dark-haired, and twentyish, in a dark suit and cow-dung smeared shoes that hadn't been designed for country walking. He looked round to see nobody was watching and slid quickly into the box as if glad of its protection from the country all around him. The number he wanted was at an East London exchange.

'Bit of luck. Their car's broken down.'

'Have they seen you?'

'Naw, we came over a hill and saw them pushing it. So we turned off before they saw us and Gribby and me followed them on foot. Bleeding miles over the fields.'

'Where's Gribby?'

'Keeping watch. Trouble is, they've all gone inside this house at the garage place.'

'They'll have to come out sometime.'

'Won't be easy, making it look like an accident.'

'You could pay a boy to bung a stone at him.'

'You joking?'

'With what I'm paying you, don't expect jokes as well. Next news I want to hear is the fight's called off. Understood.'

'Understood.'

In the parlour, Uncle Enoch was restive.

'I'm going to see how he's doing with the car. You stay here, Sonny. Rooster can have another slice of beef if he likes but no more bread and for heaven's sake don't let him even sniff those pickled onions.'

There was a tangle of briars and bushes at the back of the garden, clustering around the small stone building that sheltered the earth closet. Two rowans formed an arch over the pathway between the earth closet and the house. They'd been planted in a time when people still believed they kept away witches, all of fifty years ago, by Davy Davitt's grandfather. Davy kept threatening to cut them down but never got round to it, so they formed a useful screen for Tod and Gribby. Tod came back from making his phone call and found his partner lurking in the bushes.

'They still inside?'

'The Rooster and the tall one are. His trainer's gone inside the forge place. What's that you got?'

Tod held out his hand to show him. It was a rusty horseshoe, worn thin and sharp on one side.

'What's that for then? Bring the Rooster good luck?'

'Some kind of luck.'

Molly was in the kitchen, washing up. The Rooster was shifting around on his chair in the parlour. Because they'd started so early he'd missed his training run and his internal system was out of rhythm.

'Where's the little house then, Sonny boy?'

'Down the path, back of the house.'

The Rooster went down the path, under the rowan arch and into the stone building, latching the door behind him. Tod, watching from the bushes, gauged exactly the height of the Rooster's left eyebrow against the rough stonework of the door frame. As soon as the latch clicked down he crept out and wedged the horseshoe into place between two blocks of stone, sharp side towards the privy, so that a man coming out couldn't help but run into it. The loud sigh of satisfaction that the Rooster gave from the inside when his business was done was echoed more quietly by Tod in the bushes.

The inspector stared out of the window at Constable Price's potato patch.

'So Tod and Gribby were in one car and the British Middleweight champion just happened to be in the other,' he said.

'He wasn't that at the time, sir. He didn't take the title until the fight in London two days later. But yes, they broke down in the village.'

'Going from the Rhondda to London?'

'Yes, sir.'

'And Tod and his pal were driving from Cardiff to London?'

'Yes, sir.'

'And the shortest and best way from either place doesn't go within miles of Tadley Gate, does it?'

'No, sir.'

'So what in the world were both of them doing there?'

'The statement from the Rooster's uncle says he thought a country route might be calming for him.'

'And Tod – was he doing it to calm his nerves as well?'

'No, sir. I'd suggest that the presence of both cars in Tadley Gate was not a coincidence.'

'So you've got that far too. Go on.'

'We know Tod worked for a bookie. We know there was a great deal of money riding on the outcome of that fight. Wouldn't the bookie want to know how the Rooster was looking, the way they watch racehorses on the gallops?'

'So Tod and Gribby go all the way to south Wales and back to spy on him.'

'It's one explanation, sir.'

'And not a bad one.' The inspector gave him a reconsidering look. 'You've got a brain, constable. If you solved this one, I'm sure you could expect promotion to somewhere quite a lot livelier than here.'

Constable Price tried not to let his alarm show. He liked his garden, his hens, his pig. His wife and children were healthy in the country air. He'd been born in a city and now devoted quite a lot of his considerable intelligence to making sure he wasn't promoted back to one.

'So what goes wrong?' the inspector said. 'Assume Tod and Gribby are spying. The Rooster's people might be annoyed about it, but not annoyed enough to beat Tod over the head with an iron bar. And remember the Rooster's lot haven't a trace of a criminal record among the three of them, unless you count Sonny Nelson being fined for doing forty-two miles an hour in Llandaff.'

'Yes, sir.'

'So we come to thieves falling out, then. Gribby's got a record even longer than Tod's and on the evidence you collected, he drove out of the village on his own and he was in a devil of a hurry to get his petrol tank filled.'

The Rover was in the yard, with the repaired front axle bolted back in place. Sonny, Davy and Tick were carrying the rear axle from the forge, still warm from its welding. The Rooster had been forbidden to help so was back on the wall chatting to Molly who was sitting beside him but not getting anywhere with her because her attention was on Sonny. All of them were startled by the loud burping of a horn as a black Austin 20 drew up at the pump with a large man in a checked suit at the wheel. After a glance over his shoulder, Davy ignored him.

'He'll have to wait. Get this job seen to first.'

They put the axle down by the Rover. Uncle Enoch watched, chest heaving as if the strain of waiting had been too much for him and his face had turned grey. Sonny looked concerned and put a reassuring hand on his shoulder. The horn went on burping.

'Oh, serve him first and get him out of the way,' Sonny said. 'We can spare a few minutes.'

Enoch looked at him doubtfully and Davy hesitated, caught between the allure of repair work and a customer for petrol. An idea struck him.

'Molly, you know how to work the pump. Go over and see to the gentleman.'

She got up lightly from the wall and started crossing the yard, passing so close to Sonny that he caught a whiff of the perfume she'd bought herself in Birmingham and not used till then. Following his impulse he leaned towards her and said so softly under the noise of the horn that none of the others even knew he'd spoken: 'Delay him, long as you can.' She gave him a gleaming glance, the slightest of nods and went on across the yard to the pump. The man in the check suit was out of the car by then with the petrol cap off, quivering with impatience. The sharp smell of his sweat mingled with petrol fumes. Molly fumbled with the hinged panel at the front of the pump. The Rooster seemed disposed to go across and help her but Sonny called to him sharply.

'Rooster, I think I left my wallet on the parlour table. Go and see, would you?'

The Rooster obligingly went back into the house. By then Davy and Tick were both under the Rover with spanners. Sonny took Enoch by the elbow and led him back into the shadows of the forge.

'Get a move on please, miss,' said the man with the Austin 20 to Molly. She'd managed to get the panel open but was staring at the pump mechanism inside as if she'd never seen it before. Eventually she remembered that the little wooden handle unfolded at right angles and began to wind it slowly anticlockwise to draw up the petrol. The man wanted to do it for her but she wouldn't let him. When she'd got the first gallon pumped up she turned the handle slowly clockwise to let it down into the tank. The bronze indicator needle by the pump mechanism moved to figure one. She looked at the driver of the Austin.

'Is that it?'

'No, of course it's not. Fill her right up, for heaven's sake.'

In other circumstances Gribby would have tried flirting with her because she was undeniably a good-looking girl. Now he could hardly restrain himself from hitting her. Slowly she pumped another gallon up and down, then another, his eyes on her, willing her to hurry. He looked away from her only once and then it was because some movement at the back of his car caught his attention. He swung round and there was Sonny standing there, his hand on the big black luggage trunk. The two men's eyes met. Sonny returned the stare for a few moments then shrugged and moved away, as if he'd been admiring the car. It took Molly the best part of ten minutes to get the indicator to the ten-gallon figure and by that time Gribby was nearly gibbering with anger. He shoved some money at her, not waiting for change, then accelerated out of the yard in a cloud of dust and exhaust. Tick shouted after him as he went, 'Hey, your trunk's undone.' One of the straps round it was unbuckled and flapping. But the man at the wheel couldn't have heard because he didn't stop. Forty-five minutes later, with Sonny driving, the repaired Rover followed more sedately. Sonny made sure that nobody saw him touch Molly's hand or heard his whispered 'Thank you'.

The Rover turned on to the road past the common. 'We'll stop at the phone kiosk,' Sonny said. 'Let them know we're on our way again.'

He slowed down as they came alongside it, almost stopped then accelerated away so clumsily that he almost stalled the engine. From the back the Rooster said, 'What's wrong?'

'Nothing wrong, Rooster. Just there's somebody using it already. We'll find another one further along.'

Sonny and Enoch exchanged glances and from there on Sonny drove so smoothly that the Rooster slept most of the way to London.

'So Gribby drives off in a hurry,' the inspector said. 'Less than an hour later Rooster's lot notice a man in a telephone kiosk. An hour or more after that, Miss Davitt finds Tod dead and her father sends the apprentice to tell you.'

'And I got there as soon as I could,' Constable Price said. When Tick arrived, breathless, on an old bicycle, he'd been at a farm on the far side of his own village, investigating a case of ferret stealing. His wife sent his son running for him and he cycled from there as fast as a man could go on a police bike to the telephone kiosk in Tadley Gate.

'And judging by your report, you decided at once that whoever battered, him over the head didn't do it in the kiosk?'

Outside Price regretted giving in to the temptation to be clever in his report, but couldn't go back on it now.

'There'd have been blood splashed all over the place, sir. As it was, he'd just bled down the back of his suit and onto the floor.'

'Yes. So our assumption is that he managed to stagger to the phone kiosk from wherever Gribby hit him with the iron bar, probably intending to call for help.'

'You think that's what happened, sir?'

'Speaks for itself. Then there was that trail of blood you noticed from the road to the kiosk, as if he'd dragged himself the last few yards. So they quarrel – probably over the money they're getting paid for spying on the Rooster – Gribby bashes Tod over the head, leaves him for dead and scuttles back to London as soon as he's got a full tank of petrol. Only Tod comes round and has just enough life left in him to make it as far as the phone kiosk but not enough to pick up the telephone.'

Constable Price thought about it in his slow rural way. 'So that's it then, sir?'

'Yes, but we're never going to pin it on Gribby unless you turn up a witness. So work on it and keep me informed.'

The inspector went back to his car – smaller and more battered than either the boxer's or the villain's – and headed back thankfully for the town. Constable Price went to feed his hens. But he couldn't stop thinking about the girl watching a dead man in the phone kiosk.

When the Rover left her father's yard Molly was in a world she didn't recognise any more. Her father and Tick were tidying their tools away, pleased with their day, talking about the Rooster. The murmur of their voices, the small metallic clanks, the lingering petrol smell, should have been familiar but she felt as if she'd been put down in a foreign country. Probably a nice enough country if you got to know it, but nothing that had any connection with her. From habit, she went in the kitchen, put a saucepan of water on the stove for her father to wash, boiled a couple of eggs for his tea since their visitors had eaten everything else. But as soon as she'd finished washing up she let her feet take her towards the common and the telephone kiosk. It was the link between herself and Sonny. She didn't believe that the combined magic of her father's motor mania and the telephone kiosk would bring him here and let him go again as if nothing had happened. The squeeze of her hand surely meant he'd be back – and how would he let her know that if not by telephone? Her heart gave a jolt when, from a distance, she saw a man in the kiosk. But it wasn't Sonny, nothing like him, just a smaller man in a darker suit. Nobody she recognised, but on this day of wonders another stranger more or less made no difference. She sat on the steps of the war memorial, thinking about Sonny while the shadows of a summer afternoon grew long on the grass around her. The cooling of the air made her realise that time had passed and the stranger was still there in the phone kiosk. Curiosity, then increasing alarm, made her hurry toward it.

Once Tadley Gate knew that the body was a stranger's everybody got on with haymaking before the weather broke. When the news got out that the dead man had been a criminal from London some people in the village implied that it was the fault of the phone kiosk and the petrol pump, which would naturally attract people like that. Once the police had finished in the kiosk a woman who usually did the cleaning in chapel took it on herself to scrub and disinfect it and people went back to not using it quite normally. Davy Davitt and Tick were more interested in the Rooster's chances for the Empire and the World titles. Constable Price sometimes discussed it with them. He'd taken to dropping in at the forge quite often these days. One day he had to go to the privy and noticed a rusty horseshoe with a sharp edge lying on the earth outside. It seemed a funny place for a horseshoe, but it was a farrier's after all. Some of the bushes had been pushed back as if something heavy had landed there not long ago, but then you got boys fighting all over the place. Constable Price tried hard, but he couldn't stop thinking. As for Molly, she strolled on the common within earshot of the telephone in the long evenings but apart from that got on with the cooking and accounts like any sensible girl. Then, one day when she was scrubbing a frying pan, two boys arrived running from the common with just enough breath between them to get out the news.

'Miss, you're wanted on the telephone.'

She dropped the pan and ran to the kiosk with her apron still on.

'Miss Davitt?' Sonny's voice, distant and metallic but perfectly clear. He had to say it again before she managed to whisper a 'yes' into the receiver. He apologised for not telephoning before. He'd had to stay in London with the Rooster and Uncle Enoch but would be driving himself home the next day and wondered if he might call in. 'Yes,' she said again. For her first telephone call it was hardly a big speaking part, but it seemed to be all that was needed.

* * *

When she got back to the yard, Constable Price was there, sitting on a wall in the sun. His bicycle was upside down and her father was doing something to its chain with pliers. He was looking at a magazine, open at an advertisement for the Austin 20. He stood up when he saw her.

'Hello, Miss Davitt. Will you stay and talk to me?'

Molly didn't want to talk to anyone. She wanted to rush around shouting that Sonny had telephoned, was dropping in. But you couldn't, of course. She sat down on the wall and Constable Price sat back down beside her.

'Nice roomy cars, Austin 20s. Space for a good big trunk at the back.'

She nodded, still not concentrating on what he was saying.

'There was a good big trunk on the one the man was driving, the one who filled up with petrol here. Remember? Tick noticed it wasn't properly fastened when the man drove out, only he was in too much of a hurry to stop.'

She said nothing, but he felt something change in the air round her, as if it had suddenly gone brittle. 'Stop now,' he said to himself. But something was throbbing in his brain, like a motor engine with the brake on.

'I suppose nobody happened to open the trunk while he was getting his petrol?'

'You wouldn't.' She said it to the sparrows pecking in the dust. 'Not to put in petrol.'

He noticed it wasn't an answer, felt the brake in his mind slipping.

'So if there'd been anything in the trunk, you couldn't have known?'

She shook her head, still looking down.

'Did he go anywhere near his trunk while you were putting in the petrol?'

She murmured, 'No'.

'Or did anybody else?'

She raised her head and looked at him. Such a look of desperation he'd only seen before in the eyes of a dog run over by a cart that he had to put out of its misery. He pulled on the mental brake, told his brain it couldn't go along the road. If he persisted, she'd break down, tell him something he couldn't ignore. She was a good girl, didn't deserve trouble. He stood up.

'Looks like your dad's finished with my bicycle.'

He waved to her over his shoulder as he pedalled away.

Sonny came next day, in the Rover. He asked Davy if he'd be kind enough to have a look at the electrical starter, something not quite right about it. While he was working on it, Sonny and Molly strolled together in the sunshine on the common.

'A promise I made Uncle Enoch,' He told her. 'I'd never say a word to anybody, long as I lived, just one exception. If there was a girl I liked, I might have to tell her. If I could trust her, that is.'

'You can trust me.'

'I know. The Rooster matters to Enoch more than all the world. Anything threatening him, he goes mad. And it was my fault, partly. If I'd done what he told me and not let the Rooster out of my sight, they wouldn't have had their chance. When he came back to the parlour and I told him the Rooster was down at the little house on his own he rushed straight down there, just in time. A second later and the Rooster would have walked right into it. The wickedness of it.'

'Yes.'

'And we couldn't let the Rooster know. It would have unsettled him. But we couldn't leave the body there in the bushes because it might have caused trouble for you and your dad. So when I saw the other one driving into your yard, bold as brass, it came to me that if we put it in his trunk it would serve both of them right. And you played up to me. Without a word. Just trusted me.'

'Yes.'

As they walked, the back of his hand brushed lightly against hers.

'Only it went wrong, you see? He must have noticed the trunk strap flapping just after he drove out of your yard. So when he looked in there and saw what he saw, all he could do was dump it in the phone kiosk. Only it happened to be you that found him. I'm sorry about that.'

Their hands met palm to palm and stayed together.

'It's all right,' she said.

Later, when they'd been married for some time and Sonny was doing well in London as a boxing promoter, she had a telephone in her own home and talked to her friends on it nearly every day. Sonny was driving a Daimler by then with plenty of room at the back for the children and they sometimes used it to pop down to Tadley Gate, where her father had put up a proper garage sign and often filled up as many as half a dozen cars a day on summer weekends. Sometime between one visit and the next the Post Office took away Kiosk One and replaced it with a more imposing model, all bright red paint and glass panels. They gave it a glance as they drove past.

So many things that could have been different.

An almost infinite number of them: the flight of the ball; the angle of the bat; the movement of his feet as he skipped down the pitch. The weather, the time, the day of the week, the whatever...

The smallest variance in any one of these things, or in the way that each connected to the other at the crucial moment, and nothing would have happened as it did. An inch another way, or a second, or a step and it would have been a very different story.

Of course, it's *always* a different story; but it isn't always a story with bodies...

He wasn't even a good batsman – a tail-ender for heaven's sake – but this once, he got everything right. The footwork and the swing were spot on. The ball flew from the meat of the bat, high above the heads of the fielders into the long grass at the edge of the woodland that fringed the pitch on two sides.

Alan and another player had been looking for a minute or so, using hands and feet to move aside the long grass at the base of an oak tree, when she stepped from behind it as if she'd been waiting for them.

'Don't you have any spare ones?'

Alan looked at her for a few, long seconds before answering. She was tall, five seven or eight, with short dark hair. Her legs were bare beneath a cream-coloured skirt and her breasts looked a good size under a sleeveless top. She looked Mediterranean, Alan thought. Sophisticated.

'I suppose we must have, somewhere,' he said.

'So why waste time looking? Are they expensive?'

Alan laughed. 'We're only a bunch of medics. It costs a small fortune just to hire the pitch.'

'You're a doctor?'

'A neurologist. A consultant neurologist.'

She didn't look as impressed as he'd hoped.

'Got it.'

Alan turned to see his teammate brandishing the ball, heard the cheers from those on the pitch as it was thrown across.

He turned back. The woman's arms were folded and she held a hand up to shield her eyes from the sun.

'Will you be here long?' Alan said. She looked hesitant. He pointed back towards the pitch. 'We've only got a couple of wickets left to take.'

She dropped her hand, smiled without looking at him. 'You'd better get on with it then…'

'Listen, we usually go and have a couple of drinks afterwards, in the Woodman up by the tube. D'you fancy coming along? Just for one maybe?'

She looked at her watch. Too quickly, Alan thought, to have even seen what time it read.

'I don't have a lot of time.'

He nodded, stepping backwards towards the pitch. 'Well, you know where we are…'

The Woodman was only a small place, and the dozen or so players – some from either team – took up most of the back room.

'I'm Rachel by the way,' she said.

'Alan.'

'Did you win, Alan?'

'Yes, but no thanks to me. The other team weren't very good.'

'You're all doctors, right?'

He nodded. 'Doctors, student doctors, friends of doctors. Anybody who's available if we're short. It's as much a social thing as anything else.'

'Plus the sandwiches you get at half time…'

Alan put on a posh voice. 'We call it the tea interval,' he said.

Rachel eked out a dry white wine and was introduced. She met Phil Hendricks, a pathologist who did a lot of work with the police and told her a succession of grisly stories. She met a dull cardiologist whose name she instantly forgot, a male nurse called Sandy who was at great pains to point out that not all male nurses were gay, and a slimy anaesthetist whose breath would surely have done the trick were he ever to run short of gas.

While Rachel was in the Ladies, a bumptious paediatrician Alan didn't like a whole lot dropped a fat hand on to his shoulder.

'Sodding typical. You do fuck all with the bat and then score *after* the game…' The others enjoyed the joke. Alan glanced round and saw that Rachel was just coming out of the toilet. He hoped that she hadn't seen them all laughing.

'Do you want another one of those?' Alan pointed at her half-empty glass before downing what was left of his lager.

She didn't, but followed him to the bar anyway. Alan leaned in close to her and they talked while he repeatedly failed to attract the attention of the surly Irish barmaid.

'I don't really know a lot of them, to tell you the truth. There's only a couple I ever see outside of the games.'

'There's always tossers in any group,' she said. 'It's the price you pay for company.'

'What do you do, Rachel?'

She barked out a dry laugh. 'Not a great deal. I studied.'

It sounded like the end of a conversation, and for a while they said nothing. Alan guessed that they were about the same age. She was definitely in her early thirties, which meant that she had to have graduated at least ten years before. She had to have done something, had to *do* something. Unless of course she'd been a mature student. It seemed a little too early to pry.

'What do you do to relax? Do you see mates, or…?'

She nodded towards the bar and he followed her gaze to the barmaid, who stood, finally ready to take the order. Alan reeled off a long list of drinks and they watched while the tray that was placed on the bar began to fill up with glasses. Alan turned and opened his mouth to speak, but she beat him to it.

'I'd better be getting off.'

'Right. I don't suppose I could have your phone number?'

She gave a non-committal hum as she swallowed what was left of her wine. Alan handed a twenty-pound note across the bar, grinned at her.

'Mobile?'

'I never have it switched on.'

'I could leave messages.'

She took out a pen and scribbled the number on the back of a dog-eared beer mat.

Alan picked up the tray of drinks just as the barmaid proffered him his fifty pence change. Unable to take it, Alan nodded to Rachel. She leaned forward and grabbed the coin.

'Stick it in the machine on your way out,' he said.

Alan had just put the tray down on the table when he heard the repetitive chug and clink of the fruit machine paying out its jackpot. He strode across to where Rachel was scooping out a handful of ten pence pieces.

'You jammy sod,' he said. 'I've been putting money into that thing for weeks.'

Then she turned, and Alan saw that her face had reddened. 'You have it,' she said. She thrust the handful of coins at him, then, as several dropped to the floor, she spun round flustered and tipped the whole lot back into the payout tray. 'I can't... I haven't got anywhere to put them all...'

She'd gone by the time Alan had finished picking coins off the carpet.

It didn't take too long for Rachel to calm down. She marched down the hill towards the tube station, her control returning with every step.

She'd been angry with herself for behaving as she had in the pub, but what else could she do? There was no way she could take all that loose change home with her, was there?

As she walked on she realised that actually there *had* been things she could have done, and she chided herself for being so stupid. She could have asked the woman behind the bar to change the coins into notes. Those were more easily hidden. She could have grabbed the coins, left with a smile and made some beggar's day.

She needed to remember. It was important to be careful, but she always had options.

She reached into her handbag for the mints. Popped one into her mouth to mask the smell of the wine. The taste of it...

As she walked down the steps into Highgate station she dropped a hand into her pocket, groping around until she could feel her wedding ring hot against the palm of her hand. There was always that delicious, terrifying second or two, as her fingers moved against the lining of her pocket, when she thought she might have lost it, but it was always there, waiting for her.

She stood on the platform, the ring tight in her fist until the train came in. Then, just as she always did, she slipped the ring, inch by inch, back on to her finger.

Lee pushed his chicken madras round the plate until it was cold. He'd lost his appetite anyway. He'd ordered the food before the row and now he didn't feel like it, so that was another thing that was Rachel's fault.

She'd be in the bedroom by now, crying.

She never cried when it was actually happening. He knew it was because she didn't want to give him the satisfaction, or some such crap. That only proved what a stupid cow she was, because he couldn't stand to see her cry, to see *any* woman cry, and maybe if she *did* cry once in a while he might ease off a bit.

No, she saved it up for afterwards and he could hear it now, coming through the ceiling and putting him off his dinner.

The row had been about the same thing they were all about. Her, taking the piss.

He'd backed down on this afternoon-walking business, on her going out to the woods of an afternoon on her own. He'd given in to her, and today she'd been gone nearly six hours. Half the fucking day and no word of an apology when she'd eventually come strolling through the front door.

So, it had kicked off…

Lee was bright, always had been. He knew damn well that it wasn't *just* about her staying out of the house too long. He knew it all came down to the pills.

There'd been a lot more rowing, a lot more crying in the bedroom since he'd found that little packet tucked behind her panties at the back of a drawer. He was clever enough to see the irony in *that* as well. Contraceptive pills, hidden among the sexy knickers he'd bought for her.

He'd gone mental when he'd found them, obviously. Hadn't

they agreed that they were going to start trying for a kid? That everything would be better once they were a family? He was furious at the deceit, at the fool she'd made of him, at the time and effort he'd wasted in shafting her all those weeks beforehand.

There'd been a lot more rowing since...

Christ, he loved her though. She wouldn't get to him so much if it wasn't for that, wouldn't wind him up like she did. He could feel it surging through him as he lost his temper and it caused his whole body to shake when it was finished, and she crawled away to cry where he couldn't see her.

He hoped she knew it – now, with her face buried in a sopping pillow – he hoped she knew how much he loved her.

Lee dropped his fork and slid his hand beneath the plate, wiggling his fingers until it sat, balanced on his palm. He jerked his forearm and sent the plate fast across the kitchen.

Watched his dinner run down the wall.

He watched them.

He lay on the grass, just another sun-worshipper, and with his arm folded across his head he spied on them through a fringed curtain of underarm hair. He watched them from his favourite bench. His face hidden behind a newspaper, his back straight against the small, metal plaque.

For Eric and Muriel, who loved these woods...

He watched them and he waited.

He watched *her* of course at the other times too. He'd followed her home that very first day and now he would spend hours outside the house in Barnet, imagining her inside in the dark.

He couldn't say why he'd chosen her; couldn't say why he had chosen any of them. Something just clicked. It was all pretty random at the end of the day, just luck – good or bad depending on which way you looked at it.

When he was caught, and odds on he would be, he would tell them that and nothing else.

It all came down to chance.

* * *

They'd begun to spend their afternoons together. They walked every inch of Highgate Woods, ate picnics by the tree where they'd first met, and one day they'd held hands across a weathered, wooden table outside the cafeteria.

'Why can't I see you in the evenings?' Alan said.

She winced. 'This is nice, isn't it? Don't rush things.'

'I changed my shifts around so we could see each other during the day. So that we could spend time together.'

'I never asked you to.'

'There's things I want, Rachel…'

She leered. 'I bet there are.'

'Yes, *that*. Obviously that, but other things. I want to take you places and meet your friends. I want to come to where you live. I want you to come where I live…'

'It's complicated. I told you.'

'You never tell me anything.'

'I'm married, Alan.'

He drew his hand away from hers. He tried, and failed, to make light of it. 'Well, that explains a lot.'

'I suppose it changes everything, doesn't it?'

He looked at her as if she were mad. 'Just a *bit*.'

'I don't see why.'

'For fuck's sake, Rachel…'

'Tell me.'

'I don't… I wouldn't like it if I was the one married to you, put it that way.'

She looked at the table.

'Don't cry.'

'I'm not crying.'

Alan put a laugh into his voice. 'Besides, he might decide to beat me up.'

Then there *were* tears, and she told him the rest. The babies she didn't want and the bruises you couldn't see, and when it was over Alan reached for her hand and squeezed and looked at her hard.

'If he touches you again, I'll fucking kill him.'

She appreciated the gesture but knew it was really no more than that, and she was sad at the hurt she saw in Alan's eyes when she laughed.

Afterwards, Rachel leaned down to pull the sheet back over them. A little shyness had returned, but it was not uncomfortable, or awkward.

'I *would* tell you how great that was,' she said. 'But I don't want you to get complacent.' She turned on her side to face him, and grinned.

'I was lucky to meet you,' he said. 'That day, looking for the ball.'

'Or *un*lucky...'

He shook his head, ran the back of his hand along her ribcage.

'Did you know that a smile can change the world?' she said. 'Do you know about that idea?'

'Sounds like one of those awful self-help things.'

'No, it's just a philosophy really, based around the randomness of everything. How every action has consequences, you know? How it's *connected*.' She closed her eyes. 'You smile at someone at the bus stop and maybe that person's mood changes. They're reminded of a friend they haven't spoken to in a long time and they decide to ring them. This third person, on the other side of the world, answers his mobile phone doing ninety miles an hour on the motorway. He's so thrilled to hear from his old friend that he loses concentration and ploughs into the car in front, killing a man who was on his way to plant a bomb that would have killed a thousand people...'

Alan puffed out his cheeks, let the air out slowly.

'What would have happened if I'd scowled at the bloke at the bus stop?'

Rachel opened her eyes. 'Something else would have happened.'

'Right, like I'd've got punched.'

She laughed, but Alan looked away, his mind quickly elsewhere. 'I want to talk to you later,' he said. 'I want to talk to you tonight.'

She sighed. 'I've told you, it's not possible.'

'After what you told me earlier, I want to call you. I want to know you're OK. There must be a way. I'll call at seven o'clock. Rachel? At exactly seven.'

She closed her eyes again, then, fifteen seconds later she nodded slowly.

It was a minute before Alan spoke again. 'Only trouble is, you smile at *anyone* at a bus stop in London, they think you're a nutter.'

This time they both laughed, then rolled together. Then fucked again.

When they'd got their breaths back they talked about all manner of stuff. Films and football and music.

Nothing that mattered.

Alan lay in bed after Rachel had left and thought about all the things that had been said and done that day. He wanted so much to do something to help her, to make her feel better, but for all his bravado, for all his heroic notions, the best that he could come up with was a present.

He knew straight away what he could give her, and where to find it.

It was in a shoebox at the back of a cupboard stuffed with bundles of letters, a bag of old tools and other odds and sods that he'd collected from his father's place after the old man had died.

Alan hadn't looked at the bracelet in a couple of years, had forgotten the weight of it. It was gold, or so he presumed, and heavy with charms. He remembered the feel of Rachel's body against his fingers, her shoulder blades and hips – as he ran them around the smooth body of the tiger, the edges of the key, the rims of the tiny train wheels that turned...

After his father's death, Alan had spoken to his mother about the bracelet. He asked her if she knew where it had come from. The skin around her jaw had tightened as she'd said she hardly remembered it, then in the next breath that she wanted nothing to do with the bloody thing. Not considering where it had damned well come from.

Alan put two and two together and realised how stupid he'd been. He knew about his father's affairs and guessed that, years before, the bracelet had been a failed peace offering of some sort. It might even have been something that he'd originally bought for one of his mistresses. His father had been a forensic pathologist and Alan was amazed at how a man who exercised such professional skill could be so clumsy when it came to the rest of his life.

It wasn't surprising his mother had reacted as she had, that she'd wanted no part of the charm bracelet. It had become tainted.

Alan was not superstitious. He sensed that Rachel would like it. He wouldn't give it to her as it was though. He would make it truly hers before he gave it. He knew exactly what charm he wanted to add.

From Muswell Hill it was a five-minute bus ride to Highgate tube. Rachel leaned back against the side of the shelter. Her hair was still wet from the shower she'd taken at Alan's flat.

She'd thought so often about how she might feel, afterwards. It had been a vital part of the fantasy, not just with Alan but with other men she'd seen, but never spoken to. The sex had been easy to imagine of course. It had been gentler than she was used to and had lasted longer, but the mechanics were more or less the same. Where she'd been wrong was in imagining the feelings that would come when she'd actually done it. She'd been certain that she'd feel frightened, but she didn't. Fear was familiar to her, and its absence was unmistakable. Heady.

She waited a couple of minutes before giving up on the bus and making for the station on foot. Had there been anybody else at the bus stop, she might well have smiled at them.

Lee didn't think that he asked too much. Not after a long day talking mortgages to morons and assuring mousy newlyweds that damp was easily sorted. At the end of it, all he wanted was his dinner and some comfort.

He couldn't stand her so fucking cheerful.

Taking off his jacket and tie, opening a beer and asking just what she was so bloody chirpy about.

Had she been up to those fucking woods again?

Yes.

Who with?

Don't be silly, Lee.

Sucking off tramps in the bushes, I'll bet.

Then she'd laughed at him. No outrage like there should have been. No anger at his filthy suggestions, at the stupid suspicions that he'd only half tarted up as a joke.

A jab to the belly and another to the tits had shut her up and put her down on the floor. Now he straddled her chest, knees pressed down on to her arms, his hands pulling at his own hair in frustration.

'We were going to do the business later on. I was well up for it and tonight could have been the night we did something special. Made a new life.'

'Lee, please…'

'You. Fucking. Spoiled. It.'

'We can still do it, Lee. Let's go upstairs now. I'm really horny, Lee…'

He shook his head, disgusted, gathering the spit into his mouth. She knew what was coming, he could see it in her eyes and he waited for her to try and turn her head away as he leaned down and pushed the saliva between his teeth. Instead, she just closed her eyes, and he thought he saw something like a smile as he let a thick string of beery spit drop slowly down on to her face.

As soon as the seven o'clock news had begun, Alan reached for the phone and dialled the number.

It was answered almost immediately, but nobody spoke.

Alan whispered, realised as soon as he had that he was being stupid. He wasn't the one who needed to be secretive.

'Rachel, it's me…'

Suddenly, there was a noise, above the hiss and crackle on the line. It was a guttural sound that echoed. That it took him a few moments to identify. An animal sound: a gulp and a grind, a splutter and a swallow. It was the sound of someone sobbing uncontrollably but trying with every ounce of strength to assert control. Trying desperately not to be heard.

Alan sat up straight, pressed the phone hard to his ear.

'Rachel, I'm here, OK? I'm not going anywhere.'

* * *

He watched the comings and goings with something like amusement.

For a fortnight he watched her leave the house in Barnet mid-morning, then come home again by late afternoon. He stayed with her most of the day when he could, saw her meet him in the woods or sometimes go straight to his flat when they couldn't be arsed with preliminaries.

When they wanted to get straight down to it.

He watched her leave the flat, eyes bright and hair wet. The smell of one man scrubbed away before she went home to another.

He wondered if the man he saw climbing into the silver sports car every morning knew that he was a cuckold. On a couple of occasions he thought about popping a note under his windscreen to let him know. Just to stir things up a bit.

He hadn't done so because he didn't want to do anything that might disturb the routine. Not now that he was ready to take her. Besides, mischief for its own sake was not his thing at all.

Still, he couldn't help but marvel at the things people got up to.

On the day Alan had hoped to give Rachel the bracelet, his mother tripped on the stairs.

So many things that could have been different...

Two weeks before, the jeweller had shown him a catalogue. There *had* been charms that would have carried more or less the same meaning but Alan knew what he wanted. He'd ordered one specially made. He'd decided against the diamond spots and gone for the enamel, but still, it wasn't cheap. He'd thought of it as a dozen decent sessions with one of his private patients. He always thought in those terms whenever he wanted to splash out on something.

A fortnight later, half an hour before he was due to meet Rachel in the woods, he walked out on to Bond Street with the bracelet. Then, his mother called.

'Don't worry, Alan. It's just my ankle, it's nothing...'

A message that said 'Come and see me now, if you give a shit.'

He phoned Rachel and left a message of his own. She was probably on her way already, was almost certainly somewhere on the Northern line. He made for the underground himself, steeling himself for the trip to his mother's warden-controlled flat in Swiss Cottage.

As he walked, he realised that his mother would see the bag. It was purple with white cord handles and the name of the jeweller in gold lettering. He couldn't show her the bracelet for obvious reasons...

He decided if she asked he'd tell her he'd bought himself a new watch...

Lee wasn't stupid – God, it woud be a lot easier if he were – but it couldn't be very much longer before he noticed how often she was going to the toilet or taking a shower just before seven o'clock...

She collected her bag on the way upstairs, then, once she'd locked the bathroom door, she switched the phone on, set it to *vibrate only* and waited.

Tonight she was desperate, had been since Alan had failed to meet her at lunchtime. She'd waited in the woods for twenty minutes before she'd got a signal, before the alert had come through. She'd listened to his message once then erased it as always. Walked towards the tube, unravelling.

Sitting with her back against the side of the bath, she thought there was every chance he might not ring at all. His excuse for not turning up had sounded very much *like* an excuse. Not that she could blame him for wanting to call a halt to things; she knew how hard it was for him in so many ways...

She almost dropped the phone when it jumped in her hand.

'Where were you?'

'Didn't you get the message? I was at my bloody mother's.'

'I thought you might have made it up.'

'Jesus, Rachel.'

'Sorry...'

A sigh. Half a minute of sniffs and swallows.

'God, I wish I could see you,' he said. 'Now, I mean. I've got something for you. I wanted to give it to you this afternoon...'

'I'd like to see you too.'

'Can you?'

The hope in his voice clutched at her. 'There might be a way…'

'By the tree in half an hour. The woods don't shut until eight.'

'I'll try.'

When she'd hung up she dialled another number. She spoke urgently for a minute, then hung up again. When she heard the landline ringing a few moments later she flushed the toilet and stepped out of the bathroom.

Lee was holding the phone out for her when she walked into the lounge. She took it and spoke, hoped he could hear the shock and concern in her voice despite the fact that he hadn't bothered to turn the television down.

'That was Sue,' she said afterwards. 'Her brother's been in a car accident. Some idiot talking on his mobile phone, ploughed into the back of him on the motorway. I said I'd go round…'

Lee's team had been awarded a penalty. Without turning round to her, he waved his consent.

He was astonished to see her leave the house alone at night. The husband did of course, jumped in his sports car every so often to collect a takeaway or shoot down to the off licence, but never *her*…

He'd been planning to do it during the day; he knew the quiet places now, the dead spots en route where he could take her with very little risk, but he wasn't a man to look a gift horse in the mouth.

This was perfect, and he was as ready as he'd ever be.

He presumed she'd be heading for the tube at High Barnet. He got out of his car and followed her.

It took Alan ten minutes to get to the woods. By half past seven he'd got everything arranged.

He hadn't wanted to just give her the bracelet. He'd wanted her to come across it, to find it as if by some piece of good fortune. Luck had played such a big part in their coming together, after all, which is why he'd chosen the charm that he had. There was only really one place that he could leave it…

The light was fading fast. The few people he saw were all moving towards one or another of the various exits. He dialled her number.

'It's me. You're probably still on the tube. Listen, come to the tree but don't worry if you can't see me. I'll be nearby, but there's something I want you to find first. Stand where the ball was found, then look up. OK? I'll see you soon.'

He moved away from the tree so that he could watch from a distance when she discovered the bracelet. It worried him that it would soon be too dark to see the expression on her face when she found it. He sat down, leaned back against a stump to wait.

It was the away leg of a big European tie and one-up at half-time was a very decent result.

Lee was at the fridge digging out snacks for the rest of the game when the car alarm went off. That fucking Saab across the road again – he'd told the tosser to get it looked at once. The wailing stopped after a couple of minutes, but started up again almost immediately, and Lee knew that uninterrupted enjoyment of the second half had gone out of the window.

He picked up his keys and stormed out of the front door. The prat was out by the looks of it, but Lee fancied giving his motor a kick or two anyway. He might come back afterwards, grab some paper and stick a none too subtle note through the wanker's letterbox. Maybe a piece of dogshit for good measure…

Rachel's phone was lying on the tarmac halfway down the drive.

Lee picked it up and switched it on. The leather case had protected it and the screen lit up immediately.

He entered the security code and waited.

There was a message.

Rachel had realised her phone was missing as soon as she came out of the station. She knew Alan would be worried that she'd taken so long and had reached for the phone to see if he'd left a message. A balloon of sickness had risen up rapidly from her guts, and she'd begun running, silently cursing the selfish idiot who'd thrown himself on to the line at East Finchley, then feeling bad about it.

A few minutes into the woods and still a few more from where Alan would be waiting. It was almost dark and she hadn't seen anyone since she left the road. She looked at her watch – the exits would close in ten minutes. She knew that people climbed over fences to get in – morons who lit bonfires and played 'chase me' with the keepers – so it wouldn't be impossible to get out, but she still didn't fancy being inside after the woods were locked up.

She thought about shouting Alan's name out; it was so quiet that the sound would probably carry. She was being stupid…

Still out of breath, she picked up her pace again, looking up at the noise of feet falling heavily on the path ahead, and seeing the jogger coming towards her.

Alan rang again, hung up as soon as he heard her voice on the answering machine.

He looked at his watch, leaned his head back against the bark. He could hear the distant drone of the traffic and, closer, the shrill peep of the bats that had begun to emerge from their boxes to feed. Moving above him like scraps of burnt paper on the breeze.

He slowed as he passed her, jogged on a stride or two then backed quickly up to draw level with her again. She froze, and he could see the fear in her face.

'Rachel?' he said.

She stared at him, still wary but with curiosity getting the better of her.

'I met you a few weeks ago in the pub,' he said. 'With Alan.' Her eyes didn't move from his. 'Graham. The cardiologist?'

'Oh, God. Graham…right, of course…'

She laughed and her shoulders sagged as the tension vanished.

He laughed too, and reached round to the belt he wore beneath the jogging bottoms. Felt for the knife.

'Sorry,' she said. 'I think my brain's going. I'm a bit bloody jumpy to tell you the truth.'

He nodded but he wasn't really listening. He spun slowly around, hand on hip, catching his breath. Checking that there was no one else around.

'Well…' she said.

He'd have her in the bushes in seconds, the knife pressed to her throat before she had a chance to open her mouth.

He saw her check her watch.

It's time, he thought.

'Rachel!'

He looked up and saw the shape of a big man moving fast towards them. She looked at the shape, then back to him, her mouth open and something unreadable in her eyes.

He dug out a smile. 'Nice to see you again...' he said.

With the blade of the knife flat against his wrist, he turned and jogged away along the path that ran at right angles to the one they'd been on.

'Was that him? Was that him?'

'He was a jogger. He just...' Lee's hand squeezed her neck, choked off the end of the sentence. He raised his other hand slowly, held the phone aloft in triumph. 'I know all about it,' he said. 'So don't try and fucking lie to me.'

There were distant voices coming from somewhere. People leaving. Laughter. Words that were impossible to make out and quickly faded to silence.

Lee tossed the phone to the ground and the free hand reached up to claw at her chest. Thick fingers pushed aside material, found a nipple and squeezed.

She couldn't make a sound. The tears ran down her face and neck and on to the back of his hand as she beat at it, as she snatched in breaths through her nose. Just as she felt her legs go, he released her neck and breast and raised both hands up to the side of her neck.

'Lee, nothing happened. Lee...'

He pressed the heels of his hands against her ears and leaned in close as though he might kiss or bite her.

'What's his name?'

She tried to shake her head but he held it hard.

'Or so help me I'll dig a hole for you with my bare hands. I'll leave your cunt's carcass here for the foxes...'

So she told him, and he let her go, and he shouted over his shoulder to her as he walked further into the woods.

'Now, run home.'

Alan had given it one more minute ten minutes ago, but it was clear to him now that she wasn't coming. She'd sounded like she was really going to try, so he decided that she hadn't been able to get away.

He hoped it was only fear that had restrained her.

He stood up, pressed the redial button on his phone one last time. Got her message again.

There were no more than a couple of minutes before the exits were sealed. He just had time to retrieve the bracelet, to reach up and unhook it from the branch on which it hung.

He'd give it to her another day.

Standing alone in the dark, wondering how she was, he decided that he might not draw her attention to the newest charm on the bracelet. A pair of dice had seemed so right, so appropriate in light of what had happened, of everything they'd talked about. Suddenly he felt every bit as clumsy as his father. It seemed tasteless.

Luck was something they were pushing.

He stepped out on to the path, turned when he heard a man's voice say his name.

The footwork and the swing were spot on.

The first blow smashed Alan's phone into a dozen or more pieces, the second did much the same to his skull, and those that came after were about nothing so much as exercise.

It took half a minute for the growl to die in Lee's throat.

The blood on the branch, on the grass to either side of the path, on his training shoes looked black in the near total darkness.

Lee bent down and picked up the dead man's arm. He wondered if his team had managed to hold on to their one-goal lead as he began dragging the body into the undergrowth.

Graham had run until he felt his lungs about to give up the ghost. He was no fitter than many of those he treated. Those whose hearts were marbled with creamy lines of fat, like cheap off-cuts.

He dropped down on to a bench to recover, to reflect on what had happened in the woods. To consider his rotten luck. If that man hadn't come along when he had... A young woman with Mediterranean features was waiting to cross the road a few feet from where he was sitting. She was taking keys from her bag, probably heading towards the flats opposite.

She glanced in his direction and he dropped his elbows to his knees almost immediately. Looked at the pavement. Made sure she didn't get a good look at his face.

The next High Barnet train was still eight minutes away.

Rachel stood on the platform, her legs still shaking, the burning in her breast a little less fierce with every minute that passed. The pain had been good. It had stopped her thinking too much; stopped her wondering. She sought a little more of it, thrusting her hand into her pocket until she found her wedding ring, then driving the edge of it hard against the fingernail until she felt it split.

Alan had thought it odd that she still took the ring off even after she'd told him the truth, but it made perfect sense to her. Its removal had always been more about freedom than deceit.

An old woman standing next to her nudged her arm and nodded towards the electronic display.

Correction. High Barnet. 1 min.

'There's a stroke of luck,' the woman said.

Rachel looked at the floor. She didn't raise her head again until she heard the train coming.

Jake Arnott
Ten Lords A-Leaping

A discrepancy which often struck me in the character of my friend was that, although in his method of thought he was among the most well ordered of all mankind and in his manner of presenting an argument or pursuing an argument or pursuing a case or theory he was impeccably efficient, he was nonetheless in his personal habits one of the most untidy men that ever drove a colleague to distraction. His disorderly study was strewn with manuscripts, books and periodicals. Scattered about the room were knives, forks, cups with broken rims, Dutch clay pipes, discarded pens, even an upturned inkpot. He kept his cigars in the coal scuttle and his tobacco in the toe end of a Persian slipper. His unanswered correspondence was transfixed by a jack-knife into the very centre of his wooden mantelpiece. Everything was, one might say, 'topsy-turvy'.

His rooms reeked with the odour of the cheap tobacco that he had purchased from a small shop in Holborn, in the spirit of one of his more obscure economic inspirations. He had been taken by the slogan in the shop front that promised that 'the more you smoke the more you save' and had pointed out to me that by switching to this inferior brand he could save one shilling and sixpence a pound and, if he forced himself to smoke enough of the wretched stuff he might one day be able to live on his 'savings'. I had long since given up trying to point out the absurdity of the 'logic' to one of the greatest materialist thinkers in Europe, just as I had also given up complaining about the downright untidiness of his domestic affairs. I have become familiar enough with them to no longer take much notice of these strange habits and idiosyncrasies, but in the process of introducing the young Lord Beckworth to him on that fateful afternoon (the intercession of a complete stranger forces you to renew what the first impressions are of an old friend), I confess that there was a brief moment of embarrassment on his behalf.

Yet if the young nobleman was at all taken aback by the odd circumstances of the great man, he showed it not one jot. Perhaps in deference to my colleague's reputation for mental prowess, he simply overlooked this disordered clutter, or quietly acknowledged it as one of the vagaries of genius. I do not mind admitting my own deference to my old friend as a thinker, and resent not that his powers of reasoning and deduction far outstrip my own. I am resigned to the obvious fact that he is the dominant one in our partnership and see it as my duty to assist and support his great mind without complaint or jealousy, or even much thanks from the possessor of it. Indeed, it merely falls to me to facilitate, from time to time, the practicalities needed for this prodigious consciousness to bear fruit and to keep a sober eye on the mundane matters that he all too often neglects, his thoughts, as they say, being on higher things.

It was to this end that I had, in the first instance, invited the young Lord Beckworth to my friend's lodgings. Lord Beckworth had expressed to me, when we had met earlier that year, at the house of a common acquaintance, a progressive Manchester manufactory owner, his great admiration for the work of my colleague and, more importantly, his desire to support, or even to sponsor, the continuation of his endeavours. My old friend was, at first, reluctant to be beholden to any third party in the way, convinced as he is of the need for independence in all matters. However, I managed to persuade him that he would be in no way compromised by any arrangement with this enthusiastic nobleman, and that the work itself was important enough for him to seek help from the most unlikely of sources.

Beckworth had his manservant with him, a dark, handsome-looking fellow called Parsons. The conversation that afternoon started out amiably enough with the character of a harmless politeness, but very soon it became strangely weighted with a darker and more sinister nature. Formalities had been observed with a certain jocular awkwardness. My colleague made a seemingly harmless remark about social class, I think it was an attempt to include Beckworth's butler, when Lord Beckworth announced, one could almost say blurted out, as if wishing to unburden himself of a dark and terrible secret: 'Privilege, sir, is a curse!' My friend nodded and gave a vague and expansive gesture, as if agreeing that this 'curse' extended to us all, but the visitor shook his head vigorously and continued:

'No, sir, I speak not of a general curse, but a very specific one! The hereditary principle, the very fact of primogeniture that one might call a bane on the world of men, is for me a very personal scourge.'

'What?' My friend retorted, frowning.

'It is a matter of bad blood, sir. Parsons here is forever entreating me to deny the blight on my family name, but I cannot, sir.'

Beckworth looked for a moment at his manservant, who shrugged.

'Well,' said the butler slowly, 'I have always wanted my lord to find blessings in life, also.'

Beckworth smiled briefly at this, then his mood darkened once more. And, as the early evening light faded, with a foreboding he recounted, the 'curse' of the Beckworths. It was related to us that the first lord of this unfortunate house was a certain Ralph Beckworth, of yeoman stock, who had found employment in the household of James I. He was, by all accounts, a good-looking youth and he soon became one of that king's many 'favourites'. He gained his title and no small fortune, but did so without merit or breeding but rather from an exploitation of the baser instincts. Ambition, lasciviousness and a general moral incontinence that had secured him an elevated station in society, all conspired to corrupt him fully once he had attained his rank. His were the temptations of power, without the necessary moderations of genuine nobility. His debauched revels became legendary and culminated in a terrible scandal. It seems that in 1625, the first Lord Beckworth, now grown ugly and malicious in appearance, had taken a shine to a young footman in his employ and no doubt wished to make him his own 'favourite', just as he had himself been despoiled as a young man so many years before. The footman, however, was not as compliant as his masters had been, but despite defending his honour with vigour, found himself imprisoned by that degenerate peer in an upper chamber of his Great Hall. Lord Beckworth and a crowd of flatterers and hangers on sat down to a long carouse, as was the nightly custom. The poor youth upstairs was likely to have his wits turned at the singing and shouting and the terrible oaths which came up to him from below, for they say that the lightest words used by Beckworth, when he was in wine, were such as might damn a man who used them. As it was, that evening there were loud declarations that he intended to exercise upon his unfortunate servant a *droit de seigneur* of the most appalling and perverse kind. The hapless footman, no doubt in utter despair at his fate, threw himself out of the upstairs window to his death on the cobbled courtyard below.

After this awful incident the first Lord Beckworth grew melancholy and brooding. He quickly developed an utter terror of high places, a vertiginous fear of falling. Not of heights so much: we know after all, that vertigo is not the fear of heights. It is a fear of depths, of a fall. And it manifests itself not as a fear, but rather a compulsion, a desire even, for a return from the insubstantial loftiness of our aspirations, back down to earth, as it were. And it was, with this awful realisation, that the first Lord Beckworth went into a long decline, a descent into gloom and enervation. Cursed by a strange madness, he climbed up upon the roof of his Great Hall and hurled himself down.

Our young noble visitor then went on to recount the litany of his cursed family. The next Lord Beckworth had been part of the Royalist defence of the castle of Banbury, a stronghold that had been of strategic importance in the Civil War, or what my old friend would have insisted was the 'English Revolution'. In any case it seems, in a lull in the battle between Roundhead and Cavalier, the second Lord Beckworth had thrown himself, without apparent reason, from the battlements to his death.

The third Lord Beckworth had lived in exile until Charles II was restored to the throne in 1660, and then had tripped and broken his neck on the stone staircase of Windsor Castle. The fourth lord was thrown from his horse during a fox-hunt; the fifth, a commodore in the Royal Navy, was captured by Barbary pirates and made to 'walk the plank'; the sixth fell from scaffolding whilst inspecting repairs to the Great Hall; the seventh slipped and plunged to his death from a precipice while on a walking tour of the Swiss Alps and the eighth, after an assault by footpads on Blackfriars Bridge, had been hurled into the treacherous waters of the Thames.

'And my own father,' concluded our guest, 'the ninth Lord Beckworth, was killed in a ballooning accident five years ago, leaving me this awful inheritance. The family curse is a joke to many. We are known as the "Leaping Lords".'

He gave a hollow and humourless laugh as he ended his story. I have to admit to feeling an almost disabling bafflement at the conclusion of this extraordinary narrative. My colleague maintained a more thorough and hard-headed attitude to the bewildering unravelling of this supposed 'curse'. Knowing him as I do, I observed that expression of effrontery on his countenance which manifested itself whenever he found himself confronted with any evidence, anecdotal or otherwise, that contradicted his precious materialism. His method, after all, was a method of elimination: he always sought to eliminate the impossible in order to arrive at the truth. And yet, as the street lights were being lighted that evening, I saw my esteemed friend for once on the defensive, 'on the back foot' as prize-fighters are wont to say.

'Well, your class is tainted with superstition,' he muttered, as if trying to make sense of what he had heard. 'You're, you're feudal, barbaric. I'm sorry, I don't mean this as a personal insult nor a slur on your character but just —' his gestures for a moment looked helpless, as if he was signifying the very search for meaning, 'a, a psychology, isn't that the word? Maybe this "curse" that you speak of is merely that.'

Our young nobleman merely nodded at this and the conversation quickly turned to more practical matters. He invited us both to his townhouse in Mayfair the following day and bade us farewell, as my friend and I had an evening appointment.

I remember feeling an absurd sense of lucidity in the artificial illumination by gaslight of the darkened streets we sauntered south into Soho for our assignation that night. The words that our noble visitor had uttered that very day still affected me deeply, their insistence reverberating in my mind with a contagious fear. I was somewhat reassured to find that my old friend, despite his abundant intellect and rationality, had been no less impressed by the strange unfoldings of the story of the Beckworths' curse.

'An interesting case,' he finally admitted as we passed through Bloomsbury. 'A series of coincidences, no doubt. But what if they were not?'

We proceeded to amuse ourselves with a kind of intellectual banter, trying to apply theories of historical materialism to what we had heard that afternoon. My friend then suggested that, perhaps, the new and controversial ideas of evolution could be related to this 'curse'.

'His class is dying out, after all,' my colleagues reasoned.

'You're surely not proposing that, somehow, one branch of a social class is somehow spontaneously accelerating its own extinction?' I retorted. 'I wonder what Mr Darwin would think of that.'

'I wasn't thinking of him, but rather of the work of Pierre Trémaux.'

My friend had recently become besotted with this French naturalist who maintained that evolution was governed by geological and chemical changes in the soil and manifested itself in distinct national characteristics. I had no time for this Frenchman's far-fetched notions and did not hesitate in expressing my doubts to my esteemed friend.

'His theories are preposterous!' I exclaimed. 'No, no, not preposterous,' my colleague insisted. 'They are elemental, my dear Engels.'

When we arrived at Greek Street for a meeting of the General Council of the International Working Men's Association, our thoughts turned to the business of that evening and no more mention was made of our young nobleman and his family 'curse'. Except when one of the delegates brought up the proposal that 'All men who have the duty of representing working-class groups should be workers themselves', hastily adding with a deferential nod in the direction of my colleague, 'with the exception of Citizen Marx here, who has devoted his life to the triumph of the working class'; and my friend muttered to me: 'Well, they should have seen me hobnobbing with the aristocracy this afternoon.' But the very next morning, when we went to call upon Beckworth at his house in Mayfair, we found a police constable posted at the front door and we were informed that the young lord had died, having fallen down the stairs and broken his neck.

We were ushered into the hallway of the house and greeted by an officer in plain clothes.

'Inspector Bucket of the Detective,' he announced and took out a large black pocket book with a band around it. He produced a pencil, licked it, and ungirdled his notebook as a prelude to interrogating us both as to the movements of the young Beckworth the day before. Neither myself nor Marx has ever had much reason to trust a gendarme of any colour, particularly those who go about in mufti, as police spies and *agents provocateurs* are wont to do. But this Bucket displayed none of the underhand furtiveness one associates with such fellows. Indeed he had an altogether affable manner, if a peculiarly directed energy and purpose in his questioning. Oft-times a fat forefinger of his would wag before his face, not at us, but rather at himself as if in some form of communication. This digit seemed to have a life and intelligence all of its own and Bucket looked to it as his informant.

We learned in the course of our interview that Lord Beckworth had been found dead at the front of the main staircase that morning by the parlour maid. The upstairs rooms were in disarray and it appeared that a great quantity of alcohol and a certain amount of laudanum had been consumed. The butler Parsons was missing and his whereabouts unknown. There was one very strange clue to the death of the young lord: a small green flower, a buttonhole perhaps, was found clasped in his hand.

Marx seemed very taken by the scientific approach of the 'detective-officer' and at the end of the questioning turned to Bucket and said:

'If I can be of any assistance in this investigation, do let me know.'

Bucket's finger twitched thoughtfully.

'I certainly will, sir,' he replied jovially. 'I certainly will.'

'Why did you say that?' I demanded of my friend when we were away from the house. 'We certainly don't want to have much to do with the police, do we?'

'My dear Engels, I have a strange fascination with this case and feel sure I could apply my own skills and methods in investigating it.'

'But Marx, what possible qualifications do you have in the field of criminology?'

'I have spent my life trying to solve the greatest crime committed by and against humanity. Surely I can bring some of this intelligence to bear on what, in comparison, is a mere misdemeanour.'

He was, of course, referring to his definitive work on the political economy. *His* great case, if you like. But I feared that this was yet another excuse for him to be diverted from his historic task. Decades had passed since its outset and yet he had only completed the first part of *Capital*. Alas, I have grown used to so many excuses for the non-completion of the work. I had no idea why his great mind might be stimulated in pursuing this particular distraction, what was to become known as 'The Case of the Ten Lords a-Leaping', but I suggested to him that it was perhaps the supposed supernatural aspect of it that provoked him so.

'You may be somewhat affronted by the use of phantasmagoria,' I chided him. 'But wasn't it you yourself that described communism as a spectre haunting Europe?'

'Now, now,' my friend reproached me. 'Let us stick to the facts. But first let us retire into this tavern here.'

'Isn't it a bit early?'

'Yes, yes,' he whispered furtively. 'But I fear we are being followed.'

My colleague and I had long been sensitive to the attention of police spies and government agents. Once safely inside the pub there was a brief appraisal as to who our pursuer might be in the pay of. My friend was of the opinion that his movements were far too subtle to be that of a Prussian.

'You mean that he might be from Scotland?' I demanded.

'Perhaps,' muttered Marx, stroking his beard thoughtfully.

'Then that is all the more reason for staying away from this unpleasant business. We must not unnecessarily provoke the attentions of any government institution.'

But Marx was having none of it. It has been my experience that despite his rather chaotic approach to his work, once my friend becomes obsessed with something it is invariably impossible to dissuade him from a complete involvement in it.

'Now,' he went on. 'The manservant Parsons, he seems under suspicion, does he not?'

'I suppose so.'

'And did you notice anything strange about the butler?'

'What do you mean?'

'In his appearance. Would you say he was English?'

I remember the swarthy looks of Parsons, a peculiar accent.

'No,' I replied.

'Then what?'

'Er, Jewish?' I ventured tentatively, knowing of my friend's sensitivities.

'I thought so at first, yes. But did you notice the strange tie-pin that he wore?'

'I can't say that I did, no.'

'A curious device. I've seen the emblem before. A black M embossed on a red background. I've seen it struck on medallions and tokens commemorating Garibaldi's "Thousand".'

'You mean Parsons is an Italian?'

'Yes. And I suggest that Parsons is not his real name. Here is my theory: he was a Red Shirt with Garibaldi in the triumphant success in Sicily. After the defeat at Aspromonte, he goes into exile, and like so many of the "Thousand" finds himself an *émigré* in London. There he enters into the service of Lord Beckworth and adopts the name Parsons.'

'But how can any of this point to a motive in the death of the young lord?'

'I have no idea. But, as you know, it has always been my contention that it is not the consciousness of men that determines their being, but, on the contrary, their social being that determines their consciousness. I intend to discover more about this Parsons, or whatever his real name is. Once we have a clearer idea of his social interactions, then we might be able to deduce his intentions.'

He stood up from the table.

'Where are you going? I asked.

'There is a back way from this pub. I can slip out unnoticed if you can keep our spy occupied for a while. Clerkenwell, I believe, is where most of Garibaldi's Italians have settled. I intend to make some inquiries there. Meet me at my place tomorrow at noon.'

Marx was already entertaining a visitor when I called upon him the next day, a young lady in mourning weeds. She was so shrouded in black that her face, revealed as it was beneath a veiled bonnet, seemed a half-mask of white. I do not think that I have ever seen such a deadly paleness in a woman's face. Her eyes were speckled grey like flint, her lips a blood-crimson pout. I could not help but frown when I looked from her to my friend. Marx gave a little shrug.

'This is Miss Elizabeth Cardew,' he explained. 'She was the fiancée of the young Lord Beckworth.'

'I have been informed,' she said to me, 'that yourself and your esteemed colleague here were among the last people to see my beloved alive.'

'The butler Parsons must have been the last,' I reasoned.

'That damnable fellow!' she exclaimed.

My friend and I were shocked at such an outburst and Miss Cardew's pallor was all at once infused by a rosy flush that bloomed in her cheeks. She quickly sought to regain her composure.

'I must apologise, gentlemen,' she explained. 'I'm sorry, but the enmity that I feel towards the man known as Parsons is so strong that I find it hard to moderate myself.' She sighed. 'I do believe that he had some kind of diabolical hold over my betrothed. He certainly is not the person he presents himself as.'

'Indeed not,' my colleague concurred. 'The man employed by your husband-to-be as Gilbert Parsons was, in fact, one Gilberto Pasero, a Piedmontese fighter in Garibaldi's "Thousand", forced into exile in London. He worked for a while at the Telegraph Office in Cleveland Street, then after meeting with Lord Beckworth at a Radical meeting in Finsbury, was engaged in service as his gentleman's gentleman.'

Something like fear flashed in the expressive eyes of Miss Cardew.

'How did you know…?' she began.

'I have been conducting my own investigation. Now, you say that Parsons, or rather, Pasero, had some kind of hold over Lord Beckworth. What do you mean by that?'

'We had just become engaged when he took up with this dubious manservant.'

'When was this?' I interjected.

'Oh,' she thought for a moment. 'It was over two years ago.'

'A long engagement?' I suggested.

'Yes,' she sighed, mournfully. 'It was the curse, you see. My betrothed was terrified of it, but even more fearful of passing it on. He could not countenance the continuation of his family's bane. He had a horror that,' she gave a little sob, 'in consummating our love we might pass on something so wicked and damnable.'

She took out a handkerchief and dabbed at her eyes that were now filmy with tears.

'He always sought to try to understand his fate,' she went on. 'This led him to unconventional ideas, radical ones even. The love that I offered him seemed no consolation to his desperate temperament. Instead he seemed ever more drawn to that awful butler of his. He was enthralled in some way and I am sure that Parsons, or whatever this creature is really called, was responsible for my fiancé's death.'

'Have you informed the authorities of your suspicion?' I asked.

'Oh yes, but it seems that they are following procedure without much effect. This wicked manservant must be found before it is too late.'

'But where can he be?' I demanded.

'I think that I might know the answer to that,' claimed Marx.

The young lady looked as astonished as I felt.

'What?' I began.

'Just say that my contacts among the revolutionary émigrés in Little Italy have borne much strange fruit. Now,' he said to Miss Cardew, 'you go home. I feel sure that we will have news of this Pasero fellow this very evening.'

My friend saw the young lady out and then came back into his study.

'Now Marx,' I reproved him. 'What are you up to?'

He merely pulled out a slip of paper from his inside jacket pocket and handed it to me. Daubed with red printer's ink on the heading were indecipherable Chinese characters and, in black copperplate below, an address in Limehouse.

We took a hansom with a good horse down to the Docks that night. A skull-like moon hung low above the river, casting a jaundiced shimmer on the dark and filthy waters below. Gaslight grew thinner, the streets more narrow, as we came closer to our appointed address. We passed gloomy brick-fields, their kilns emitting a sickly light in the dripping mist. The public houses were just closing, befuddled men and women clustered in disorderly groups around the doorways. There were shrieks of awful laughter, loud oaths and raucous outbursts of brawling and disorder.

We rattled over rough-paven streets. The roads were clogged with muck and grime. The stench of putrescence hung in the air, a wraith of dreadful contagion. Most of the windows were dark, but here and there fantastic shadows were silhouetted against some dreary lamplight like magic-lantern shows of penury and degradation. Here dwelled the sordid secrets of the Great City.

'My God, Engels!' Marx exclaimed. 'Such squalor!'

I was somewhat surprised that he should be so shocked at the appalling poverty we witnessed that night. But then it always amazed me that, despite my friend's prowess in commentary and observations of conditions, his lucid approach to theoretical social analysis, he could, for the most part, be strangely inattentive and unmindful of the actual destitution that surrounds us. His detachment of thought, however, did not impair a particular attentiveness of his, no doubt born out of his many years of exile, intrigue and subterfuge, and he confided to me that he had noticed another carriage on the same trail as ours and consequently it was likely that we were once more being followed.

The hansom drew up with a start at the top of a dark lane, nearly at the waterside. The black masts of ships rose over the squatting rooftops of the low hovels. We got out and made our way towards the quayside along a slimy pavement and found a shabby house with a flickering oil lamp above the door that illuminated the same Oriental characters that were printed on the slip of paper that Marx had shown me earlier that day.

We knocked and were greeted by a sallow Chinaman who showed us into a long room, heavy with the sickly odour of opium, and edged with low wooden berths, like the forecast of an emigrant ship. The low flare of gaslights glowed feebly, their scant illumination diffused by the miasma of the foul-smelling drug. A group of Malays were hunched around a stove, clattering ivory tokens on a small table. Our attendant offered each of us a pipe. Hastily we demurred and proceeded to search amongst the stupefied occupants of the bunks on either side of us.

We were watched with suspicion by the more sober patrons of that den. Harsh oaths were uttered as we moved through the room; one of the Malays looked up from the game in our direction and hissed something to his fellows in their alien tongue. I began to feel a concern for our safety, though Marx seemed quite oblivious to any danger, driven as always by his relentless curiosity.

'I've always wanted to see what one of these places looks like,' he commented with a quite inappropriate jocularity.

Through the gloom we could make out contorted figures reclining in strange twisted poses; some muttered to themselves, others appeared to be in a trance, but all were possessed by a mental servitude to that merciless narcotic. In the corner a man lifted himself up from his bed and reddened eyes blinked against the vaporous light. He looked with a docile astonishment upon us, as if not sure if what he was seeing was real or a phantasm of his contorted imagination. He then gave a rasping and mirthless laugh. It was Pasero.

'Ah!' he called out to us. 'Comrades! Citizen Marx, now you may prove the accuracy of your aphorism as to the anaesthetising effect of religion.' He relit his pipe and taking a ghastly inhalation, held the glowing red bowl towards my friend. 'Here is to oblivion, comrade.'

Marx pushed the foul object away.

'Oblivion from guilt?' he demanded. 'Is that what you seek here?'

Pasero coughed and shook his head.

'From sorrow,' he croaked, mournfully.

'Elizabeth Cardew, the fiancée of Lord Beckworth, seems convinced that you had some hold over your late master and believes that you were responsible for his death. What do you have to say to that?' demanded my colleague.

'That bitch!' hissed Pasero. 'It was her fault. It was she that drove him to his death.'

'Explain yourself, man!' Marx exclaimed. 'And why you absented yourself from Beckworth's household just after he had met his terrible fate.'

'Because no one would understand. Do you think you could understand?'

This enigmatic query was, of course, a direct provocation to the great mind of my friend. He stroked his beard, thoughtfully.

'Go on,' he insisted.

Pasero sat up on the edge of the bunk and rubbed at his sore eyes. He sighed and shook his head, as if trying to rouse his dulled mind into some sort of coherence.

'I was a young man when I joined Garibaldi's Red Shirts,' he began. 'I hardly knew myself back then. But I was drawn, I know now, to the dear love of comrades. We were a band of brothers and, through danger and action, some of us could find comfort in each other, and secretly believed in that Ancient Greek ideal: that we were an army of lovers. Ah, the Thousand! A true company of men. After Aspromonte I came here in exile, lost and alone in a cold city. I tried to involve myself in the political movements like so many other *émigrés*, but these dull meetings with their endless arguments and empty resolutions were nothing compared to the solidarity I had known with the Thousand. Then, one night, at a Chartist gathering in Bloomsbury I met with Beckworth. He was kind and generous. Although we were from entirely different worlds we were drawn to each other and we soon discovered the desire that held us in common. We shared another curse, as you would call it, like that of the first Lord Beckworth who was a king's favourite. I strove to make Beckworth see it was a blessing also.'

'You mean the abominable sin of sodomy!' I gasped.

Pasero groaned.

'Really,' Marx chided me. 'We are trying to understand the social circumstances of this case.'

'Understand gross and unnatural vices?' I retorted.

'My dear Engels,' my colleague went on, 'I would have thought that you, as the author of *The Origin of the Family*, might have a more scientific curiosity concerning this problem.'

'And encompass human perversion as part of my thesis?' I demanded.

'If you have both quite finished!' Pasero declared boldly, his voice suddenly becoming clear and emphatic. 'I am a man of action, I have little time for your analysis. You theoreticians, you have no idea what real rebellion is! We were revolutionaries of the heart, ours was the sedation of desire.'

Marx saw that I was about to make a reply to this and glared to me to keep quiet.

'We had so many plans for our liberation. Utopian ideas maybe, but we both dreamt of a world where we could be free. When we were alone there was no servant and no master but equal souls, true comrades joined together in love. But *she*!' he seethed through gritted teeth. 'She ruined everything!'

'How?' asked Marx.

'That Cardew woman's designs upon poor young Beckworth were for securing herself a social position. She preyed upon his sensitive nature and his vulnerability. When she discovered where his affections really lay she tried to insist upon my dismissal. She threatened to expose His Lordship to open scandal if he did not honour his promise to elevate her to her long-desired status as Lady Beckworth. On the night of his death she had sent him a hateful letter and a green carnation.'

'Oh, that,' Marx interjected. 'What is the significance of that flower?'

'It is a symbol of our condemned nature. She wanted him to know that she knew the truth about him. He was utterly distraught, at his very wits' end. He had so much to lose. We argued, we had drunk much and taken laudanum in an attempt to quell our anxiety. We ended up fighting and in a struggle Beckworth slipped at the top of the stairs and fell to his death.'

Just then came a loud banging on the front door of the squalid den. There was a chorus of groans as the pitiful wrecks roused themselves from their berths. The game-playing Malays stood up and started jabbering at each other. After two or more heavy thuds the door was broken down and a shrill whistle pierced the night air.

'Police!' a voice called out as a group of uniformed men, with a plain-clothed man at their head, stormed into the smoke-filled room.

'Gentlemen,' the leader hailed us. 'I thought you might lead us to the quarry.'

It was Inspector Bucket of the Detective.

'But where...?' he went on.

We looked to Pasero's bunk. In the commotion he had slipped out of the den through a back way.

'I've men posted outside,' said Bucket. 'He won't get far.'

We rushed out into the cold air. A figure could be seen making its way to the dockside.

'There he goes, then. And get on, my lads!' called Bucket to his men.

But it was myself and Marx that were closest to him as he reached the edge of the slippery quayside. He looked at us for a second, panting like a hunted animal, his breath steaming into the night. He gave a defiant laugh, then dropped out of sight. There was a muffled splash. As we reached the waterside we saw him flounder in the dank waters below. He struggled awhile, his body protesting against its fate, though there seemed a strange tranquillity in his countenance, as if his mind had already given up the ghost. The policemen arrived and made an attempt to drag him out of the dock with a boat-hook. But by the time he had been fished out of the dirty water he was quite cold and dead.

We gave our statement to the affable Inspector Bucket, whose curious forefinger wagged with increasing agitation at our strange testimonies. The 'Case of the Ten Lords a-Leaping' was, as they say, closed, and it seemed likely that the inquest into the death of the last Lord Beckworth would record a verdict of accidental death. A perturbing conclusion perhaps, but I must confess that our minds were reeling at the unfolding of events over the last few days. My friend's great intelligence seemed particularly vexed at all these provocations of meaning; confounded, even.

'Struggle,' he murmured to me as we made out way back to his lodgings as the dawn broke. 'It's all struggle.'

A week later I was much relieved, when I met with my colleague as he came out of the British Museum, to see that he had been coaxed back to his great work after this strange diversion. A curious-looking young man was with him who bore an intense expression on his countenance, and wore some kind of tweed hunting-cap on his head. After the briefest of formalities the young fellow left us.

'Who was that?' I asked Marx.

'Oh, a student, or, rather, he had just left university with prodigious talents and is unsure of how, exactly, to apply them. Very much like myself when I was his age,' Marx mused. 'He has lodgings in Montague Street and is using the Reading Room to develop methods of analysis. He feels sure that a scientific approach to criminology is to be his vocation. I told him of the Beckworth case and he was most interested. I believe he wants to pursue a career as a detective.'

'As a police officer?'

'No, as a civilian.'

'What a peculiar notion,' I commented.

'Yes, it's a pity that such a gifted mind cannot be persuaded to apply itself to our cause but I'm afraid he's utterly unpoliticised.'

'The youth of today,' I sighed.

'Yes. Though he is a committed materialist. It's just that he is content to analyse human behaviour and interactions without a desire to change them. Though I must confess that I can now see the fascination in uncovering evidence, interpreting disclosures and clues. One could get lost in the deduction of class and society. He is working on a puzzle presented to him by a high-born friend of his from college, a superstitious observance of an ancient family known as the "Musgrave Ritual". It is a litany of questions and answers that have no apparent meaning but —'

'Marx!' I barked at him.

He stared at me in shock for a second then his face broke into a broad grin.

'No more of this amateur sleuthing,' I reproached him. 'There's work to be done.'

'You're quite right, my dear Engels,' he assured me, patting the thick sheaf of notes he had been making for the next part of *Capital*. 'We've the greater crime to solve.'

To the end of his days, Charles Dickens forbade all talk about the slaying of Thaddeus Whiteacre. The macabre features of the tragedy – murder by an invisible hand; the stabbing of a bound man in a room both locked and barred; the vanishing without trace of a beautiful young woman – were meat and drink to any imaginative mind. Wilkie Collins reflected more than once that he might have woven a triple-decker novel of sensation from the events of that dreadful night, but he knew that publication was impossible. Dickens would treat any attempt to fabricate fiction from the crime as a betrayal, an act of treachery he could never forgive.

Dickens said it himself: *The case must never be solved.*

His logic was impeccable; so was his generosity of heart. Even after Dickens's death, Collins honoured his friend's wishes and kept the secret safe. But he also kept notes, and enough time has passed to permit the truth to be revealed. Upon the jottings in Collins's private records is based this account of the murder at the House of the Red Candle.

A crowded tavern on the corner of a Greenwich alleyway, a stone's throw from the river. At the bar, voices were raised in argument about a wager on a prizefight and a group of potbellied draymen carolled a bawdy song about a mermaid and a bosun. The air was thick with smoke and the stale stench of beer. Separate from the throng, two men sat at a table in the corner, quenching their thirsts.

The elder, a middle-sized man in his late thirties, rocked back and forth on his stool, his whole being seemingly taut with tension, barely suppressed. His companion, bespectacled and with a bulging forehead, fiddled with his extravagant turquoise shirt pin while stealing glances at his companion. Once or twice he was about to speak, but something in the other's demeanour caused him to hold his tongue. At length he could contain his curiosity no longer.

'Tell me one thing, my dear fellow. Why here?'

Charles Dickens swung to face his friend, yet when he spoke, he sounded as cautious as a poker player with a troublesome hand of cards. 'Is the Rope and Anchor not to your taste, then, Wilkie?'

'Well, it's hardly as comfortable as the Cock Tavern. Besides, it's uncommon enough for our nightly roamings to take us south of the river, and you gave the impression of coming here with a purpose.' He winced as a couple of drunken slatterns shrieked with mocking laughter. The object of their scorn was a woman with a scarred cheek who crouched anxiously by the door, as if yearning for the arrival of a friendly face. 'And the company is hardly select! All this way on an evening thick with fog! Frankly, I expected you to have rather more pleasurable company in mind.'

'My dear Wilkie,' Dickens said, baring his teeth in a wicked smile. 'Who is to say that I have not?'

'Then why be such an oyster? I cannot fathom what has got into you tonight. You have been behaving very oddly, you know. When I talked about Boulogne, you didn't seem to be paying the slightest attention.'

'Then I apologize,' Dickens said swiftly. 'May I thank you for your patience.'

Collins was not easily mollified. 'Even when you mentioned your jaunt with Inspector Field the other night,' he complained, 'it was as if your mind was elsewhere. May I finally be allowed to know what lies in store for us during the remainder of the evening?'

Dickens pushed his glass to one side with a sweep of the hand as though, after wrestling with an intractable dilemma, he had at last made up his mind. 'Very well. I shall enlighten you. Our destination lies at the end of this very street.'

Collins frowned. 'By the river?'

'Yes.' Dickens took a deep breath. 'You cannot miss it. There is a fiery glow in the window of the last house in the row. In these parts, people call it the House of the Red Candle?'

'Ah!' Collins's eyes widened in understanding. 'I take it that the name speaks for itself?'

'Indeed. Unsubtle, but you and I have agreed in the past that even the most refined taste can have too much of subtlety.'

'Quite.' Collins chuckled. 'So you favored a change from the houses of Haymarket and Regent Street?'

'Even from those of Soho and the East End,' Dickens said quietly.

'A writer must indulge in a little necessary research!' Collins laughed, his cheeks reddening with excitement. 'Whatever strange resorts it takes him to. Do you recall telling me about your experiences at Margate, years ago? Margate, of all places!'

Dickens shrugged. 'At the seaside there are conveniences of all kinds.'

'And you knew where they lived! Very well, tell me about this House of the Red Candle. Come on, spare me no shocking detail!'

'Later,' Dickens said. 'I have no wish to spoil your anticipation.'

Collins belched. 'Really, I must complain. You should have mentioned this an hour ago. I would have been more abstemious if only I had realised the nature of the entertainment you had up your sleeve. You old rascal! I wondered why you were wearing such a mysterious expression and only taking ladylike sips from your glass!'

Suddenly Dickens leaned across the table and stabbed a forefinger toward his companion's heart. 'Tonight, Wilkie, tonight of all nights, whatever happens, I beg you to repose your trust completely in me. Do you understand?'

His massive forehead wrinkling in bewilderment, Collins exclaimed, 'Why, my dear fellow!'

'I must have your word on this, Wilkie. Can I rely upon you?'

A light dawned in the younger man's eyes. 'Oh, I think I understand! Go on, then, you rascal! What is her name?'

Contriving a sly grin, Dickens said, 'Ah, Wilkie, you are always too sharp for me.'

'Go on, then! Her name?'

'Very well. Her name is Bella.'

'Splendid! And is she as pretty as her name?'

'She is beautiful,' Dickens said softly.

'Ah! I do believe you are smitten. Now, don't forget you are a married man, Charles, old fellow. How long have you known this – Bella?'

'I have answered quite enough questions for the moment,' Dickens retorted, springing to his feet. 'Come, it is time for us to be away.'

Outside it was bitterly cold and fog was rolling in from the Thames, smothering the dim light from the sparse lamps. As Dickens led the way down the cobbled street at his customary brisk trot, Collins heard the restless scurrying of unseen rats. He knew this to be a part of the city where life was as cheap as the women, but he found the temptation of the unknown irresistible. Like Dickens, he always felt intensely alive during their late-night wanderings in dark and disreputable streets and alleyways. One never knew what might happen. For a writer – for any man with red blood in his veins – that shiver of uncertainty was delicious.

Just before they reached the river, they paused in front of the last house. A red candle burned in the ground-floor window, its flickering light the only colour in a world of grey. The curtains at all the other windows were drawn.

Dickens tugged at the bellpull beside the front door, but at first there was no response. Collins shivered and rubbed his hands together.

'I shall be glad when I am warmed up!'

'Patience, Wilkie, patience. I promise you one thing. You will not readily forget tonight.'

Collins was still chuckling when the door creaked open. A small and very fat woman peered out at them. Her hair was a deep and unnatural shade of red – Collins surmised that she wore a wig – and perched on her nose were spectacles with lenses so thick that they distorted the shape of her porcine eyes.

'What d' you want?' Her voice was as sharp as a hatchet.

'Mrs Jugg? Splendid!' Dickens greeted her with gusto. 'My friend and I have been given to understand that you have a young lady lodging with you by the name of Bella?'

'What if I do?' The woman had several chins, and each of them wobbled truculently as she spoke.

'Well, the two of us are eager to make her acquaintance.'

'Bella's a lady,' the harridan hissed. 'A proper lady. She has very expensive tastes.'

'Expensive and exotic, I understand,' Dickens murmured.

'There's no one like her. If you've been recommended...'

'We have.'

'Then you'll know what I mean.'

Dickens glanced over his shoulder, making sure that he was not observed by prying eyes. They could hear the rowdy harpies, presumably tired of baiting the sad woman with the scar, spilling out of the tavern in search of better entertainment. In the distance hooves clattered, but the fog was a shroud, and anything farther than five yards away was invisible. Satisfied, he put his hand inside his coat and extracted a wallet, from which he made a fan of banknotes.

'My friend and I are not without means.'

The woman took a step toward them, as though keen to check that the money was not counterfeit. Collins caught the whiff of gin on her breath as she grinned, showing damaged and discoloured teeth.

'Well, you look like respectable sorts. Proper gentlemen. I have to be careful, y'know. Come with me.'

She shuffled back inside, the two men following over the threshold and into a long and narrow passageway. The air reeked of damp and rotting timber. She led them into a cramped front room where a slim scarlet candle in a dish burned on the window-sill.

'So you both want to visit Bella at the same time?' she asked with a leer.

'You read our minds, Mrs Jugg.' Dickens contrived to step backward onto Collins's toes, stifling his companion's gasp of surprise as he passed a handful of banknotes to the brothel keeper.

The woman's myopic gaze feasted on the notes for a few seconds before she secreted them among the folds of her grubby but capacious dress. 'That's very generous, sir. Very generous indeed. You'll both be wanting to stay the night here, I take it?'

'Not exactly,' Dickens said. 'I am on good terms with a man who keeps an inn not far away from here, and it would please us if Bella accompanied us there.'

The fat woman frowned and indicated their surroundings with a wave of a flabby hand. 'This is her home, sir. She doesn't care to go out much.'

Dickens said with animation, 'But this is our one and only night in the locality! Who knows when we will return? My friend and I wish to enjoy a memorable finale to our sojourn south of the river!'

He passed her another sheaf of notes, and the woman caught her breath. So did Collins. Clutching the money tightly in her fist, as if fearing that he might change his mind, the brothel keeper whispered, 'Well, sir, the circumstances are obviously exceptional. Very exceptional indeed.'

'I'm glad we understand each other. Now, if we can be shown to Bella's room?'

The woman glanced at a battered old clock on the sideboard and let out a snort of temper. 'I'm sure she won't be long. Perhaps you'd like to make yourselves comfortable in the parlour while I see what's what?'

She shuffled back into the malodorous passageway, and they followed her into a rear hall, from which a narrow flight of stairs ran up to the floors above. Opposite the bottom of the staircase was an open door leading to another room. A bald, unshaven man in shirtsleeves, heedless of the chill of evening, was standing there, a tankard in his hand. He glanced at the two visitors, but seemed more interested in savouring his ale. Collins surmised that he was a 'watcher', retained to keep an eye on the girls and customers of the House of the Red Candle.

Someone was coming down the stairs, taking them two at a time, stumbling over her skirts so that it seemed that she might at any moment trip and fall head over heels. The fat woman demanded, 'Where d'you think you're hurrying off to, Nellie Brown?'

Nellie came to rest at the foot of the stairs. She was a stooping, round-shouldered woman in a lace cap and a maid's uniform. Pulling a handkerchief from a pocket, she blew her nose long and loudly.

'Nowhere, m'm,' she croaked.

'I have two gentlemen here with an appointment to see Bella. You took His Lordship up a good three-quarters of an hour ago. You left the key with him, didn't you?'

With eyes downcast, Nellie said, 'Yes, m'm.'

'Well, he never needs longer than thirty minutes. What are they doing up there?'

Nellie, evidently reluctant to meet Mrs Jugg's gaze, bowed her head and declined to speculate.

'Lost your tongue, girl? Why, he was supposed to be out of there a good fifteen minutes ago!'

'Yes, m'm.'

'I can't abide cheats, whatever their airs and graces! He paid for half an hour, no more. If he wanted longer, that could have been arranged.'

Nellie's shoulders moved in a hapless shrug as she considered the threadbare carpet.

Dickens shifted impatiently from foot to foot, and the woman snapped 'Well, I can't keep these two gentlemen waiting. You'll have to rouse her.'

Nellie darted a glance at Bella's visitors before shrinking away from them, as if fearing a slap, or worse. Collins thought she was afraid of Dickens; he had a fleeting impression of dark, secretive eyes and a disfiguring mark on her left cheek that she was striving to shield from his gaze.

For a moment Dickens seemed taken aback, but then he said, 'Yes, my friend and I have made a special journey. We prefer not to waste our time.'

Collins was disconcerted by the sudden urgency in his friend's tone. His mood of excitement had given way to fascinated apprehension. The whole evening had taken on an *Arabian Nights* quality. Dickens had a hedonistic streak, but his taste did not usually extend to houses of ill fame quite as unsalubrious as this.

'Take them up with you, Nellie,' the fat woman commanded. 'Bang on the door until he leaves her be. I don't care if he hasn't got time to button up his trousers, d'you hear? He's long overdue!'

'But…' Nellie sniffled. Her distress was unmistakable.

'At once, or it'll be the worst for you!'

The maid began to drag herself up the stairs as if her limbs were made of lead. At a nod from the old woman, the two men followed. When they reached the landing on the first floor, Collins whispered in his friend's ear, 'Both of us with the same girl? Taking her to a nearby inn? For heaven's sake! What are you thinking of?'

'I asked you to trust me,' Dickens muttered.

The only illumination came from the faint glow of the moon through a skylight. The ceiling was low and a taller man would have needed to bend to avoid banging his head against it. Three doors led from the landing. From two of the rooms issued the unmistakable cries of men and women in the throes of ecstasy. Nellie halted in front of the thin door, and it seemed to Collins that a tremor ran through the whole of her body.

Dickens hissed, 'Is that Bella's room? Come, there is no need to be frightened. You can see we are gentlemen! I swear, we mean her no harm.'

She shot another glance at them, taking in Dickens' extravagant clusters of brown hair and Collins's fancy yellow waistcoat. Her lips were pursed, as if she were thinking: *not quite gentlemen, actually*. Her dark eyes, misty with suspicion, held something else as well. Collins realised that it was terror. Did this pitiful creature really believe that she would be called to join Bella in satisfying their lusts? The thought had the same effect as a drenching by a bucket of icy water.

'My friend is right,' he said. 'And we mean you no harm either. What are you afraid of, Nellie? That Bella's customer will want to punish you for disturbing him? We won't allow it, do you hear? We simply won't let him take out his anger on you, will we?'

Dickens nodded. 'The sooner the blackguard is gone, the better.'

Tears began to form in Nellie's eyes. 'But, sir…'

Dickens patted her on the shoulder. 'I am *sure* you are a good friend to her, Nellie,' he said meaningfully. 'So let me tell you this. The sooner you introduce us to Bella, the better for everyone.'

The maid seemed to have been paralysed. Even when Collins gave her an encouraging nod, she did not move an inch.

'He has the key to this room,' she said. 'All I can do is knock. If he don't answer…'

Dickens took a step toward her. 'Does he hurt her, Nellie?'

She choked on a sob. 'I…I can't say.'

'We must stop this,' he said. 'Will you knock at her door?'

'Sir, I —'

She was interrupted by a sound, from inside the room. A low groan. And then, unmistakably, a man's hoarse voice.

'Please…help me!'

As the voice fell silent, Nellie screamed. Dickens leapt forward, hammering the door with his fist. 'Let us in! For pity's sake, let us in!'

Collins rushed to his friend's side and pressed his ear to the keyhole, but he could detect no further sound from inside. The door was locked. Nellie's head was in her hands and she had begun to weep. Dickens put his shoulder to the door in an attempt to shift it, but to no avail.

The commotion must have roused the watcher down below; for a coarse voice roared, 'What's to do? What's to do?'

One of the doors to the landing was flung open, and a half-dressed man appeared. 'What's happening, for God's sake? Are the peelers here?'

Within moments the place was in uproar. The man who feared the arrival of the police was fastening his britches with clumsy desperation. A grizzled old fellow emerged from the second room, wheezing so frantically that Collins feared that he might succumb to a heart attack at any moment. The bald ruffian from the parlour was lumbering upstairs, with the fat brothel-keeper trailing in his wake. Looking into the other rooms, Collins could see two naked girls cowering in the shadows. Their clients jostled past the bald watcher, the younger man taking the steps two at a time in his haste to escape.

The watcher grabbed Dickens by the arm. 'Causing trouble, mister? Why did she scream?'

'We heard the voice of Bella's client,' Dickens said.

'He sounded frightened and in pain. But the door is locked and I cannot force it open.'

The man pushed him aside and heaved against the door. Timber splintered, but the lock held. Puffing furiously, the fat little woman arrived on the landing.

'What's all this to-do?' she demanded, turning furiously to Nellie. 'Where's Bella?'

The maid was sobbing piteously and unable to speak. Fearing that the fat woman would strike her servant, Collins interposed his squat frame beween them and said, 'We heard her visitor. Something – is very wrong.'

The watcher grunted and took a step back before charging at the door. They heard the wood giving way. He charged again and this time the door yielded under his weight. Bella's room was no more than twelve feet square. Apart from a tall cupboard and a double bed, the only furniture was a cracked looking glass and a battered old captain's chair on which were piled a pair of tweed trousers and an expensively tailored jacket as well as a man's underthings, evidently discarded in haste.

Stretched out on the bed lay the body of a naked man. His wrists were tied to the bedstead by lengths of rope, his glassy eyes staring sightlessly at the ceiling. Collins had a sudden fancy that he saw in them a look of horrified bewilderment. Tall and broad-shouldered, with heavy jowls, the man had a shock of jet-black hair. His lips had a sensual curve. Blood dripped onto the sheets from a gash in his stomach, an inch above the navel.

The watcher uttered an oath. 'She's done for him!'

'Murder!' the fat woman cried. 'Oh, Bella, you stupid little bitch!'

Behind them, Nellie retched. Dickens was the first to move. He rushed into the room and bent by the corpse, searching for a pulse. After a moment he said, 'Nothing. Nothing at all.'

'There's her weapon,' the watcher said, pointing to a pair of scissors lying on the floor. They were dark with blood.

The brothel-keeper lifted the man's coat from the chair.

A leather wallet tumbled from one of the pockets. She picked it up and folded it open. They could all see that the wallet was empty.

'So she's a thief as well as a murderess! She'll swing for that. Precious little bitch, just see if she won't!'

Only four of them were in the room: the fat woman, the bald man, Collins, and Dickens. Outside the door Nellie was wailing, her head in her hands. Of Bella there was no trace.

'She must be in there!' the fat woman cried, waving at the cupboard.

The two friends held their breath as the bald man flung open the cupboard door. Collins was not sure what he expected to see: a cowering woman, stripped and covered in blood, he supposed. The cupboard was crammed to overflowing with gaudy gowns and dresses. As well as a pair of tasselled boots, there was a mass of lace and ribbons piled high on the cupboard floor. The watcher tore the clothes aside, as if to unmask his quarry, lurking behind them. But there was no sign of her.

The room had a small rectangular window set high in the wall above the end of the bed. Collins could detect no other means of egress. The watcher ripped the blankets from the mattress, but found nothing. He got down on his hands and knees and peered underneath the bed, discovering only dust.

Unable to help himself, Collins cried, 'Where is she?'

The fat woman clasped a podgy hand to her heart. 'The window is bolted shut. Besides that, there are bars outside.'

'Could the bars have been tampered with?'

The bald watcher clambered onto the bed and shoved at the window. There was no hint of movement. Shaking his head, he said, 'I couldn't move 'em, never mind a young slip of a girl like her.'

'How can she vanish into thin air?' Collins demanded. 'This Bella, is she a wraith, a phantom?'

'All her clothes are in the cupboard,' the fat woman gasped. 'Every stitch. But where is the key?'

'The girl must have it,' the watcher said. 'She is hiding somewhere.'

'Not in here,' Dickens murmured.

Beyond argument, he was right. Dickens pointed to the corpse. 'This man came here alone, I take it?'

'Oh, yes. He was one of her regulars. Always paid handsomely for her time.'

'When he arrived, you handed him the key and asked Nellie to escort him up to this room?'

Mrs Jugg nodded. 'Ain't that right, Nell?'

The maid, still snivelling out on the landing, managed a grunt.

Dickens said, 'You saw him enter the room?'

'As he put the key in the lock,' the maid croaked, 'he told me I could go.'

'So you did not see Bella herself?' Collins asked.

The maid shook her head, but the fat woman said impatiently, 'Of course, Bella was in the room, waiting for him. She was here all evening, same as usual. Nellie brought her up and locked her in, same as always. The gentleman had an appointment. He called upon her every Thursday at nine, regular as clockwork.'

'She must have done him in and then locked the door on him,' the bald man said. 'It's the only way.'

'If she'd come down to the ground, you'd have stopped her, wouldn't you, Jack, my lad?'

'She could never get past me,' he boasted. 'She's tried it once or twice and I made her pay for it, so help me.'

'Then,' Dickens suggested, 'if she is flesh and blood and not a poltergeist, she must be concealed in one of the other rooms on this floor.'

'He's right,' the watcher said.

'What are you waiting for, then?' the fat woman demanded. 'Let's find her, quick!'

They hurried out and into the adjoining bedroom. Dickens moved swiftly to Nellie's side and whispered something to her before returning and pulling the door shut behind him.

'What did you say to her?' Collins asked.

Dickens was staring at the pale flesh of the dead man.

'Do you recognise him, Wilkie?'

'The face seems familiar, but —'

'This is the Honourable Thaddeus Whiteacre. You heard the woman refer to him as "His Lordship"? He liked to play up his noble origins. Besides that, he fancied himself as something of an artist, although to my mind his daubs were infantile. John Forster introduced me to him a year ago at a meeting of the Guild for Literature and Art.'

'You are acquainted?'

'Regrettably. *De mortuis*, Wilkie, but he struck me as one of the least agreeable men I have ever met. I recall a conversation in which he sought to convince me of the pleasure that could be gained from inflicting pain – and having pain inflicted upon oneself.'

Collins shivered as he considered the corpse's face. Even in death, the saturnine features seemed menacing. He found it easy to imagine that they belonged to a man with vile and sinister tastes.

'Do you believe that Bella killed him?'

Dickens put a finger to his lips. 'Come, let us join the search.'

The watcher and his mistress were opening and slamming shut cupboard doors and drawers scarcely large enough to accommodate a box of clothes, let alone a full-grown woman. It was absurd, Collins thought, to imagine that the missing girl could have taken refuge in a room where a colleague was entertaining a client – but where might she have concealed herself? The brothel-keeper was cursing and describing in savage terms what she would do to Bella once she was found. Nellie had scuttled off downstairs, while the shivering prostitutes hugged each other in a corner and tried not to attract the fat woman's attention.

'She's been spirited away!' one of the girls said. Her face was blotchy and tear-stained, her body covered in yellowing bruises. Collins doubted if she was yet sixteen years of age. 'It's the Devil's work!'

'Bella would never hurt a fly!' the other girl cried. 'Someone else has done this! Or some*thing*. Killed His Lordship and then kidnapped Bella!'

'Shut your mouths!' the brothel-keeper shouted. 'Bogeymen don't stab strong fellows to death with scissors. And as for you, Jack Wells, don't think I've finished with you – not by a long chalk!'

'I told you, she couldn't have passed me,' the bald man said mutinously. 'I never take my eye off the stairs when there are visitors in the house.'

'Then where did she go? I've been by the front door ever since Nellie roused me at five.'

'You reside on the premises, I suppose?' Dickens said.

'In the basement, that's right. But it would have been impossible for her to get down there. Jack or I would have seen her. And there aren't any windows she could have climbed through to get out of the building. Besides, her boots were in the cupboard. That's her only pair. She can't have got far without her boots!'

'The fact remains,' Dickens said, 'that Bella has vanished. It is as if she never existed. Yet my friend and I have not enjoyed the privileges for which we paid handsomely. May I ask for reimbursement of —'

The bald man took a couple of paces toward them and seized Dickens's collar. 'So you want your money back, do you? Well, you'll have to whistle for it!'

'That's right!' the fat woman shouted, as if glad to find a target for her fury that was made of flesh and blood. 'If you two know what's good for you, you'll clear off now like these other lily-livered bastards!'

'Please assure me,' Dickens said, rubbing his neck as the bald man released his grip, 'that there is no question of your summoning the police.'

The fat woman stared at him. 'Think I was born yesterday? No fear of that, mister. Them peelers would like nothing better than to pin something on me.'

'But the body —' Collins began.

'Jack will find a graveyard for it,' she interrupted. 'Don't you fear.'

'At the bottom of the Thames, I suppose?' Dickens said.

The bald watcher scowled at him. 'You heard what she said. It's as easy for me to chuck three bodies in the river as one.'

Dickens caught his friend's eye and nodded toward the stairs. 'Very well. We will go.'

'And don't come back,' the fat woman said. 'You've brought trouble to this house, you two. Theft and murder. Now, Jack, you see to the body while I get Nellie to help me look for that murderous little bitch.'

Dickens hurried down the stairs, with Collins close behind. As they reached the ground, they heard the brothel-keeper calling Nellie's name, but Collins could not see the maid in the parlour. He presumed that she was in the front room, where the red candle burned. Dickens caught hold of his wrist and manhandled him down the passageway and out into the fog.

* * *

An hour later the two friends were ensconced in the more congenial and familiar surroundings of the Ship and Turtle in the heart of the City. Exhausted on their arrival after racing from Greenwich, they had quaffed a couple of glasses of ale to calm their nerves with scarcely a word of conversation.

'An extraordinary evening,' Collins said at length. 'Expensive, too.'

Dickens shrugged, his expression shorn of emotion. So energetic by nature, he seemed in an uncharacteristically reflective mood. 'For the Honourable Thaddeus Whiteacre, undoubtedly.'

'Well, I realise you are a man of means, old fellow, but you must be bitter at having spent so much for so little reward.'

'Oh, I'm not so sure about that, Wilkie.'

Collins stared at his friend. 'I really think that it is time that you were frank with me. Your behaviour tonight has been most extraordinary. I thought that we were out for a little innocent amusement...'

'I agree that what happened was neither innocent nor amusing.'

'...and instead we ended up running through a peasouper, fleeing from a madam's hired ruffian. Even since we've arrived here, you've spent most of the time staring into space, as if trying to unravel the most ticklish conundrum.'

'In which endeavour I believe I have succeeded. You are right, Wilkie. I do owe you an explanation. But first – let us have another drink.'

'You almost sound as if you are celebrating a glorious triumph,' Collins grumbled as a waiter replenished their glasses.

'In a sense,' Dickens said calmly, 'I am. Your health, dear Wilkie!'

'But we have been present at the scene of a brutal slaying!' Collins protested. 'What is worse, the circumstances are such that we cannot inform the police. I might be a young nobody, but you are Dickens the Inimitable, the most famous writer in England. Not even your friendship with Inspector Field could save you from disgrace if the truth came out. He could not hush up your presence at the scene of the crime, even if he wished to do so. The author who patronised a house of ill repute on the night of a murder – how the scandal sheets would love that story!'

'True, true.'

'You have not yet told me how you became acquainted with Bella,' Collins grumbled.

'Forgive me, Wilkie,' Dickens said. 'Undoubtedly you deserve an explanation for the night's events.'

'In so far as you can explain the inexplicable.'

'Oh, I shall do my best,' Dickens said, with an impish smile. 'I met Bella one night when my nocturnal ramblings took me to that God-forsaken tavern the Rope and Anchor. I was sitting just where you and I sat this evening. Looking round, I noticed a young woman in the company of Jack Wells, whom you met this evening. Her profession was apparent from her dress, if not from her demeanour, yet I was struck by her quite astonishing beauty. She is no more than seventeen, Wilkie, but her face and figure were as fine as any I have seen in a long time. More than that, there was an innocence and purity about her that I found mesmerising. It was as if, by some miracle, she had yet to be tainted by her profession. But it was plain that she was in the depths of misery, above all that she was in mortal fear of her brutish companion. I surmised that she was a dress lodger and that the madam of the house where she plied her trade had instructed Wells to keep an eye on her.'

'That is the way these people run their business, is it not? A watcher dogs the dress lodger's footsteps to make sure that she does not run away from the brothel.'

'Exactly. As I studied the girl, I found myself speculating about her history, imagining the sequence of events that had reduced her to such dire straits. It can happen easily enough, you know.' A dreamy look came into Dickens's eyes. Collins had seen the same expression when he acted before the Queen at Devonshire House, throwing himself body and soul into his part, so that any deficiencies in thespian talent were amply compensated by the intensity of his imaginative investment in his performance. 'A young woman, perhaps an orphan, becomes destitute and is "rescued" by an apparently kind-hearted older lady. She is offered salvation in the form of board and lodging, only to learn – too late! – that the price is higher than she can afford. Possibly she is accused of a petty theft – a put-up job, with the threat of criminal prosecution supposedly bought off by the bribing of a bogus police officer. By whatever means, the madam ensures that the victim stays deeply in her debt. The poor wretch must repay by selling the only wares that she possesses. Oh, yes, Wilkie, there are female slaves in plantations across the ocean that enjoy liberty for which a dress lodger in a mean London brothel can only offer up hopeless prayers!'

Collins swallowed a mouthful of beer. 'It is pure wickedness.'

'Indeed. I hold that a woman is free to sell herself, just as a man is free to buy. That is the way of the world, and has been throughout history. But when all that the woman earns goes to the harridan who keeps her in thrall... Well, emboldened by drink, I decided that I must do something. This young woman might only be one of a thousand dress lodgers in this city, but I vowed to myself that I would set her free.'

'But you knew nothing of her.'

'Only what I had seen in her lovely, wistful face. Yet it was enough, Wilkie. I decided to bide my time and when the watcher succumbed to a call of nature, I approached the girl. I urged her to come with me and escape from her guard while she had the chance. But she was terrified and suspected a trap. I could see in her eyes that she yearned to believe that I was offering her a chance to start a new life, but her fear of Jack Wells and his mistress was stronger than the faith she could muster in the words of a complete stranger. Within a minute I realised it was no good. I had time merely to ask her name and where she lived.'

'Bella, from Mrs Jugg's lodging, the House of the Red Candle in Greenwich,' Collins murmured.

'Precisely. Even as she gave me those few details, a look of panic crossed her face, and I realised that Jack Wells was returning to take charge of her. I made myself scarce – but not without whispering a promise that I would see her again and set her free.'

'Hence tonight?'

'Hence tonight.' Dickens sighed. 'I had not reckoned that Fate would intervene in the sordid shape of her regular client, the Honourable Thaddeus Whiteacre.'

'I suppose he abused her terribly.'

'No doubt,' Dickens said softly. 'Yet Bella does not lack spirit. She did not trust a stranger in a tavern to rescue her, but she was prepared to save herself. So she conceived an audacious scheme of her own, to kill Whiteacre and escape with all the funds he kept in his wallet.'

'You are sure that she did murder him?'

Dickens gave him a pitying look. 'Who else?'

'Indeed. But *how*?'

'There, my dear Wilkie, I can only speculate.'

'For the Lord's sake, Dickens, you can't leave it at that!'

For a moment Dickens eyed his friend, scarcely able to contain his amusement. 'Very well. If you wish to hear my theory, then I shall be glad to share it with you. I make just one condition.'

'Name it.'

'That, after tonight, we never speak of this matter again. No matter what the circumstances. Can I trust your discretion?'

'Naturally,' Collins said in a stiff voice.

'I mean it, Wilkie. We must hold our tongues forever. Two lives depend upon it.'

'*Two?*'

'Those of Bella and the maidservant Nellie Brown.'

Collins frowned. 'It was hardly the maid's fault that she led Whiteacre to his death and that Bella contrived to flee from the House of the Red Candle. If indeed she did escape.'

'Oh, I think she did.'

'But *how*?'

Dickens finished his ale and put the tankard down on the table. 'I helped her to escape.'

'We have been together all evening,' Collins said. 'How could you have done so?'

Dickens grinned. 'When I saw the chance for her to get away, I whispered that she should seize it. My fear was that she might be overcome by remorse at the enormity of her crime and confess her guilt to the madam. I do not condone the taking of life, but tonight I am tempted to make an exception.'

'But I don't —'

'She masqueraded as Nellie Brown,' Dickens interrupted. 'You saw the real maidservant yourself. She was waiting at the Rope and Anchor for her friend. Remember how the drunken women mocked her, and all because of the scar on her cheek?'

'That was Nellie?'

'I am sure of it. Bella had borrowed her clothes, so as to fool Mrs Jugg. I suppose they slipped out of the house while Mrs Jugg was dozing and under cover of the fog sliding in from the Thames, Bella put Nellie's garments on under her own dress. Once she was back in the upstairs room, she reversed the outfits. She must have strapped her bosom down – I recall that she was quite formidably endowed, Wilkie! – and used cosmetic preparations to mimic the scar on her friend's cheek. She is a couple of inches taller than Nellie, and she needed to stoop and kept her head bent so as to avoid close scrutiny. She was relying on Mrs Jugg's poor eyesight and Jack Wells's lack of imaginative intelligence. When, in Nellie's character, she showed Whiteacre into the room and then revealed herself as Bella, no doubt he was amused by the impersonation, perhaps even excited by it. We can speculate as to the inducement she offered to persuade him not only to strip for her but to allow her to tie him up. When he was at her mercy, she stabbed him, but with insufficient force to kill him straight away. Then she stole his money. Knowing Whiteacre's penchant for heavy spending, I suspect she found enough to keep her and Nellie out of the brothels forever and a day. She committed a wicked crime, but I cannot find it in my heart to condemn her for it.'

'She must have been trying to escape when we saw her coming down the stairs.'

'One can scarcely imagine her feelings when she was forced to take us back to the room,' Dickens said softly.

'And when she heard her victim's dying words. No wonder she vomited when faced with the horror of his corpse. But how did you guess what had happened?'

'Guess?' Dickens raised his eyebrows in amusement 'The scar was my clue. It bore such an uncanny resemblance to that which disfigured the woman in the Rope and Anchor that the whole scheme revealed itself to me. But Bella made one mistake.'

'Which was?'

'When she put on the make-up, she forgot that she was applying it to an image in a looking-glass. And so her scar ran down the right cheek. But Nellie's was on the left.'

'Above all was the sense of hearing acute. I heard all things in the heaven and in the earth, I heard many things in hell.'

—Edgar Allan Poe, 'The Tell-Tale Heart'

One night, many years ago, I found myself wandering in an unfamiliar part of the city. The river looked like an oil slick twisting languidly in the cold moonlight, and on the opposite bank the towering metal skeletons of factories gleamed silver. Steam hissed from tubes, formed abstract shapes in the air, and faded into the night. Every now and then a gush of orange flame leapt into the sky from a funnel-shaped chimney.

I was lost, I know now. The bar where I had played my last gig was miles behind me, and the path I had taken was crooked and dark. The river lay at my right, and to the left, across the narrow, cobbled street, tall empty warehouses loomed over me, all crumbling, soot-covered bricks and caved-in roofs. Through the broken windows small fires burned, and I fancied I could see ragged figures bent over the flames for warmth. Ahead of me, just beyond the cross-roads, the path continued into a monstrous junkyard, where the rusted hulks of cars and piles of scrap metal towered over me.

Out of nowhere, it seemed, I began to hear snatches of melody: a light, romantic, jazzy air underpinned by wondrous, heart-rending chords, some of which I could swear I had never heard before. I stopped in my tracks and tried to discern where the music was coming from. It was a piano, no doubt about that, and though it was slightly out of tune, that didn't diminish the power of the melody or the skill of the player. I wanted desperately to find him, to get closer to the music.

I walked between the mountains of scrap metal, sure I was getting closer, then, down a narrow side path, I saw the glow of a brazier and heard the music more clearly than I had before. If anything, it had even more magic than when I heard it from a distance. More than that, it had the potential to make my fortune.

Heart pounding, I headed towards the light.

What I found there was a wizened old black man sitting at a beat-up honky-tonk piano. When he saw me, he stopped playing and looked over at me. The glow of the brazier reflected in his eyes, which seemed to flicker and dance with flames.

'That's a beautiful piece of music,' I said. 'Did you write it yourself?'

'I don't write nothing,' he said. 'The music just comes out of me.'

'And this just came out of you?'

'Yessir,' he said. 'Just this very moment.'

I might lack the creativity, the essential spark of genius, but when it comes to technical matters I'm hard to beat. I'm a classically trained musician who happened to choose to play jazz, and already this miraculous piece of music was fixed in my memory. If I closed my eyes, I could even see it written and printed on a sheet. And if I let my imagination run free, I could see the sheets flying off the shelves of the music shops and records whizzing out of the racks. This was the stuff that standards were made of.

'So you're the only one who's heard it, apart from me?'

'I guess so,' he said, the reflected flames dancing in his eyes.

I looked around. The piles of scrap rose on all sides, obscuring the rest of the world, and once he had stopped playing I could hear nothing but the hissing of the steam from the factories across the river. We were quite alone, me and this poor, shrunken black man. I complimented him again on his genius and went on my way. When I got behind him, he started playing again. I listened to the tune one more time, burning it into my memory so there could be no mistake. Then I picked up an iron bar from the pile of scrap and hit him hard on the back of his head.

I heard the skull crack like a nut and saw the blood splash on the ivory keys of the old piano. I made sure he was dead, then dragged his body off the path, piled rusty metal over it, and left him there.

I had to get back to the hotel now and write down the music before I lost it. As luck would have it, at the other side of the junkyard, past another set of crossroads, was a wide boulevard lined with a few run-down shops and bars. There wasn't much traffic, but after about ten minutes I saw a cab with his light on coming up the road and waved him down. He stopped, and twenty minutes later I was back in my hotel room, the red neon of the strip club across the street flashing through the flimsy, moth-eaten curtains, as I furiously scribbled the notes and chords etched in my memory on to the lined music paper.

I was right about the music, and what's more, nobody even questioned that I wrote it, despite the fact that I had never composed anything in my life. I suppose I was well enough known as a competent jazz pianist in certain circles so people just assumed I had suddenly been smitten by the muse one day.

I called the tune 'The Magic of Your Touch', and it became a staple of the jazz repertoire, from big bands to small combos. Arrangements proliferated, and one of the band members, who fancied himself a poet, added lyrics to the melody. That was when we really struck the big time. Billie Holiday recorded it, then Frank Sinatra, Tony Bennett, Peggy Lee, Mel Torme, Ella Fitzgerald. Suddenly it seemed that no one could get enough of 'The Magic of Your Touch', and the big bucks rolled in.

I hardly need say that the sudden wealth and success brought about an immense change in my lifestyle. Instead of fleabag hotels and two-bit whores, it was penthouse suites and society girls all the way. I continued to play with the sextet, of course, but we hired a vocalist and instead of sleazy bars we played halls and big name clubs: the Blue Note, the Village Vanguard, Birdland, and the rest. We even got a recording contract, and people bought our records by the thousands.

'The Magic of Your Touch' brought us all this, and more. Hollywood beckoned, a jazz film set in Paris, and off we went. Ah, those foxy little mademoiselles. Then came the world tour: Europe, Asia, Australia, South Africa, Brazil. They all wanted to hear the band named after the man who wrote 'The Magic of Your Touch'.

I can't say that I *never* gave another thought to the wizened old black man playing his honky-tonk piano beside the brazier. Many times, I even dreamed about that night and what I did there, on instinct, without thinking, and woke up in a cold sweat, my heart pounding. Many's the time I thought I saw the old man's flame-reflecting eyes in a crowd, or down an alley. But nobody ever found his body, or if they did, it never made the news. The years passed, and I believed that I was home and dry. Until, that is, little by little, things started to go wrong.

I have always been of a fairly nervous disposition – highly strung, my parents used to say, blaming it on my musical talent, or vice versa. Whiskey helped, and sometimes I also turned to pills, mostly tranquillisers and barbiturates, to take the edge off things. So imagine my horror when we were halfway through a concert at Massey Hall, in my home town of Toronto, playing 'Solitude', and I found my left hand falling into the familiar chord patterns of 'The Magic of Your Touch', my right hand picking out the melody.

Of course, the audience cheered wildly at first, thinking it some form of playful acknowledgement, a cheeky little musical quotation. But I couldn't stop. It was as if I was a mere puppet and some other force was directing my movements. No matter what tune we started after that, all my hands would play was 'The Magic of Your Touch'. In the end I felt a panic attack coming on – I'd had them before – and, pale and shaking, I had to leave the stage. The audience clapped and the other band members looked concerned.

Afterward, in the dressing room, Ed, our stand-up bass player, approached me. I had just downed a handful of Valium and was waiting for the soothing effect of the pills to kick in.

'What is it, man?' he asked. 'What the hell happened out there?'

I shook my head. 'I don't know,' I told him. 'I couldn't help myself.'

'Couldn't help yourself? What do you mean by that?'

'The song, Ed. It's like the song took me over. It was weird, scary. I've never experienced anything like that before.'

Ed looked at me as if I were crazy, the first of many such looks I got before I stopped even bothering trying to tell people what was happening to me. Because that incident at Massey Hall was, I soon discovered, only the beginning.

* * *

Playing in the band was out of the question from that night on. Whenever my hands got near a piano, they started to play 'The Magic of Your Touch'. The boys took it with good grace and soon found a replacement who was, in all honesty, easily as good a pianist as I was, if not better, and they carried on touring under the same name. I don't really think anyone missed me very much. My retirement from performing for 'health reasons' was announced, and I imagine people assumed that life on the road just got too much for someone of my highly strung temperament. The press reported that I had had a 'minor nervous breakdown', and life went on as normal. Almost.

After the Toronto concert, I developed an annoying ringing in my ears – tinnitus, I believe it's called – and it drove me up the wall with its sheer relentlessness. But worse than that, one night when I went to bed I heard as clear as a bell, louder than the ringing, the opening chords of 'The Magic of Your Touch', as if someone were playing a piano right inside my head. It went on until the entire song was finished, then started again at the beginning. It was only after swallowing twice my regular nightly dose of Nembutal that I managed to drift into a comalike stupor and, more important, into blessed silence. But when I awoke, the ringing and the music was still there, louder than ever.

I couldn't get the song out of my head. Every minute of the day and night it played, over and over again in a continuous loop tape. The pills helped up to a point, but I found my night's sleep shrinking from four hours to three to two, then one, if I was lucky. Only with great difficulty could I concentrate on anything. No amount of external noise could overcome the music in my head. I couldn't hold intelligent conversations. People shunned me, crossed the street when they saw me coming. I started muttering to myself, putting my hands over my ears, but that only served to trap the sound inside, make it louder.

One day in my wanderings, I found myself back in the city where it all began and retraced my steps as best I could remember them. I don't know what I had in mind, only that this was where the whole thing had started, so perhaps it would end here, too. I don't know what I expected to find.

Soon the landscape became a familiar one of decaying warehouses, oily river, and factories venting steam and belching fire. I saw the junkyard looming ahead beyond the crossroads and followed the path through the towers of scrap metal, rusty cars, engine blocks, tires, axles, and fenders. Then I heard it again. Uncertain as first, hardly willing to believe my ears, I paused. But sure enough, there it was: 'The Magic of Your Touch' played on an out-of-tune honky-tonk piano, the music outside perfectly matching the loop tape in my head.

I could see the brazier now, a patch of light at the end of the narrow path between the columns, and when I approached, the wizened old black man looked up from his keyboard with fire dancing in his eyes. Then I saw what I should have seen in the first place. The flames weren't reflections of the brazier's glow. They were inside his head, the way the music was inside mine.

He didn't stop playing, didn't miss a note.

'I thought I'd killed you,' I said. 'Lots of people make that mistake,' he replied.

'Who are you?'

'Who do you think I am?'

'I don't know.'

'You took my song,'

'I'm sorry. I don't know what got into me.'

'No matter. Now it's taken you.'

'I can't get it out of my head. It's driving me insane. What can I do?'

'Only one thing you can do, and you know what that is. Then your soul will come home to me, where it belongs.'

I shook my head and backed away. 'No!' I cried. 'I'm dreaming. I must be dreaming. This can't be real.'

But I heard his laughter echoing among the towers of scrap as I ran, hands over my ears, the insufferable melody I had come to detest now going around and around for the millionth time in my head, gaining in volume, just a little bit each time, and I knew he was right.

When I got back to my hotel room, I took out paper and pen.

You have no idea what a struggle it was to write just this brief account with the music, relentless, precise, and eternal inside my head, what an effort it cost me. But I must leave some kind of record. I can't bear the thought of everyone believing I was mad. I'm not mad. It happened exactly the way I told it.

Now, like a man who can't get rid of hiccups might contemplate slitting his throat, I have only one thought in mind. The pills are on the table, and I'm drinking whiskey, waiting for the end. He said my soul would go home to him, where it belongs, and that scares the hell out of me, but it can't be worse than this eternal repetition driving out all human thought and feeling. It can't be. I'll have another slug of whiskey and another handful of pills, then I'm sure, soon, the blessed silence will come. *Amen.*

Acknowledgements

A TALE OF ONE CITY by Anne Perry, © 2004 by Anne Perry. First appeared in *Death by Dickens*, edited by Anne Perry. Reprinted by permission of the author and her agent, MBA Literary Agency.

FOUR CALLING BIRDS by Val McDermid, © 2004 by Val McDermid. First appeared in *12 Days*, edited by Shelley Silas. Reprinted by permission of the author and her agent, Jane Gregory.

THOROUGHLY MODERN MILLINERY by Marilyn Todd, © 2004 by Marilyn Todd. First appeared in *The Mammoth Book of Roaring Twenties Whodunnits*, edited by Mike Ashley. Reprinted by permission of the author.

THE LADY DOWNSTAIRS by Christopher Fowler, © 2004 by Christopher Fowler. First read on BBC Radio 4. Reprinted by permission of the author.

OLD BAG DAD by Keith Miles, © 2004 by Keith Miles. First appeared in *Ellery Queen's Mystery Magazine*. Reprinted by permission of the author.

RUMPOLE AND THE CHRISTMAS BREAK by John Mortimer, © 2004 by Advanpress Limited. First appeared in *The Strand Magazine*. Reprinted by permission of Peters, Fraser, Dunlop Limited.

LIVING WITH THE GILT by Judith Cutler, © 2004 by Judith Cutler. First appeared in *Ellery Queen's Mystery Magazine*. Reprinted by permission of the author.

LOVE-LIES-BLEEDING by Barbara Cleverly, © 2004 by Barbara Cleverly. First appeared in *Ellery Queen's Mystery Magazine*. Reprinted by permission of the author.